Praise for Sariah Wilson

The Hollywood Jinx

"Wilson nails the small-town setting, complete with nosy but well-meaning residents, and delivers a sweet happy ending. This is a treat."
—*Publishers Weekly*

The Chemistry of Love

"Abundant pop culture references and nerdy quips only enhance . . . This is utterly adorable."
—*Publishers Weekly* (starred review)

"In this adorable romantic comedy, the fake dating trope is taken to another level with banter and nerdy references Anna and Marco throw around. Adding to the fun, Anna's grandparents and their pet birds will have readers in stitches. A fresh and fun romance from Wilson."
—*Library Journal*

"*The Chemistry of Love* is full of funny moments . . . that will have readers cringing and laughing out loud in turns."
—Bookreporter

Cinder-Nanny

"Diana and Griffin's slow-burn closed-door passion is authentic."
—*Kirkus Reviews*

"*Cinder-Nanny* is a definite must-read. This cute play on the age-old fairy tale will surely worm its way into your heart and leave you feeling all warm and fuzzy."

—*Harlequin Junkie*

"Wilson's ability to weave a sweet tale of two people, each of whom needs what the other has to offer, is magical."

—Bookreporter

The Paid Bridesmaid

"Combining a fast-paced plot with a slow-burning romance, this is sure to give readers butterflies."

—*Publishers Weekly*

"Wilson's (*Roommaid*) funny, sweet stand-alone about marriage, friendships, and mistaken identities is full of witty dialogue, endearing characters, and fast-paced narrative. Will appeal to fans of feel-good romances, rom-coms, and plots about weddings and social media."

—*Library Journal*

The Seat Filler

"Wilson (*Roommaid*) balances the quirky with the heartfelt in this adorable rom-com."

—*Publishers Weekly*

The Friend Zone

"Wilson scores a touchdown with this engaging contemporary romance that delivers plenty of electric sexual chemistry and zingy banter while still being romantically sweet at its core."

"Snappy banter, palpable sexual tension, and a lively sense of fun combine with deeply felt emotional issues in a sweet, upbeat romance that will appeal to both the YA and new adult markets."

The #Lovestruck Novels

"Wilson has mastered the art of creating a romance that manages to be both sexy and sweet, and her novel's skillfully drawn characters, deliciously snarky sense of humor, and vividly evoked music-business settings add up to a supremely satisfying love story that will be music to romance readers' ears."

"Making excellent use of sassy banter, hilarious texts, and a breezy style, Wilson's energetic story brims with sexual tension and takes readers on a musical road trip that will leave them smiling. Perfect as well for YA and new adult collections."

"*#Starstruck* is oh so funny! Sariah Wilson created an entertaining story with great banter that I didn't want to put down. Ms. Wilson provided a diverse cast of characters in their friends and family. Fans of *Sweet Cheeks* by K. Bromberg and Ruthie Knox will enjoy *#Starstruck*."

Party Favors

The Royals of Monterra Series

Royal Date

Royal Chase

Royal Games

Royal Design

The Ugly Stepsister Series

The Ugly Stepsister Strikes Back

The Promposal

Party Favors

SARIAH WILSON

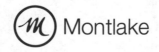
Montlake

Published by Montlake, Seattle

www.apub.com

Amazon, the Amazon logo, and Montlake are trademarks of Amazon.com, Inc., or its affiliates.

ISBN-13: 9781662514241 (paperback)
ISBN-13: 9781662514234 (digital)

Cover design by Caroline Teagle Johnson
Cover images: © surachet khamsuk / Shutterstock; © Liliia Hryshchenko / Shutterstock; © Karlygash / Shutterstock; © melissahelddesigns / Getty Images

Printed in the United States of America

For my mom—
thanks for being the best mother in the world

CHAPTER ONE

"Everly, can you come in here?"

I'd been getting a bottle of sparkling water from the fridge for my boss and happened to pass by the door of our events director Claudia Delgado. She was at her desk, working on her computer.

I glanced down at the bottle in my hand. It was important to bring it straight from the fridge to Adrian because he somehow could detect if the water had warmed even slightly. While I knew that he might be upset about the delay, I did as she requested. "Is there something I can help you with?" I asked.

"Sit down," she said, gesturing toward one of the chairs opposite her. She finished typing and then gave me her full attention. "I know I've only been here for a few months, but I wanted to let you know how impressed I am by the work you're doing."

"You mean the work Adrian's doing," I said, suddenly feeling a little anxious. Getting recognition always made me feel nervous.

"No, the work *you're* doing. I know that it's you from start to finish. You're the one making the budgets, contacting the vendors, finding sponsors and event partners, taking care of the scheduling, overseeing all of the staff for the event, making sure everything goes off without a hitch. And it's not just your organization and communication skills, impressive as they may be. I've watched you running events. You are in your element—you inspire confidence, and the clients trust that you'll take care of them."

My heart started beating even faster. I didn't know why she was saying this. I didn't see myself the way she was describing me. I'd never wanted to be in the spotlight or get a lot of attention. I mean, yes, I did want to get promoted. I'd been Adrian's administrative assistant for the last four years, and now that I'd graduated from college, I was ready to become an official event planner for Elevated Events. I'd been ready for three years, wondering when it would be my turn. Every other administrative assistant who had worked for an events director had been promoted within a year.

Not me.

But I was happy to labor on the sidelines. If no one ever heard my ideas, that was okay, right?

I loved being Adrian's assistant and I liked doing a good job for him. I didn't mind that he got the credit. His success was my success, and vice versa.

Which meant that I wasn't sure what to say to Claudia right now. She and Adrian were one step below the CEO, a man I'd met only once, right after I started, as he didn't seem all that concerned with the day-to-day operations of Elevated and had never come into the office.

Claudia and Adrian were in charge. Adrian hadn't been happy about Claudia being hired—the last events director had retired and Adrian thought it was unnecessary to bring in someone new. He'd seen it as a slight against the work he was doing. He felt like she was his rival.

Which made it so that I wasn't sure how to respond to her or what she was getting at. I was so fiercely loyal to Adrian—so protective of him. I wouldn't ever say anything bad about him.

I sat there silently, not knowing what I should say.

Claudia studied me, and it felt like she could read my mind. As if I were broadcasting my innermost thoughts onto my forehead.

"Tell me one thing you'd change about Elevated," she said.

What? She had gone from seeming like she wanted me to take credit for the work both Adrian and I were doing, to tear him down, to now seeming . . . encouraging? "One thing?"

"Yes. I'm sure someone as talented and driven as you has a lot of ideas on how to move Elevated forward into the future, but I'd like to start with just one thing you'd change if you could."

She was right about that—I had so many ideas on how I would improve things at the company and the way we did business. "I would take on new clients. I know that corporate clients have been very good to us, but I've never understood why we don't take on individuals as clients. Why we don't do luxury parties or showers or celebrity events."

She nodded thoughtfully. "I've thought the same thing. I don't understand the reluctance to broaden our market, either."

I could almost hear Adrian's voice in my head, going on about how it was better to focus our efforts on one type of clientele and that we didn't need to go looking for new clients, especially not ones who would completely alter the kind of work we currently did.

There was a pang of guilt for my disloyalty that made me uneasy.

"Well, there are lots of reasons why—" I started, but she cut me off.

"If I bring in a potential client, an individual, would you be willing to ask Adrian if you could pitch?"

She was challenging me, and again I worried about her possible endgame here. It was true—I never participated in pitch sessions with clients. I was there, taking notes, but I always stayed quiet.

Even when I had good ideas of my own.

I glanced over at the bottle of water. Adrian was going to call me soon to ask what was taking so long. I had to get going, despite wanting to respond affirmatively and take that leap.

"Yes."

And I didn't know which one of us was more surprised by my answer. Me, because I had been intending to say no, or her, because I'd actually agreed to it.

Her face broke out in a huge smile. "Excellent. I think it's long past time for you to be given the official title of event planner. I've scheduled this new client to come in two days from now, and I hope that you'll be one of the people pitching an idea. I'll forward you the email with all the relevant details."

I nodded. "Thank you. I have to go. Adrian's expecting me."

At that, she pointedly glanced over at the large clock hanging on her wall. It was nearly nine o'clock at night and her own assistant had left hours ago.

But as long as Adrian was in the office, so was I. Just in case he needed something.

Like his favorite brand of water.

My roommate and best friend, Vella, kept trying to tell me that Adrian took advantage of me and that I should stand up to him and create professional boundaries, but she didn't understand.

Neither did Claudia.

I wanted to be here with him.

There was a definite flash of pity in Claudia's expression, and I ignored it as I headed back to my desk.

I rushed down the hallway, eager to escape to the comfort and familiarity of my own workspace. I was excited at the prospect of pitching while still feeling as if I'd betrayed Adrian somehow. I hadn't corrected her about the work that I'd done, because she was right. It wasn't Adrian who took care of all the major and minor details of the events—it was me. I was the woman behind the scenes who got everything done, and much as I hated being the center of attention, it felt good to be recognized for my hard work.

Would I be brave enough to ask Adrian to let me pitch? I'd hinted over the years about being promoted and becoming an event planner, but he always changed the subject.

And I hoped that it was because he couldn't bear to lose me.

Not just because I was good at my job.

I sat down in my chair and wondered what Adrian would do if I marched into his office and asked for the opportunity to pitch the potential new client that Claudia had found. Would he be upset?

Supportive?

Change the subject without giving me an answer?

I didn't know.

And that bothered me.

I took my cell phone out of my pocket, intending to open my email, and saw that I had a text from my mother.

DID YOU SEE THE PICTURE OF NICO AND KAT AND THEIR CHILDREN? SO, SO CUTE! MOM SEND

Nico and Kat were King Dominic and Queen Katerina of Monterra, but in my family we always referred to them as Nico and Kat. Like we knew them or something. I responded quickly.

Of course I did.

As if I didn't have the same Google alerts set up as she did.

DO YOU THINK CHIARA IS GOING TO RELEASE AN EARLY SKETCH OF HER WEDDING DRESS? MOM SEND

I'd told her on numerous occasions that she didn't have to sign her texts, that I knew they were from her, but she didn't believe me. She also insisted on writing her texts in all caps, despite me explaining that it was the equivalent of yelling at someone, because she had decided it made it more likely that her texts would go through.

She also dismissed me when I told her that she didn't have to write the word *send* and that just pushing the button made the text arrive on my phone.

She was a stubborn woman, and there was no point in arguing with her or trying to use reason.

My mother was texting me about Princess Chiara (Nico's younger sister) because her wedding was set to take place in a couple of weeks, and because she loved fashion the most out of all of her royal siblings, we were expecting wedding-dress greatness.

> I don't know if Chiara will. She loves her
> privacy and I'm sure we'll have to wait until the
> actual wedding to see.

I HOPE SHE WILL! MOM SEND

If there was one thing the women in my family loved, it was royal families. And we were especially obsessed with the royal family of Monterra. My grandma had started the whole thing, and while some families passed down silverware or noble titles, our love of royalty was what bonded us all together.

I remembered viewing Nico and Kat's wedding on TV eight years ago. We'd all gotten up at four in the morning to watch. Kat McTaggart, an American girl, had met the crown prince of Monterra while on vacation in his country, a small kingdom situated between Switzerland and Italy. Nico was gorgeous and had the sexiest accent I'd ever heard, and I completely understood why Kat had fallen head over heels in love with him.

I was fourteen years old when they got married, and it was the most romantic thing I'd ever seen, a real-life fairy tale.

I'd been chasing that dream for myself ever since and had continually come up short. I wanted my own Nico but hadn't been able to find anything even close.

ARE YOU STILL WORKING? MOM SEND

I made a disgruntled noise but didn't respond. She'd be upset if I told her I was still at the office.

The intercom on my desk phone buzzed and I reached for the button. "Yes?"

"Everly?"

Adrian's warm, rich voice came over the loudspeaker and I couldn't help but smile. He had called me Beverly for the first three months after I started as his assistant, and there had been a period of time when I'd considered giving in and just letting that be my new name, but I'd resisted and gently corrected him each time.

And I was glad that I had, because I got a flutter of happiness each time he said my name.

"Everly? My water?" he said when I didn't respond.

Oh, right. I'd totally forgotten. I rushed into his office and handed it to him. He was very handsome. I'd expected that at some point I'd become more accustomed to his appearance, that light blond hair and those deep, dark brown eyes.

He was my own personal Nico. Not that they looked anything alike—but Adrian Stone was the heir to one of the richest families in New York. Adrian was working at Elevated to learn the ropes so that someday he could take over all of his father's businesses.

Adrian and his family were constantly showing up online, dressed to the nines, going from one fabulous event to another.

I imagined that being his girlfriend would be like an Americanized version of being a princess.

This was probably an HR crisis waiting to happen, but I'd had a crush on Adrian since I'd started at Elevated. Both Vella and my mom told me I'd eventually outgrow it, but it hadn't happened yet.

I knew he didn't think of me that way. That he probably couldn't think of me romantically, given that he was my boss. He was seven years older than I was, and while that might have been a big deal when I was eighteen and had just started here, now I was twenty-two.

I'd grown up, and I'd been waiting a long time for him to notice.

Not that he would. While he'd initially been the kind of guy who dated a different woman every week, he had been in a serious relationship for the last two years.

I wanted him to be happy, but a tiny part of me was jealous.

I also recognized that I wasn't his type. His girlfriend was petite and perfect-looking and blonde and unbelievably sweet. I wanted to be okay with his relationship. But a small piece of me thought that if he ever got to really know me, he might like me.

He didn't say anything about the water, but I saw the grimace he made when he took the bottle and felt a pang at disappointing him. This was another reason I wanted my crush to be over. So that I'd stop being so emotionally tied up in him and his reactions.

Adrian preferred it as cold as it could be, and I'd let myself get distracted by Claudia and then my mom and I had let him down and I hated how this felt.

"Is everything ready to go for Origin Telecom next week?" he asked.

"Yes." As if I'd ever let a client as important as Origin Telecom fall to the wayside. "Everything is set up and we have multiple contingency plans in place just in case anything goes wrong."

And in my experience, something always went wrong. Part of being a good event planner was having a backup plan for your backup plan when the AV system blew up or the bathrooms flooded.

Some sliver of my brain noted how easy it was for me to talk to Adrian now. It had taken a long time to get to this point. I'd been so bowled over by his good looks the first few days on this job that every time I'd had to speak to him, it was like I was having a series of mini-strokes.

But now we could have actual conversations. Progress.

"Good." He put the water down and leaned back in his chair, giving me a charming smile. "I always know things will go well as long as I have you by my side."

I felt his words from the top of my head all the way down to my tingling toes. Adrian didn't give compliments often, but when he did? It was like Christmas, my birthday, and a royal wedding all wrapped into one. I lived for that approval in his voice.

This is your chance, an inner voice whispered. *Ask him if you can pitch Claudia's new client.*

Without my brain's permission, my mouth began speaking. "Adrian? There's something I wanted to ask you."

CHAPTER TWO

For the second time that evening, I was caught off guard by the way words had unintentionally spilled out of my mouth. It was entirely unlike me—I was the kind of person who was careful with what I said at work and who I said it to.

Immediately I began to consider the potential consequences and worst possible outcomes. What would Adrian think of my request to pitch? Would he be annoyed? Turned off by it? Angry? I couldn't predict his reaction, and that made me uncomfortable.

I shouldn't have said anything. I was ready to tell him "Never mind" and beat a hasty retreat from his office.

Despite what I'd promised Claudia, I wasn't ready.

"Shoot," he said.

My mouth went dry, and I couldn't form the question. This was too big and scary. I could feel sweat beading up on my lower back, and I pulled my blouse away from my skin in an attempt to cool off.

He looked at me expectantly, and I couldn't do it.

"Not ask you, tell you," I amended. "I found a receptionist to replace Amy."

Amy had quit suddenly earlier today, with no notice, and we needed someone to cover the front desk.

"Who?"

He was asking which temp agency I'd called. But I had forgotten. While I never let anything fall through the cracks when it came to an event, the same wasn't true for everything else. Event planners were notorious for running other people's events extremely well while the rest of our lives were often out of control.

Needing an answer, I seized on the only one I could think of. "My friend Vella."

"Which agency is she with?"

My brain went completely blank—she wasn't currently with a temp agency, although she had been in the past. "She's been with a few different ones. She's done this before."

"Sounds good. Have her here first thing tomorrow and get everything squared away with Human Resources."

"You got it," I said.

He nodded and his gaze returned to his computer screen. Recognizing that I had been dismissed, I headed back to my desk.

Why was I so afraid to ask Adrian for what I wanted? Of course I couldn't tell him about my crush—that would be unprofessional and uncomfortable and someone would have to pry that particular secret from my cold, dead hands. If I were ever forced into a confession about it, well, that was what deathbeds were for.

But I should have been strong enough to tell him that I wanted the opportunity to pitch. That I was more than ready to have the title of event planner. I had put in my time, and even Claudia recognized that.

I needed to take the next step. Somehow I was going to have to get a lot braver where Adrian was concerned.

For right now, though, I needed to focus on the next impossible thing I needed to accomplish.

I had to convince Vella to take the job.

~

When I got back to the apartment, Vella wasn't home yet. She'd been doing gig work lately, delivering takeout and groceries.

She'd had more jobs than anybody could reasonably count, as she changed her career aspirations approximately every three months. She had recently reenrolled in college since she'd decided she wanted to be a professor of Russian literature.

This was after she'd graduated from cosmetology school to be a hairstylist, and prior to that she was going to specialize in cybersecurity programming and had been interning at a tech company.

Before the internship she'd had plans to be a math teacher, a veterinarian, an acrobat in the circus, a professional wrestler, a neurologist, a bar owner, a writer . . . The list was ever changing and apparently endless, and she moved around to different internships and schools depending on her whims.

We lived in a one-bedroom apartment in Manhattan. I had found her listing for a roommate online while I still lived in Alabama and I'd initially assumed we would share the bedroom. When I arrived I discovered that she had a dining alcove that would be my space. It was relatively large, but I did not have any privacy. Just a room divider.

Vella scared me a little bit, too—she looked like a more murderous Wednesday Addams. Jet-black hair, heavy eye makeup, always dressed like she was about to attend a funeral.

Given what I'd heard about real estate in New York City, I should have been suspicious that she was charging me so little. I later discovered it was because she hadn't been able to get anyone else to agree to move in. I assumed that was partly due to her one rule—under no circumstances was I to ever, ever go in her locked bedroom.

I had slept with a butter knife under my pillow for the first few weeks because she was so unlike anyone I'd ever met that I feared a bit for my safety. I probably should have grabbed a more heavy-duty knife, but I was pretty sure that I'd accidentally stab myself while sleeping.

But the apartment was only a couple of blocks from work, so I told myself that I could buck up and deal with my situation.

My overactive imagination did not help my resolution, though, especially when I came up with so many different scenarios for what she had hidden in her room that she didn't want me to see.

We had lived completely separate lives, barely even speaking. I'd wondered how she could jump from job to job while affording rent and finally asked her about it.

"My father covers my rent," she said with a glum tone that indicated she wasn't on the best of terms with her dad.

"What does he do for a living?"

"Violates the planet." At my raised eyebrows, she added, "He owns an oil company."

I never would have guessed that Vella came from that kind of money.

After we'd lived together for about four months, everything changed. I came home one night to find Vella lying in the middle of our living room, arms and legs spread out like a starfish.

I wasn't sure if I was supposed to ask or not, but I couldn't help myself. "Are you okay?"

She turned her head toward me. "My grandfather just died. He was the only person in my family who was nice to me."

I sat down next to her on the floor. "I'm so sorry. Is there anything I can do to help?"

She considered my words and then said, "I want to go to church and light a candle for him."

I attempted to conceal my surprise. "I didn't peg you as being religious."

"I'm not. But church was important to him, and I think it would make him happy to know that I'd done it."

So we found a nearby church and went in and took turns lighting candles. We stood there in silence for a minute or two.

"Who are you lighting a candle for?" she asked in a solemn voice.

"My aunt Louise."

"When did she pass?"

"Oh no, she's not dead, she's just a really bad person," I said. "I don't think she'll ever die. I'm pretty sure she's just going to change form."

A couple of beats passed, and then Vella started to giggle. I couldn't help myself and laughed along with her. The fact that we were doing it at such an inappropriate time and place made the giggles worse. We got some disapproving looks and had to go back out to the sidewalk, where we collapsed against each other, hysterically laughing.

We opened up to one another that night, realized how much we liked each other, and had been best friends ever since.

People always seemed surprised when they saw us hanging out together. That was probably because we were like what would happen if you opened up an internet browser and did an image search for *total opposites*. She was dark and gloomy and scary, and I was overly optimistic and loved everybody and blonde.

Well, I used to be blonde. It had been actual eons since I'd last dyed my hair, and my brown roots were just my hair color now.

I got on my laptop and had started making a list of ways to convince Vella to take the job when she breezed into the apartment, slamming the front door. "Are you interested in hearing what our neighbors were loudly discussing at five o'clock this morning? I recorded them. I'm going to download the file and send it to them with the title 'You Two Should Break Up.'"

Our neighbors had ridiculously loud arguments, and while I understood that the noise of people around you was part of living in an apartment building, they seemed to consider it their particular mission to be as obnoxious as possible. I used earplugs to sleep through their early-morning fights, but given that her bedroom adjoined theirs, Vella was directly in their arguments' flight path and couldn't escape the sound, no matter how many white-noise machines she used.

"I've been trying to figure out what I should do to get revenge," she mused. "Remember when I was in that grunge band? I was considering going over to my storage unit, getting my amplifier and my electric guitar."

"You're planning on annoying them with your bad playing?" I teased, but her face was completely serious.

"No, I'm going to leave the guitar on top of the amplifier, turn the volume all the way up on both, and let our lovely, considerate neighbors enjoy the high-pitched shriek of feedback for the next twelve hours. Or maybe I'll put superglue in their locks."

"Could you not plot out loud?" I asked her. "I'm not married to you, so I would have to testify against you."

She nodded. "Right. I'll keep my plans to myself, and that way when you bail me out of jail, you can honestly say you had no knowledge of my successful and hilariously on-point revenge schemes."

"I will be happy to bail you out." I paused for a second and then said, "And maybe in return you can do something for me."

Vella had gone into the kitchen and was opening and closing cabinets, as if she were trying to find something to eat but nothing sounded appealing. "I told you, you have to ask me about your outfits *before* you leave for work if you want me to fix them."

"Oh, ha ha," I responded sarcastically. "You've already done that joke earlier this week, by the way."

"It's one of my greatest hits. When you see Taylor Swift in concert, you want her to play 'You Belong With Me,' don't you?"

"You listen to Taylor—" I cut myself off. That wasn't the point right now. I had to persuade her to take the job at Elevated, and I knew she wasn't going to want to because she'd once compared working in an office to being actively and continuously tortured.

"Did you just get home?" she asked suspiciously, breaking me from my train of thought.

"Adrian was still working. If he's there, I have to be there." I was trying to sound factual, but even I could hear the defensiveness in my voice.

"Why does he have to work so late when you're the person who does everything?"

It was the second time in the last couple of hours that someone had said this to me, and I didn't handle it any better the second time than I had the first. "I don't do everything. Adrian does stuff."

"Name one thing."

"He . . ." My mind went blank. Secretly, I had wondered on more than one occasion what he did all day. But surely he wouldn't keep me there so late if he was just messing around on his computer.

"Does nothing," she finished for me. "If he was my boss, I would set his hair on fire."

"Why is it your first instinct to light someone's hair on fire when they annoy you?"

"Why isn't it yours?"

Again, we'd gotten off track. "If you want to see what he does, come work with me. The receptionist quit and I told Adrian that you'd take the job temporarily until we find someone new."

I squared my shoulders, expecting that I'd have to spend the rest of the evening convincing her, but she surprised me by saying, "I'd love to be your receptionist."

"Wait, really?"

"Yes, really. When do I start?"

"Tomorrow, at a time you're unused to. It's called 'morning.'"

"I feel like my sarcasm is rubbing off on you." Vella said this approvingly, and looked at me the way I imagined a mother lion would as her cub made its first kill.

Shrugging, I said, "I have to speak to you in your mother tongue. And please remember that you're going to be the face of Elevated, so you have to get along with people."

She rolled her eyes at this. "I know how to get along with people, Everly."

"Knowing and doing are two entirely different skill sets. You have to be nice."

"I was nice once. It wasn't for me." She pulled a frozen dinner out of the freezer and popped it into the microwave.

"Then be less scary," I suggested.

"I'll see what I can do. Do you have the show cued up?" she asked.

I nodded. Vella and I had been watching television shows from different eras. We were currently on the 1970s and had been watching *The New Adventures of Wonder Woman*. We'd just started season 2.

The microwave beeped and she pulled her food out, cursing as she burned her fingers. She put it on a plate and came over to join me on the couch. I held up the remote, intending to press play, but stopped.

"All kidding aside, you really do have to behave." I didn't want to lose my job because Vella let a raccoon loose in the duct system after someone stole her afternoon yogurt.

"I will, I promise." She hesitated for a second and then, like she couldn't help making another joke, added, "But if Adrian makes me mad, is it okay if I set his hair on fire?"

"No, because despite my joke earlier, I don't have enough money to get you out of prison if you get arrested for arson and attempted murder."

"Fine," she playfully grumbled as I started the show up. "But I absolutely will put superglue on his keyboard if I see him being mean to you."

That seemed like a fair compromise considering her original intention.

And while I knew Vella was more bark than bite, it worried me that maybe I'd just made a big mistake.

CHAPTER THREE

The next morning I had to pound on Vella's door for several minutes before I heard grumbling on the other side.

"We're going to be late!" I told her.

"I'm going to scream into my pillow for six minutes and then I'll get ready," she yelled back.

Or at least that's what I thought she said. I couldn't be sure. "Scream later, get ready now. I'll feed you if you do."

I went into the kitchen and made her some turkey bacon and eggs. She stumbled into the room, her eyes barely open, and mumbled, "What's this?"

"Breakfast. I know you may not have much familiarity with it, given that you're normally asleep when it happens, but it is known as the most important meal of the day."

She collapsed onto a chair. "The most important meal of the day is the one you eat before you go out for the night so you don't get too drunk." I laughed and she began devouring her food, like she was a grizzly bear and I'd just served her up a heaping pile of fresh salmon.

After she finished eating, I managed to corral her into the bathroom, reminding her about the time situation and ignoring her protests that nothing should happen this early in the day.

Despite her complaints, it took her only about ten minutes to get out the door. I was impressed, but then she complained the entire walk to the office. "Don't we have public transit for a reason?"

"I'd rather not get my neck licked today," I told her. "Plus, walking is good for you and it's actually faster." I'd timed it just to be sure.

"People always say things are good for you when they want you to do something terrible and unfun," she said, and I couldn't disagree, given that it was partly true.

We arrived at the office and I took her to HR, where they had her start her paperwork. I hurried to the kitchen to make Adrian's favorite green smoothie. I'd just put it on his desk when he came into the office.

"Good morning, doll!" he said to me with a big grin.

My heart fluttered in my chest. Whenever Adrian was in a particularly good mood, he would call me *doll*. While part of me knew I should object on behalf of womankind—it was a bit demeaning for him to call me a term that Don Draper of *Mad Men* might have used—I did like that Adrian had a pet name for me. It was something personal that we shared.

"Nice shoes," he said, glancing at my feet.

I was wearing flats. I always wore flats to the office. Because I was 5'10" and Adrian said he was six feet tall but seemed to be the same height as me. When I'd started at Elevated, I'd always worn high heels and I'd towered over him. He'd made a couple of comments about how tall I was, and so I had quickly stopped wearing them.

Which was a shame because I had high arches and had always found heels much more comfortable.

"Thank you. Your agenda is on your computer, and you have a follow-up meeting with the head of events from Origin Telecom this morning. She wants to go over a couple of last-minute details."

When Adrian looked at me with concern, I smiled back at him, knowing why he looked worried. I added, "I've already set up the program on your computer to record the entire meeting, and I'll give her a call later on today with answers that you might not have."

Answers he won't have because he didn't do any of the work, a voice said inside me, but I ignored it.

"What would I do without you?" he asked, again giving me that approving smile that felt like the sun beaming directly onto my face.

There was a short coughing sound behind us and I tried hard to not let my face fall.

It was Colette, Adrian's girlfriend.

"Hello, Colette," I said.

She smiled at me, her mouth full of perfect, gleaming white teeth. "Everly! You look gorgeous! How are you?"

It would be so much easier to dislike her if she weren't such a fantastically sweet person. I couldn't help but like her, though. She was also gorgeous—her blonde hair wasn't mostly brown and was probably her actual hair color. She had dark green eyes and looked like a little girl had wished for her Barbie to come to life. Colette was so tiny that she made me feel overly aware of my height and general awkwardness. She seemed to glide more than walk.

Today she had her little fluffy white dog, Bijoux, in her designer handbag. I had so many questions about purse dogs. How often did they relieve themselves and ruin the bags? Was that why purse-dog women had so many different handbags? Did the dogs get bored? Were they happy with the arrangement, or did they just put up with it to get treats later?

The thing I wondered most, though, was why I wasn't allowed to pet Bijoux. Adrian had mentioned something about an anxiety disorder once, but I loved animals and it was a struggle every time to not pet Bijoux.

Plus, every time I saw Bijoux, it made me miss my dog back home, Princess. Even though she was ten years old, she still had the energy and mischievousness of a new puppy.

And as much as I missed my mom and my grandma, it might have been a tiny bit harder for me to leave Princess behind.

Then I remembered that Colette had asked me a question. "I'm good! How was Paris?"

She split her time between New York and Paris, where she'd grown up. "Paris is Paris, wonderful as always. You should come and visit! You could stay with me."

Yes, that was absolutely the first thing I would do when I saved up enough money to travel. Fly to Paris to stay with my boss's girlfriend, who had no idea that I'd been harboring a secret crush on her boyfriend for years.

Because that wouldn't be at all awkward.

"It's on my list," I told her. I'd much rather take a trip to Monterra, but there was no way I'd be able to afford that anytime soon, either.

"Thank you for the flowers," she said to me with a twinkle in her eye.

"Hey, I sent you those flowers!" Adrian protested.

She glided over to him and wrapped her arms around his waist, kissing him on the cheek. "I know you paid for it, but I also know that Everly picked them out and made all the arrangements."

She was better at standing up for me than I was for myself. Maybe I could learn something from her.

Adrian turned to capture her lips in a kiss, and I felt extremely awkward. I snuck out, closing his door behind me. I went to HR and found Vella had finished up her paperwork. To the manager's great relief, I offered to train Vella and show her how the phones worked at reception.

"I know how phones work," she said dryly as we went down the hallway.

"Yes, it's not really a difficult skill to master," I responded.

She tugged on my arm and pulled me to a stop. "Are you okay? Your eyes are a bit glassy and frenzied-looking. Like that time when you didn't sleep for two days straight because you had too much to do and I found you eating honey by the spoonful."

I didn't even remember that happening. While Vella might have been a lot of things, she did not lie, so I believed that I had weirdly eaten honey because I hadn't had enough sleep. Weirdly enough, I didn't even like honey.

We arrived at her desk and she took a seat, adjusting the chair to the right height.

"How about I take you out to lunch to celebrate your first day and I'll tell you all about what's going on with me and why I look like I just ate spoonfuls of honey?" I offered.

"Okay." She drew the *A* sound out, like she was annoyed I wasn't telling her immediately and intended to pull every detail out of me later. It always amazed me how much she could convey with a single syllable.

"Hang on," I said, and sent a quick text to Adrian reminding him of his meeting.

"Who are you texting?" she demanded as I put my phone down. When I didn't answer, she easily guessed. "Adrian? About that meeting? You know, he is a big boy and he can remember his own meetings. He can even set his own alarms on his phone. You shouldn't have to text him like he's an infant."

"Who texts an infant?" I asked.

She just sighed loudly and waved her hand at me, like she was dismissing the entire situation. "Never mind. Show me how this phone thing works. I'm assuming it rings and then I pick it up and put it to my ear and speak."

It was a good thing she didn't have an immediate supervisor, or else her grade A sarcasm would probably ensure that her first day was also her last.

I spent the morning checking up on Adrian, reminding him about what was next on his agenda, and showing Vella the ropes. She managed to keep her sarcastic comments about my boss to just four, which I took as a good sign.

She also got to attend her first department-wide meeting, where the expectation was that she would take notes. I could tell how bored she was, given the comical faces of distress and exasperation she kept making, and I had a hard time not laughing.

At one point she texted me, This meeting is sucking my will to live. Stay strong, I texted back.

How do you do this every day?

Mostly caffeine and a love for my job, but I knew she didn't want to hear that. I just shook my head at her and went back to listening to Claudia talk about new possible clients. She made deliberate eye contact with me, and I glanced over at Adrian. I was going to have to ask him. Claudia would absolutely check up on whether or not I had done it.

At lunchtime I knew that Adrian had plans to take Colette out, so that freed me up to actually go out somewhere to eat instead of having lunch at my desk. I took Vella to a little bistro around the corner that I'd had cater many meetings at work.

The manager greeted me by name. "Everly! I'm so happy you joined us. I've saved the best table for you."

"Thank you, Joe."

"How do you do that?" Vella asked, actually sounding impressed. "How do you know everybody in New York?"

"I have a lot of contacts," I said, picking up my menu.

"You like everybody." She said it accusingly, like it was a bad thing. "It must be exhausting being you."

I did like everybody. "Only sometimes. How's your first day going so far?"

"Other than that torture method you called a meeting? Pretty good."

I laughed. "It wasn't that bad."

She made a face at me. "Not that bad? My mother once told me after I got my first tattoo that I'd never be able to work in an office because tattoos weren't professional, but she was so mistaken. If anything, they should show potential employers that I have the ability to stay still for long periods of time while sharp needles prick my skin over and over, because that's what that meeting felt like."

I laughed again and thanked the waiter who brought us over some glasses of water.

"Spill," Vella said when he'd left. "What's going on with you?"

I filled her in on everything that had happened last night with Claudia, but I left out how Colette's showing up this morning was probably what had made me appear a bit off. Because I already knew how my best friend felt about my crush.

When I finished, she nodded. "Okay, here's what's going to happen. You're going to stop waiting for that spine donor and tell Adrian you want to pitch. Today. When we get back from lunch. If you put it off, you'll never do it."

She was right. I couldn't wait. The new-client meeting was tomorrow. I was running out of time.

"I'll do it," I said, determined.

If I wanted things to change in my life, I was going to have to be the one to take that first giant leap forward.

No matter how scary it was.

CHAPTER FOUR

When I'd pictured myself being brave, I'd never imagined that I'd be in the office bathroom splashing water on my face and trying to calm down.

It didn't help matters that Vella was glued to my side, encouraging me like a demented goth cheerleader. "You can do this. I believe in you!"

"Right. I can."

There was a fleeting expression on her face, so quick I nearly missed it, but I saw the annoyance mixed with pity, and it made all my nervous feelings intensify. I had to calm down, to focus. I remembered a trick my mother had once taught me and put my fisted hands on my hips, widening my stance.

"What are you doing?" Vella asked.

"It's a superhero stance. Apparently there's studies that say it actually improves your confidence."

"That's not going to work," she said. She was right—it wasn't inspiring positive feelings. All I felt was a little silly. "Try spinning around like Wonder Woman."

"Seriously?"

"Yes."

It couldn't hurt. I shrugged and did as she suggested. I spun around several times with my arms out wide, imagining that I was a powerful Amazon about to conquer Elevated.

I came to a stop and put my hands on the sink until I regained equilibrium.

"How do you feel?" she asked.

"Honestly? A little dizzy."

"Maybe that's a good thing. You'll be focused on your spinning head and not your anxiety. Go ask him now. And we'll go shopping after work as a reward for your bravery."

I nodded. I wasn't going to get what I wanted if I didn't go after it. Even if I liked staying on the sidelines, I knew that I had to march onto the field and ask for my chance to play the game. I opened the bathroom door and started walking toward Adrian's office.

"I don't know why I've been put into this position. You're supposed to be the encouraging one," Vella said.

"Maybe we're rubbing off on each other."

She scowled. "I don't want to be cheerful."

"Sorry not sorry."

We arrived at my desk, and I took a couple more deep breaths. Despite her protesting that she wasn't interested in cheering me on, she said, "You've got this."

I went into Adrian's office before I could change my mind, trying to calm my erratic breathing. I wanted to do a Kool-Aid Man exit through Adrian's wall, but I stayed put.

"I need to ask you something," I said to him.

He didn't even glance up from his phone. "Yes?"

Part of me wanted to chicken out again, but I steeled my spine and squared my shoulders. "Tomorrow, I want . . . I want to pitch at Claudia's potential-client meeting. I know I don't have the title of event planner yet, but I'd like to head that direction and so I wanted to ask you if that would be okay." My words came out in a big whoosh and my heart thudded hard in my chest as I waited.

"Yeah, sure. That's fine with me. Hey, what is the password for my TikTok account again? I can't remember it."

I took his phone and put in the password and handed it back to him. He thanked me, and in a daze, I walked back to my own desk. I texted Vella, letting her know that I'd done it, he'd said yes, and the Wonder Woman spin had worked.

She sent me back a bunch of emojis I didn't understand, including a witch's hat and a left-pointing arrow.

I set my phone down and thought about how Adrian had agreed so easily that I felt incredibly embarrassed for not asking him earlier.

Maybe after the pitch meeting, if my idea was selected, he and I could revisit the idea of my getting a promotion. I'd promise to train my replacement really well, but I wanted the chance to do more.

To stand in the spotlight for a little bit.

And it had been a long time since I'd felt like that.

Adrian left early in the afternoon without telling me where he was going. Which meant that I was able to leave promptly at five o'clock and go shopping at Vella's favorite thrift store with her. She had a long list as to why we were only allowed to shop for clothes at secondhand stores, but my primary reason for shopping there was that it was the only place I could afford.

Within a few minutes Vella already had a big pile of clothing draped over her arm and I absentmindedly flipped through their dress section.

Until I came across something that made my heart start racing and my hands fall to my sides.

It was the blue-and-white Monti dress that Queen Katerina had worn on her visit to India with her husband a few years ago. She wore only Monterran designers, and this had been one of my favorite looks on her. I loved her style. The dress had sold out within minutes online after she wore it, so even if I could have afforded it, I never would have been able to grab one before they were gone.

There was no way this was her actual dress, given that I was in New York and Kat's dresses were probably in a museum somewhere, but it looked exactly the same. I wanted to see if it was an actual Monti dress, but there was no tag. It could be a replica. But none of those things mattered. I had to buy this. I didn't even care how much it cost.

Or what size it was. If it was too small, I'd put on some Spanx or something to force it to fit. I checked the tag, sure it wouldn't be my size, but to my sheer delight, it was.

I took it off the rack and held it in front of me, marching over to the cashier. I couldn't believe this was about to be mine.

It felt like a sign from the universe that things were about to turn around for me.

~

I wore the dress to work the next day. It was a bit more casual than the sort of attire I usually wore, but it was giving me an incredible boost of confidence to wear something exactly like what Kat had worn. She was always so sure of herself, of her place in the world, and she went after the things she wanted.

As bizarre as it might have sounded, I felt like this dress was imbuing me with some of her strength.

Last night, after I'd hand-washed the dress and left it out to dry, I'd spent the rest of the evening working on my plans for today.

The potential client was a teenage girl named Hyacinth Albrecht. Her family was from the Washington, DC, area, where her father had some kind of business. I didn't fully grasp what they did exactly, but whatever it was, it seemed to involve owning actual money trees.

Hyacinth was about to turn sixteen years old, and she wanted an extravagant, luxurious party here in New York City to celebrate. I'd spent a lot of time looking at her social media, trying to get a feel for what she'd enjoy, and I had tons of ideas running around in my head. I figured that after meeting her, I'd have a better sense of what she might gravitate toward.

I went into the meeting feeling like a million bucks. I wondered how much a tiara would cost and whether it would be too ridiculous if I wore that to the office, too.

Everybody filed into the conference room, and Adrian sat in his usual spot at the head of the table. He looked annoyed, while Claudia seemed very sure of herself and pleased with the situation.

Vella led Hyacinth and her mother, a woman named Marie, into the conference room. Claudia greeted them, shaking Marie's hand.

Hyacinth didn't look up from her cell phone, even when they sat down in their chairs. Claudia told them a bit about what we did, and how we would love it if they would choose us to plan their event. "We have some of the best event planners in the industry right here in this room. You will get personalized, concierge-level attention, and you won't have to worry about a single thing. We will handle every single detail for you."

Marie glanced at Hyacinth, maybe hoping for some engagement, but the teenager ignored all of us.

Claudia continued, "What kind of budget were you planning on? And how many guests were you planning on inviting?"

Marie mentioned a mid–six figures number that made me want to gasp. It was more than some rich people spent on their weddings! I'd never had a budget that high. Marie added that they were expecting about two hundred and fifty people, making it a bigger budget than most of our corporate clients would spend on a much larger audience. We were going to be able to do so much with that.

"We had an event planner prior to this, but we had to part ways when we realized that our visions didn't align," Marie said, and there was a slightly bitter tone to her voice. "As I mentioned in my email, we already have a venue secured and the invitations sent. We are planning on most of our guests flying in and staying at the hotel. We are short on time—Hyacinth's birthday is only three weeks away."

There was some fidgeting and mumbling around me, but no one expressed their surprise out loud. We usually had months and months to plan events. Less than thirty days? That was fast. It could easily be done with enough money, though, so long as the clients were decisive and would trust our input. We would also need to have the vendors return phone calls and follow through with their promises.

Eighty percent of event planning was babysitting vendors.

But again, with the kind of cash Marie was willing to spend, I guessed that the vendors we contacted would be very happy to do as we asked.

"Do you have an idea of what you'd like, Hyacinth?" Claudia asked.

"Something not stupid," she mumbled, again avoiding eye contact. At least she would speak when spoken to—that was good.

But it wasn't a lot to go on.

She and her family weren't from New York, which would take the party in a different direction. Had Hyacinth grown up here, the party probably would have been themed something like *Existential Crisis of the Ongoing Ennui of Euphoria.*

Claudia introduced a couple of the more senior event planners and two of the event designers. They began to share some of their ideas, complete with mood boards and suggestions for how they could potentially decorate the selected venue.

No response from Hyacinth.

The longer this went on, the more aggravated Marie became. I understood it—she was about to spend a lot of money to make sure her daughter had an unforgettable party, and Hyacinth didn't seem like she cared at all.

Several people on the team exchanged looks, as we were all aware that nothing seemed to be getting through to her.

Kat could do this. She could speak out.

So could I.

I stood up and realized that I didn't know the protocol for pitching. I'd been in these meetings before, and the planners and designers seemed to instinctively know who should go next and what they should say. If I asked for my turn to pitch, it might make me look like I didn't know what I was doing. Several people looked surprised, but Claudia just beamed.

I couldn't do a Wonder Woman spin here, so I settled on doing a quick mental one before starting to talk.

"I'm Everly Aprile. I'm . . ." My voice trailed off. I couldn't say I was an administrative assistant. I would undermine myself before I'd even begun.

An awkward silence filled the room, and I heard a person off to my right whisper, "I hope someone knows the Heimlich, because she's about to choke."

No, I wasn't. I did another mental Wonder Woman spin before I launched into the beginning of my pitch.

"There are a lot of directions we could go in. Modern or vintage, sophisticated or more playful." My voice wasn't shaking, which was good. I had been hoping that Hyacinth might respond to one of the things I'd listed so that I'd have an idea of what direction to go, but again, she didn't look up.

I glanced down at my dress and thought of Hyacinth's Instagram account, which I had pored over. I'd noticed in some of her older posts that she liked fairy tales, and had reposted images with dreamy, gauzy backgrounds featuring glass slippers or castles in them. Nothing recent, but it was worth a shot.

"What about a fairy-tale party?"

Hyacinth winced. "I'm not turning six years old. Besides, Cinderella has been so done to death."

I wished I'd thought to prepare visuals. "You're right. We don't need another interpretation of an old fairy tale, and this definitely would not be a party for little girls. What about a modern love story, full of gorgeous castles, formal ball gowns, and handsome princes? Based on a country known for its beautiful landscapes and snowy mountains, with a distinct and vibrant culture that would be unlike anything else you've ever seen. Monterra has so many unbelievably romantic and true stories of royalty finding their soulmates. Your party will be fit for an American princess."

I knew hardly anything about Monterran culture, but I would figure it out later. Especially since I could see that it was working. Hyacinth had finally torn her gaze away from her phone.

She studied me for a few moments and then said, "Whatever. Let's do that."

My mouth dropped open. I knew we were competing with some other big firms who had much more experience with these sorts of events, and I'd thought we'd have to wait to find out whether or not they'd chosen us.

Not to mention that I knew there were other senior staff members who were waiting for their turns to present. Now they wouldn't need to.

I couldn't believe it had worked.

"Excellent!" Claudia said, standing. "We will get those contracts drawn up tonight, and Everly will be in touch."

Marie's expression had completely changed, and she looked both relieved and delighted. Hyacinth's attention was back on her phone, but she managed to follow behind her mother as they went back out to the lobby.

I stood in place, my heart hammering. I'd done it. This felt unreal.

"Well done," Claudia said, as she came over to shake my hand. "You just landed your first big account. You'll be handling the entire party from beginning to end. Are you ready for that?"

I glanced behind her, thinking I'd see Adrian. I wondered what he thought about all of this.

But he had already left the room.

I ignored the twinge of disappointment and smiled at Claudia. "I am ready."

"This is going to be a huge responsibility, and a lot is riding on this. I will need you to check in with me every couple of days and update me as to how things are going."

That was entirely fair. "I will."

"Good. There should definitely be a promotion at the end of what is sure to be your very successful event," she said. "Keep me in the loop."

Yeah, no pressure or anything.

I couldn't believe she was putting so much faith in me.

Sinking into my chair, I thought about my immediate future. Now I had to do all of Adrian's work and plan this elaborate birthday party?

I was never going to sleep again.

I hoped we didn't have any honey at home.

Adrian came back into the conference room, and my stomach fluttered in response. Had he returned to congratulate me? He was beaming, and I took that as a very good sign.

But he didn't have any words of praise for me. "Everly, I need you to call some jewelry stores for me. I've decided that I'm going to propose to Colette, and you have to find the perfect ring. We're leaving tonight so that I can meet her family in Paris. I need you to buy tickets for us—I'm planning on being there for two weeks. You can arrange to have the ring sent over to me later. I'll be sure to text you the address. Let Claudia know, will you?"

He was getting engaged?

CHAPTER FIVE

After Adrian's announcement, I had a strange mixture of emotions. I was happy for him and Colette, but disappointed that I'd never get a chance to go out on a date with him to see if there could be anything between us. Excited that my pitch had worked, worried that Adrian might not react well to it. Unaware of my inner turmoil, my colleagues congratulated me and offered help if I needed it.

They were excited because this event was unlike anything else that we had ever done. To be honest, corporate events were boring. There was very little opportunity to put our own spin or design on it. Typically there was a seminar/conference with speakers and we provided snacks and swag. That was it. There were no decorations other than a banner or a backdrop, or basics like a podium and an AV system. Everything had to be professional.

Translation—sterile and boring.

But a rich teenager's birthday party? That could be a lot of fun.

I had lunch with Vella again and found myself distracted. I shouldn't have been surprised that Adrian was getting engaged. It made sense. He and Colette had been dating for a long time, and she was a great person. Marriage was the next logical step. Of course he wanted to marry Colette, and of course she would want to marry Adrian. I completely understood it.

It still made me a bit sad.

"Earth to Everly!" Vella said, waving her hand in front of my face. "You're not still moping about that lump of clay getting engaged, are you?"

"Lump of clay?" I repeated. "What does that mean?"

"That is a man not yet fully formed. He needs a lot of molding and spending time in a kiln before he'll actually be relationship material. I don't envy that French chick."

That was the problem—I did envy Colette. Being jealous of someone while still liking them as a person was a very confusing problem to have.

I wanted to change the subject. "So I now have to design and plan a luxury birthday party based on a culture I know next to nothing about. I should have pitched something British themed."

"What do you know about British culture?"

My mind went blank. "Uh, *Doctor Who*, those guards with the big hats, and the royal family."

Vella made a scoffing sound. "Americans caring about British royals is like asking Protestants to be super invested in the pope. I wouldn't have allowed that theme. No culture who calls cookies 'biscuits' should be a theme of anything."

I laughed, knowing she was teasing me because she knew how much I loved all royal families worldwide. "Seriously, though, I am going to have to study Monterran culture."

"Good thing we have the internet."

"No, I need to experience it. I've always been more of an auditory and tactile learner. I do better having someone explain things to me, or physically doing stuff myself."

She narrowed her eyes at me. "And how are you planning on experiencing Monterra? Are you going to fly there?"

Ha. Even if I put all six of my credit cards together, I still wouldn't have enough money to buy a ticket to Monterra. "I wish, but that won't happen. My lack of knowledge is concerning, though. I don't even know how they celebrate birthdays."

Vella picked up her phone, typed something, and then studied her screen for a bit. "I looked it up. Monterrans celebrate birthdays with a birthday cake and by singing 'Happy Birthday to You' in Italian. The party is planned. You're welcome."

Our lunch came out—she had ordered a salad, while I'd gotten the hamburger and fries. She gave my food a wistful look and sighed.

"I get your jealousy," I told her, while pointing at her food. "That looks like the lunch of someone whose doctor told them they would die if they didn't make major changes to their eating habits."

She grumbled in response but ate her slightly wilted lettuce. "I can't eat things that used to be alive."

"Lettuce and tomatoes used to be alive."

If Vella rolled her eyes any harder, she was going to spin the earth off its axis. "You know what I mean. I've watched too many YouTube videos. I can't eat meat. Even if it does smell really delicious."

Her phone buzzed and she checked it. "Why am I getting messages from your office manager to contribute money for birthday cupcakes? I don't even know who Dan from Accounting is." Her eyes widened. "They want me to pitch in one hundred dollars? For cupcakes?"

I shrugged. Elevated liked big parties. The bigger the better.

"What is in those cupcakes?" she asked in disbelief.

"Gold flakes and cocaine," I promptly replied and she laughed.

Joking with her made me feel better, a fact she seemed to pick up on quickly. "Does this mean you're over Adrian now?"

Was I over the crush I'd nursed for the last four years? Not so much. "Teasing you doesn't mean I'm suddenly done with my residual feelings."

"That's too bad. Because now that I've worked with him, I have to tell you, I don't get it."

I had a french fry halfway to my mouth when she said this, and I froze. "What do you mean?"

"I'd like to tell you, but my New Year's resolution was to stop insulting people at work." She paused. "But given that it's been over ten months since New Year's Eve and I've already broken it repeatedly, here it is. Adrian is not very bright."

Indignation swelled up in my chest. "He is, too!"

"You really do always try to find the best in others. It must be so exhausting and disappointing."

I'd actually discovered the opposite to be true. I had faith in other people, and I'd found them to generally be who I thought they were.

"I've been going through his social media," she said, gearing up for what was presumably going to be a long rant. "He wears sunglasses inside and calls people 'doll' and 'champ.' He posts pictures of his food every day. It's not like his four hundred and sixty-two pictures of lobster risotto are going to wind up at MoMA."

"That doesn't mean he's not smart."

"He is absolutely the kind of guy who has unironically called a woman 'milady' at some point in his life. He's a human golden retriever. And not the lovable, adorable kind, but the inbred one that isn't very smart. His brain cells have to huddle together for warmth. And he's lazy and lets you do everything for him while he takes all the credit."

That one stung a little. "You don't understand. Adrian and I are a team. We do things together. His success is my success."

My phone beeped with a message, and my cheeks flushed when I realized who it was from. As if he'd somehow intuited that we'd been discussing him.

"Is that your assignment?" she asked. "What are you supposed to bring to the birthday celebration for Dan from Accounting? The *Mona Lisa* and a Fabergé egg?"

I didn't want to lie to her, but I also didn't want her to see the text. I wasn't sure what to do.

Vella noticed my expression and took my phone from my hand, while I protested. "Hey!"

She started reading Adrian's text out loud. "Hey doll, could you feed the kids and get my dry cleaning? I also need you to be at my apartment tomorrow between noon and four o'clock because I have an electrician coming to install some new lights for the aquarium. Could you also water my plants and grab my mail while I'm gone?"

My cheeks got even hotter.

"Are you kidding me with this?" she said, squeezing my phone so tightly I worried she was going to break it. "Are you going to scrub his toilets and wash his windows, too?"

"I don't do windows," I tried to joke, but she wasn't having it. "It's fine. I don't mind helping him out." I didn't mention that I had done these sorts of things for him many, many times. Because I sensed she wouldn't be happy about that.

At all.

"You're like his girlfriend with none of the benefits," she muttered. "And who are 'the kids'?"

"He has a pet python and some sharks."

For a second she didn't speak, her mouth opening and shutting again like she was trying to form words but couldn't. Her voice returned quickly. "Nobody should own a shark! Just so you know, they say the type of pet you have is a representation of who you are as a person." I made a dissenting noise at this, but she pressed on. "I guess the kind of people who have decided it's okay to own a shark should be allowed to because, more likely than not, this is going to end up in some kind of Darwinian natural-selection situation."

I tried to say something, but she kept going. "A shark is the kind of pet a serial killer would own."

"He's not a serial killer."

"Yay for him?" she said sarcastically. "One point in the pro column—he doesn't unalive people. It doesn't outweigh all the negatives. It's like you're his beck-and-call girl."

"I am most definitely not his call girl," I responded.

"No, but you'd like to be."

That was so ridiculous it didn't even merit a response. When Vella got worked up like this, it wasn't worth arguing with her. I just nodded and said nothing.

She didn't understand how things were between me and Adrian. As I'd said, we were a team. I liked that he relied on me. Needed me.

I enjoyed being useful and good at my job.

"Just so you know, I don't like him," she added.

"But you don't like anybody." It was hard to take her judgment of Adrian seriously, given that she had been at Elevated for only two days and really did hate everybody else in the world besides me.

Vella studied me for a moment, chewing on her lettuce the same way an evil, demented bunny might. "Regardless of how you feel about him, the bottom line here is that Adrian's getting married to someone else. You need to move past it."

She was right. Even if I didn't want to admit it, I had to find a way to go forward and let go of this silly crush.

"Do you have plans tonight?" she asked. I was immediately suspicious.

"Yes, I do."

"Sitting alone in the dark and drinking excessive amounts of beer while watching videos of royal weddings does not constitute plans."

"Sure it does."

"Nope. We're going out and having a good time."

I started to protest. "But I won't have—"

Vella held up her hand. "Adrian's out of town. You don't have hours and hours of sitting at your desk waiting on him ahead of you. You'll get to leave the office at a reasonable hour, and you can come out and have irresponsible fun like the twentysomething that you are."

Again, she was right. My schedule had opened up considerably. Without having Adrian here assigning me busywork or needing me to babysit his time, remind him constantly about meetings, or follow up with vendors for him, I could go out and act my age.

I did have Hyacinth's party to plan, but I already had a bunch of vendors in mind that would be responsive and easy to work with. I couldn't imagine that Hyacinth was going to change her mind multiple times about what she wanted, as she'd barely agreed to the theme I'd presented.

And now I was going to have a full eight hours at the office to devote to her event.

"Okay." I nodded. "Let's go out."

"Yes!" Vella pumped her fist in triumph, as if she'd just won a victory. "But on one condition, though."

Uh-oh. "What condition?"

"You have to speak to at least one man before the night's over."

I nodded. I could manage that.

"An attractive, age-appropriate man," she added on, trying to close off any loopholes. "You're not going to chat up some middle-aged bartender and claim that it counts."

That made my stomach feel a little queasy. It had been an actual eternity since I'd spoken to a cute guy outside of the office. I'd had zero work-life balance for so many years that I was pretty sure the part of me that knew how to flirt had dried up completely, like the Sahara.

"And bonus points if you get his number."

"Sure." I was as likely to run into the Easter Bunny as I was to get a hot guy's phone number, so it was easier just to placate her.

Vella was still revved up, though. "Because you know the best way to get over someone—"

I interrupted her. "Is this where you tell me it's to get under someone else?"

She pressed her lips together. "No. The best way to get over someone is to light his hair on fire."

That made me laugh.

She smiled slightly, then let out a long sigh. "You've turned me into your unintentional cheerleader, Everly. Because you are altering the core of my personality, the least you can do is to get out there and find the man of your dreams. If for no other reason than I wouldn't mind having the apartment to myself a few times a week."

No way was that going to happen.

Poor Vella was about to be so disappointed.

CHAPTER SIX

"What is this place?" I asked her as we stood outside an actual hole in the wall. Well, not really. It had a door. But one that was so battered that it looked like it had survived an explosion and been welded back into place.

"You'll see," Vella said. "I think you're really going to like it."

Now I was concerned. She usually wasn't a very good judge of things I would like.

We'd gone home after work and changed our outfits. She had insisted I wear something low cut and short, and I gave in. I did wear my coat, though, because November in New York was cold.

Vella had put on black pants, a black shirt, and black combat boots, and heavy eye makeup. She had a very "back off" thing going on, but she looked fantastic. I'd reminded her to wear a coat, but she'd ignored me. And predictably enough, within a few minutes of leaving the apartment, she was shivering, although she pretended she was fine.

I didn't get it.

She had lent me a purple, clingy dress. It wasn't the kind of thing I'd normally wear, and it surprised me that she actually owned something that wasn't black.

She yanked on the busted door, and it creaked loudly as she got it open. We stepped inside and I gasped in surprise.

I had expected a tiny room, smoky air, and the general scent of desperation and resignation.

But the outside was deceptive. This bar had high ceilings, was brightly lit, and boasted several television screens all showing the same soccer game. The floors were polished, the countertop of the bar gleaming. There were a lot of people laughing, watching the game. It wasn't overly crowded, but was definitely bustling. The most surprising thing was that it had a coat check—most bars in New York City didn't. I gave them my coat. Vella took the ticket and stuck it into her back pocket. I was about to tell her that I could put it in my purse, but she was heading into the main area of the bar. I hurried behind her, tugging on the bottom of my dress.

"Are you going to tell me where we are?" I asked.

"This is a Monterran sports bar!" she announced, spreading her arms wide. "It's the only place in New York that's Monterra-themed, and I thought you could hang out here, get the vibe of the place, and use that as part of your research."

"That's . . ." I trailed off, my mouth hanging open. "Incredibly thoughtful."

I'd been mistaken. She could find things that I'd like.

"Don't say that so loud," she grumbled. "I don't want anyone to hear you."

"You don't have to worry. The secret that you're a nice person is safe with me," I said.

She nodded, satisfied. "I also thought it would be the perfect place for you to meet someone. Maybe you'll find your own . . . What's that king guy's name again?"

"Nico."

"Yes. Maybe there's a Nico here," she said, and it had me scanning the crowd of people gathered there with sudden interest.

The king of Monterra had a metric ton of paternal cousins who were also princes. They were most likely all in their home country, but some of them had to travel, right? What if one of them had come to New York and was here in this bar at this very moment?

And what would I do if I met an actual Monterran prince?

Honestly, I'd probably make some inarticulate sound and then pass out.

Vella said, "Okay, we need to divide and conquer. I'll be over at the bar and you go sit at one of those tables."

I felt my throat seizing. I put my hand on her arm. "Wait, you're making me try and meet someone alone?" At the very least I had thought she'd be sitting next to me.

"I have faith in you. There, those people are leaving." She ushered me over to a booth that hadn't been cleaned yet. It was too big for one person, but Vella was determined.

"You should stay," I told her, wanting to use her security blanket-ness to keep me feeling safe.

Vella shook her head. "Since I know you're not going to approach anyone, someone will have to come over and talk to you. And sitting next to me will make you unapproachable."

"Why do you say that?" I asked.

She gave me a pointed look. "We both know I'm very good at scaring men off. And the kind of guys who would be brave enough to say hi are not the type you'd be interested in."

Vella was right about that. She and I had polar opposite tastes in men. She tended to like hipsters who cheated on her constantly because of their deeply held beliefs that monogamy was a social construct, while I was apparently drawn to men who were getting engaged to other women.

"Do a quick Wonder Woman spin," she said.

"What?" My eyes darted around, making sure no one was watching us, because Vella was going to get her way. She usually did.

"Spin. It'll give you a boost."

I swallowed hard and then did as she requested, spinning a couple of times before settling back into place. No one seemed to have noticed and I didn't hear any mocking laughter, so I figured I was safe.

"Good luck!" she said. She made her way over to a barstool and waved the bartender down.

Not seeing another option, I sat in the booth, scooting over toward the middle. I felt silly sitting there by myself and a bit pathetic. The waitress came by, apologized for the messy table, and quickly started cleaning it.

"Are you from Monterra?" I asked, recognizing her accent.

"Sì," she said. "Most of the waitstaff are. Many of the patrons, as well."

That made me feel a little better because it was honestly exciting to be surrounded by so many Monterrans.

"What can I get you?" she asked.

"I'll have a bottle of Heineken," I told her.

She said she'd be right back and I surveyed the room. This booth was in a far corner, which was probably going to defeat Vella's plans of a guy coming over to hit on me.

Although that was fine with me.

I watched Vella for a couple of minutes. She gave off a very do-not-speak-to-me vibe, but it didn't keep men away. If anything, they seemed to take it as some kind of personal challenge, and to nobody's surprise, there were two men vying to chat her up already.

It was probably why she assumed that she could stick me in this corner and men would be lining up to come over and speak to me. I wished she understood that for the rest of us, life did not work that way.

But to my great delight, someone did come over to meet me.

It was a big, beautiful, all-white dog, a breed I didn't recognize. She climbed up onto the bench, coming over to sit next to me.

"Hello there," I cooed at her, offering her my hand. She leaned her head forward, as if expecting a pet, and I happily obliged. Her tongue lolled out as I started scratching behind her ears.

She was wearing an ID tag.

"Basta," I read. "Is that your name?" I asked, still petting her. I grabbed my phone with my free hand to look it up. It meant *stop* or *enough* in Italian. "Which means your owner is probably from Monterra and you are a particularly mischievous girl."

She gave me the sweetest expression, as if that were the furthest thing from the truth, and I smiled at her.

"You know, I read once that scientists say dogs get a rush of oxytocin when they look at people, just like we get when we look at you," I said as I continued to rub her ears. "That dogs think humans are adorable."

Basta made a short grunting noise, like she agreed with me.

My phone beeped and I had a message from Vella.

Not a dog, a man! You had one job. Also, if you have to pee, hold
it because the bathroom here is a human rights violation.

I had only a moment to wonder when she'd checked out the bathroom when I got another text from Adrian.

When will you be able to go to the jewelers to pick out a ring?

I texted back, Soon.

Another notification came in from Facebook. My stepmother had posted a picture of her kids and my dad.

Happy family! #blessed

My father had abandoned us when I was young and had gone through a long string of women before settling on my stepmother. They'd had four kids together in the last five years. I'd never met any of them, was never invited to holidays or events. I didn't matter in my father's life at all. The only acknowledgment I'd ever gotten from them was her accepting my friend request. He absolutely doted on his new kids, and it always made me feel like there was something I personally lacked because he'd never loved me the same way.

Those twisted, painful feelings returned, and I couldn't help myself. I started to cry. Not huge, heaving sobs because that would have been humiliating to do in public. My throat felt tight from trying to stay quiet, and my eyes burned. I could feel my shoulders shaking and kept my head down.

Basta reached over to lick the tears on my cheeks, and I found myself putting my arms around her neck, hugging her tightly.

"Are you all right?"

I glanced up and saw the most handsome man I'd ever met in real life standing at the edge of the table.

My heart started to pound hard in my chest as I blinked my tears away. I had an immediate response—it was like steel striking against flint. I felt an undeniable spark when our eyes met.

It had been years since I'd felt that way.

He had dark hair, almost black, and light eyes. Most likely blue, but it was hard to tell in this lighting. I flashed to an early interview Kat had given, before the royal family had helped her refine her image, back when she would be completely honest and overshare. When the interviewer asked her what she'd thought the first time she'd met Nico, she said she had thought he looked like Superman's hotter cousin. I completely understood the sentiment because the man in front of me blew both Nico and Superman out of the water.

"Are you all right?" he repeated, looking so sweetly concerned. My fizzy, overexcited brain registered that he rolled his *R*s the same way Monterrans did. It was faint, but there.

The still-functioning part of my mind reminded me that I had been sitting there not responding to his initial and repeated question for an uncomfortable length of time.

"Yes!" Whoops, needed to modulate my voice. I shouldn't be shouting. "I'm okay. Well, okay-ish."

I wondered if he was lost or something and needed directions. I couldn't figure out why else he'd be talking to me right now.

So I was completely shocked when he asked, "May I join you?"

You can do anything you want to me. My hands flew up to my flushed cheeks, as I didn't know if I had just thought that sentence or said it out loud.

"Yes." I croaked the word out and cleared my throat and loudly repeated it. "Yes. Please."

Given that he sat down instead of running screaming into the night, it seemed I'd managed to keep my thoughts about letting him have his way with me all to myself.

The waitress returned with my beer, handing it to me. "Ciao, what can I get you to . . ."

Her voice trailed off when she looked up from her pad to make eye contact with him.

She put a hand over her chest and I completely understood her reaction.

"Drink?" she squeaked, as if she suddenly realized she hadn't finished her question and was staring. Not that anyone would blame her. "What can I get you to drink?"

Some part of me felt relief because the fact that she was speaking to him meant I hadn't hallucinated him and he was really sitting next to me, being impossibly handsome.

He smiled at her and asked, "What would you recommend?"

His voice sounded seductive, and I wondered if he was the kind of person who flirted with everybody and I wasn't special. Deflating, but expected.

"Uh, everything. Everything's good," she said, leaning against the table and batting her lashes at him. I'd never seen anyone do that in real life. The detached part of my brain that wasn't experiencing vivid jealousy wondered if he was going to respond to her.

Then my ovaries went up in flames when he ordered his drink in Italian. It was so sexy I wanted to faint like one of those sickly girls from Victorian times. She responded to him in Italian and I didn't know what she was saying, but based on her body language and tone, I was guessing it was something like, "So, fellow sexy person, would you like to get out of here?"

But he shook his head and just said, "Grazie."

That I understood. *Thank you.*

Was it a *thanks but no thanks*?

It seemed to be, given that waitress's look of disappointment as she left.

"I told her I'll have what you're having," he said. I guessed there was more to it than that, but he didn't elaborate and I didn't ask for specifics. He went on, "But if someone had asked me to guess your favorite drink, I probably would have picked chardonnay."

He didn't need to know that my drink of choice was usually whatever was on sale at the bodega two blocks from my apartment. I found myself preening a bit that he thought I was more sophisticated than I actually was.

"I'm from a small town in Alabama, and drinking beer was the only thing to do there."

His eyes crinkled in amusement, and heaven help me, I wanted to kiss those sexy little creases. "But you don't have an accent."

"I worked hard to get rid of it. It comes back out when I'm drunk or around other southerners." I lifted my beer up, intending to take a drink because I definitely needed the liquid courage, but I hesitated because I didn't want to risk getting sloppy. Not that I was ever going to see this incredibly hot man again, but when I looked back at this night as one of my fond yet unbelievable memories, I didn't want my throwing up in a sewer grate to be part of it. I set the frosty bottle back down on the table. "When I started at my job, people would make fun of my accent, and it seemed like my superiors didn't take me as seriously. I wanted to move up the ranks and thought that might be a way to do it."

I briefly thought of who I had been at eighteen, how much more driven I'd been then, willing to eradicate my southern accent to get ahead. I wondered where that girl had gone.

He leaned toward me, looking at me like I was the most interesting woman in the entire world. "That's a shame. You should be allowed to be yourself."

His words were so innocent, the sort of thing one kind stranger would say to another, but it made me feel understood in a way that I hadn't for a while. It was disconcerting.

Out of total nervousness I smiled at him and said, "Speaking of accents, I noticed yours, too. You're Monterran, right? My roommate and I came here tonight specifically to meet someone from Monterra."

"Why is that?" he asked, genuinely curious.

I hadn't had a man pay this much attention to me, well, ever, and I started to gush. "I have this birthday party I have to plan that's based on your culture and I've never actually spoken to somebody from Monterra before and it feels like divine intervention that you're here and you just made my whole night."

As if my mouth were a horse, my brain pulled at the reins to get it to slow down. When I was nervous like this, I either babbled or clammed up completely, and right now both of those reactions were bad. I told myself to try to act like someone who had actually spoken to another human being.

"I'm glad I'm here to help. I see you met my favorite girl, Basta."

Oh my, I had completely forgotten about the dog curled up on my left side. That spoke to the power of his hotness, because I never forgot about adorable furry friends.

"Is she yours?"

He nodded. "She is."

"What kind of dog is she?"

"A Spinone Italiano."

"I've never heard of that breed before. She is one beautiful dog, though." Basta put her head in my lap so that I would keep scratching her ears.

"She knows it, too. Do you have a pet? Are you a dog or a cat person?"

"I'm an everything person. I'd pet an alligator if the little jerk wouldn't try to bite my hand off."

He laughed, and it was the most glorious thing I'd ever heard. I actually got chills from it.

"No wonder Basta came over to say hello. She must have sensed that. She's been starved for attention lately. She just got out of quarantine and I didn't want to leave her home tonight. Fortunately, they're dog friendly here."

"Quarantine?" I repeated, wondering if she'd been sick.

"I just moved to New York."

A newbie. "Well, I've been here for four years, so if you need a tour guide, just let me know and I'll be happy to help." I'd also be happy to bear his children, but I figured I should leave that part out.

"Thank you, I'll remember that. I'm Max, by the way."

He offered me his hand and I hesitated for a moment before shaking it—given how I was reacting to him just from our proximity to each other, I didn't know what would happen if we touched. Realizing that I was going to make this more awkward than it needed to be, I took his hand. When we made contact, his warm palm against mine, it was like static electricity times ten thousand. Like he was a live wire, sending volts directly into every nerve ending in my body. All the cells in my body lit up at his touch.

I quickly pulled back because my inclination was to sit there and keep his hand in my possession all night long, which he might object to, and he'd probably be so unreasonable as to want said hand returned to him.

And it shouldn't have made me giddy that I knew his name. "Max? Is that short for Maximus or Massimo?" I couldn't think of any other Italian names that might have Max as a nickname.

"I don't know you well enough to share that information with you," he said with the sexiest wink that had my stomach doing somersaults.

"Do I at least get your last name?"

He hesitated for a moment before he said, "Colby."

Max Colby. If I were still in middle school, I would be writing his name in my notebook over and over again. Mrs. Max Colby. Everly Colby. Max and Everly.

Colby didn't sound like an Italian surname, but thanks to the research Vella had done this afternoon out of boredom, I now knew that people from all over Europe immigrated to Monterra.

"And you are?" he prompted.

Why was I so awkward? "Everly Aprile."

"Like the month?"

"Yes, but it has an *E* on the end."

"I suppose you're fortunate that your parents didn't name you March," he teased.

"Oh, I don't think you can make fun of anyone else's name, Mr. Cheese." I was rewarded with another laugh, and even if the conversation ended at this very moment, I would consider the night a complete success.

"Everly Aprile," he repeated, and I felt a little lightheaded at the way his accent caressed my name. "I like the alliteration."

Technically it started with two different vowels, but I wasn't going to correct the sexy man. "It kind of makes me sound like a superhero, right?"

"Are you?"

Ha. "Not quite."

"You seem to me like the kind of woman who has a secret superpower."

While I wished that were true, he could not have been more off base. "Do you mean besides making the worst possible decisions in my personal life and the ability to whip up the world's most perfect grilled cheese?"

He grinned, and that "I'm about to faint" feeling was back. "What about your power to put men under your spell?"

I couldn't help but laugh before I said, "I think I'd know by now if that was true."

He seemed to move even closer to me. "It might be truer than you think."

CHAPTER SEVEN

Heart palpitations. Actual heart palpitations. I wondered if the bar had an emergency defibrillator.

While I knew Max was just being nice and probably flirted the way other people breathed, I couldn't help my giddy and embarrassed reaction, which was currently rendering me speechless.

My phone buzzed with a text from Vella, and I was grateful for the excuse to break eye contact, as I was about to do something completely socially inappropriate with this gorgeous man.

Good job on talking to a human. He's cute.

Cute? The man was retina-melting hot. If I actually were a super-hero, he would be like what my archnemesis would construct in her lab to distract me while she conquered the world.

And her evil plan would work.

"Trouble?" he asked, probably due to my annoyed expression.

"No, my roommate is checking up on me," I said. "She forced me to come out tonight so that I could meet someone."

"I'm supposing that means you're single."

Was that a hopeful note in his voice or was I projecting? "To quote my meemaw, I am only single because none of mankind's champions have yet proven worthy." That sounded so much better than "Yes, I am desperately alone and have been for a very long time, thank you."

"What's a meemaw?" he asked, appearing confused. "Did you grow up in a Dr. Seuss book?"

I laughed and said, "No, 'meemaw' is a nickname for 'grandma' where I'm from."

"Ah. So you were saying that your roommate is trying to get you to meet someone—I'm assuming there's a reason for it."

"There is. I've had a crush on my boss for the last four years and he told me today that he's marrying his longtime girlfriend. She's worried that I'm only interested in unavailable men."

While I knew there was a rule that you shouldn't talk about this kind of thing when you were meeting someone you might date, my brain could logically accept that there was zero chance of that happening. It was kind of freeing, knowing I could just say whatever I wanted and it wouldn't change the outcome of this night.

I didn't have to play any games.

"Ouch. I'm sorry," he said.

He might have said it out of politeness, but I detected a real sincerity there that touched me. "Thank you. I don't think I'm ready to meet anyone, though. I feel . . . a bit emotionally unavailable myself."

Although if Max made me an offer, I would seriously consider it.

I added, "She wants me to get someone's phone number."

"I have a phone number. I can give you mine."

"That's . . ." I trailed off, not sure how to respond. Was this like, a pity thing? His good deed for the day? I didn't want to be his charity case. "You don't have to do that."

"Last time I checked, phone numbers were meant to be shared." He put his hand out for my cell and I unlocked it and then handed it to him, a little thrill going through me. He sent himself a text, and I heard when it buzzed.

"There," he said, giving the phone back to me. "Now you can tell your roommate you fulfilled all of her demands."

"Thanks." It had been a kind gesture on his part.

"You know, I get the pushy-loved-one thing. My relationship ended a few months ago, and ever since then, my cousin has been nagging me to go out and have fun. I keep telling her I'm fine. I'm not depressed, I've just moved to a new city. She doesn't listen, though. She was particularly relentless tonight, and I thought it would be fun to come out and watch the Reali game."

"Reali?" I echoed.

He pointed at the television screens. "The Monterran Reali football team. 'Reali' means 'royals.'"

Another reminder of how little I knew about Monterra. "Is your cousin here babysitting you, too?" I asked.

"No, but she did make me send her a picture of myself at the bar to prove I'd left the house."

"So we're both here under duress."

"It doesn't feel quite like that now," he said with what could only be called a shy smile, but I was pretty sure this man had never been shy or unsure of himself a day in his entire life.

Heaven save me from a kind man who was just being nice, because I was fully misreading everything he was saying and doing as if he were hitting on me.

It really had been too long since I'd been in a relationship. Or even had an actual date. And this was the result—attributing all kinds of flirtatious meaning to regular conversation.

Maybe dating was something I needed to make time for in my real life. If I wanted to get over my crush, then I should start trying to meet people.

People who weren't unrealistically hot and weren't still hung up on their ex-girlfriend.

What kind of woman would Max date? I found myself intensely curious.

"Do you have a picture of her?" I asked, knowing it was entirely inappropriate for me to be asking. He had every right to shut me down and tell me I was being too invasive.

Instead he looked adorably confused. "A picture of who? My cousin?"

"No, your ex-girlfriend." I knew I was being weird and that it was an odd request. I wondered if he'd ask me the reason why.

It was partly due to my insatiable curiosity, but mostly because I wanted to prove my theory about the kind of woman he'd be in a relationship with.

He frowned slightly. "Probably. Hold on."

Max scrolled through his phone and then turned it toward me. There was a picture of him with a dark-haired woman, both of them smiling at the camera.

She looked like someone had given an illustration AI one instruction—to create an image of the most beautiful woman on the planet.

My good mood evaporated as my suspicion was confirmed. It was replaced by a sinking feeling because I knew that a man who dated a woman who looked like that would never, ever date someone like me.

Max Colby was completely out of my league.

I'd understood this since he'd sat down, but the picture took away any tiny sliver of hope I might have held on to.

"Why did you break up?" I asked.

He put his phone down on the table. "There were a lot of reasons. At some point I realized she had become a selfish person. It got worse the longer we were together, but she was my college sweetheart and I kept thinking she'd go back to the person she used to be, the woman I'd first fallen in love with. It never happened and I'm upset with myself that I tolerated it for so long. For the last year or so, we weren't even living in the same country. I think we stayed together long after the relationship actually ended because it was familiar. Comfortable."

"How old are you?" I asked him.

"Twenty-five."

I heard the question in his voice, as he wondered why I'd asked him that. Depending on when he'd met her, he had been with her anywhere from three to seven years.

That was a long time either way. It showed he could obviously commit to a long-term relationship, and in my experience, that wasn't true for most of the men I'd come across so far in New York, who all suffered from Peter Pan syndrome. "So what made you finally end it?"

"She sent me a text clearly meant for another man."

"Oh no," I said, feeling so much sympathy for him. Obviously his ex-girlfriend was the stupidest person alive. Who would cheat on Max? "That completely sucks. The lying would be the worst thing for me. My dad used to always lie to my mom and me about everything. We would know he was lying, but we were all supposed to pretend like he was telling the truth. I hated it."

Something flickered across his face and I wondered if he'd had a similar situation growing up.

"It did indeed suck," he agreed. He leaned toward me, radiating warmth and some delicious scent that I wanted to bottle up and sell to other single women because I would make a fortune.

Even though he'd put his phone down, I could still see the picture of the two of them together.

I told my overeager hormones to calm down and face reality that this wasn't going anywhere. Not only because I still had my own emotional hangups from my soon-to-be engaged boss and my emotionally distant father, but because I understood how the world worked. So I said brightly, "Given that you're new to the city, I'd offer to set you up, but I honestly only have the one friend and I'm pretty sure she'd eat you alive."

I gestured toward the bar and saw that Vella was kissing someone. I let out a groan.

"What is it?" Max asked, turning that direction.

"My roommate is kissing Otis." I would recognize that raggedy, oversize hipster beanie anywhere. What was he doing here?

"And that's bad because?"

"He's her ex and their relationship was terrible. Their love language seemed to be humiliation and toxicity."

Our waitress returned then and handed the bottle to Max. He thanked her, but she didn't respond and instead hurried off.

"She left the cap on and didn't give me a bottle opener," he said to me, sounding slightly bewildered.

Was it because he'd turned her down, or because she was really busy?

"Seriously?" I teased. "You can't open it? Hand it over."

He gave it to me, a bemused expression on his face.

"Do they not have bottled beer in Monterra, city boy?" I took the bottle and lined the cap up with the edge of the table, slamming it down with my other hand to pop the cap off.

"Impressive," he said as I gave it back to him.

"I can also open it with my teeth, but nobody wants to see that."

He gave me a look that made me think he very much wanted to see me do it, and it sent little shivers up and down my spinal column. "That sounds like a good skill to put on a dating app. 'Can open beer bottles with my teeth.'"

"Yes, I'm sure that will have all the men of New York City beating a path to my door. I'm not on dating apps, though. I hate that whole mutual scamming/hobby arms race going on there. I wish you could be honest and just say, 'I'll like you fine, but please don't make me hike or row a canoe.'"

That earned me another laugh. "No hiking or canoeing. Noted. What kind of guy do you like?"

I like guys named Max Colby, I thought.

He added, "Maybe I'll meet someone I could set you up with. What's your type?"

Mortal men with actual flaws were my type. Not this demigod and whatever heaven he'd obviously fallen out of.

Sadly, though, I couldn't have asked for a clearer sign that he wasn't even a little bit interested in me, given that he wanted to set me up with someone else. Message completely received. "My type is a man who can open his own beer bottles."

Another laugh, but I felt a bit deflated. Even though I knew better, I had let myself get the tiniest bit caught up in what was clearly a fantasy.

"I guess that rules me out," he said with a grin.

His perfect face ruled him out. "I guess so," I agreed.

"Why is it that you're throwing a party based on Monterra but you don't know anything about the people there?" he asked.

"I'm currently working as an administrative assistant at an event planning company, and I was trying to sell a moody teenager on a theme, so I used something I love and get excited about. I'm kind of obsessed with Monterra's royal family. All the women in my family are. Princess Chiara's wedding is coming up, and my mom and meemaw are so excited about it they can't stand it. Royal weddings are kind of like our Super Bowl. Or whatever the soccer equivalent is."

"The World Cup?" he offered with a charming grin that made my insides flutter.

"Yeah, that," I said as I tried not to sigh. It should be a crime to be this good-looking.

Because some people, like me, had absolutely no defense against it.

"What would you like to know?" he asked, and for a second I wasn't sure how to respond. I wanted to know everything about him. What did he eat for breakfast? How long had he had Basta? Why had he fallen for an evil, stupid woman? Why was he alone when probably every woman in this bar would have gladly gone home with him, including the ones in relationships?

"About Monterra?" he added when I didn't say anything.

"Everything. I mean, I know what I see in the sanctioned photo ops the royal family puts out, but I'm not up to speed on like, the minutiae of everyday life there. Or how they celebrate events. But let's start with birthdays." I grabbed my purse and pulled out a notebook and a pen. I opened the notebook and clicked my pen, waiting for him to start talking.

"Pen and paper?" he said.

"Yes. I have to handwrite when I'm taking notes. It really sears it into my brain, and it's also faster. I've never quite mastered the art of typing with two thumbs on my phone. Which I know is an embarrassment to my peers and I should probably turn in my Gen Z card."

He grinned. "I won't tell if you won't."

Why did I like the idea of sharing a secret with him? Also, did he think it was ridiculous that I carried around a notebook? "I'm always prepared," I said by way of explanation, a little embarrassed. "It's part of being an event planner. So many things could go wrong in this bar right now and I have something in my purse that would fix it."

"Too bad you didn't have a bottle opener."

I grabbed my keys and triumphantly showed him that I did, in fact, have one.

"Why didn't you get it earlier?"

"How would I have impressed you, then?" I asked, putting my keys back in my purse.

"Good point," he said with a laugh.

"Back to birthdays. Do Monterrans have an equivalent of Sweet Sixteen?"

He thought for a moment and then said, "No. The big birthday that's celebrated is eighteen—when a child becomes an adult. It's often a formal event, and all of the celebrant's friends and extended family come to it. There's no other special traditions, though. It's basically good food, a cake and singing, maybe fireworks, and dancing all night long."

He had the best voice. There was almost a melodic feel to it, and I could have happily sat next to him all night just listening to him talk. I forced myself to take notes, though.

It was discouraging that they didn't have something special or unique to celebrate a birthday. The formal part was interesting, though. We could require ball gowns and tuxedos.

"Are there any holiday events around this time of year?" I asked.

"One of the big ones is the carnival that takes place in the capital city every winter, usually right around Christmas."

That sounded vaguely familiar to me. I was sure I remembered an interview with Kat when she'd talked about going to that carnival with Nico.

My mind was flooded with ideas. A winter wonderland. Ice sculptures of a castle, a carriage, a prince. I'd get candles, cascading blue and white flowers as centerpieces, glass ornaments, snow falling, white trees covered in white lights, garlands of flowers with blue lights intertwined coming down from the ceiling like giant icicles, and we'd have everybody in their fanciest clothes. It would be elegant and fun. I'd get performers and the most incredible food. I knew exactly who to call.

"Where did you just go?" Max asked.

"I think you just helped me figure out what I'm going to do for this party. If the client agrees."

"I'm glad I could be of service."

He could service my—I told my inner voice to knock it off. That wasn't what was going on here.

I managed to say, "Thank you," instead.

Unfortunately, my mouth started speaking before my brain could stop it. "Why did you come over and talk to me tonight?"

I wasn't sure why I was asking. Some part of me believed that we'd been fated to meet, that like in some mythological story or fairy tale, he had shown up right when I needed him. The perfect person to help me on my path, like a birthday party fairy godfather.

He looked down at his bottle and my stomach dropped. "I saw that you were crying and I wanted to make sure you were okay."

My fears earlier about him seeing me as someone to be pitied came rushing back. I was over here having a great time with him, and he'd felt compelled to sit and talk to me in an attempt to make me feel better.

I felt crushed.

Out of the corner of my eye, I saw someone approaching and heard them ask, "Do you mind if I interrupt you?"

CHAPTER EIGHT

I didn't mind Vella interrupting us at all. Three minutes ago I would have told her to scram, but now that I knew Max pitied me? I wanted nothing more than to make my escape.

"Vella, this is Max. He's from Monterra. Max, this is Vella. My best friend and roommate."

"The one who made her come out tonight. I'm grateful that you did." He gave her a heart-stopping smile and I saw the effect it had on her.

Despite her protestations that we weren't attracted to the same kind of guy, Vella melted when he shook her hand.

Of course in the moment when I needed her to be strong, she was just as whipped as the rest of us. I'd never seen her with that goofy-looking expression on her face. She was going to start twirling the ends of her hair in a minute.

"Hi," she said, drawing out the *I* in a long exhale. "So nice to meet you. You're from Monterra? How long have you been in New York?"

He answered her questions, and all I could think about was that he'd come over here because he'd seen me cry. My ears started to ring as I was crushed by the memory of one of the worst things that had happened to me in high school. My mom's best friend was the mother of the most popular boy in school, and without my knowledge, she forced him to ask me to the spring formal our senior year.

My mother and I weren't well off, and I was stuck with a dress that didn't fit me very well and shoes that were way too tight. I'd had hopes of feeling like a princess, but instead I was dressed up like an ugly stepsister.

My so-called date didn't say a word to me during our drive to the school and then ditched me entirely once we got to the dance. It was humiliating, knowing he and his friends were making fun of me while I stood there in a too-short dress, feeling gangly and awkward, my shoulders hunched forward in an attempt to make myself smaller. I'd had to call a rideshare to get back home.

And Max's confession that he'd only approached me because he'd felt sorry for me was making me feel like that gawky teenage girl all over again.

Someone else approached the table, and it was Otis. I scowled at him, but he didn't take any notice of me. He kissed Vella on the cheek and said, "I'll meet you outside, babe."

Why did she let him call her that? She hated that kind of thing.

"Be right there," she said, and then directed her words at me. "I'm leaving with Otis. Will you be okay getting home by yourself?"

"Really? Otis?"

"He's hot and I'm bored. You can do the math," she said. "See you later."

She walked off before I could object further, and my phone beeped. I looked down to see a message from her.

I'm taking your coat. Borrow Max the Monterran's and have him take you home. The apartment will be empty! Or you can go back to his place and let him warm you up.

She added an emoji with suggestive eyebrows and some other explicit symbols that I couldn't think about because Max was sure to notice my embarrassment.

Did she not realize that there was no possibility of either one of her suggestions happening? Not to mention that she had officially abandoned me to freeze to death—she and I had walked here and I didn't currently have enough money in my checking account to pay for an Uber.

Now that I knew Vella was gone, it was like this built-in security to keep me in line and behaving had disappeared. With her here, I wasn't going to do something like make out with a random stranger, because she would have teased me endlessly about it.

But with her leaving . . . all bets were off.

Which made me a danger to myself.

"I should probably get going," I said to Max, alarmed at the direction of my thoughts.

"Really?" I couldn't read his reaction. Was he disappointed that I was leaving? Or relieved, glad that his duty of keeping an eye on the crying girl was over? It was hard to tell. He added, "No one's here to watch you, so it's time to duck out?"

That, and I was concerned that despite how pathetic I currently felt, I still wanted to ravage his mouth or else spontaneously combust because he was sitting next to me. There was no in-between that I could see, so staying was not an option. "Something like that."

"You strike me as the kind of kid who stayed put in her seat if the teacher left the classroom."

"Guilty. I've always been a big rule follower."

"That's too bad," he said in a low, raspy voice, and all of my desire to leave instantly evaporated as his words made me desperately regret all of my life choices up to this point.

If I were bolder, more sure of myself, maybe I would have made a move and I wouldn't care about why he'd come over. It was what Vella would have done. But despite how I might look on the outside, I was still that teenage girl who'd been abandoned at the dance.

Time to get back to real life. "I should head out. Thanks for everything. I really appreciate all your help."

"Any time."

I packed up my notebook, put it away, and slid my purse onto my arm. I was trapped in place, a sleeping Basta on my left and Max on my right.

"Oh, right," he said. "Sorry. Let me get out of your way."

He scooted along the bench and stood up. I gave Basta one final pet and then scooched over to the end of the booth.

Max offered me his hand just as I was about to stand up, and I had a serious internal debate as to what I should do. Take it one final time to experience that delicious electricity again? Or be strong, ignore his hand, and leave with some of my dignity intact?

I opted for the weaker option and let him assist me even though I didn't need it. The surging warmth and tingling sensations were there, just as sharp and strong as they had been the first time.

"You're really tall," he said.

"Am I? I never noticed." I let my hand fall. What I did notice was the fact that he was a good two inches taller than me, and I had heels on.

That made him even yummier.

"I'm guessing people say that to you a lot," Max said with a smile.

"Pretty much every time I get up from behind a desk or a table."

We stood there and I felt so awkward and didn't know what to do with my hands. I clasped them in front of me. "Well, I'm going to go pay for my drink."

He had put his hands into his front pockets. "It was very nice to have met you, Everly Aprile."

"And you, Max Colby."

"If you have any other questions about Monterra, you should text me."

He was just being nice, I told my lady bits. Someone had raised him to be a gentleman. I hadn't encountered a lot of his peculiar species since moving to the city, so I needed to be sure not to read too much into it. "Sure. Good night."

Despite everything, I'd had fun. I was glad for that, at least. I went over to the bar and waved my hand for the bartender. He was busy mixing a drink and flirting with the cute redhead he was creating it for.

This might take a while. I wondered if Max was still here or if he'd left. I wished I'd thought to bring cash with me—then I could have just left some money on the table and made a dignified exit.

I refused to turn around and check, though. I was going to keep some of my pride tonight.

"How are you?"

A man on my right was slumped against the bar, obviously drunk. He wore an expensive suit that was going to cost an arm and a leg to dry-clean when he inevitably vomited all over it. I realized that he was addressing his question to me.

My creep radar immediately went off. It was one thing to try to see the good in people—it was another entirely to be a lamb walking into a lion's den.

I might have been nice and optimistic, but I wasn't stupid.

I ignored him.

"Can I buy you a drink?" he slurred with his thick British accent.

"No, thanks." I didn't make eye contact with him.

"Come on, just one pint." Alcohol fumes radiated off him. "My name's TC. What's yours?"

If Vella were here, she'd use some colorful language as her response, but I didn't want to engage him. I leaned against the bar, trying to see if I could catch the bartender's attention. He was still busy.

I looked behind me, wondering if I could find my waitress. Or any waitress.

"Oi, I asked you a question. You're being very rude."

"I was just leaving," I said, worried about escalating the situation with this very inebriated and possibly unstable person.

"I'm here from England. I work on Wall Street. I have a lot of money."

A finance guy being gross? What a shock. "I'll bet your mom is very proud." I had a slight hint of some of Vella's sarcasm in it, but I figured he was too drunk to tell.

"If you want to get out of here, you can come home with me. You're not really pretty enough to date, but if you want to shag, I'm game."

A sickly taste entered my mouth and my heart started to beat erratically. "No, thank you. I'm not interested."

"What, do you think you're too good for me? You're not. You're lucky I'm willing to lower my standards."

Adrenaline coursed through me and I reached into my bag, ready to get my pepper spray. But then I felt an arm going around my shoulders, and even though I shouldn't have, I instantly relaxed.

It was Max, and it was like my body knew it was him before my brain registered it.

"Are you ready to go, la mia lei? I paid for the drinks." He was holding on to Basta with his free hand and she let out a low growl, staring at TC.

"Yes, I'm ready. Let's go home."

"Why didn't you say you had a boyfriend, you stupid cow?" TC called behind us, and Max's arm tightened slightly around me.

Max kept his arm around me until we reached the coat check. I was trembling slightly and didn't know if it was because I was coming down from the rush of adrenaline from being afraid that TC guy was going to hurt me, or because Max was touching me.

Maybe both.

"Are you all right?" he asked, and I realized it was the third time he'd done so that evening. I felt silly that he had to keep coming to my rescue.

"I'm fine."

"Do you have your ticket for your coat? I can grab it for you." He handed over his own ticket, and the checker returned quickly with his black coat. Max put it on.

"Vella stole it because she was cold." I didn't tell him the part about her suggesting I go back to his place to warm up.

"You should borrow mine."

"Oh, I can't do that."

"I insist," he said, taking it off and handing it to me. "I'm wearing a sweater and you're . . ."

His voice trailed off, and was it my imagination or had Max just given me a thorough once-over? And was that an appreciative gleam in his eyes, as if he liked what he saw?

It was then that I realized I hadn't even paid attention to what he was wearing, as I'd been so fixated on his gorgeous face all night. He had on jeans, casual shoes, and a light blue sweater that I was willing to bet was probably the exact same shade as his eyes.

He could have sat down next to me naked earlier and I probably wouldn't have noticed.

Okay, that was a lie. If he'd sat down next to me naked, I wouldn't have wasted my time looking at his face.

"I'll be fine," he said, and I snapped out of my not-safe-for-work thoughts to take his coat. "Do you have a car coming?"

"No, I was going to walk."

His eyes narrowed at me and he said, "Is it okay if Basta and I walk you home? I don't want you to walk home by yourself when . . ." He gestured toward the bar, where TC was in a loud fight with the bartender and probably about to get thrown out. I shivered at the possibility of having to walk home with him following me.

"Yes," I said gratefully. I slid his coat on, and it smelled like Max. I wondered if it would be weird if I sniffed it. It was too big for me, but I liked having it on.

Definitely sad. I really needed to fix my life.

He went to the door and shoved it open for me, and it creaked loudly again. Basta surged out onto the street, but with a couple of words in Italian, she relaxed and stopped straining against her leash.

"I would have enjoyed punching that man in the face," he said as we went outside.

"Me too."

"I was more concerned with getting you out of there."

His concern was touching and it was nice to feel protected and safe. Given his broad shoulders and the big biceps visible through his sleeves, I was pretty sure Max could have destroyed that TC guy if he'd wanted to.

"Which way?" he asked. I pointed south and we started walking in that direction. I noticed when Max moved positions so that he was closest to the curb. Most women probably wouldn't have picked up on a detail like that, but my meemaw had told me once that it was a sign of a good guy—one who put himself between you and potential danger.

And it was the second instance where Max had been protective in the short time I'd known him.

"You don't have to walk me home," I said after we'd walked for a bit in silence while Basta sniffed every available surface. I thought I should give him an out. He had done his princely duties for the evening and could go home. There were plenty of people out and about. I would be safe.

But I found myself holding my breath, waiting for his response. I realized that I wanted him to stay with me and was actually worried about what he might say.

He came to a stop and considered my words before responding, "I know I don't have to walk you. I want to."

I tried pressing my lips together and couldn't help but smile at his words. I wondered if being gallant like this was a Monterran thing. Even if he was one of those guys whose moms had taught him to be chivalrous and polite and that was the only reason he was still hanging around me, I would take it. I wanted the opportunity to spend more time with him.

Obviously I wasn't ever going to see him again after tonight, so I realized I should probably enjoy it while I could.

"Shall we?" he asked, and he offered me his arm.

It was so old-fashioned and romantic that I had to swallow back the nervous but excited lump in my throat. "We shall."

CHAPTER NINE

Max was so warm and strong. It took every ounce of willpower I possessed not to lean against him completely.

I cleared my throat and said, "Thank you for rescuing me. And for paying for the drinks."

He raised his fingers slightly, like he was waving my words away. "Consider it payment for the pleasure of your company."

His eyes went wide as he seemed to realize how that sounded. "I didn't mean, that is to say, I meant, it was a small price to pay for getting to spend time with you."

I couldn't help but smile. I liked him flustered. I bet this happened sometimes when English was your second language.

"I feel bad that you paid for beers we didn't actually drink," I said.

His arm seemed to flex under mine and I tried not to get distracted by it. "I was more interested in talking to you."

"So was I." Now I was the one tripping over my words. "To you. Not to myself. Not that I ever talk to myself."

Great, now I was the one who was flustered.

Being so close to him was obviously scrambling my brain. I needed to talk about something, anything, else. "When you came up to me at the bar, what did you call me?"

"La mia lei."

"That's pretty. What does it mean?"

"It means 'my her.' It's a way of saying that out of all the women in the world, you are the only one who belongs with me."

While I knew he didn't actually mean me and was using *you* in a more general sense, I couldn't help the flapping that started up in my stomach.

He went on, "Italians and Monterrans are notorious for their paroline dolci. Sweet words. We make fun but we all use them for the people we love."

I internally sighed as I tried to imagine what it would be like if I were the woman Max felt that way about.

"So besides birthday parties, what other kinds of events do you do?" he asked, and I wondered whether he kept asking me questions because he was curious about the answers or because I kept getting lost in my own thoughts and daydreams about him and wasn't holding up my side of the conversation.

"I work on mostly corporate events."

"Like the kinds at hotels where you sit around and listen to people talk?"

"Yep."

He had to redirect Basta, who saw something that interested her and pulled against her leash. "I'm getting the sense it's not your dream job."

"Right now I'm just an administrative assistant and don't even have the official title of event planner. I'd really like to get a promotion, and this birthday party is my ticket to make that happen. I'm already planning events; I just don't have the title."

"That doesn't sound fair."

"You have to pay your dues," I said. "I've paid mine about four times longer than anyone else, though." I felt a tiny bit of resentment creeping in and shook my head, determined not to let myself get down. "My dream is to do showers."

"Like installing them?" He sounded so adorably confused.

I held in my laugh. "No, 'showers' as in 'parties.' Here in the States we have like, baby showers or bridal showers. It's a gathering to celebrate a new life or a new relationship. I love how much emotion is involved, all the joy. It feels like an honor to join in on something that is so important to the people involved."

"We have those types of parties in Monterra, too."

I felt a bit embarrassed that I had assumed he wouldn't know what I was talking about. "You're right—they have them all over the world, and it's a tradition that's been carried on for a long time in some cultures. I looked it up once, and they started calling them 'showers' because of a custom in the nineteenth century where presents were put inside of an umbrella and then they would shower it down on the bride."

"I would guess that getting smacked in the head with a high chair wouldn't be fun."

Now I did laugh. "Maybe that's why they stopped doing it." I realized that for our whole walk home, he'd been the one asking me questions. My mother would be so upset with me for being so impolite. "What do you do for a living?"

"I work at a nonprofit."

That caused me to stumble as I basically tripped over my own feet. A nonprofit? Really, Universe? He couldn't have been like, a professional dog kidnapper or a loan shark or a scammer telemarketer? He worked for a charity?

Then I considered the fact that Nico also devoted all of his time to charitable causes, and it made my attraction to Max grow even stronger.

He let me fall against him until I found my footing. I just knew he was going to ask me if I was all right again and I couldn't take it a fourth time. This poor man did not have to keep coming to my rescue.

"I'm okay. Just having some staying-vertical issues that aren't my fault," I said.

"Yes, I saw the way that sidewalk leapt out at you," he agreed, seriously. I smiled.

"Do you like your job?" I asked.

"Very much. My father thinks it's a waste of my education."

"Where did you go to school?"

"Yale."

I was impressed. He didn't strike me as wealthy, though. He was too down-to-earth for that. "Did you have to put yourself through school?"

"Basically, yes."

"I've noticed that you use some American expressions and phrasing." It made sense. Nico's younger twin brothers, Prince Dante and Prince Rafe, also attended American universities and their Monterran accents were much lighter than their older brother's as a result.

"Have you noticed?" he asked playfully, calling attention to the fact that I'd been observing him so closely that I'd been able to detect speech patterns.

Back to feeling pathetic again.

"My mother is from California, and growing up, I spent my summers there with my cousin, Sunny," he added when I didn't respond to his question. "I've spent a lot of time in America."

That piqued my interest. Monterran royalty did have a tendency to marry American women. Maybe that had happened with his family and Max was a secret prince. "Are you like, nobility or a lord or something?"

"Like *Lord of the Dance*?" He sounded confused.

"No, I . . ." How was I supposed to explain that I was attempting to make sure that he wasn't royal?

"What does that have to do with my speech patterns?" He was teasing, but I no longer wanted to discuss this particular topic because of the potential traps and pitfalls waiting for me and my assumptions.

"Working at a nonprofit seems pretty noble to me. What did your dad want you to do instead?" I asked, changing the subject.

I wondered if he might tease me, challenge me, but instead he just answered, "Go into the family business."

"Which is?"

"Deceiving people for money."

Were they lawyers? Actors? Writers? Max had sounded a bit prickly, and I got the sense that I shouldn't ask him specifics. I settled on, "That doesn't sound great."

"It's not. My mother isn't much better. Growing up I had a babysitter who was really dedicated to helping other people, and I guess it stuck with me. But all in all, I'm a disappointment to everyone in my life."

"I get it," I told him with a sigh. "Even the family business part. My mother wanted me to come work with her at her nail salon after I graduated from college, but I didn't want to, which did not make her happy. She didn't want me to move to New York, either. She also seems to be upset with my personality. She thinks I'm too much of a people pleaser."

"You can't be that much of a people pleaser if you came to New York City over her objections."

That mollified me slightly. That was sort of true. "There are things I'm not willing to back down on and will stand firm, but she's not wrong. I usually want to make other people happy."

He considered this information and then said, "Did your parents fight a lot when you were a kid?"

"Constantly. All the time. They would have arguments that would last for days where they would just scream at each other. I hated it so much. It was actually kind of a relief when my dad left."

"I understand," he said. "Same in my home growing up. And the arguing is what made you a people pleaser."

"What makes you say that?"

"I was in therapy for a long time as a kid. My parents also fought constantly before they got divorced. I wanted to make everything okay for them by making them happy. Thinking that if I could just be the perfect kid, then they'd stop fighting all the time. I took on that burden of wanting to make others feel better. Because if I could do whatever they asked, then maybe my life would have been okay."

It was, in all honesty, probably one of the most profound and insightful things anyone had ever said to me. It was like Max had cracked open my soul and peered inside. His revelation shook me. "That was exactly how I felt, too."

He looked at me then, his face close to mine. And if we'd been just regular people who'd met for the first time at a bar, felt an attraction for one another, and were walking home together, this might have been the part where he kissed me.

My pulse went haywire and my lips tingled with want. There were two heartbeats, three, four, where he just looked into my eyes. I wanted so desperately to see what color his were in sunlight. The streetlamps weren't doing him justice.

"I suppose that makes us kindred spirits," he said, facing forward again and breaking the spell. "My dysfunction manifests less as people-pleasing, more savior complex. I like to rush in and save someone."

"You like to rescue people." I nodded, finally understanding what had happened tonight. "Which explains why you came over to talk to me in the bar and why you work for a nonprofit."

"That's not why I . . ." But whatever he'd been about to say, he stopped. I held my breath, hoping he would finish his sentence and that he might confess something—that he'd thought I was pretty or he felt the same spark I had when we'd first met. But he didn't and instead just said, "It's complicated, I guess."

I got caught up in imagining what he could have said and fell silent. I didn't know him well enough to accurately predict it but was coming up with some very outlandish explanations.

"What is the worst thing you've ever done?" he asked me, probably because I'd fallen silent again and was forcing him to single-handedly carry the conversation.

"Oh. Let me think." I hadn't done a lot of bad things. Pettiness hadn't ever really been a part of my personality. Except for that one time. "I had auditioned for the Christmas nativity at my church. When I was twelve, I really wanted to play Mary, but they picked Ellie Macon to play the part. The director just did not like me, and to this day I have no idea why. This was right around the time my parents divorced, and I had a lot of pent-up anger."

"I'm almost afraid to find out what you did," he said, sounding amused.

"I downloaded and printed out a copy of Imagine Dragons' 'Radioactive' sheet music. I took off the name and entitled it 'Baby in the Manger' and put it on the piano the night of the performance. Sure enough, the pianist played it all the way to the end before Ellie Macon ratted me out to the pastor and the director. I got yelled at by a bunch of church leaders."

He laughed.

"What about you?" I asked. "Worst thing you've ever done or your deepest regret?"

"I've never been yelled at by religious leaders. The worst thing I've ever done—it's probably how I treated my father. He fought my mother hard for custody, and I think it was more about how much he hated her than wanting to be with me. He got primary custody of me for years and I resented him the entire time, so I did everything I could to make him miserable. Especially since he married my stepmother six months after the divorce was finalized. My stepmother couldn't have children and she wanted to mother me, but I wouldn't let her. I've been angry with both of them for a long time. I've been trying to work through it."

"How is that going?"

Max grimaced. "It's going. Slow and steady."

"Well, the tortoise does win the race. Although now you have me thinking I have to revise my answer because I don't speak to my dad. To be fair, he doesn't speak to me, either."

"Why not?"

"He didn't want to be a husband or a father, and he's much happier somewhere out in Oregon pretending I don't exist. With his new wife and new children that he spends all kinds of time with."

"I'm sorry," he said.

"Don't be," I said with a wave of my hand. "What's sad is I don't even miss him. I did a lot in the beginning, but after someone rejects you so many times, there's only so much you can take. I had to figure out a way to move on with my life and be happy, and I did."

"Someday I hope to be as evolved as you."

I didn't feel very evolved. Sometimes I felt like I had made the wrong choice and that maybe I should have tried harder and not written my dad off completely. "I think maybe it's better to have the relationship if you can. Not if it's toxic or harmful, obviously. But I do worry that I'll regret things when my father passes away. That I'll wish I'd tried harder. So good for you that you are."

He shrugged. "We'll see."

"Can I tell you something?" I asked as we turned a corner, approaching my building.

"You've known me for about an hour. You can tell me anything. I have an open-shoulder policy." At my confused expression, he added, "In case you need a shoulder to cry on."

I smiled. "No crying. I just needed to let you know that it is entirely unfair that you are both nice and hot. No one should have two ways to get free stuff."

"And here I was thinking the same thing about you."

Panic and elation slammed into me at the same time. Was he serious? Kidding? Being polite? Facetious?

I had no way of knowing.

While I would usually keep such thoughts to myself, to my dismay I admitted, "Max, I know I'm not hot."

He came to a halt. "What liar told you that?"

Uh, every man I'd had feelings for since I'd hit puberty? You didn't get stood up, rejected, abandoned, and ditched out on as many times as I had without developing an inferiority complex.

I studied his face, adrenaline flooding through me as that temporary bravado left my system. I saw a slight smile. Kindness. Friendliness.

What I did not see was overwhelming desire, lust, or any indication that he was about to take me in his arms and kiss me senseless. As if he couldn't resist me for one more minute.

He devoted his life to charity and rescued people. That apparently included sad, insecure women with no love life to speak of.

Feeling ridiculous, I started walking toward my building. I was always creating castles in the sky. Which was fine when it came to my work but wasn't very practical for my personal life. I was sure it had something to do with my father being terrible and wanting a fairy tale, because reality, so far, had pretty much sucked. I dug into my purse and got my keys out, preparing myself to make a quick and nonhumiliating exit.

When I reached my building, I nodded to Casimir, the night doorman. He opened the front door, greeting us. I said hello and Max actually introduced himself to Casimir, proving that he was just nice to everyone he met.

I tried to swallow down the nervous blob that had lodged there. Vella didn't care what other people thought. She did whatever she wanted when she wanted all the time.

I'd never been that brave.

He went to the elevators with me. "Thank you so much for walking me home," I said, ready for this night to be over and for my heartbeat to return to a normal rhythm. It hadn't pumped correctly since Max had walked into my life.

"Thank you for letting me," he said.

Now what? "Okay, good night." I pushed the up button and he reached out to touch my arm.

"Can I tell you something?" he asked.

"Sure."

"You're really easy to talk to."

Like a good buddy or a kid sister? That somehow just made everything worse. "You too." I crouched down and rubbed Basta's ears, which she seemed to enjoy.

The elevator dinged and the doors opened. "Bye."

"Have a good night," he said. Max hesitated for a second, and then he gently pulled on Basta's leash and they headed off. I watched as he walked away, allowing myself one last good look.

I figured I deserved it, given that I was never going to see him again.

CHAPTER TEN

It wasn't until I got back into my apartment that I realized I still had Max's coat on. This whole night had been so strange and surprising that it was like I'd forgotten about everyone and everything else. I collapsed onto the couch, kicking my shoes off.

Since I was all alone, I gave in to my impulse and smelled his coat. It had the same clean, fresh, and masculine scent as Max. I took it off and set it on the couch next to me.

I reached into my purse and grabbed my phone, sending him a text to let him know that I had his coat, ignoring the part of me that was overjoyed at the notion that I was going to see him again.

His coat started to buzz.

I searched through it until I found his phone in his pocket. I registered that he had an Android and it buzzed a second time, and then again.

Both new texts were from different women—one named Emanuela, the other Jade. Muscle memory had me swiping up the screen, and to my surprise, he didn't have a security lock on his phone. That was weird.

I was in his messaging app and couldn't help my curiosity—I quickly scrolled through it, and every message seemed to be from a different woman. Natalia, Coco, Alana, Elle, Kate . . . did he date supermodels exclusively?

Violetta? As in Princess Violetta, Nico's sister? My rational brain reminded me that wasn't possible because she was married and Max did not seem like the kind of guy who would cheat.

Especially not after it had been done to him.

I put his phone down, feeling guilty for having even glanced at the names. I didn't read any of the messages because I wouldn't have been able to live with myself for violating his privacy even worse than I already had.

My cell buzzed, and for one brief, clearly stupid moment, I hoped that it was a text from Max.

Which was obviously impossible.

No, it was from Adrian.

Can you call someone at the hotel I'm staying at and have them bring me toilet paper?

For the first time in, well, forever, I found myself feeling annoyed at Adrian. In the time it had taken him to write a text and send it to me, he could have called the front desk himself.

I did as he asked and texted back that his toilet paper was on its way.

After I pushed the send button, I realized that I hadn't thought about Adrian even once after I told Max about him. When I had been talking to Max, if someone else had said Adrian's name to me, I probably would have asked, "Adrian who?"

It was like I had completely blocked him out of my mind.

Or Max had inadvertently pushed him out.

This felt significant.

I leaned back and took a deep breath, staring at the ceiling. Was it a good thing or a bad thing? Was I just trading one impossible crush for another?

The door opened and startled me. Vella dramatically strode inside and slammed it shut.

"Never. Again."

She stomped into the kitchen and took a log of cookie dough out of the fridge. She threw it on the counter and grabbed a serrated knife and started sawing through it.

"Did you want to talk about it?" I asked. "Did you light Otis's hair on fire and you need me to be your alibi?"

"The bar for men is so low it's in hell and those idiots still try to play limbo with the devil."

She finally cut through the entire thing and brought half of the log into the living room, sitting on the couch next to me. She squeezed the dough like a tube of toothpaste and took a big bite.

After Vella had chewed and swallowed, she said, "He wanted us to get back together, which, as you know, I'm morally opposed to because he's the actual worst. When I asked him why, he said he has to go out of town for a week and wanted me to take care of his cat."

A pulse of unease began to throb at the base of my stomach. Now was not the time to tell her I was doing the same thing for Adrian. "Like, he wanted you to go over and feed it? Change the litter box?"

"No, he wanted me to stay over at his place so that she didn't 'feel lonely.'"

"Does he know that you're—"

She didn't let me finish. "Yes! He should know that I'm allergic to cats!" Her allergy was the only reason I didn't currently have a menagerie of animals. "When I made the huge mistake of dating him, I had to take a Benadryl every day just to go over to his place and I was still miserable with my red eyes, stuffed-up nose, and scratchy skin. The fact that he can't even remember the most basic of details about me is why I broke up with him in the first place."

"I thought it was because you caught him cheating."

She rolled her eyes so hard I was surprised she didn't sprain them. "Obviously, that too. I just broke up with him again for conduct unbecoming a boyfriend."

"I still can't believe you left with him."

"Am I perfect? No. But more importantly, am I trying to make better choices? Also no."

I laughed and she devoured another chunk of cookie dough.

"How long was that?" I asked. "An hour? Is that a new record for your shortest relationship ever?"

"Possibly." She nodded.

"I'm glad it's over. I was worried that if you did start things up with him again, it would end up as a special *Dateline* episode where I'd have to tell the world that I saw this coming."

"Enough about the train wreck that is my life. What happened with you and David?"

"His name is Max," I reminded her.

"Oh, I'm aware. I said David meaning he looks like Michelangelo personally sculpted him."

"Yeah, I noticed that you thought he was attractive." She'd been so unlike herself when she'd met him.

"No argument from me. And he's not even my type."

"Gorgeous isn't your type?" I asked skeptically.

"He seems too . . . clean cut and *nice*," she said with distaste before taking a quick bite.

"Yes, heaven forbid someone treats you well," I teased.

"Nobody wants that," she agreed.

I smiled at her. "You're right, though. He was very nice."

She waited a moment, chewing her cookie dough. With a mouthful of food, she said, "And?"

My smile got even bigger as I thought about him. "He walked me home because some guy at the bar was weird and creepy."

"Look at you grinning like a fourteen-year-old girl who just met her favorite pop star."

And here I was trying to downplay my attraction to him.

She went on, "I haven't seen you this giddy about a boy since Lumpy."

"Who?"

"I already told you that's what I'm calling Adrian Stone because he's unformed and not worth your time, especially since he's older than twenty-five and his frontal lobe is fully developed, so there is no excuse."

I didn't even bother correcting her this time. Vella was welcome to her opinion. "Hanging out with Max? It's probably the best date I've ever been on and it wasn't even a date."

"How do you know he didn't feel the same?"

"Uh, because when he left, he didn't even bother to offer up any of those token fake promises to text me soon or that we should do it again sometime."

Vella blinked slowly at me. "I'm not understanding the problem here. You thought he was cute, he obviously thought you were cute, you're sickeningly nice, he probably is, too. Seems like a good situation with possibilities."

"He's not attracted to me. He felt bad for me because he saw me crying." Even saying it out loud made me feel deflated. "I would have done the same thing if the situation had been reversed."

"So?"

How was I supposed to make her understand? If I didn't, she was going to badger me. No one was supposed to offer their opinion on her life, but Vella had long ago decided that she was going to loudly share with others what she thought about their choices and decisions. If I didn't make her see reason, she was going to be relentless.

"I saw his phone. He has an actual army of women texting him. While I'm flattered that he would even consider inviting me to join his harem, I'm not interested. I told you about how my dad cheated on my mom constantly. Even if Max did want to date me, which he does not, I couldn't be with someone like that." I was a relationship kind of girl.

"When did you see who was texting him?" she asked.

"Your evil plan worked and he lent me his coat when he walked me home."

"My evil plan was for you to go back to his place, so no, it didn't work."

Ignoring her, I said, "I forgot to give his coat back to him, and he must have put his phone in his coat pocket without realizing it."

I hoped she wouldn't point out that I'd invaded his privacy, although I had been telling myself it had been innocent, given that I didn't read any of the texts. Not that I hadn't been tempted, but that was a step too far.

"He likes you," she said with a triumphant smile.

"What makes you say that?"

"Max did a leave behind. It's more serious than you realize."

"A what?"

"It's when you leave something behind intentionally so the person you were with has to see you again so you can get your stuff back."

"I don't think it was intentional." It had happened because every time I looked at Max, my brain felt like it was having a heart attack and I couldn't think straight or remember to do stuff like returning things that had been lent to me.

Why hadn't he asked for it back, though?

"Does it actually work?" I asked, wanting to distract myself and not think about things that couldn't possibly be.

"One time I accidentally left my favorite pair of earrings at a guy's place and wanted them back. It took me almost four weeks because he decided that I'd done it deliberately and was obsessed with him. He thought I was trying to mark my territory to warn off other women and attempted to ghost me."

"Did you get your earrings back?"

"Only after I sarcastically told him that if I'd wanted to mark my territory, I would just pee in his ficus and leave my droppings on the floor. Why do men think a random scrunchie or scarf is some power play?"

Sometimes people just forgot things. It wasn't their fault if unreasonably attractive people distracted them.

When I didn't answer her rhetorical question, she asked, "Does he pass that test?"

"Test?"

"The one your moomah or whatever told you about."

"Meemaw," I corrected, trying to recall what Vella was talking about. "Oh! The two-drinks-and-a-puppy test?"

She nodded. "Yes."

My grandmother had found an article about how to divide up potential friends and mates and had taught it to me like gospel. She said that men were easy to put into categories. The first question to ask was whether or not you would have two drinks with him. The second was if you would let them babysit your puppy for a couple of days.

A man who was no to both was a person to stay completely away from.

Someone who was a yes and a no might be good for a fun time, but you should probably steer clear, as you didn't need people you couldn't trust in your life.

A no and a yes was someone who wasn't very fun and, while responsible, probably wouldn't make for a good long-term relationship.

I was supposed to be searching for a man who was a yes to both questions. Someone I could talk to, someone I would trust, someone who was a lot of fun but who took their responsibilities and me seriously.

Max was someone I would want to get two drinks with, and I would leave a puppy with him for any length of time.

Vella didn't ask me how I rated him on that scale. Given the smug look on her face, it seemed like she could already tell what my answer was.

She let me off the hook, though, and instead asked, "Did you google him yet?"

"No. Why would I?"

Her mouth went wide in disbelief. "I looked up my barista this morning and the UPS guy who delivered packages today at the office because you never know. And I'm not interested in dating either one of them. What's Max's last name?"

I probably shouldn't have told her, but I said, "Colby."

She got her phone out and started furiously typing. "I'm . . . not finding anything. As far as I can tell, he has no social media presence whatsoever. I am both impressed and disturbed."

That was weird. Not a picture or anything?

I got my own phone out and tried spelling Colby several different ways, just to make sure. She was right. Nothing.

"Maybe he just really values his privacy?" But even as I said it, I knew that couldn't be the case, given that his phone didn't have any security on it. I briefly considered the option that he might be an international spy or something and had to hide his true identity, but again, his phone would have had a password.

She asked, "You said he dated around a lot? Shouldn't one of those women have posted a picture of him? What about a more serious relationship? A girlfriend?"

"He said he had a serious girlfriend for a long time but that she cheated on him," I responded. "Which implies that there is a man out there hotter than Max Colby, and I'm not sure I can accept such a mythological thing as being a possibility."

"Max is a mythological creature," she said as she finished off the last of her cookie dough. "I don't know what to tell you. You should definitely ask him about it, though, because I would like to get totally off the grid, too. Anyway, I'm going to bed. Have fun with your unicorn when he calls you."

She padded off, stopping in the kitchen to throw away the wrapper before going to her room.

I thought about what she'd said—that Max had done this deliberately because he wanted to see me again. And I just couldn't reconcile that with how the evening had gone. Wouldn't he have said something if that were true?

Then a truly horrible thought occurred to me.

If Vella was wrong and his actions hadn't been intentional . . . when he got back to his apartment and realized that I had his coat and his phone, what if he thought *I'd* done it deliberately?

That I had kept his things on purpose so I could see him again?

CHAPTER ELEVEN

I'd stayed up way too late working on a mood board for Hyacinth's birthday party. It was so easy to assemble my ideas, as I knew exactly how I wanted things to look, but I needed to run everything past Claudia before I presented it to Hyacinth and Marie. I had a chef/caterer in mind who specialized in delicious Italian dishes and a baker who made the most incredible cakes; I knew both were more than capable of filling in last minute. For a substantial fee, of course.

Because it had been a few years since I'd been a teenager, I went online to do research for what Hyacinth might enjoy.

It occurred to me that Nico's youngest sister, Princess Serafina, was close in age to Hyacinth, so I looked up some of the princess's interests. Her favorite American band just happened to be a local one called Silver Cup. I made a note to get in touch with their manager in the morning. If they had availability, they would be perfect for the event.

Staying up most of the night meant that when my phone rang at seven o'clock in the morning, I was completely out of it.

"Hello?" I mumbled.

"Everly? Why aren't you awake yet?"

I stifled a groan. It was my mother. I loved her dearly, but she always made me feel like I was falling short—in my personal life, at work, with exercising and eating healthy food—whatever it was that I participated in, my mom thought I could be doing it better.

She was an extremely early riser, preferring to get up before the sun, and thought the rest of the world should do the same.

"It's the weekend," I told her with a groan, but she breezed past it.

"Did you go out last night like you'd planned?"

I turned over and put an arm across my eyes. I could hear our neighbors yelling next door and wondered whether Vella would make good on her threats and glue their front door shut.

This was all my fault. Not the next-door argument, but me telling my mother that I couldn't call her back yesterday because I was going out with Vella. I had given her ammunition.

"Yes, I went out last night."

"And did you meet someone?"

"I did," I said, trying not to sigh because I knew exactly where this was going. It was like my mother was starring in a one-woman play called *You're a Disappointment* and performed it every night of my life.

I figured it was one of the reasons why we bonded so much over our mutual love for royals. My mom never criticized me when it came to that kind of stuff. When we talked about our favorite princes and princesses, I could just enjoy her as a person without her trying to fix me.

"And?" she prompted.

"He gave me his number." Along with his actual phone.

"Are you going to see him again?"

Probably when I returned his cell, but other than that, no. "I don't think I'm his type," I told her.

She sighed. "If you just made a little more effort with your appearance and tried to be more outgoing, I think that—"

Now it was my turn to sigh loudly. My whole life my mom had been trying to turn me into someone I wasn't and I'd never understood why. "Don't worry about it, Mom. Things are well under control here."

Someday I would meet a man, and hopefully he wouldn't make my life as miserable as my dad had made hers.

Part of me wondered what she would do if I said that to her. If I was completely honest—that I didn't understand why she pushed so hard for me to get into a relationship when her own had turned out so badly.

I didn't, though. If there was one thing southern mamas taught their children, it was to be respectful.

I had never told her about my crush on Adrian, either. She would be like a dog with a bone and I wouldn't ever hear the end of it. She would push me to make a move or tell him about my attraction or wear a padded bra and high heels to catch his attention.

As if she somehow intuited that I was thinking about my job, she asked, "What about work? You have to be more assertive and go after what you want. Don't let people boss you around and not recognize you for all the hard work you're doing."

"I'm actually in charge of planning an event where, if it goes well, I'll get a promotion."

"Which is how it should be," she said with satisfaction. "It's about time. You have let them take you for granted for too long."

It made me sad that my mom saw only my shortcomings, and not my awesome parts. When I was at an event, I was the person who inspired confidence, who kept my cool in difficult situations and always found a solution.

But just because I wasn't actively pursuing meeting someone or being the girl boss my mom thought I should be, it didn't mean that I was falling short.

"Speaking of that event, I need to go. I have a lot of work to do." Technically it wasn't a lie. I wasn't planning on doing any of that work right now, but I did have a lot of work to do for the birthday party.

"Okay, I'll text you soon. Love you!"

"Love you," I said.

There was a crashing noise from Vella's room, and I wondered whether she had busted a hole through her bedroom wall so that she could deal with our neighbors, who apparently had no concept of time or social boundaries.

I put my phone down on the table near my bed and lay there for a bit, thinking about my call with my mom and my encounter with Max.

Before last night, I would have said that I had some sort of feelings for Adrian. I knew him better than anybody else in the world, and he was very handsome and wealthy and on paper was a total Prince Charming.

But all it had taken was Max smiling at me and being polite and I'd been ready to drop Adrian like a bad habit. It made me think that my feelings for Adrian were pretty superficial and I was a much shallower person than I'd realized.

Or maybe it was a knee-jerk reaction to Adrian getting engaged—latching on to someone else as a way to make myself feel better.

I wasn't sure.

And I wished I had someone to talk to about it. My mom would have taken it all wrong, and Vella only seemed to care about whether or not I hooked up with Max for the good of all womankind.

Meeting Max last night and my mother's comments this morning had me reevaluating my life.

I didn't want to be alone. I absolutely wanted to find my person, my prince, who would make me feel like I was in my own fairy tale. My own parents' relationship had been so spectacularly unhealthy that I had resorted to wanting a mythological romance that seemed to exist only in books. Like I had to find the opposite of what they'd shared. Work hadn't really allowed that to happen, as I always had so much to do. I'd been stuck in a holding pattern for a very long time.

My phone beeped—it was one of the online alerts I'd set up for Nico and Kat. They had gone to the opening of a new hospital with their kids, and I looked at the picture of their family.

Kat had been a regular American girl just like me who'd turned her life into something worthy of storybooks.

Why couldn't I do the same?

If she were in my position, what would Kat do?

Huh. Maybe I should make that my motto. WWKD?

I started writing a list with changes I was going to make in my life. They included:

- Put myself out there more—in business and in my personal life. I would try to meet people and stop hiding in this apartment so much and using work as an excuse. I would speak up in the office because I had good ideas.

- Fake confidence until I felt it for real. I would stop second-guessing myself at work.

- Be a good friend. Kat was an amazing friend, fiercely loyal and loving.

- Remember to be kind. The queen was thoughtful and caring to the people around her.

- Let go of my crush on Adrian. In some ways it was holding me back. I used our "what if?" potential to shove other men away as possibilities.

- Do more charitable work. It had always felt good to help other people; I didn't know why I had forgotten about that part of myself.

- Look fabulous while doing it.

I worried a little about the last one. Despite being annoyed by my mother's suggestion, I knew that I probably should spend more time on my appearance. It made a difference in my industry, whether or not I wanted to admit it. I'd always gone for comfort over style.

My rack of clothes was against the wall next to the foot of my bed, and I looked at it, remembering how I'd felt when I wore the dress that looked like Kat's. It had given me faith in myself, confidence. A belief that I could be like Kat.

I wanted that feeling again.

I opened up my laptop and did a search for "how to dress like Queen Katerina." I found a website run by fans who called themselves "Copy-Kats," and the content was devoted to Kat's fashion sense. Not only did they have pictures of her in various outfits, but they also included links to where to buy either the same dress or a close replica.

This would be my first step in my WWKD journey.

Choosing to believe in myself and that I would get the promotion when my event was successful, I maxed out my credit cards and bought a bunch of her outfits. It probably wasn't a wise financial decision, but fortunately being smart with money wasn't on my self-improvement list.

I'd have to hope the money followed as I improved myself and my situation.

This was going to work. I'd get my life back on track and manifest the things I wanted. I decided that when I had the chance, I was going to make a vision board for my new future.

A big portion of that was probably going to be dedicated to men with dark hair and light eyes. If I wanted to date someone like Max, I was going to have to actually do the things on my list.

I suspected it wouldn't be too hard, especially the whole moving-past-my-Adrian-crush thing. All I'd have to do was remember Max offering me his arm and Adrian would be completely banished from my brain.

The thought made me grimace. Maybe I was just trading one obsession for another. I should put a rubber band around my wrist to ward off my intrusive thoughts—if I was feeling nostalgic about Adrian or wishing that I could date Max, I'd snap it to remind myself to not be ridiculous.

Because Max was a pipe dream—a romantic comedy hero come to life for a single night before disappearing back into the genie's bottle he'd popped out of.

Since I was already up, I went ahead and got ready for my day and had breakfast. I worked on the party for a few hours until it was time to go over to Adrian's apartment to let the electrician in.

Just as I was about to leave, I heard a phone ringing.

It wasn't mine, and Vella was still in bed asleep and made a point of turning her phone off so that it didn't inadvertently wake her up.

Then I realized that it was Max's phone.

His coat was still on the couch and I reached into the pocket. I checked the screen, but the call was from an unknown number. It might have been one of Max's many women, but I felt like I should answer it just in case.

"Hello?"

"Everly? This is Max. It seems you have my phone."

"I do," I said breathlessly, sitting down because it was exciting to hear his voice again. "Accidentally. I'm sorry I didn't return it to you last night."

"It's okay," he said. "I'm sorry I didn't ask for it back. I would have called you last night but I didn't want to wake you up."

"That was very considerate of you. My mom called me so early this morning it felt like I traveled back in time."

I wanted to smack myself in the forehead. Why had I said that? He didn't care.

He laughed, and I didn't know if it was out of politeness or if he thought I was actually funny. "This works out well because we can hang out again. Can we meet up today? Like in an hour or so? We could have lunch."

Disappointment welled up inside me. I wished that I were free and could have a meal with him. It would fit into my whole putting-myself-out-there-more resolution, but I'd made a commitment. "I have to go over to my boss's place to let an electrician in."

There was silence and I worried he might ask me to leave his stuff with Vella so that he could just pick it up.

"If you want to meet me there, I could give you the address," I said hopefully. I didn't want to pressure him or anything, but if this was going to be the last chance I had to talk to him in person, I should take it so that I could appreciate his extremely symmetrical face one more time.

"Sure, why don't you . . ." His voice trailed off and he laughed. "I was about to say 'Why don't you text me the address,' but that's not going to be possible. And I don't have a notebook and pen at the ready like some people, so hang on a second."

I nodded and then immediately felt stupid because he couldn't see me. "Okay."

While I waited, I tried not to grin too hard. It had been only a couple of hours since I'd come up with my list of ways that I could be more like Kat and it was already paying off.

CHAPTER TWELVE

Seeing Max again was going to be the perfect opportunity to practice my new resolutions. Asking myself WWKD, I changed into her blue-and-white dress I'd worn to the pitch meeting. I figured it would be a good visual reminder to myself that I was trying to do things differently.

Walking into Adrian's apartment didn't feel the way it used to. There had always been this little thrill about being in his home, his private sanctuary. I'd sometimes imagined myself living there, married to a prince of New York society, wearing ball gowns and tiaras.

Today was different. It was just an apartment, and what I currently felt was panic and annoyance.

Annoyed that I had to be there instead of being able to have lunch with Max, and panicked that he was going to show up any minute and I wasn't sure exactly when to expect him as he hadn't given me a specific time. The waiting was driving me to distraction.

I tried to work but felt too jittery and unable to concentrate. I attempted to water Adrian's plants, but I ended up making a huge mess by knocking the watering can over in the kitchen. After I cleaned up the spill, I decided to sit on the couch, where I couldn't do any more damage.

The electrician had arrived right after I did, and now he was coming into the living room to tell me that he had finished up. He had me sign some paperwork and then gathered up his tools. I walked him out and thanked him for coming.

Right as I opened the front door, I had to stifle a gasp because Max was standing there with his hand lifted, as if he'd just been about to knock. All the cells in my body jumped with joy at seeing him again and I couldn't quite catch my breath.

Max was every bit as gorgeous as I'd remembered. If anything, my memory had failed to do him justice.

With the bright sunlight streaming in, I noticed that his eyes were an icy, light blue. Sharp and piercing, but beautiful.

I wanted to sigh.

He and the electrician nodded at each other as the electrician left. Max let himself into the apartment while I stood there with the door-knob in my hand, not able to move.

"Nice place," he said, taking it all in.

Okay, time to get myself together. *WWKD, remember?* I needed to act with some decorum, to be regal and elegant like Kat, but it wasn't happening.

Instead I was a bumbling mess.

"Thanks," I said, finally managing to shut the door. Then I realized how stupid I probably sounded, given that it wasn't my apartment. "I mean, it's my boss's place."

"The same boss that you have the crush on?" he asked as he walked over to the glass doors to the balcony, taking in the view.

Now I was regretting that I'd spilled my guts so easily to Max. "That's him. The same one that's getting engaged."

I wasn't really sure why I felt compelled to tack on that last part— I'd already shared that information with him.

Okay, that was a lie. I knew why I had said it. A not-very-bright part of me wanted to oh-so-subtly let Max know that Adrian was not an option for me. It was not a great inclination, given that I'd already had many talks with myself to not get swept away in an impossible romantic fantasy.

But then I noticed Max's expression had turned into a mixture of distaste and terror when I'd said Adrian was going to get married.

"What is that face for?" I asked.

His eyebrows flew up his forehead, as if he were surprised that I'd caught him. "What face?"

"The one you made when I said he was getting engaged."

He made the expression again, and this time I laughed. "Just the mere mention of the word is enough to freak you out? Marriage is not an epidemic. You're not going to catch the commitment flu and find yourself at an altar against your will."

While his reaction was amusing, it also let me know that we were fundamentally incompatible because I one hundred percent wanted to get married and have a family. This realization felt like a large stone sinking down from my chest and settling into my stomach.

Such a shame.

"I know that," he said. "I just can't imagine myself getting married. I prefer having fun."

That sinking feeling intensified, but I focused on the indignant flame that was coming to life inside me. As I'd suspected, a total playboy just out to have a good time, moving from one woman to the next. I knew he didn't mean it as some kind of attack on my personal choices, but it sort of felt like one. "I guess that'll be sustainable for a while, especially while you look . . ." It probably wouldn't have been a good thing for me to say "Like someone asked Santa Claus for the hottest guy imaginable as a Christmas present and he brought you." I settled for vaguely waving my hand in his direction. "Like that. But as my meemaw loves to remind me, looks fade and you'll want to find somebody you enjoy being with all the time, someone you can build a life with, someone who has the same goals and aspirations that you do. It's not a bad thing to spend your life with your best friend."

"Your Dr. Seuss grandmother sounds like a wise woman," he said with a smile.

He was avoiding what I'd said by skirting the subject and redirecting my attention. I wasn't going to let him do that. "Do you think your feelings about marriage are a reaction to your last relationship not working out?"

Considering that my own mother hadn't dated anyone seriously since her divorce, it would have been valid for Max to feel that way.

He looked a bit surprised, as if I'd taken him off guard. "Possibly. Maybe I am scared to go down that road again. To trust somebody with my heart a second time. It seems easier to just stay casual."

Yes, casual as he flitted about, sharing himself with all the women of New York. "If you don't trust anybody, if you don't take that risk, you'll also miss out on all the rewards," I said. I paused and then added, "Not that I'm the expert at that sort of thing. Like Alice in Wonderland, I am good at giving out advice, but I very seldom follow it."

Max smiled at me, and even though Adrian's apartment had new lighting, the wattage of Max's smile put every other light source to shame. "Which is why Vella forced you to go out last night. Have you thought about her theory?"

I blinked slowly, not sure what he meant. "About reptilian aliens secretly running the government?"

His smile somehow got bigger and brighter. "No, her theory about why you go after emotionally unavailable men."

"Oh, she's made sure I know the reason why. As she so often tells me, I've always been attracted to men who aren't attracted to me because it's safer." She spent six months majoring in psychology in college and felt like this gave her some sort of license to psychoanalyze me.

"Safer how?" he asked.

"If I keep everyone at arm's length, then I don't have to worry about my heart getting broken." While I was attributing the words to Vella, I did have some insight as to why I made the choices I did. I decided to go for broke. "I use my workload as an excuse, and even though it is a valid one, the truth is I'm too scared to be with anybody. Relationships terrify me."

Adrenaline made my limbs feel shaky. Why was it so hard to admit that? This being more open and putting myself out there more thing sucked.

"Because of your parents' divorce?" he asked.

"Probably," I said. "Which I know is super cliché. My dad being completely unfaithful, never being there for my mom or me, messed me up and gave me some serious self-esteem issues. We were never good enough for him. That's not the only reason, though. The few times I've let my guard down and let myself be excited about someone, it's never turned out well."

"In what way?"

So I told Max the story of what had happened to me in high school at the dance, how humiliated I'd been when I was ditched and mocked. The time in college when a guy who had invited me to meet him at a basketball game stood me up and then ghosted me. When a girl in my economics class had offered to set me up on a blind date with her brother and he'd stayed for about ten minutes and then made up an excuse about a sick ferret and all but sprinted to his car.

While part of me was freaking out at telling Max all these things, internally warning me that I was presenting myself as so unattractive and undesirable, the other part of me wanted to be honest.

I wanted to be seen.

Even if it made him come up with an excuse for his own hasty exit.

But when I finished, he didn't run off flailing his arms like Kermit the Frog.

He stayed.

I felt compelled to fill in the silence. "My dad constantly cheating on my mom is probably the main reason why it's hard for me to trust men. I think some part of me expects that it will happen to me, too. I want to protect myself."

Max was silent for several beats and finally said in a rough voice, "And then when you take a chance, you get let down time and time again. All of that must have been incredibly difficult to deal with."

I felt tears burning at the edge of my eyelids, and I was not going to cry in front of the hot man who just wanted to get his phone back. "Well, you know what they say. What doesn't kill you makes you weird about intimacy."

His eyes crinkled, like he wanted to laugh, but he didn't. He gave me a sad but supportive look that somehow made me feel worse, even though I could tell he wanted to comfort me.

To my dismay, he kept his hands to himself. I would have bet his hugs were fantastic. I let out a big breath. "Wow, I'm glad we skipped over the playful-banter portion of our day and went straight into our own personal therapy session."

"Yes, I appreciate the insight, Dr. Aprile," he said, giving me a slight nod.

"Sorry for going deep. I've never been a big fan of small talk."

"Me either." He paused and then looked the tiniest bit uncomfortable. Had I shared too much about my dysfunctional childhood? "Here. I got you this."

He reached into his coat pocket and pulled out a single red rose.

I caught my breath and put a hand over my stomach. "What's this for?"

"To thank you for taking such good care of my things," he said.

It felt a little like a freight train slamming into my chest, knocking the wind out of me. He meant it as a token of his appreciation. Not as an indication of something more.

When was I going to stop reading so much into every innocent thing he was doing?

Last night I'd been worried that he would accuse me of keeping his stuff deliberately and being obsessed with him, like that guy Vella had gone out with. It was a relief to see that wasn't the case. That he had even brought me a thoughtful gift to thank me.

Or if he'd thought it, at least he'd had the courtesy not to say as much.

I reached for the rose and was careful to avoid brushing my fingers against his. It was the first time anyone had given me a flower. I wanted to thank him but worried that if I did, I might actually start to cry. I joked instead. "You don't know that I took good care of your stuff. I might have taken a hammer to your phone screen and dragged your coat through the streets."

"You wouldn't." He said it with such surety and confidence, like he knew me and didn't have a single doubt in his mind.

"You're right. I didn't. But I am sorry about inadvertently committing grand theft coat." I walked over to the coffee table, where I'd put his things, and handed them back to him.

Now he was going to say his goodbyes and someday I would tell my grandchildren about the time I met and hung out with a hot Monterran man who made my knees wobble and how he had been very nice to me.

"Have you been up to anything exciting since I last saw you?" he asked, as he walked over to the couch and sat down.

I was in such shock that he didn't head for the door that I wasn't sure what to do or how to react. I stood there for a few beats, my heart pounding and my mind racing. Why had he sat down?

As if he sensed my inner turmoil, he gave me a quizzical look. Which was well deserved, given that I was behaving like someone who had never spoken to a man before.

I had to head this off before I wound up in some embarrassing place. Which was kind of where I was currently living. Mayor of Humiliationville, Population: Me.

Taking in a deep breath, I walked over and sat in one of Adrian's extremely uncomfortable and weirdly shaped chairs that flanked his coffee table. It took me a second to figure out how to sit in it but I finally settled in.

"I've decided that I'm going to revamp my life. Make new choices," I told him. "I made a list this morning."

"What brought this on?" He put his arm along the back of the couch, and it took every bit of strength I had not to go over there and snuggle up next to him.

And meeting him was what had made me want to change things, but that wasn't something I was going to confess. Because I knew how this conversation was going to go. I would indicate interest in him; he would look at me sympathetically. I couldn't bear to hear him say, "You're a really nice girl, but . . ." He'd tell me he wasn't looking for anything serious. Nobody ever wanted to hear that from a cute guy because it was so demoralizing. But from a man like Max? Perfect Saint Max?

It would be devastating.

Despite me telling him he should take risks, I was not willing to risk my own heart just to get it inevitably bruised, if not broken.

This would all be a lot easier if I said it. Then I wouldn't have to wait for the axe to inevitably fall. I'd just rip off the Band-Aid now.

I tried to shrug nonchalantly, sure that I hadn't pulled it off. "I realized that if I wanted something else, something better, in my life, I was going to have to do things differently. And one of my resolutions is to make more friends. As much as I don't want to sound like I'm in first grade right now, I'd really like it if you and I could be friends."

There. I was the one who said "friends only" so that he couldn't do it first. I was going to keep my potential humiliation in check. I recognized that this was probably coming across strangely to him—but I had put myself up on a shelf for so long that I no longer knew how to have a normal interaction with a guy.

Holding my breath, I studied his face for a reaction. Part of me desperately wanted him to disagree. To tell me he wasn't interested in being only my friend.

To say he wanted something more.

CHAPTER THIRTEEN

An emotion flitted across his face so quickly that I couldn't register what it was. But then he smiled and said, "Of course. Who couldn't use more friends?"

Happy, relieved, and disappointed. All at the same time.

"That's what I always say! Although I haven't had the easiest time making friends since I moved here. The people I get along with the best also don't want to leave their houses."

"Is that why you're close with your roommate?"

"Yes, it makes it much easier when you both don't want to go out and you live in the same place."

He grinned and said, "Tell me about her."

My hackles went up. I reminded myself that I was not allowed to be suspicious or to ask him why, as if I were jealous. Which I was. Although I figured I probably shouldn't act that way with him right after I'd said I wanted us to be just friends. Talk about a mixed message.

It was just that guys always went for Vella, and much as I loved her, I wanted to keep Max for myself. Even if we were only going to be pals. "She's scary smart, but never really finishes anything. I always joke that she has a black belt in Partial Arts. She is the most sarcastic person I've ever met. If snark was a science, she would have her PhD. She tries to scare people off, but she's a big old softie underneath. When I first met her, I was kind of worried that she was going to kill me and make it look like an accident, but she's great now."

"She doesn't really seem like the kind of person someone like you would be friends with."

Our day doorman, Yiannis, had once referred to us "Workaholic Barbie" and "Scary Goth," so Max wasn't the first person to comment on it. "That's fair. But we just really click and enjoy spending time together. She always says we balance each other out. She makes me be more realistic and I keep her from committing homicide."

He laughed and I loved that he got my sense of humor. I'd been on a couple of dates where I'd made the same kind of Vella-inspired dark joke and had been met with a strange silence.

"Are you busy now?" he asked, and it was such a sharp turn from where our conversation had been headed that it took me a second to respond.

"I still have to feed my boss's pets."

He frowned slightly. "I haven't seen any pets."

"Come with me. I have to grab their food in the kitchen. They're in Adrian's . . ." I wasn't going to say *man cave* to Max. Mostly because he didn't seem like a video gaming / loud movie sort of guy. More of the reading a good book by a roaring fire while looking extremely sexy type. I swallowed down that image and finished my sentence. "They're in Adrian's office."

"What kind of pets does he have?"

"A python and three sharks."

"Did you say 'sharks'?" Max asked behind me as we went into the kitchen. "Is he a supervillain? Am I in a lair right now?"

I laughed, ready to agree that Adrian's place did have that chrome-and-white furniture one would find in a lair when I heard a grunting sound and then a loud thud.

Max was laid out flat on the tile, blinking up at me.

What had happened? I glanced down and realized that I hadn't mopped up all of the water from when I'd taken care of the plants.

"I am so sorry," I told him, crouching down next to him on the floor. "I spilled some water earlier and I thought I got it all. Are you okay?"

He gave me a devastating smile. "I'm fine. It isn't the first time I've hit my head."

He hit his head? Now I felt worse and kept apologizing, but he brushed it off and slowly got up.

"Are you sure you're okay? I'm so sorry that I caused you bodily harm." It was like I'd ripped a hole in Van Gogh's *The Starry Night*.

"Everly, I'm fine," he said with a gentle smile. "Now what were you doing in the kitchen? Other than bowling me over?"

I appreciated that he was teasing to lighten the mood, but I still felt bad. "The food is in the freezer. A mouse for the python, and shrimp and tilapia for the sharks."

It didn't take me long to locate the packages, as they were the only things kept in the freezer besides vodka. Adrian always ate out. But I stood in front of the freezer for a moment, letting the cold air blast against my face.

Regal and confident, I reminded myself as I closed the freezer door.

"This way," I said, and we left the kitchen.

But I was so scattered that I was heading in the wrong direction. I had gone down the hall that led to the bedrooms and came to a sudden stop, twirling around.

I'd only managed to say, "Whoops, wrong—" before I turned and crashed into Max, pressed flush against him.

He grabbed me by my elbows and held me in place so that I wouldn't fall. Our faces were so close together that I could smell the minty toothpaste he must have used before coming over here. I desperately hoped he couldn't smell the calzone I'd eaten earlier.

His sweet, warm breath caressed my face, and my heart started to pound against my ribs, like it was trying to break free. Our chests were pressed together and I prayed he couldn't feel my reaction to him.

My skin burned where his fingers held on to me, and blood rushed into my ears so that for a few moments all I could hear were my own ridiculously loud, harsh breaths.

I swallowed down a gulp and looked up into his sparkling blue eyes. Something in his expression made the air in my lungs solidify and my lips tingle in anticipation.

I had never wanted to be kissed so badly in my whole life.

"You good?" he asked in a low voice that made all of my nerve endings light up.

"I . . ." I was never going to be good again. Without my permission, my body leaned into his so that I could revel in his strength, and in the planes and ridges of his body that felt so delicious against my own softness. He made a sound in the back of his throat that had my stomach tightening in response.

This was an impossible situation. I didn't want to waste any more time on men who were not interested in dating me. He'd just told me he was only looking to have fun. I couldn't kiss him and recover from that. If I crossed that line, we would have to stop being friends, and I wanted to be his friend.

"I'm good," I finally managed to breathe while disengaging myself from him. I was not a clumsy person, but his touch made me feel like he'd detached my central nervous system from the rest of my limbs and I was no longer in control of them.

I had managed to drop the food on the floor and stooped down to pick it up, grateful for the distraction from my thundering heartbeat and shaky extremities.

Unfortunately, Max bent down to help me and I miscalculated how close he was and we smacked our foreheads into each other. I yelped and we both apologized at the same exact time.

"Let me get it," he said, and I quickly stood, ignoring the blood rush from standing up too quickly combined with the heat of him being so close. I put a hand over my forehead and wondered if that ringing feeling was from bumping heads with him or just from his nearness.

I dropped my hand when he straightened up. I didn't need him to check in on me. I would be fine.

Eventually.

"Which way?" he asked.

"Over here," I said, and walked quickly to Adrian's man cave . . . er, office. I opened the door and went inside.

One entire wall was devoted to Adrian's saltwater aquarium.

Max let out a low whistle. "How big is that?"

"Hundreds of gallons? Thousands? I'm not really sure." My brain still felt disconnected from the rest of me. I got out the step stool and opened the cabinet doors above the aquarium to throw in the food. Two of the sharks were extremely interested in what I was doing, but even if the third one was ignoring me, they'd all eat every last bite.

After I finished, I found Max studying the python in his terrarium behind Adrian's desk. A desk that was for looks only, because as far as I could tell, Adrian had never actually used it.

I hated feeding the snake. I knew he wasn't going to leap out and bite me on the face, but I still pictured it every time I had to open the top of his terrarium.

"Here, let me," Max said, gently taking the package from my hands and opening it. I had no idea how he could tell that I was afraid, but I was thankful for his assistance.

After he'd put the frozen mouse in and reclosed the top, he said to me, "I thought you loved all animals."

"I'm willing to make an exception for snakes. I have always been afraid of them. One of the two things Indiana Jones and I have in common."

"What's the other?"

"I look great in a fedora," I said, and he laughed. I took the wrappers from him and threw them away in the trash.

He looked around the room, taking in the expensive stereo system, the gaming consoles, the imported Italian leather armchairs, the custom-made pool table. "Your boss has a lot of money."

There was a disapproving note in his voice and I wondered what it was. That Adrian wasted it? It would be hard to argue with that.

Or was Max, like Vella, against people having a lot of money? Given his line of work, maybe he was thinking how many people he could have helped with what Adrian had spent in here.

Strangely enough, despite the fact that I'd defended Adrian every chance I got to my mom and Vella, I didn't want to defend him to Max.

"I would say he should get to spend it how he wants since he earned it, but he didn't really do that. Everything he has was given to him." It was easily the most disloyal thing I'd ever said about my boss.

But I didn't even feel guilty about it.

"And you don't respect that?"

"I like it when people make their own way in the world instead of relying on a trust fund."

"Me too," he said with a nod. "I find it very impressive."

His eyes met mine and another charged moment passed between us. The air felt heavy, like something exciting was about to happen, and my brain turned sluggish, hazy, ready to slip into some netherworld where the only thing that would matter would be Max's lips on mine.

"When it comes to furniture, I much prefer comfort over aesthetics," he said. There was something in his voice that pierced through my befuddled mind and revved my adrenaline up, even though he was saying something ordinary with no subtext to it whatsoever.

"Me too," I whispered, and that connection I felt to him, like we were similar in so many ways, overwhelmed me.

He took a step toward me and my heart stopped.

"I'm, uh, going to wash my hands," I said. "The bathroom is this way."

Needing to escape, I left the room and went into the guest bathroom, turning on the faucet and pumping out some liquid soap. Max stood just behind me, waiting for his opportunity to do the same.

After I dried my hands off, he entered the bathroom just as I exited it, which caused us to have to brush past each other again, and despite the fact that we were both fully clothed, every inch of my skin prickled with delight, as if he were making skin-on-skin contact.

"Excuse me," he said, right as I managed a "Sorry."

I went out into the hallway and leaned against the wall as I closed my eyes, asking for heaven to give me strength.

Because I wanted to go back into that bathroom and throw myself at Max Colby.

What was wrong with me?

I tried to catch my breath while reminding my overeager body of the facts.

He was out of my league.

I'd had feelings for Adrian five minutes ago and was basically transferring my crush from him to someone else because he'd gotten engaged, which wasn't fair to Max or to me.

Max had an army of women texting him. I wasn't willing to be one of many.

But most importantly? He had just agreed with me that he wanted us to be only friends.

I was not going to be this pathetic.

He came out into the hallway and I immediately straightened, smiling at him. "Thanks so much for helping me. I should walk you out."

Before he could respond, I headed to the front door and opened it. This was better. I knew that Max couldn't be interested in me that way, and as much as I'd enjoyed talking to him and seeing him, this was it and I had to accept that.

Better to end things now, on a high note, than to have a thoroughly regretful interaction that I'd run through my head over and over again every night just before I fell asleep for the next ten years.

I did allow myself to feel sad that I wasn't going to get to hang out with him again. I knew that maybe we'd text occasionally until he picked one woman in his rotation to be his new girlfriend, and I'd have to content myself with that.

He got his phone and his coat, which effectively snuffed out any sad hope I might have had that he'd forget them again and make it so I'd get to see him a third time. I drank in his masculine beauty, feeling a little depressed this was my last opportunity.

But when he came over to the door, he stopped. "Now that you've fed the pets, are you free?"

"For what?" I asked, bewildered, my heart throbbing from him standing so close to me.

"Last night you offered to be my personal New York City tour guide. I was wondering if I could take you up on your kind offer this afternoon."

CHAPTER FOURTEEN

Despite the fact that I had a pile of work at home, I immediately said yes and began to walk out into the hallway.

"Wait, don't you need to get your stuff?" he asked.

"Hold me a minute," I said, and my eyes widened as I realized what I'd just said. "I was going to say 'hold on' and then 'give me a minute,' and instead it came out . . . the way it did."

Not at all mortifying.

I could feel the color rising in my cheeks.

He gave me a playful smile. "We all misspeak sometimes."

"I'll be right back." I paid careful attention this time when I spoke so that the right words came out and not some weird combination that made it seem like I was hitting on him.

Max waited by the door while I got my coat. I slipped the rose he'd given me into my purse. I wished I had a second to collect myself, or to do a Wonder Woman spin before I went out the door with him.

For a second I hesitated, wanting to cry off and tell him that I had a lot of work to catch up on and wasn't free, but my body wouldn't let me. My feet were already bringing the rest of me over to join him at the door.

"Let's go," I said. "What are you in the mood for? Something very touristy, or something more real New York?"

"I pick touristy," he said.

"Okay." I took out my phone and looked down my vendor list. "I know a guy who can get us orchestra seats to any Broadway show the day of the performance for like, a quarter of the price." I sent a quick text and got an immediate response. "Done. We have to hurry, though—the matinee show is going to start soon. Then afterward we'll go to Times Square, and if you'd like, I know a great restaurant with this chef that does the most amazing catering. I was thinking of getting him for that Monterra party I'm doing. Maybe you could tell me what you think of the food."

"That sounds like a plan. Where can I send you money for my ticket?" he asked as we got to the elevator. The doors opened immediately and he held them open, letting me step inside first.

Another gentleman point for him.

"I'm the tour guide, it's on me," I said as I sent the money to cover both tickets over to Peter via an app. Again, Max was making it very clear that this was not a date by offering to pay for his half. Which was entirely my fault for the friends-only thing, but it was still deflating.

Then I quickly texted Vella to tell her that I wasn't going to be home this afternoon to start watching *Columbo*, the next show in our rotation. I'd made it a habit to text her when I had a date. My mother and grandmother were utterly convinced that I was going to get mugged or assaulted every time I went outside because they thought New York City was so dangerous, and some of their paranoia had managed to rub off on me.

Instinctually I knew that Max was safe, but I still sent the text.

Sending that note to her was probably more because I couldn't believe that I was about to spend the afternoon with him.

Vella didn't respond, which surprised me. Her phone was usually glued to her hand. I had expected another string of inappropriate emojis.

The elevator reached the ground floor and we stepped out into the lobby. The doorman, John, waved to me. "See you soon, Everly!"

"Have a good day!" I called back to him.

"Do you know everyone in New York?" Max asked as we went outside.

"It's part of being a good event planner. You'd be shocked at the kind of people I have at my fingertips. I know someone who can set up a petting zoo at the last minute. Another who has a portable tattoo parlor. A hot-air balloon girl. A balloon-animal maker. Tent, table, linens people. Floral arrangers. Caricature artists. Arcade vendors. Hairstylists and makeup experts. Caterers of every kind of food imaginable. I never know what a client will ask for, and most of my job is connecting clients with the right vendors for their events, and then making sure those vendors do their jobs. It helps to have good relationships with them."

"That's impressive," he said, and I preened over his admiring tone.

"It's a good thing I've built up this kind of network. That birthday party is going to be a very last-minute thing, but I'll be able to pull it off because they're spending a lot of money and I know the perfect people to call. That's what you're hiring when you get a good event planner."

"Have you always wanted to be an event planner?"

"I mostly wanted to be a princess when I was younger," I told him. "I joined student government in high school and discovered that I really enjoyed planning our activities. Then when I found out it was an actual job, I moved here to New York and did college online while working full-time to get practical experience. I figured the best events in the world would be here, and I was right."

Never mind that most of the events I'd done so far hadn't been very much fun. "What about you? Did you always want to work for a nonprofit?"

"I changed my mind a bunch of times growing up," he said. "But what I'm doing makes me really happy. I love giving back."

"What kind of work are you doing?"

"Right now we're assisting single mothers from under-resourced communities in getting their degree. We pay all their bills for them and their children, including their room and board, and pay for their tuition. We help them find their first job in their chosen field and their own place to live. One of the unexpected side benefits they've discovered over the years is that the children go on to get college educations as well, emulating what their mothers have done. In a small way we're helping as many families as we can to break the cycle of poverty."

"Wow," I breathed. I really loved my job and making people happy, but Max was doing real, lasting, serious work. Things that were changing the lives of people for generations to come.

It made me like him so much.

Which intensified when he said, "We've also started a program to help mothers of infants to get all the necessary supplies they need. I had no idea how expensive diapers and formula were."

Oh, my heart and my ovaries were aching. He was the absolute kindest, sweetest person ever and all of this was just making me want him more.

I cleared my throat. "That's really neat. It must be so rewarding to do that kind of work."

"It is." He nodded.

Then he proceeded to make everything worse. There was a green glass bottle on the ground in front of us. He picked it up, took it over to a recycling bin, and threw it away. It made my insides flutter. If someone had stepped on it, they could have gotten seriously hurt. He was thoughtful, aware, and considerate. He hadn't done it to impress me—it was just instinct—and so it impressed me even more.

Meemaw had always wanted me to find a gentleman, and they were a dying breed as far as I could tell.

Max was apparently launching a one-man effort to revive the species.

I desperately needed to think about something else. "No Basta today?"

"She has a doggy playdate."

"Like she has a boyfriend?" I asked with a laugh.

We came to a stop at the corner, waiting for the light to change. "In a way. There's a woman in my building who goes to the same dog park nearby, and we met. Basta and Champ hit it off right away, so she offered to take them to the park with her a couple of times a week, and then they hang out afterward at her place."

"Do you go, too?" I asked.

"Not usually."

I pressed my lips together so that I wouldn't smile. That poor woman. I bet that really frustrated her clever plans of getting to spend some alone time with Max. Well, if nothing else, she was getting in good with his dog, and that seemed as smart a scheme as any other, given how attached he was to Basta.

"How long have you had her?" At his quizzical expression, I added, "Basta, not the neighbor."

"For a couple of years. I had another dog before her named Gelato, which was her favorite thing to eat. Her favorite thing to do was to chase squirrels."

"Do you have a lot of squirrels in Monterra?" I asked.

"The same as anywhere else, I guess."

"Well, maybe Gelato is still chasing squirrels up in heaven."

"You're not the first person to say that to me," he said with a smile. "Although it makes me feel bad for the departed squirrels. They have to spend their eternity evading dogs?"

I thought about that for a second. "Maybe squirrel hell is doggy heaven. Like a two-birds-with-one-stone situation."

That earned me another one of his delicious smiles. "And what sorts of mortal sins have squirrels committed on Earth that warrant that kind of torment?"

"Squirrels are just rats with fluffy tails," I told him. "Adorable, and I would keep one as a pet if I could get away with it, but they can be very devious and destructive. Plus, they know those bird feeders are not intended for them."

"What about the good ones?"

"Maybe the reverse is true. Squirrel heaven is dog hell. Because no dog would ever end up being eternally punished. They're too pure and perfect."

"I totally agree with you," he said as we went down the stairs to get on the subway. "I also think dogs are much smarter than we give them credit for. Basta knows a lot of human words, but I don't understand any dog barks."

This led to a long but interesting debate on what we thought of animals' levels of intelligence—like how an ape could communicate with sign language or parrots could speak and comprehend things, but like Max had pointed out, it never seemed to work the opposite way.

It wasn't really date-like material, but I found myself fascinated with all of his thoughts and ideas and couldn't agree with him fast enough. He was easily one of the most interesting people I'd ever met. I loved the way his mind worked.

I also probably stood a bit closer to him than was necessary on the subway. We were both holding on to the handrail and standing, as there was nowhere to sit. A man was edging closer and kept "accidentally" bumping into me even though the car was not that full. I moved away from him—I knew where this was going and wasn't in the mood to be randomly groped.

Max seemed to understand what I was doing and wedged himself in between me and the other man. I was pressed up against Max's side and discovered a well of self-control that I didn't know existed as I refrained from wrapping my arms around his waist.

It got worse when he put his arm around my shoulders, like he had at the bar last night, in a protective gesture. My brain basically short-circuited entirely and I could only nod and listen as he talked, incapable of contributing anything to the conversation.

We got off on the Times Square–42nd Street stop. Max took his arm away from me and I mourned the loss of his touch.

How was I supposed to be friends with this man?

I'd somehow managed to keep my hands and lips to myself with Adrian for the last four years. Surely I could do the same with Max.

The only problem was that it all felt completely different.

Like I'd never been as attracted to Adrian as I was to Max.

We walked a few minutes to the theater, where they had begun letting people in. I showed them our tickets and we got our programs. I made my way down to the second row, scooching past people to get to our spots.

"These are really good seats," Max said as we both settled in.

"They are!" I agreed. "Peter always delivers." I leaned forward, trying to take my coat off, and struggled with the position I was in.

I felt Max's fingers against my shoulders, moving down my arms as he helped me remove it, and everywhere he touched left tiny fiery trails of sensation.

I tried hard not to shiver.

When he had my coat off entirely, I said, "Thank you." I sounded breathy and desperate.

Not good.

"My pleasure," he said in a growly way that made all the tingling feelings inside me intensify.

I could only gape at him, wishing I had another article of clothing that he could remove for me without us both getting arrested for public indecency.

His gaze held mine, and then it drifted down to my mouth and my breath hitched.

"Everly, I wanted to ask you something," he said.

"Yes?" That was a question, but it also felt like my answer. Anything he wanted, I was going to say yes.

But whatever he'd planned on asking was drowned out by the orchestra playing the overture.

I cursed the rotten luck that kept him from finishing.

And instead of enjoying the show, I spent the next three hours wondering what Max had wanted to ask me.

CHAPTER FIFTEEN

I didn't question him about what he was going to ask me when the show finished, worried that he might have forgotten completely and would think me ridiculous for bringing it up.

He might have been about to ask me something completely innocuous, like what my favorite brand of bubble gum was. Or if I thought squirrels should have some kind of purgatory so that they could work their way up to squirrel heaven. It could have been anything, and I cursed my overactive imagination for wanting what I couldn't have.

The rest of me did not get that message, though. Max and I stood up to put our coats back on, but no matter how hard I tried, I just could not get my left arm in the sleeve.

Max gave me an amused and indulgent look and reached forward to hold my coat in place for me so that I could easily slide my arm in.

He smelled so good and was so warm and strong.

I wanted to tell him I hadn't done it intentionally.

Okay, maybe it had been intentional on my body's part—to inhibit our coordination so that he would have to help and we could stand close to each other.

"What did you think?" I asked him as we spilled out onto the street with the rest of the audience.

"It was really good! What about you?"

Although my dating history in New York was not that extensive, I could say that I hadn't gone out with a single man who would have admitted to enjoying a musical.

More and more I was beginning to believe that Max was some figment of my imagination that I had wished into being.

"This is like the seventh time I've seen it. It's my favorite." It was why I'd chosen it, wanting to share it with him. I was so giddily happy that he'd liked it.

"I could have guessed. You sang along to all of the songs."

That made me gasp. I had an absolutely terrible singing voice and did not ever sing voluntarily where others could hear me. "I did not sing," I whispered in horror.

"Oh, you did. It's okay, though. It was adorable."

Like a puppy. Wonderful.

"Why didn't we go to something you haven't seen before?" he asked as we approached the traffic light.

"I'm not one of those people that need constant variety or novelty. I'm very happy with the things I love."

"I'm the same way!" he said.

The horde of women on his phone told me differently, but I stayed quiet.

"I eat the same breakfast every day and my—" He stopped himself. "People have made fun of me for it in the past."

By *people* did he mean his ex-girlfriend? Why would that incredibly evil, stupid woman make fun of Max for anything?

My opinion of her dropped lower every time he mentioned her.

"What do you like to have for breakfast?" I asked, knowing that it was something I was probably never going to witness personally but still feeling intensely curious about it.

"Bacon and eggs. What about you?"

"Coffee and panic, mostly."

Max laughed and I grinned at him. It took only a couple of minutes to walk over to Times Square, and I got several pictures of him with various people dressed up in costumes of famous animated characters. We walked through the crowded and busy stores, talking about other things we liked and disliked. Our conversation was easy and flowed well. It had been a long time since a man had paid this much attention to me, or had seemed so interested in learning things about me.

He stayed close, so close sometimes that when he spoke, his words would stir the hair next to my ear. That feeling made my eyes roll so far back in my head that it nearly teleported me into another dimension.

Somehow I managed to keep myself together long enough to direct him to Roma Vida, the Italian restaurant I'd mentioned to him earlier. Max didn't seem to detect that anything was amiss with me, that I was barely hanging on to my sanity and sense of self.

All I wanted to do was get lost in him, and it was very, very distracting.

I'd been so careful in drawing boundaries with him to be just friends, but no part of my body agreed with my brain's decision, and it was actively trying to sabotage me and get closer to him.

I "accidentally" bumped into him so many times he probably thought I had an inner-ear issue.

When we arrived at the restaurant, the hostess said she could seat us immediately, despite the fact that there were a bunch of people waiting for a table.

"I guess it pays to know the owner," Max said to me, and his lips were close to my ear again and my head buzzed as we followed behind the hostess.

If someone had asked me to re-create the sound I made in response, I would not have been able to because it lacked any recognizable vowels or consonants.

"This place looks expensive," he said, and it hadn't occurred to me to take his financial situation into consideration. I didn't know exactly what it was, but considering his comments today, my guess was that working for a nonprofit didn't pay very well.

I didn't have a ton of money, but given that I'd gotten paid today, I could cover dinner. It would probably mean ramen noodles for the rest of the month, though.

"It's only expensive if you buy stuff," I teased him. "But don't worry about it. I've got it."

"Everly, you can't keep paying for things when I—"

We arrived at our table and Max pulled a chair out, standing behind it. He obviously intended to assist me.

Like he'd stepped out of some novel from the nineteenth century. I sat and scooted myself in while he went to the other side of the table.

Just as he'd sat down across from me, Bartolomeo, the owner, made his way over to us.

"Everly! Cara mia!" He leaned down to kiss me on both of my cheeks and I returned the greeting. "To what do I owe this pleasure?"

"I'm introducing my friend Max to your excellent food. And if my client agrees, I have an event I'll need you to cater."

"No talk of business tonight," Bartolomeo said, waving my words away with both of his hands. "You will call me later. We will talk. Tonight is for amore, eh?"

"No," I said, hoping that I wasn't blushing as I tried to set the record straight. No amore here. Just . . . whatever the Italian word for *friendship* was.

Max held out his hand and introduced himself to Bartolomeo, and the two men began a rapid dialogue in Italian. I had no idea what either one of them was saying and cursed the fact that I'd never bothered to learn the language despite my Monterra royal obsession.

What I did notice was Bartolomeo pointedly looking at me several times while he made multiple hand gestures that I couldn't interpret. Max's smile got bigger and wider until I felt like I was going to throw my fork in an attempt to get them to stop talking.

"Dinner is my treat," Bartolomeo said, finally shifting back to English. When I tried to object, he said, "No, I insist."

Then he winked at Max and went back into the kitchen.

"What was that about?" I asked him.

Max shot me a mysterious smile and opened the menu. "He had some very nice things to say about you."

"Like what?"

"What's good here?" he asked, avoiding my question.

I wanted to probe further, to find out what exactly had happened in their conversation, but I got the sense that Max was going to keep his secrets. "I've never actually eaten here at the restaurant before, but I have tried his food at several events. You can't go wrong with the lobster risotto or the spaghetti alla gricia. Both the branzino with capers and the tagliata di manzo are incredible. I'd recommend any of those."

"If you recommend it, that's good enough for me."

His words sent little effervescent bubbles through my veins, making me lightheaded. He was probably just being nice, but I appreciated the vote of confidence.

The hostess came by our table. "Bartolomeo asked me to let you know that he's going to serve you our tasting menu."

"So much for my recommendation," I said as Max and I handed our menus to the hostess.

"This way we'll get to try a bit of everything," he responded, and then hesitated a beat before adding, "Can I ask you a question?"

I nodded. This man could do anything he wanted to me and I would thank him for it.

Ugh. I had to knock it off with those kinds of thoughts.

"What's the rubber band for?" He reached for my wrist and my breath caught, but he stopped short, his hand hovering. I was busy watching his actions, longing for the moment when his fingers would make contact with my skin. I glanced up and realized that he was waiting for my permission to touch me. I nodded quickly, my pulse ricocheting wildly the second his fingers stroked the sensitized skin of my inner wrist.

This reaction could not be normal. Something had to be wrong with me that I was in this constant heightened state around him.

Especially when I knew it couldn't go anywhere.

"You still haven't explained what it's for," he said, and I had to blink several times to reorient myself to my current surroundings. He had hooked his index finger under the rubber band, tugging at it slightly.

I had to swallow down the longing feelings that were overwhelming me. "It's a technique where if you have intrusive thoughts, you snap the rubber band against your wrist to bring yourself out of it." The band was there to remind me to do better, be more like Kat, move forward with my life.

"What are you having intrusive thoughts about?" Now his fingers were just gently gliding against my wrist and he was searing my skin with every slight movement.

What was I having intrusive thoughts about?

You.

I felt my lips forming to make the *U* sound, as if my brain were battling against my mouth to get me to say it out loud.

A waitress approached and announced the first course, which was tagliatelle al ragù. Max took his hand away, and it was like he'd torn off that patch of my skin and taken it with him. I put my hands in my lap, trying to regain some composure, snapping my rubber band over and over again.

"This is amazing," he said after he took his first bite.

"Told you," I said. "Bartolomeo is one of the best chefs in the city. I've used him for so many events."

"Have you ever planned weddings?" he asked, settling his linen napkin across his lap.

I did the same with mine, and given how clumsy Max made me, I should have done it sooner. I was just glad I hadn't spilled anything yet. "Why? Are you in the market for one?"

"Most definitely not."

"You're not engaged, right? Or about to get engaged?" He'd already told me that he was single, but I wanted to make sure. Maybe I had some weird in-a-committed-relationship sensor in my brain that made it so I was attracted only to men already involved with someone else.

If he was at all concerned about my line of questioning, he didn't show it. "I'm not and have absolutely no plans to."

While I was happy he was very single, I was also annoyed at the reminder that he wasn't looking for a relationship at all and was allergic to commitment. "I will never plan weddings, because most brides are sociopaths. I like doing events where there's a personal stake and happy emotions are involved, but brides are like skilled thieves/assassins planning some high-stakes mission, willing to strike down anyone in their path to get what they want. I did one wedding for a cousin while I was in high school, and never again. I got personally attacked on a daily basis and I'm too thin-skinned not to let it bother me. Which is probably something I should work on. Thin skin is not a good thing when you're an event planner."

I kind of felt like I'd been talking for too long, but Max didn't look bored. If anything, he looked intrigued. "I don't know. There must be some situations where thin skin could be an asset. Like what if you're getting your blood drawn by a weak phlebotomist?"

"Or a lazy mosquito?"

"An elderly vampire."

We were both grinning at each other as the next course arrived—tortellini with braised greens.

"Do you have any photos of your one wedding attempt?" he asked, and I wondered whether he was just being polite or if he was really curious.

I got my phone and went through my social media to find some of the photos of the reception from my cousin's wedding. I told him that she had been so terrible through the entire planning process that we hadn't spoken for three years. She had finally reached out and apologized and we'd been working on rebuilding our relationship.

"Here." I handed him the phone.

He was looking at the pictures, scrolling through them, when my phone buzzed. "Oh. You have a message. Sorry, I didn't mean to read it—it just popped up. Who is Mom Send?"

The universe just had to make sure it really and truly messed with me, didn't it? Plus, I couldn't be mad at him for inadvertently reading my text when I'd scrolled through messages from his female horde. "That's from my mother. She always signs her texts and thinks she has to write the word 'send' to get it to work."

"And it's in all caps because?" he asked as he handed my phone back to me.

"Because she doesn't know how caps lock works? I don't know. I've told her so many times but she never listens."

I glanced at the message. It said:

T MINUS 8 DAYS AND COUNTING UNTIL THE WEDDING!!!
MOM SEND

With a growing sense of dread, I knew the next question he was going to ask me. Sure enough, he said, "What wedding are you counting down to?"

Oh, how could I say this without him questioning my sanity? It was very hard explaining to someone who had only a passing familiarity with something you were over-the-top invested in.

"The Monterran royal family. Princess Chiara is getting married next week, and like I told you, it's our Super Bowl. We're getting up at four thirty in the morning to watch it."

That was okay, right? It didn't sound too bizarre?

I was about to ask him something about his life, to steer him away from getting deeper into this minefield. He already knew I was weird about it—I just didn't think he understood to what extent.

He beat me to the punch, though, and asked a question first. "Do you have a good relationship with your mom?"

I took another bite of the tortellini dish before I answered. "I love my mom. But I think she wishes I was a different person. I always feel like I'm not measuring up to who she wants me to be."

He let out a small sigh. "I know how that feels."

Max's phone rang and he picked it up to glance at the screen. One of his many female admirers? "Speaking of intrusive family members, it's my cousin Sunny. She knows I haven't checked my voice mail in ten years, so she'll keep calling until I pick up. Excuse me a second. Hello?"

I ate my pasta and watched as his face dropped.

"It's okay. Breathe. What do you mean? What did she say? What did you say? I can't understand you when you're crying. How soon?"

Then his eyes flicked over to me.

"I think I know someone who can help. Let me call you back."

He hung up and with a very somber expression said, "I hate to have to do this, but Everly, I need to ask you for a favor."

CHAPTER SIXTEEN

Again, there was very little that I would refuse this man. I already knew I was going to say yes regardless of what he needed.

I'd even plan a wedding for him.

"Sunny and her husband, Todd, are about to have a baby. She wasn't planning on having a baby shower because my aunt, her mom, passed away a few years ago and she said she couldn't imagine having one without her."

"I'm so sorry. That must be so hard." Max had mentioned his cousin before—she was the one insisting that he get out of his apartment. Without thinking, I reached over to squeeze his hand. I left it there for a beat too long, convincing myself that this was something friends did to comfort one another and it wasn't at all about wanting to feel his warm skin against my fingers.

"It has been. Todd's family are very wealthy, old school, and traditional, and his mother expects that there will be a baby shower for her friends. She spoke to Todd about it, but he didn't communicate it well to Sunny and my cousin found out this afternoon when she and Todd went over for a family brunch that his family expects someone to throw her a shower in three weeks. Invitations have already been sent, as apparently Todd agreed to have it at his parents' place."

At my surprised look, he added, "I love the guy, but Todd can be a little absent-minded. He works in biotechnology and only partially pays attention to the real-life stuff going on around him. It is entirely believable that his family would have made plans that he'd somehow agreed to without realizing it."

I slipped into planning mode. "What will her budget be?"

"Todd's got a trust fund. I don't think money will be a concern."

The words *unlimited budget* danced through my head, making me feel tingly. It was one of the reasons I had moved to New York City. To be in charge of events on a scale unimaginable anywhere else. But I had the Origin Telecom conference coming up, followed by the birthday party. I wasn't sure I could add on an event for the week after that one. "I have a lot of last-minute things going on right now."

I glanced down at my dress and asked myself what Kat would do if she were in this situation. I could see from the expression on his face that he expected me to say no, and I couldn't bring myself to do it.

It would be the smart thing to do, but not the right thing.

"But I'd love to help out," I said.

His face broke into the most glorious smile. It was payment enough for going without sleep for the next three weeks.

"Are you sure?"

"Absolutely," I assured him. I had no idea how I was going to make it work, but I would.

"Anything I can do to assist you, let me know," he said, and I was worried about the ways my subconscious mind might find to take advantage of his offer. "She also mentioned that they're giving her a hard time about who is officially throwing the event. According to etiquette guides, which are very important to them, it's supposed to be a distant family member or a friend who throws the shower for her."

I was going to suggest he do it, given that they were cousins, but if her in-laws were traditional, they probably wouldn't want a man to be the host. It seemed like such a stupid thing to get upset about, but if I could help ease Sunny's mind, I would do it. "Tell her not to worry about it. I'm now her friend, too, and I'm throwing it for her."

Now Max was the one reaching across the table to take my hand, and while I told myself to calm down, I did not listen. His palm was so warm and firm.

"Sunny is the most important person in the world to me. It means so much to me that you would do this. Thank you."

I was ridiculously happy to just bask in the glow of his approval and gratitude. His hand tightened around mine and I loved the way it felt to hold hands with him.

"What can I do to repay you?" he asked, his voice soft and enticing.

I'd happily take payment in kisses, but I wasn't going to say as much and put myself in that kind of awkward position. He was just grateful to me, he wasn't making a move.

My overstimulated glands did not care, though.

We were interrupted by our waitress bringing out the next course, beef cheek ravioli with black truffles, and I was both glad for and annoyed by the interruption.

The food was so exceptional that we both ate in silence for a bit, and I contemplated what was happening to me. I barely knew this man. Why was I so ready to pledge my allegiance to him?

Probably because everything I did know, I really liked. He was smart, kind, down-to-earth, and thoughtful, loved animals, admired hard work, cared about his family, had a good sense of humor, and was a perfect gentleman.

That wasn't even taking into account his fallen-angel face, which had been created solely to tempt me.

If Meemaw ever met him, she would force me into a shotgun wedding with him.

And I wouldn't object.

The rest of the dinner seemed to fly by, while Max entertained me with stories from his job, things he and Sunny had done when they were children, and best of all—stories of what it was like to live in Monterra.

Dessert was something called torta Barozzi, which was a dense, flourless chocolate cake flavored with coffee, rum, and almonds. It was one of the most sinful things I'd ever put in my mouth.

After my first bite I let out a little groan of delight and briefly closed my eyes. When I opened them again, Max had fixed his hot, intense gaze on me, watching my mouth move. His eyes flicked up to mine, and I saw hunger and wanting there. My blood sizzled in response, my breathing growing labored.

But as quickly as it appeared, it was gone. Making me think it had been a figment of my imagination.

Bartolomeo came out to see us after dinner was finished, and we both lavished him with praise, which he could not get enough of. "No, please, it was my pleasure, you don't need to thank me," he said, while waving his fingers to let us know that we should continue.

After we'd sufficiently complimented and thanked him, Max and I stood up to leave. Since he'd comped our dinner, I didn't feel right about lingering and keeping the table from a paying customer. I told Bartolomeo that I would be in touch soon, so long as the client approved him as a vendor, but that it would all be very last minute.

"For you, cara mia, I will clear my schedule."

"Thank you again for everything," I said as he walked us out.

"Di niente. It was nothing. Buonasera con il tuo ragazzo." He kissed me on each cheek, shook Max's hand, and then we went out into the wintry evening.

I didn't even feel the cold, though. I was glowing on the inside. "What did Bartolomeo say?"

Max gave me a playful smile. "He said, 'Have a good night with your boyfriend.'"

My cheeks were bright red, I just knew it. I didn't know how to respond without making a bigger fool of myself, so I just stayed quiet. It was actually flattering that Bartolomeo thought that someone like Max would be interested in dating me.

Totally unrealistic, but nice nonetheless.

I was thankful that Max didn't make fun of the situation or ask me what I'd said to Bartolomeo that had led him to believe the two of us were together.

"Is it all right if I walk you home?" Max asked, which was going to bring our evening to a close. It made sense, given that I hadn't planned anything past this point.

If we actually had been on a date, it was still early enough that we could do more.

But since we were only friends, we probably should call it a night.

My hormones definitely needed a break.

"Sure," I said, and we walked toward the subway.

"Everly, there's something I want to clear up," he said, and my heart skipped a beat.

Maybe he was going to say he wasn't interested in us being only friends. Maybe he'd agreed to it only because I'd said it. Maybe . . .

"I don't want you to think that I'm taking advantage of your good nature." He sounded worried. "You can say no to helping Sunny. I should have told you that earlier. I know you're busy."

"Max, it's fine. If I didn't have the time, I would have said no." I was going to have to give up some unnecessary things, like showering and sleeping, but I would find a way to make it work.

And not because I was a people pleaser. I genuinely wanted to help him, someone who had been nothing but sweet to me. He had gone out of his way to be helpful to me last night when we met; I could do the same for him.

Max came to a stop and I heard the guy behind us cursing as he nearly crashed into us. New Yorkers hated when people blocked sidewalks. Max pulled me by the hand, leading me over to a storefront so that we were out of the way.

"I don't know anyone like you, Everly. You are truly kind and selfless."

We stood there, neither one of us speaking. My heart was pounding so hard I was sure he could hear it.

I coughed and then licked my lips so that I could talk. He seemed to be watching me intently, and he was wrecking my ability to regain my composure. I started walking toward the subway stop because I needed to move.

If I kept standing there staring at him, I was going to do something that friends did *not* do.

His long strides made it so that he caught up to me quickly.

I didn't want him to think those sorts of things about me. His admiration weakened my resolve.

"My motives are entirely selfish," I told him as I crossed my arms over my chest. I was not the person he seemed to think I was.

"How so?"

"Have you ever heard that story about Abraham Lincoln? He was on his way to give a speech somewhere and he was arguing with his traveling companion. Lincoln said that all actions, both good and bad, were always motivated by selfishness. His friend disagreed."

Max went to my left, putting himself between me and the street again. I wondered if he even realized that he did it, or if it was just instinctual.

"You were saying?" he prompted me.

Oh, right. The Lincoln story. "They heard a mother pig squealing because her piglets were trapped in mud. Lincoln had the driver stop, and despite the fact that he was about to appear in front of a large crowd, he waded into the mud to return the piglets to their mom. His friend was smug, saying Lincoln had just proved his point with a good, selfless act. Lincoln responded that it had been motivated by his own selfishness—that he would have spent the rest of the day worrying about that mother pig and had saved the babies for his own peace of mind."

"Are you trying to convince me that you helping people is completely selfish?" he asked with a laugh as we headed down the stairs into the station.

"I'm saying there is an element of it. If I had said no to you, I would have worried about Sunny and what she would do."

"You don't even know her."

"I don't have to." Max had spoken so highly of her, and I knew how close they were. That was good enough for me.

Because somehow, in the space of less than twenty-four hours, Max Colby had become very important to me.

I would have done a lot more if he'd asked for it. This was kind of a drop in the bucket.

The lighting in the subway station was terrible, and so it was impossible for me to read his expression.

There seemed to be something there, though. Something that made my breath catch in my throat.

We were surrounded by a throng of noisy people and it smelled disgusting, but all I could see, hear, and sense was Max.

The subway arrived and we got on, standing close together again. We didn't speak. His eyes searched mine and a smile played at the end of his lips, as if he liked what he saw.

No man had ever looked at me like that.

Again I worried over the possibility that I was creating a mountain out of a molehill. Making up and/or hallucinating things that weren't there. Misreading the actions of a nice person.

When we got to my stop, we pushed our way through the crowd, up the stairs, and onto the busy street.

I didn't have to tell him which way to go—he remembered.

"In case I didn't mention it earlier, you look nice today," he said.

I couldn't help my pleased grin.

"Your dress looks familiar," he added.

Despite my resolution to keep my insanity tucked in, I said, "It's a copy of the one Queen Katerina wore on her official visit to India." I regretted the words as soon as I'd said them.

But all of my regret immediately dissipated when he said, "You remind me a lot of the queen."

Swoon, swoon, swoon. I was going to pass out.

It was the most romantic thing a man had ever said to me.

I floated the rest of the way, his words echoing in my mind. He was talking about some trip he'd recently taken and I wasn't even paying attention.

I reminded him of Kat? I didn't think there was a bigger compliment.

His words made me want to spin in a circle with my arms out. Not because I was trying to get some Wonder Woman confidence, but because I was so elated it was the only thing I could think to do.

We arrived at my building and Max walked me into the library, where he greeted Casimir like a long-lost friend. We got to the elevators and I just stood there, waiting. Oh, right. Button. I needed to push the button. Silly me. I leaned over and pushed it while grinning at him to show him that I could still function like a regular person.

Not like someone who was living in her own personal fantasy world where Max and I were some alternate version of Nico and Kat.

"Should I have Sunny call you?" he asked.

It took a second for my hazy mind to make sense of his words. "Yes. Or tell her to come to my office Monday morning. And it would help if you could send links to her social media so that I can get a better sense of who she is and what she likes. That way I'll have something to show her when she comes in to meet me."

"Done," he said. He put both of his hands in his pockets and started walking backward, still facing me. "Thanks for everything."

"You're welcome." I didn't want the evening to end and I was sad that it was.

"Maybe we can get together soon and you can make me one of those grilled cheese sandwiches that you're so good at."

"If you play your cards right, I'll even use Colby cheese on it."

He grinned at me and I felt it in my knees. "I'll keep that in mind. I'll be in touch soon."

Then he started to leave for real, walking a few feet away. He stopped and turned back to face me.

"Everly?"

"Yeah?" I couldn't help the way my spirits lifted with hope.

"I'm glad we're friends."

And even though I'd told him that was what I wanted, it was like a dagger to the heart.

CHAPTER SEVENTEEN

The next day, Max texted me.

> Thanks so much for yesterday. I had a great time.

I debated on how to respond to him. When Vella texted, I would usually answer right away. But if I replied immediately, he might think that I had no life. Which I didn't, but I preferred he not know that. If I waited, then maybe he would believe I couldn't text back because I was oh-so-busy.

I spent so long struggling with what to do that not choosing became the choice. I didn't respond for three hours. And I settled on:

> You're welcome.

Super profound and eloquent. I wondered whether I should thank him, too, but he might read too much into that. This was better.

Maybe.

I didn't know.

That made me sigh very loudly because one of the reasons I'd said "just friends" was to avoid situations exactly like this one. I didn't want to play games with Max. Not only because I was bad at it and didn't know or understand any of the rules, but because I wanted to hang out with him and have fun without wondering if I was sending out weird and/or mixed signals.

Or obsessing over what it would be like to kiss him.

Because I had come to the conclusion that he would be very, very good at it. Vella shared my opinion and offered to find out for sure.

Max sent me links to Sunny's social media accounts and I spent a long time poring over them. This always made me feel slightly stalker-y, but it was really helpful.

Sunny was a second-grade teacher and loved her job. Her Instagram feed was full of bright and fun pictures, most of them with her cute husband. She seemed to embody her name, grinning and bubbly in every photo. Her wedding surprised me—there was a sharp contrast to her other pictures. Her reception was refined, elegant . . . uptight and stuffy. It wasn't what I would have chosen for her. I wondered how much of an influence her in-laws had played in those decisions.

Because Sunny was the opposite of straitlaced. There was a picture of her doing a keg stand on her honeymoon.

I scrolled down and time came to a complete stop. The earth no longer rotated on its axis. The sun faded out of existence.

There was a picture of Sunny with Max at her reception.

He was in a suit.

"Wow," I breathed. He looked supernaturally good all the time, but in a suit?

The world was not ready for that.

I had to close down the tabs I had open so that I didn't comb her accounts for more pictures of him. I had what I needed, and despite suited Max distracting me, I had enough to create my plan. I didn't even bother with a backup because I was pretty sure the theme I had settled on was going to appeal to her.

It might not be what her stuffy in-laws would have chosen, but this was Sunny's baby shower, and I was going to make sure she would have exactly what she wanted.

~

Monday morning was unbelievably busy. I had worn one of my new Copy-Kat dresses and it made me feel like I could do anything. Claudia started the day off with a mandatory meeting for the entire staff, which included a grumbling Vella, who wasn't fully awake yet.

When everyone was seated, Claudia stood up. "Thank you all for coming."

"Some of us didn't have a choice," Vella muttered, and I shushed her.

"I've started working my connections and have set up several meetings this week with new potential clients, mostly individuals with private events," Claudia said. "I will be sending around a link to an in-house document with all of the pertinent information so that we can start preparing our pitches."

This flew directly in the face of what Adrian wanted for Elevated. I knew it would make him mad, and part of me wondered whether or not I should contact him. But he was the one who'd run off to Europe and left Claudia hanging.

If he hadn't wanted this to happen, he should have stayed here and done his job.

Again, that feeling of disloyalty made me uncomfortable. It didn't help matters that I was on Claudia's side. I thought it was a good idea to find new clientele because it would help our company to grow.

"And along those lines, I was contacted this weekend by a former colleague of mine. She is currently organizing an event that she would like us to assist on. Ambassador Preston Wainscott and his wife, Fiona, are celebrating their twentieth wedding anniversary. This will be the social event of the year, and my former colleague reached out because she needs help, as she's had some issues with her vendors. This will be an excellent place to showcase our capabilities and find new clients. I wanted to pitch for this event when I first heard of it, but . . ." Her voice trailed off and we all knew what she meant but didn't say.

Adrian hadn't let her do it.

"You will be receiving your assignments today, and please come to me if you have any questions," Claudia added.

One of the designers raised his hand. "When is this party taking place?"

Claudia paused before responding, and I knew the answer would be bad. "In three weeks."

The reaction was the same as when the Albrechts had told us that Hyacinth's birthday was in less than a month, only instead of quiet rumbles, people openly expressed their disbelief.

Claudia raised both of her hands. "I know it is not our policy to take such last-minute events as we have been, but we're doing it to get our foot in the door. Once we get established in this space, we won't do it again. I have faith in you and in us as a team. My door is open if you have any concerns. Thank you!"

The meeting broke up. Several people stayed put, chatting in small groups. It was obvious they weren't pleased. The name of the ambassador seemed familiar to me, so I looked it up.

He had been the American ambassador to Monterra and had gone to all the recent royal weddings. That was why I had recognized his name.

It felt kind of fated that we were going to do an event for him. Like everything was connected.

Claudia came over to Vella and me. I put my phone down and sat up straighter in my chair. "What can I do to help with the anniversary party?"

"That's the attitude I'm looking for," she said, smiling at me. "But I want you to focus on the Albrecht event and making that as successful as you can. The Wainscotts and Albrechts socialize with the same type of people, so if we can get their seal of approval, it could really change things for Elevated."

"Speaking of the Albrecht event, I have some boards I want to show you."

"Excellent. Come run them past me this afternoon, and if I like what I see, which I'm sure I will, I'll bring them to the client."

Excited, I nodded. "I also might know of someone who could be a new client. Her cousin spoke to me about putting together a baby shower for her and—"

"Not a baby shower," Claudia said. "We're not doing weddings, funerals, or showers."

"Oh." I didn't know what to say. I wondered why but didn't feel like it was my place to question her. I had promised Max that I would do Sunny's shower. I could do it myself, like freelancing. I hadn't done something like that since high school. I'd do it in what little free time I had.

Then Claudia turned to Vella. "I'm going to be having a lunch meeting today. Two people are vegan, one is keto, another is dairy- and gluten-free, and I need you to order lunch to arrive at noon. Thank you!"

Once Claudia had left, Vella whirled her chair toward me, wide-eyed. "What am I supposed to get them that they can all eat? Do you know of a restaurant that serves air and water?"

I stood up and started to walk back to my office with my best friend right behind me. "It'll be fine. Make sure to get sparkling and still."

"Air?"

"No, water," I said with a smile. "I'll bring you the menus of local restaurants that fit those criteria." I had ordered many very specific lunches since I'd started here. "I'll highlight the ones that I recommend."

"You are a lifesaver," she said.

"Didn't you think today's meeting was energizing?" I asked her, feeling so enthused about the direction the company was heading. "I love that we are going to make magic here."

"Yes, it's truly magical to be working in a place you can't leave for eight hours a day because you're afraid you won't be able to eat."

I sat down at my desk, shaking my head at her. "It's not that bad."

"Your company is kind of like prison, only without the hope."

I was glad we were at my desk and not still in the conference room, where someone could have overheard her.

"Go back to work," I told her, shaking my head.

"Sure thing, warden. Back to the salt mines."

"You don't work in salt mines. You answer a phone!" I called after her.

"And I order fairy food that doesn't exist for dietary restrictions that may or may not be real!" she called back. I glanced around me to make sure no one had overheard. I didn't want her to get fired. I really liked having her here.

I gathered up the menus, putting the best options on top, and walked out to the reception area to hand them to Vella.

"Do you think I have anger issues?" she asked me. "I took an online quiz earlier during that meeting that said I do."

"I wouldn't call it an issue because an issue is something you can fix," I told her with a wink. "And online quizzes at work?"

"It's either that or reading motivational posts from people that I personally know are toxic and horrible in real life."

I supposed there wasn't a lot for her to do otherwise. She was only here temporarily. "That cousin of Max's should be coming in close to lunchtime. The one having the baby shower."

"Baby showers are weird," she said. "You basically get presents for having sex, and all your relatives are there."

"Maybe don't say that to Sunny," I suggested.

"I will let you know when she arrives," Vella said with a salute. "And I'll get the inside information about Max."

"Do not do that," I told her, feeling panicky. Why hadn't this scenario occurred to me? Vella trying to interfere now that she had access to someone in Max's life?

"I won't," she said in a way that suggested it was exactly what she was going to do. The phone rang and she answered. "Elevated. No, we don't service elevators."

I had two options. I could stand here and keep an eye on her or I could go back to my desk and get actual work done. There was no choice but to do the second; I had too much to do. I just had to hope that whatever she said to Sunny would be manageable.

I returned to my desk and worked on finalizing my board for Hyacinth's birthday party. I was completely caught up in what I was doing when my phone buzzed. It was Vella. I pushed the intercom button. "Yes?"

"There's someone here to see you. Sunny Belmont."

"I'll be right there!" I felt a nervous but excited anticipation in meeting her. I sort of felt like I already knew her after hearing Max talk about her and seeing her online life.

She had bright blonde hair that went down to her waist and the same blue eyes as Max. She was shorter than I'd expected and very, very pregnant.

"Sunny! So nice to meet you!" I held out my hand, but she brushed it aside and pulled me into a hug.

"Everly! I feel like I already know you!" Sunny said. "You're so tall. Max didn't mention that."

My stomach fluttered at the thought that Max was telling his beloved cousin things about me. "Follow me and I'll show you what I've come up with."

I decided to take her into Adrian's office because the conference room was booked for the rest of the day and I wanted to be somewhere that I could shut the door.

Claudia wanted me to focus on the Albrecht party, and I didn't think she'd be happy about me picking up some side work. My free time was my own, and I was taking my lunch break now, so I figured it would be fine.

"Thank you so much for meeting with me," Sunny said as she took a seat. I sat across from her in Adrian's chair.

"I'm happy to do it. Any cousin of Max's is someone I will make room in my schedule for."

She grinned at that, and her smile was so much like Max's that it momentarily threw me. But her expression fell quickly as she said, "My mother-in-law has very high expectations for this party. I need for it to be successful and up to her standards."

"I hear that, I do. And Max sent me links to your socials and I saw your wedding reception. It didn't seem like the kind of thing you'd like, but more of what your in-laws preferred."

Sunny nodded, her eyes bright with what looked like unshed tears.

"And this is your baby shower. Not anyone else's. It should be something that makes you happy."

"I would love to have something that's more me while still making the Belmonts happy."

Hopefully what I'd come up with would satisfy both of those requirements. "Max told me that after his parents divorced, he used to spend his summers with you in California."

I'd meant for that to be the lead-in to my pitch, but I noticed the way Sunny went rigid. "Max . . . talked to you about his parents' divorce?"

"Yes."

Her mouth dropped slightly and she blinked rapidly. "He doesn't share that with anyone. Not even me."

"Really?" He had given me all the details the first night we'd met.

She smiled, but it didn't quite reach her eyes. "So, you were saying?"

Feeling like I'd ruined things before I'd even started, I tried to get the pitch back on track. I'd had this whole bit about her Californian upbringing and how I wanted to bring that casual and, well, sunny vibe to her party, but we had gotten off course.

I decided to just go straight for the jugular. "We can do what's always been done. We could have tea and finger sandwiches on bone china with everybody wearing their pearls and twin sets. Or we could do something truly unique, something you—bright and upbeat and colorful."

The smile was real this time. "Like what?"

"You're a teacher, and I thought it would be fun to incorporate your love of kids into this celebration. I was thinking an upscale carnival." I turned around Adrian's computer screen so that she could see the images I'd selected. "We'll have a focal point here and will drape white linens to look like the inside of a fancy big top. We'll string pastel flags and white lights, have pastel balloons hanging here, and make arches at the entrances. We'll use this circus font to print the signs, and we will have upscale carnival food—funnel cakes, sliders, cotton candy, popcorn. Maybe we could get some performers like jugglers and magicians to work the room."

I paused, wondering what she thought. Or if this was so far from what her mother-in-law had envisioned that Sunny would say no.

"And the best part—we'll set up carnival games. A ring toss, balloon pop, maybe Skee-Ball or something like it. And there will be prizes for your guests to win, but we will be asking them to make a donation to Max's charity for mothers of newborns instead of giving you a gift. Whatever prizes they win, we'll have donation bins for the charity and they can donate those as well. And the prizes will be like, onesies, stuffed animals, packages of diapers, blankets."

Sunny put both of her hands over her eyes and I worried that this was all going very wrong. "How did you know? I didn't say anything to Max."

"About what?"

She put her hands down. "Whenever I mention I need something, my husband orders it online because he spoils me. We already have everything we need for the baby, and I've been dreading the idea of getting things we wouldn't have any use for. This whole shower felt like a gift grab. So your idea is perfect. Absolutely perfect. That I could use my baby shower to help other moms and for it to be fun and light and . . . so me? Yes to all of it. Yes, yes, yes. Where do I sign?"

I laughed at her enthusiasm, just as thrilled as she was. "I will set up some shared documents tonight so that you can see everything I have planned, the vendors I recommend using, and the contract. But you should know that it will just be me, and not Elevated."

"That's totally fine."

"Good. And the sooner you sign off on everything, the sooner I can make sure you have an absolutely perfect day."

"Done. You know, Max said you were amazing, but I had no idea."

My heart stopped beating as a buzzing noise filled my head. Was that hyperbole? Or had Max actually told her I was amazing?

Friend amazing? Or something else amazing?

"He did?" I croaked the words out.

Sunny nodded enthusiastically and then threw a wet blanket over my excitement. "Yes! He also said I would like you and he was right. He told me that you're a very down-to-earth and simple person."

The joy flooded out of me. That was a death knell if ever I'd heard one. He might as well have said that I was boring and had nothing interesting going on in my life.

This was supposed to be what I wanted, but it still hurt that Max had made it so clear to his cousin that he wasn't interested in me.

CHAPTER EIGHTEEN

My pulse seemed to be throbbing in my head, blocking out all sound. I realized that Sunny had said my name and forced myself to pay attention. She asked, "Does Max know about the charity part of it?"

"No, I wanted to run it past you first to see if it was something you wanted to do."

"I do. And he's going to be so happy when you tell him," she said.

When *I* told him? She said it so casually, like he and I were in constant contact and of course I'd be filling him in.

Like we were dating or something.

Before I could ask why she wouldn't tell him herself, someone walked into the office who almost made my jaw drop to the floor. I jumped out of Adrian's chair, standing there awkwardly.

It was the CEO, Topher Crawley. He was a middle-aged man in a well-tailored suit who had been bald the last time I'd seen him. I wondered if he'd gotten hair plugs. Maybe that was why he hadn't been in the office for so long.

"Is Adrian here?" he asked.

I was so befuddled by him being there that it took me a bit longer to respond than it should have. "He's in France," I finally managed.

What was Mr. Crawley doing in the office? I wondered if Claudia's changes had anything to do with it.

"I need to get in touch with Adrian," he said, and I nodded. I picked up my phone and sent the message immediately just so that I wouldn't forget.

Then, as if he had suddenly remembered his manners, Mr. Crawley stepped farther into the office and offered his hand to Sunny. "I'm Topher Crawley, CEO of Elevated."

"Sunny Belmont."

"Any relation to Frank Belmont?" he asked.

"That's my father-in-law."

"We have golfed together a few times. Small world. Well, it was good to meet you." Then he directed his attention back to me. "Have Adrian call."

"I've already texted him," I said. He nodded and then left.

Sunny got up slowly, one hand on her stomach. "I should get going. I have to pee for the fortieth time today. Thank you so much for doing this."

"I'm happy to help."

"Could you come over tomorrow night to see the apartment? My in-laws will be out."

"I need to take measurements, so that works for me." I walked her to the lobby and showed her where the bathrooms were. She hugged me and thanked me again.

Vella wasn't at her desk, and I went into the break room to grab something from the vending machine because I wasn't going to have enough time to go out. I brought my chips and soda back to my desk. Not exactly nutritious, but better than the air and water Vella had wanted to serve at the conference room meeting.

My phone buzzed and I saw that I had a text from Max.

I HEARD THINGS WENT WELL AND I'M LOOKING FORWARD TO SEEING THE END RESULT.

Had Sunny texted him from the bathroom? Or the cab? How did he already know? Then I wondered why he was shouting at me.

Why are you texting me in all caps?

Isn't that what your mother does? Plus, you said you didn't like small talk. So . . .

I didn't want to be amused. I wanted to be upset that he thought I was boring. But he was so charming it was hard to resist.

My guess is the party won't be coed,
given the Belmonts and their traditions. You're
not invited.

I know the event planner. I think she can sneak me in.

I grinned, and then laughed out loud when I saw the next text.

You're smiling right now, aren't you?

Nope. Serious as a preacher.

I don't think that's a saying.

Somber as a preacher?

What do you have against preachers?

I got yelled at by one, remember?

Now I was wondering whether he was smiling, imagining him doing just that.

Sunny said to tell you that you're perfect.

That shouldn't have hurt. I should have been pleased. But if anything, it felt ironic, given what he'd told her.

She's biased.

So am I.

What did that mean?

And why did it seem like the exact opposite of what he'd told
Sunny?

Despite my best friend's assertion that men shouldn't be treated like
skittish horses, I was going to do just that. If I asked him to explain
himself, he might bolt. Better to wonder in private.

A voice inside me whispered that this was not what Kat would do.
But I didn't know how to be braver without scaring him off.

~

Claudia signed off on my presentation for Hyacinth's party, and both
Hyacinth and her mother approved my plans. When I mentioned my
recent idea to hire Italian and Monterran models to dress up in royal
uniforms to mingle with the guests, Hyacinth even managed to look
up from her phone with one of her eyebrows slightly lifted—was that
interest? It was hard to tell since the rest of her face was so impassive.

Tuesday evening I met with Sunny to look at the Belmonts' massive
apartment. "They want it to be outside," she said.

"Are they aware that it's winter?" I asked.

She showed me the terrace. It was very large, but weather was the
bane of every outdoor event. Snow and rain I could handle—I could
put up tents and have space heaters. It just meant that I'd have to
make multiple contingency plans. I asked Sunny to verify her final guest

count as soon as possible because nothing else could be organized until we knew exactly how many people would be there.

Adrian kept texting me with inane requests, like wanting me to tell the staff at his hotel not to chew spearmint gum around him and for me to find out whether or not the water in France was different than New York because he thought it tasted so much better.

I wasn't sure if he wanted an environmental report or what, so I told him I'd look into it when I had the chance.

And in between all of this, Max was texting me.

While I had to remind myself on an almost hourly basis that we were just friends, it was so hard to remember.

It started out with him asking me about Sunny's shower and what he could do to help. When I told him I had it covered, he asked about my day. After I filled him in, I asked about his and we texted for hours. My evenings had turned into working on my projects and texting Max, giggling at the things he would say.

"You two text constantly. Like he's your boyfriend," Vella had commented one night while heating up a quesadilla in the microwave.

"That's what friends do," I countered. "It's what you and I do."

"I do not ask you about your day, and I am not at all interested in event planning. Unlike this lovesick fool who thinks you're some goddess and every word you say is scripture he has to memorize."

"That could not be further from the truth."

"You only smile like that when Max is texting you," she said.

"Do you not remember the part where I told you he said that I was 'down-to-earth and simple'?" Saying it again made me feel sick to my stomach.

She shot me a look that implied something was wrong with me. "You told me that he was down-to-earth."

"Yes, but I meant it in a humble, not-full-of-himself kind of way, which is surprising, given how he looks."

"How do you know he didn't mean it in the same way?"

For some reason, this literally had not occurred to me until Vella brought it up.

"You're always telling me people should have the benefit of the doubt and so I recommend extending it to your new *friend*," she said. "You should also stop pretending that you want to be just friends with this man. If I fed that line into a lie detector, it would explode." She took her food out of the kitchen and into her room, where she locked the door.

While I considered what she'd said, my phone rang and I answered without looking to see who was calling. I'd been on my phone nonstop over the last few days, trying to get everything lined up for the birthday party and the baby shower.

"Hello?"

"Everly?" Max's voice made me happy sigh.

"Hi!" Was that too enthusiastic? Did I need to tone it down? I tried to modulate my tone. "How are you?"

"Good." He paused and it felt a bit awkward. We never had any issues while we were texting, but this was different. It was the first time we'd spoken with our actual voices since I'd taken him out for a mini-tour of New York City.

Max cleared his throat. "So I talked to Sunny and she said she showed you around the Belmonts' apartment."

"Do you mean their palace?" I asked.

He laughed, and it was like that broke the tension for both of us. I lay down on the couch. "I haven't personally been there, but I've heard the same thing."

"It's ridiculous-looking. I can see why she's so worried about impressing them." I'd only seen apartments like that on *Gossip Girl.* "But her in-laws want her to have it out on the terrace. Which I'm not thrilled about."

"How come?"

"One, it's winter, which is never good for an outdoor event, and two, I'm not very happy about how high up it is."

"Everly Aprile, are you afraid of heights?"

"Yes, I would run the opposite direction if I encountered them in the wild."

"You're not supposed to run from heights," he said. "You're supposed to raise your arms above your head and make a lot of loud noises to scare them off first."

"That's bears."

"Same thing," he said, and I could hear his smile. I wished I could see his face. "So you do have an Achilles' heel."

"Everyone does."

"Everyone has Achilles tendons, not heels. *Heels* means figuratively. That you have an actual weakness. And here I thought you were Wonder Woman."

I sat straight up. Okay, that was freaky. How had he known about my Wonder Woman confidence-boosting thing?

There was no way he could know. It was a coincidence. "I have many flaws and weaknesses."

"So do I," he said, but I had a hard time believing him. "And one of my flaws is not being able to navigate the city easily on my own. I know you're incredibly busy and that's partially my fault, but today I was thinking about how you haven't shown me everything yet."

My mind immediately went to a very not-safe-for-work place and I managed to squeak out a "What?"

"Are you still my official tour guide?"

Oh, he wanted me to show him the city. "Yes, I'm your tour guide." I would be anything he wanted me to be.

"Then I was hoping you might guide me through some of your culture."

"My culture?" He wanted to watch reality shows and eat junk food?

"Something that's southern, like where you grew up."

"Oh! Like you want to fly to Alabama? I personally have neither the funds nor the time—"

He gently interrupted me. "No, I figured there must be someplace here that we could go."

"There is! There's this bar not too far that has live music and line dancing!" I'd always wanted to check it out, but Vella had said she'd rather have her fingernails torn off by a rabid monkey than go with me.

"This Friday? Are you free?" he asked.

I would be, no matter what it took. "Yes."

"Do I need to dress up for this? Cowboy boots, hat, that kind of thing?"

"You can wear whatever you want. Or don't want." Oh no, impure thoughts again.

"I'll keep that in mind. I just wanted to take you out to thank you for all that you're doing for Sunny."

That feeling of being a balloon with a fast leak returned. This was for the best. I knew that. Some part of me had still hoped, though. "Okay. I'll text you the address and meet you there at nine o'clock, if that's okay." No coming to my door with flowers and being all charming and irresistible.

It wasn't a date. I needed to make that clear.

To both him and me.

There was silence on his end and then he said, "That works. I'll see you then."

I hung up my phone, my heart ramming against my chest.

Why did it feel like I'd just made a big mistake?

CHAPTER NINETEEN

"I can't believe you talked me into this," Vella said, shivering next to me. While I had opted for a Kat-inspired outfit she'd worn on her last American tour topped off by my pink cowgirl boots, my roommate was wearing a black corset and leather pants with stiletto boots and no coat, again.

"I needed you here tonight," I told her.

"Can we at least go inside?"

My hesitation was enough to tip her off.

"What is happening right now?" She sounded alarmed.

"We're waiting for someone."

"For Max?" she asked, and I couldn't tell what her tone was. Incredulous? Excited? Annoyed? Probably all three. "You have a date with Max and you made me tag along? I'm guessing he doesn't know that I'm coming."

"What difference does that make?" I needed her to be a buffer. To keep me from hitting on him.

"I think we're about to find out." She nodded her head to the right and I looked in that direction and nearly had a heart attack.

While I had witnessed a couple of different incarnations of Max—casual, in a suit—nothing could have prepared me for the overwhelmingly sexy sight of him in cowboy boots and a cowboy hat. Like every teenage fantasy I'd ever had come to life.

It was freezing outside, but I was perspiring from desperate longing. I actually reached up to my mouth to check and make sure I wasn't drooling.

"You have to behave," I said to Vella, but I suspected that I was also saying it to myself.

"Are you threatening me right now?" She was delighted.

"I would, except you don't own anything valuable or have anything you love that I could hold hostage."

"Why do you think I wouldn't behave?"

"You know how you are."

She had a look of pure evil on her face. "Uh, a total delight? A virtual ray of sunshine? Like a unicorn with a rainbow horn and pink cotton candy hair?"

"Never mind. Let's just have fun and be ourselves." Another reminder to both of us.

"With your requirements, I hate to tell you that it's going to be one or the other. Max!" she exclaimed, holding out her arms to hug him hello.

Keeping my jealousy from spilling over was not easy.

"Good to see you again, Vella. I'm glad you're here. Everly has told me so many good things about you."

"Really? I'm not very nice."

He grinned. "She also told me you were funny."

"I'm just mean and people think I'm joking."

When he laughed, she turned to me with a "see?" expression, like he'd proved her point.

"Everly." He said my name and my heart stuttered in response. He reached for me and pulled me to him. He hugged me, holding me tight. As if he'd missed me.

"Max," was all I could manage to say in response to being held in his arms. This felt so perfect, like I'd been made just to be held by this man. I couldn't help myself. I buried my face against his neck, breathing in his warmth and that amazing scent of his.

It hadn't been that long since we'd last seen each other, but he was acting like he'd just returned home from war.

He let go of me only when Vella very loudly cleared her throat and said, "Should we go inside? Some of us are freezing."

We walked over to the door and I reached for my purse, but Max held his hand out. "Tonight it's my turn. I'm taking you out to thank you, remember?"

Oh, I remembered. Very clearly.

"Nice getup, Tex," Vella told him.

Max smiled at her. "I figured when in Rome."

He paid the cover charge and we went into the bar. A band I'd never heard of was playing on the stage, and people were dancing in formation. I might have bounced up and down a couple of times in excitement. I hadn't danced like this in so long.

"You're going to have to show me the steps," Max said in my ear, and all of my ramped-up energy focused away from the dancing and to the way his lips were so close to my skin.

"Sure!"

"Country music?" Vella said, leaning against the bar and glaring at everyone. "I've never understood it. All the songs by men are about wanting to marry and/or knock up girls in tiny shorts while getting drunk, and all the songs by women are about murdering their husbands."

"That's basically it," I confirmed with a smile.

"And why are there so many men in here with unironic mustaches? Half the guys in here look like they're villains who escaped from a silent black-and-white movie. I don't know why I even bother. Men suck." She glanced at Max. "No offense."

"Some taken," he said.

"Should we get something to drink?" I asked, realizing that it might have been a mistake to invite Vella if she was in one of her moods. I supposed that on the plus side, she was definitely making sure that this evening was not at all date-like.

But I was worried she might end up annoying Max and chasing him off. And even though I knew we could only be friends, I wanted to spend as much time with him as possible.

Even if it wasn't a good idea.

A brave cowboy swaggered up to us, sporting his villain mustache, and doffed his hat at Vella. "Do you want to dance, darlin'?"

She looked over at me with a dramatic expression and said, "I guess I have to do what your farm emo songs suggest and save a horse by dancing with a cowboy."

"Riding a cowboy," I corrected, and flushed when I saw from her sneaky smile that she'd set me up for that one. She went onto the dance floor and nobody was more shocked than I was when she fell into line perfectly, never missing a step.

"Shall we give it a whirl?" Max asked, offering me his hand.

There was absolutely nothing on the entire planet that I wanted more than to have him hold me in his arms while we swayed to the music. "Yes!"

More enthusiastic than I'd intended, but hopefully the band covered it up.

I explained to him the two-step, figuring we should get that down before I tried to teach him the moves for one of the line dances.

But Max was . . . bad at it. There was no other way to describe his total lack of coordination.

I had to bite the inside of my cheek to keep from laughing.

"You think this is funny, don't you?" he asked with a wry smile.

"Not even a little."

"You're a terrible liar," he said.

"You're trying, and it's the trying that counts."

"You mean it's the thought that counts."

"In this case," I countered, "you already did the thought part. So I'm giving you points for the attempt. But those are the only points you're going to get, because you are not lord of the dance. You're more like peasant of the dance."

"Hey!" he protested, but he was laughing.

Vella made her way over to us and said to Max, "Are you okay? You're moving like you're allergic to music."

Her cowboy spun her away before Max could respond.

"Is she always like that?" he asked.

"No, she's usually meaner."

He laughed again. The upbeat song ended, and the band started to play a ballad. For one panicky second I wasn't sure what to do.

"I may not be able to two-step, but I can do this," he said as he took me into his arms, pulling me against his chest. His hand went to the small of my back and he used his left hand to hold my right. Without thinking, I put my free hand on the back of his very strong shoulder.

"Is this okay?" he asked.

Which part? The internal combustion that made me feel as if he were revving me up like a race car? Or how all of my limbs were uncooperative and were melting against him, so that if he let go, I was going to turn into an Everly pool?

Then he squeezed my hand to let me know that that was the part he was talking about and then added, just in case it wasn't clear, "If I hold your hand."

I made an indecipherable sound and then commanded my vocal cords to work. "Y-yes. It's fine. We're dancing."

"What about after we're done dancing?" he asked, and again his mouth was close to my ear, my neck, and I shivered. I felt his hand at my back flex, pressing me closer. Like he felt my reaction and enjoyed it.

Wanted it to continue.

"Would it be okay then, too?" he asked.

"Yes." I breathed the word out, not caring what ramifications it had or whether or not this was going to screw up our friendship. In that moment I did not care.

"So is Vella right?" he asked as we swayed together.

"About?"

"That I dance like I'm allergic to music."

My inclination was to rest my cheek against his shoulder so that I could be even closer to him, breathing him in, and maybe press a kiss against his throat, so I decided it would be better to do something that might put some distance between us.

"You are a terrible dancer," I said, and he smiled at my response. I added, "Why didn't you tell me?"

"I didn't know. I've never had any complaints before."

I was sure that was completely true. His past women had probably lied to him about his prowess on the dance floor. "It's okay. It's a good thing. It makes you seem more human."

"What makes me seem not human?"

"Your face." The words were out even though I hadn't intended to say them.

"I have a very normal, human face," he said.

Apparently him holding me this way, with us pressed against each other, was destroying all of my defenses and making me be completely honest. "Uh, no. You have a face that looks like Aphrodite sculpted it personally for her own benefit."

A long silence stretched between us, and I was internally beating myself up for saying something so blatant to him. I might as well have just announced that I was completely attracted to him and wished he would kiss me.

It wouldn't have been any less humiliating than how I felt right now. He was going to reject me so gently and kindly, but it wouldn't take the sting of rejection away at all.

"I can honestly say that's the first time anyone's said that to me. With that accent."

"Accent?" I repeated.

"Ever since we stepped foot into this bar, your southern accent has been on full display."

I hadn't realized. "I guess it happens when I get around other southerners or listen to country music. Or when I go home. I didn't realize it would happen here since it's the first country bar I've been to since I got to New York."

I was having a hard time paying attention to what I was saying and suspected it was all coming out gibberish.

Why did he smell so good? And why was he so strong and broad and just yummy?

"I assumed this was where you brought all your boyfriends."

Ha. "I have never brought a boyfriend here."

He raised one eyebrow. "Didn't you want to share this part of yourself?"

"I've never had a boyfriend to bring."

"You haven't dated anyone seriously? I find that hard to believe."

Well, Max could find it as hard to believe as he wanted, but it didn't make it any less true.

And he had no idea how far it went. "I have never dated anyone seriously. I've never even . . ."

But I clamped my lips together. I was not going to tell this beautiful man that I was a virgin. That was sure to make him run screaming into the night.

My heart was pounding so hard that it was the only thing I could hear. Maybe he'd misunderstood. Maybe he wouldn't be able to fill in the blanks. Maybe I hadn't just shared my most personal, deepest, darkest secret with the most handsome man I'd ever met.

I wished I could unsay it.

"Really?" he asked in a tone that let me know he'd gotten my meaning completely, and I stifled a groan. This was going to go one of two ways—he would either be intensely curious about it and ask me a bunch of follow-up questions or he would excuse himself and call it a night.

To my complete shock, he went a different route.

"So I guess it would be a bad idea for me to try and seduce you."

CHAPTER TWENTY

I practically choked on my own tongue. Max was teasing. I could hear it in his voice, see it in his eyes, but it sounded like the most delicious prospect ever, and I wished there were a way to say *yes, please, do that,* without risking rejection.

His eyes shuttered. "Everly, I was only—"

"Why did you come over and talk to me the first night we met?" I asked before he could finish his sentence and tell me that he'd meant it a platonic way because we were pals. "Was it just because you wanted to save me?"

I didn't want him hanging out with me because he thought he needed to rescue me. I couldn't deal with his teasing and joking if I knew that was the reason behind it—that he was doing all of this out of pity.

He considered my question before answering. "I came over because I saw you doing a Wonder Woman spin and it made me want to talk to you."

There was nothing he could have said that would have surprised me more. Well, other than reiterating seriously that he'd like to seduce me. "Why?"

He shrugged the shoulder that I was holding on to. "It was just sweet and . . . What's that expression? It tugged at my heartstrings."

This was so much worse than I had thought. "I made you sad?"

"What? No."

Maybe it was just a translation thing and he wasn't saying he'd thought I was pathetic. "If something tugs at your heartstrings, you feel sad."

"I didn't feel sad. I felt . . . enchanted. I wanted to meet the girl who would so fearlessly twirl around in front of all those people because I wanted to know why she had done it."

Enchanted? Was that another language mix-up? I tried to not let it give me too much hope.

"I did it to give myself a boost of confidence," I confessed. "Which didn't work, given that right after, I cried all over your dog."

"That part did tug at my heartstrings." He took my hand and laid it against his chest, putting his own hand on top of it.

I couldn't help my sharp intake of breath at the intimate gesture. I could feel his heart beating beneath my fingertips. I wanted to flatten my hand and explore him, to feel his heartbeat and warmth against my palms.

"There's something I want to tell you," he said in a voice that I felt more than heard.

"You can tell me anything."

"I know I can," he said, and I swore I felt him nuzzling the side of my head. I sighed while my synapses sparked with excitement and anticipation. "I've thought a lot about something we talked about—how my past affects my future. I have a hard time trusting people. I didn't expect to get cheated on."

His evil, stupid ex-girlfriend. "People in relationships usually don't."

"I haven't really dated since Arabella and I broke up."

Now the evil, stupid ex had a name. Arabella. Of course it had to be pretty and delicate like that. It couldn't have been Gertrude or Agatha, something I could have secretly relished. "Now it's my turn to say that I find that hard to believe."

He flashed me a brief smile. "It's not because of a broken heart or not being over it. It was not really finding anyone that I wanted to spend time with. Someone I could trust. But Everly . . . I know that I can trust you."

Were those things all connected? Him trusting, talking about wanting to spend time with someone, considering it dating? Or was I reading into things? I came to a stop. Max still held me in his arms, but we were no longer moving in slow circles. "You trust me?"

He nodded. "I wanted to thank you for that—for being someone I could trust."

I would forsake sleep for a year if he would keep looking at me the way that he was right then—like I was the actual Wonder Woman and he was in awe of me.

Was I supposed to say *you're welcome*? It felt like it would be anticlimactic.

When I didn't speak, he filled in the gap. "I knew I'd be able to trust you from the moment we met."

"How could you know that?"

"Basta liked you and she doesn't like many people."

That made me smile, but I understood that he was joking, maybe as an attempt to lighten the mood, which felt very heavy and serious between us.

But his smile faltered when he added, "And I hope you feel the same way."

Did he mean whether or not I trusted him? Because while I understood logically that I hadn't known him long enough to make this kind of declaration, I would trust Max Colby with my life.

Or was there some deeper subtext here that I was completely oblivious to?

"Did you notice that the music changed like, two songs ago?" Vella asked, interrupting us. The band was playing another upbeat number and I'd been totally unaware, caught up in the spell Max was weaving.

The spell he continued to weave. Because even with the interruption, he didn't release me.

"Excuse us girls a second," she said to him. "I have to go to the bathroom and Everly's coming with me."

I tried to protest, but she clamped down on my wrist and wrenched me away from him, and with every step I took, my body protested at this drastic, unnecessary, and very unwanted change.

We got in line for the women's bathroom and all I wanted to do was go back to Max.

"So I saw you two holding hands," she said in a conversational tone that I knew was a cover for what she really wanted to say. "Isn't that like, third base or something for your people?"

"We were dancing." I didn't mean to tell her anything beyond that, but I couldn't help myself. "He did ask me if it would be okay to hold my hand later."

She blinked at me a couple of times. "Is he a fictional hero from a Victorian novel?"

"I like that he's old-fashioned," I said defensively.

"I suppose it's perfect for you and where you're at. Or it may be an indication of what's to come. And that sucks."

We moved up a spot. "What does?"

"Max being bad at dancing. I don't understand why it was so hard for him. It's literally two steps."

"He kept starting on the wrong foot and miscounting," I responded.

"I'm just sorry for you because it means he'll probably be uncoordinated when it comes to other physical activities."

My mind went blank. "Like racquetball?" I immediately realized how stupid that sounded and what she had been implying.

"No, Everly, not like racquetball. Dancing is a vertical expression of a horizontal one."

"I know what you meant," I mumbled. "It's not like I'm ever going to have to worry about that with him. He doesn't want to date me. I don't see it ever happening."

"When you hang out with him, are your eyes closed? Because that is the only explanation possible for you not being able to see what's going on. Even if you dismiss everything else, he paid for you tonight. That's a date."

"He also paid for you," I reminded her. "So unless you're ready for us to be sister-wives, neither one of us is dating him. He took me out to thank me for helping Sunny."

"That is not a thing. People don't do that."

"Sure they do."

Vella crossed her arms over her chest. "Name one time you've done it."

"I—"

She was right. I couldn't think of a single instance. I had brought people gifts or sent them thank-you notes or emails, but I had never taken someone dancing to thank them.

"This bicycle only needs two wheels," she said as we reached the front of the line.

"You're not a third wheel."

"I am, and I'm taking off with Cowboy Troy. He said something about showing me a silver belt buckle he got for bareback riding. I'm not sure what any of that means, but I'm interested in finding out." At my look, she added, "Don't worry. I have my stun gun and pepper spray."

"Is that his name? In case I need to call the police?"

"I'll be fine. And it's not his name. I just like how Cowboy Troy sounds. I'll text you with his actual information. Just in case," she said in an exaggerated way, as if I worried too much.

Which I probably did, but I didn't want anything to happen to her.

"I know you don't like to take my advice, but at least consider this one thing. Max is interested, but you're the one shutting it down. With your body language, the things you're saying. I've seen you around him twice now, and please believe me when I tell you that if you want something to happen, which deep down I know you do, you have to be more open."

"I don't do that!"

"You do and I don't understand it. You're finally getting your magical fairy tale you've always wanted and you're pushing it away with both hands. Enjoy your time with Max. Try to be more open." A stall opened up and she headed into it.

Was I doing that? All of my interactions with Max had this slightly unbelievable feel to them, as if they should have been happening to someone else. Or like I was watching a movie starring me.

Here I'd thought Vella was the one broadcasting do-not-disturb vibes, but if she was right, *I* had been the one doing that. I was scaring people off.

How long had I been doing it for? Was I so afraid of any kind of intimacy, of being publicly humiliated or secretly heartbroken, that I'd pushed away every possible chance at romance?

I used the bathroom, washed my hands, and checked my phone. Vella had texted me a note to tell me that she'd already left, and I was feeling subdued over what she'd said to me in line.

Max was at the bar and my spirits lifted at seeing him again, but that discouraged feeling didn't completely disappear.

"There you are," he said. "I was starting to get worried about you."

"Vella left," I told him.

He nodded. "She said goodbye. Are you ready to try this dancing thing again?"

I didn't feel like dancing anymore. I was worried that I was going to get caught up in this negativity that my best friend had accidentally planted in my head. I opened my mouth, intending to tell him that we should call it a night.

Instead I said, "Can we get out of here?"

He nodded. "Where do you want me to take you? Are you hungry?"

I was. I'd been so nervous about tonight that I hadn't eaten in a while. "Yes."

"Is there anywhere special you'd like to go?"

Mustering up my courage, I reached out and took his hand. I saw the momentary shock on his face and I half expected him to pull away, but he didn't. He gently squeezed my hand in return.

Then I told him, "I don't care where we go so long as I'm with you."

He gave me the sexiest smile I'd ever seen. "Then let's go."

CHAPTER TWENTY-ONE

When we got outside, Max asked, "Do you know of any good places to eat?"

Did I . . . "Are you ready for this conversation?"

He laughed.

"I'm going to need some parameters so that I can narrow it down," I said as we started walking along the sidewalk. I glanced down at where our hands were joined and was thrilled that I was doing something so . . . typical. Something other people did all the time without thinking. It shouldn't have been a big deal and Vella would have teased me mercilessly if I waxed poetic about it in front of her, but it was a big step for me.

And it was exciting.

"Okay, how about something good, American, and open?"

"And no waiting," I told him. Ever since he'd brought up food, my stomach hadn't stopped rumbling. There were a lot of different restaurants I could have taken him to, but they would have had long lines.

"I don't want to wait, either."

Why was I reading something into that? He was agreeing with what I'd said, not making some comment on whether or not he wanted to be in a relationship with me.

If I wasn't mistaken, and I was entirely willing to concede that I might have been, there had been a tone in his voice that caused me to believe he'd meant something else.

"There's a diner not too far from here that meets the criteria of being American, open, and available. The good part might be more subjective," I said.

Max laughed and said, "Lead the way."

As we walked, he asked me how the birthday party was coming along.

"I'm trying to get in touch with my teenage self, but it's been a while. I wish I knew more about Monterran teenagers."

"They definitely live in a different environment than kids in America. Their secondary school, which might be comparable to high school in the States, requires students to choose a major to focus on."

"What did you choose?"

"The same thing I studied at Yale. Languages."

As in plural? "What other languages do you speak?"

"French and Spanish, some Portuguese. I've been using an app to work on Mandarin, but it's very different from Romance languages, so I'm struggling a bit."

A distant part of my brain registered that he had just admitted that something wasn't coming easy to him and it made me like him more, but the rest of me could only focus on the fact that he was fluent in French.

After Monterran and Italian accents, French rounded out my Top 3.

"You speak French? Can you say something?"

"What do you want me to say?"

"Whatever you want." It wouldn't really matter because I wouldn't be able to understand him anyway. He could have read me his grocery list and I still would have found it sexy.

I had taken two years of French in high school but had retained none of it. Which became entirely evident when he started speaking.

His words apparently disconnected my eyeballs from my brain and I wasn't processing visual information correctly or paying attention to what was happening around me.

And as a result I stepped off the curb and directly into oncoming traffic.

"Everly!" Max jerked on my hand, whirling me back so that I collided directly into his chest, almost knocking him over. Icy panic flooded through me as a car sped past us, blaring its horn. My heart beat inside my chest like a fast drum, and I clung to him. I couldn't quite process what had just happened, how close I'd come to being run over. One second I'd been swooning over his French and the next I'd nearly been flattened.

I couldn't stop shaking and felt incapable of getting my breathing under control. I'd never had a panic attack before, but I imagined it would feel something like this.

As sensations started to return to my limbs, I became more aware of the situation I currently found myself in. Max was holding me tight, his own heart thundering inside his chest. I felt his lips brush against the top of my head.

He reached up to put both of his hands on the sides of my face, angling it up so that he could look me in the eyes. His voice was thick with fear. "Are you okay?"

"I'm okay," I finally said, trying to calm both of us down.

Max let go of my face and wrapped his arms around my waist again. This time he was the one burying his face into my neck, and I instinctively reached up to stroke his hair, to soothe him.

I was the one who'd almost become a human pancake, but he seemed more freaked out.

Maybe it was because I was just so happy to be held by him again that the fear had quickly evaporated. Some detached part of my brain realized that Max must have lost his cowboy hat when he'd rescued me, because I was able to run my fingers through his dark, soft hair. I thought about pointing it out to him but I didn't want him to release me in order to look for it.

"I'm okay," I repeated, feeling like he needed to hear it.

"The world would be so much worse without you in it." He said it like the words were being wrenched from him. He clung to me like he needed the reassurance that I was there and safe.

A few minutes passed and we stood there on the corner, holding each other. I felt his heartbeat slow, his breathing even out. He finally released his hold, but he didn't move away. We stood there, staring at each other, and I'd never experienced anything like it.

Oh, I liked him so much. So, so much. I didn't want to be just friends. I never had.

I'd been so busy protecting my heart that I'd done exactly what Vella accused me of—I'd had Prince Charming waltz into my life and I'd told him I wasn't interested in becoming his princess.

"Max—" I said, but I lost my ability to speak when he reached up to stroke the side of my face. He ran his fingertips along my chin and down to the bottom edge of my lip. I wondered if he even knew he was doing it.

"Are you sure you're okay? The car didn't clip you?" His voice was rough and laced with something I couldn't quite identify.

"I'm fine," I promised him. "Thank you for saving me."

He cupped my face again. I reached up and wrapped my hands around his wrists. I held on to him as we breathed together.

Was he going to kiss me?

My pulse had recently returned to a normal rhythm, but now that I thought there was a possibility that I'd finally get to know what it was like to kiss Max Colby, it started racing like it was in the Indy 500.

I hadn't had anything to drink tonight, but I felt very drunk on Max. My brain was hazy, I wasn't reacting as quickly as I should, and it seemed like I was about to make a very poor decision.

And I don't know how long we would have stayed in that moment if it hadn't suddenly started pouring. The forecast hadn't predicted bad weather, but the skies opened up and rain was barreling down onto us, like little heat-seeking water missiles.

"This way!" I said, grabbing his hand and running for the diner.

This time I made sure to look both ways before I went into the street. It took us a couple of minutes and we were completely drenched by the time we got to the diner. We ran inside and a bell chimed. Nearly everyone turned to stare at us as we came in.

I turned to look at Max, ready to share a laugh with him about having to dart through the rain, when stuff started happening in slow motion.

Max reached up to push his soaked hair away from his forehead and I practically heard music watching him do it. He smiled at me while rivulets of water ran down his face, tracing paths I wished I could follow with my fingers.

Or my mouth.

I wasn't picky.

"I'm so wet," he said, shaking the rain off.

All I could do was nod, shivering. And whether that was from being cold or my brain stem being detached from the rest of my body due to the overwhelming amount of sexiness I was witnessing, I wasn't sure.

"Grab a table anywhere," a waitress said as she passed by with a pot of coffee.

"How about over there?" Max said, pointing to a booth near the back.

"Sure." My teeth were chattering as I followed him to the table. He slid in on one side and I took the other, resisting the urge to follow him in so that we would be seated side by side.

As soon as we sat, a different waitress came over and handed us some menus. We thanked her and I pretended to look it over while I was actively trying to calm myself down.

Had we nearly kissed out there? Or was that a product of my overactive and wishful imagination?

Why was he so gorgeous? And why was he even hotter soaking wet? It was disconcerting.

As I pretended to read the menu, my brain floundered for something to talk about. I couldn't bring up what had almost just happened a few minutes ago. I didn't have the ability to shrug it off and pretend like it was nothing. As if it didn't matter to me, like the entire earth hadn't temporarily shifted off its axis completely.

Oh hey, we almost kissed, right? Or was I making that up?

Nope, not a suitable conversation for people who were supposed to be friends.

"What are you in the mood for?" he asked, and although it had been a perfectly normal and innocent question, it still had my blood pounding in my veins.

Because I was in the mood for Max and to follow through on where things had been going until Mother Nature had decided to personally interrupt us.

I finally settled on, "I always love getting breakfast for dinner. It was a big treat for me growing up. My meemaw used to do it the first Sunday of every month."

"Me too! I love breakfast for dinner."

Some part of me thought he was saying it to be nice, but I heard the sincerity. Another thing we had in common.

They seemed to be piling up.

The waitress returned, asking if we knew what we wanted. I ordered the chocolate chip pancake platter and Max asked for the protein breakfast—scrambled eggs, bacon, and sausage.

"I'll get that right out for you," she said, taking our menus, and I nearly asked for mine back.

Because Max was looking at me with that intense gaze of his, the one that made me feel like he could see into my soul, and it made me shift in my seat. I liked him. I felt safe with him.

But he also caused these inexplicable feelings of uneasiness and discomfort. In a good way.

I didn't know how to explain it.

"What are you working on currently?" I asked him, desperate to fill the silence between us.

He explained how his organization was in the process of trying to acquire a building that they could fix up to provide housing for the women in his program who were obtaining their degrees. He said that they were having a hard time finding donors to help cover the cost.

I internally sighed. He was so selfless and kind and I hadn't ever met anyone else who had devoted their entire life to serving others. I never would have guessed that altruism could be this sexy.

"It's just difficult to line up donors in general," he said with a grimace.

How could anyone ever tell Max no? I would have guessed that he could have just walked into a roomful of rich people and they would have had their checkbooks out before he even opened his mouth.

He said, "We need a lot of supplies for our first-time mother program and we've been struggling."

It suddenly occurred to me that I was supposed to have told him about my upcoming plans. "I know it's not going to be a lot, but I'm going to use Sunny's baby shower to help you stock up."

"You are?"

I explained to him my idea for the shower to be a charity event with all of the gifts and prizes going to him and how excited Sunny was about it.

He had gone still while I talked, and I worried that I might have somehow inadvertently offended him. I hoped he didn't think I was implying he couldn't do his job.

"So we'll just need to coordinate how to get everything over to you," I finished up, feeling a bit foolish. Maybe I should have asked his permission?

But he reached across the table and enveloped my hands with his own. Would this ever not feel amazing? Could it become commonplace?

"Thank you," he said, and I was surprised at the emotion in his voice. "How are you like this?"

"Like what?" I asked.

The waitress returned with our food and Max let go of my hands so that she could put our plates down.

He thanked her, but all I could think about was what he'd just said. He'd obviously meant it in a good way, but I needed more information.

An explanation, even if things didn't end up the way I hoped they might. But before I even skirted the subject of whether or not he and I might be something more, there was something I needed to know first.

When the waitress left, Max picked up his fork and the words fell out of me.

"Why did you tell Sunny that I was down-to-earth and simple?"

CHAPTER
TWENTY-TWO

"Did that upset you?" Max asked, sounding confused.

"Uh, yes." Might as well be honest about it. That phrase had been stuck in my head for a while now. "You think I'm boring and plain."

"What?" he said it with so much incredulousness that I felt kind of stupid for saying it in the first place. "That couldn't be further from the truth. What I meant by it was that you're not a snob and you're real, just yourself without a bunch of pretension. Those are qualities that I appreciate. They've been in short supply in my life."

"Oh." His words filled my veins with tiny fizzy bubbles of lightness, like I'd been carrying something heavy around and now I could put it down.

"Do I need to explain it more, so that you don't have the wrong idea?" he asked, and I knew that he would. That he wouldn't be angry about me misinterpreting it or roll his eyes and tell me to get over it. He would sit with me and talk about it for as long as I needed him to.

That made the fizziness in my veins intensify.

"I think I've got it," I said.

"Good." He reached for the ketchup bottle, and like some minion of the devil, he proceeded to pour it on top of his scrambled eggs.

"What are you doing?" I gasped.

He paused, holding the bottle midair. "Putting ketchup on my eggs. They taste better this way."

"Whatever demon is whispering lies into your ear telling you to do this abomination, I'd advise not listening. Although I suppose it is your right to let that creature lead you astray."

Max grinned at me and continued to douse his eggs. "I didn't know my eating habits would put my eternal soul at risk."

"Maybe you should have paid more attention in church."

Now he laughed. "One more thing I have to be worried about now."

"If you need more stuff to add to your 'Worry About This' list, I can recommend a whole bunch," I said as I poured syrup onto my pancakes.

"Do you have a lot of fears?" he asked.

"I do scary stuff," I responded, bristling a bit at what felt like an implication. "I moved to New York, which is not easy when you initially get here. I thought I was a somewhat sophisticated person, and the first time I was surrounded by skyscrapers, it overwhelmed me. All the people, the cars, the noise. It was a lot."

"Monterra is very different," he said. "Very quaint and self-contained. New York is the opposite."

"How so?" I asked, and while we finished up our food, he told me everything he loved about his home country, the beauty and serenity, the amazing skiing, the privacy, given that no paparazzi were allowed.

His last declaration felt a bit odd—I'd never worried about paparazzi ever because they had no reason to take my picture.

I was about to ask for clarification, but he spoke first. "Do you ever think that your fears might be holding you back?"

"Some fears are good," I countered. "They keep you alive."

"And sometimes they keep you trapped," he said. "Sometimes they keep you from experiencing something that might be great for you because you're too afraid."

There was some truth there. My fear of rejection was keeping me from being open and honest with him. What if it was holding me back in other ways that I hadn't realized?

He threw some large bills onto the table, tipping an insane amount. "Can I show you something?"

Anything you'd like, my hormones purred. "Sure."

"Let me grab some tickets first," he said, pushing buttons on his phone. "There. Let's go."

While the rain had lightened up, it wasn't completely gone. He got us a rideshare and we drove to a building I didn't recognize.

"Where are we?" I asked.

"It's a surprise."

He took me into an elevator and pressed the button for the ninety-second floor.

"I am not BASE jumping or walking on a tightrope," I warned him. He was cute, but not that cute.

Okay, he was, but I still wasn't willing to risk my life just because he was hot.

We went out into a giant room filled with mirrors and massive windows. There were people everywhere, taking photos. I could see the entire New York skyline spread out beyond the windows. It was a gorgeous view, but not one I wanted to examine more closely.

He held on to my hand firmly as we walked toward the edge. I realized that there were glass skyboxes that jutted out over nothing. There was just blackness, empty space, with lights sprinkled in.

Max stepped out onto that glass ledge, and for one hysterical second, I imagined him being like a cartoon character who would realize too late what he had done, hovering in place until gravity finally reasserted itself.

I tried to swallow back the lump of fear in my throat. "I did tell you that I nearly had a panic attack last year at a rooftop event, right? And that I was nowhere near the edge?"

"We can leave if you want," he said. "You are totally safe, though. I'm here with you and I won't let anything happen to you."

I believed him, but I couldn't chase off the clawing panic I felt in my gut. "How high up are we?"

"A bit over three hundred meters."

"I don't know what that is in actual distance!"

"About a thousand feet."

I put my hands on my knees, bending over slightly. That was so very many feet. "Is there a weight limit in that thing?"

He smiled sweetly at me. "Do you trust me?"

Then he held out his hand.

I let out a giant breath, straightened up, and took his hand. "Yes, I trust you."

Without letting myself think or my body react, I stepped out onto the glass ledge. We were completely encased in glass, I logically knew that I was safe, but I was still trembling.

I took several deep breaths and was intensely grateful that it was nighttime. If it had been during the day, I would have been able to see everything beneath me. As it was, it was almost like standing in a night sky with the lights of the city twinkling like stars all around us. I could appreciate the view even if I was still slightly terrified.

"Beautiful," I said.

"Beautiful," he echoed in agreement, only I turned to see his gaze fixed on me.

I swallowed hard and turned my face back to the skyline. "There's the Empire State Building," I said. "I should take you there sometime. No tour of New York City is complete without it."

"Are you doing okay?" he asked.

Admittedly, my limbs were still shaking and my breaths were coming out in sporadic bursts, but I was managing. "I think so."

"I'm sorry if I sprang this on you," he said. "I think so highly of you. I wanted you to see that you can do things that scare you."

I can if you're with me.

While I didn't say the words, he seemed to sense them and pulled me against his side, wrapping his arm around my shoulders, and we stood there, pressed together, staring out into an endless night.

I had stopped shaking, his presence soothing me. "I'm ready to leave," I told him.

We walked back through the bigger part of the room and Max mentioned that there were other exhibits that we could visit, but I'd had more than my fill of being up so high. "I'm good."

"Then I should probably get you home. It's late."

"Sounds good." It didn't sound good, though. I wanted to stay with him.

We went back down in the elevator, and he used an app to get another ride, as the rain was still dripping down. I was very grateful to step foot onto the sidewalk. Even if I'd faced my fear, I much preferred having the firm earth beneath my feet.

Our car arrived and Max opened the door for me so that I could climb in first. He got in and there wasn't much room for both of us. His legs were pressed against mine, and I was tingling from the contact. He took my hand and held it near his knee. He was rubbing his thumb along the back of my hand and it was all I could focus on. He was sending out little waves of pleasure along my skin and I didn't know if anything could feel more amazing.

And I held that belief until the moment when he lifted my hand to his lips, pressing a soft kiss there. "You were really brave tonight."

I certainly didn't feel brave now, his gentle lips causing tremors that traveled along my nerves. "I don't know about that."

He put our hands back on his knee. "You were. Sometimes the only way to get over something you're afraid of is to just do it."

Everything Max said felt like it was loaded with some double meaning that I couldn't figure out. Like we really were speaking two different languages.

"And sometimes things aren't as scary as you thought they would be," he added.

"Uh, that was every bit as terrifying as I would have imagined," I said.

He smiled. "But you did it anyway."

"Because you were with me."

There was something in his eyes I couldn't read. Not only because it was dark, but because it was unfamiliar.

We arrived at my building and he got out, offering me his hand to help me onto the sidewalk. I took it and we walked over to the door. I expected to say our goodbyes, but he asked, "Is it okay if I walk you up to your apartment? I can assure you that it's motivated purely by selfishness."

His words had me feeling lightheaded. "Oh?"

"I won't be able to sleep well tonight if I'm not a hundred percent sure you got into your apartment safely."

That made me grin. "I wouldn't want you to suffer, Mr. Lincoln." Casimir opened the door for us and we went into the lobby, over to the elevators.

While we waited he asked, "What are your plans tomorrow?"

"Working mostly. Coordinating, calling people, following up, getting things arranged. All the fun organizational stuff. I'm also going to watch that royal wedding at like, four thirty on Sunday morning. What about you?"

"I was going to go for a run in Central Park tomorrow with Basta, if you wanted to join us."

"I only run if something is chasing me," I told him as the elevator doors opened. We stepped inside.

"I could chase you," he offered.

Ha. I would lie down and let him catch me. "I'll pass."

"You don't do the whole jogging-in–Central Park thing?"

"Alone? Given that I'm female? No. I choose life."

We arrived on my floor and started walking toward my apartment. Every step ratcheted up my heartbeat another notch until I felt like I actually had gone for a run.

But was Max chasing me?

Or was it all in my head?

"This is it," I told him, reaching out to touch my door. I wasn't sure why I'd done it; I'd never done it before. Maybe I just needed to feel grounded by something that I knew was real.

"Thank you for walking me up, even if it was selfish," I added.

Max moved closer to me, his icy blue eyes glittering in the low light of the hallway.

My breath caught at his expression.

"Thank you for letting me dance with the prettiest girl at the bar tonight."

I could feel my face fall. "You don't have to say that kind of stuff to me, Max."

He blinked, confused. "Do you mean the truth? I do have to say it. According to thousands of years of religious and governmental laws, anyways."

I didn't want him to joke his way out of this. "You shouldn't say things you don't mean."

He studied me, and the air between us was charged, like the storm outside. As if lightning were going to strike at any moment, only I would have welcomed it. He brought my hand up to his lips for the second time tonight and kissed the back. As if he really were an escapee from an old romance novel, like Vella had said.

The kiss lasted longer than what would have been considered proper back then, though.

Then he flipped my hand over and pressed another hot kiss onto my palm and I hissed as my fingers curled inward. I was unprepared for that onslaught of sensation.

But he released me, letting my hand drop, and started back down the hallway. I collapsed against the door, needing the physical support.

What was that?

He stopped, squared his shoulders, lifted his head, and then turned around slowly to face me.

"Just so you know, I never say things I don't mean, Everly."

CHAPTER TWENTY-THREE

I woke up with a start the next morning as Vella was perched on my nightstand, staring down at me like a vulture. I made an undignified sound.

"What are you doing?" I asked her.

"Imagine my disappointment when I returned home last night to find you here alone," she said.

Like there was going to be any other outcome.

"Speaking of last night, how was your date?" Maybe I could distract her. I turned onto my back, rubbing my eyes.

"It went very well. Why didn't you ever tell me how much cowboys know about ropes and knots?"

I held up my hand to stop her. "I do not want more information."

"That makes one of us. What happened with Max?"

Knowing she was going to badger me until I told her everything, I did just that. I recounted every moment that had happened between Max and me from the time Vella ditched me at the country bar until he made his enigmatic statement and then went off to the elevators.

When I told her how I'd nearly been run over and didn't quite get his reaction to it, she said, "Didn't you say he has like, a savior complex?"

"He did tell me that."

"It probably freaked him out that he almost let something happen to you."

That made a certain kind of sense. "Maybe." But that whole incident had felt like something more than just him not living up to a specific idea he had of himself as a rescuer.

Vella interrupted my train of thought. "What I don't get is that you had the chance to kiss him in the rain and you didn't take it. Isn't that like, the most aspirational thing that can happen in a rom-com?"

"I—" It hadn't occurred to me until she pointed it out that Max might have kissed me if I hadn't rushed us out of the rain, and I wanted to kick myself.

It would have been fantastically romantic.

"I just cannot with you and your incredible denseness right now," she said, throwing her arms up as she stood. "Nobody can actually be this clueless."

She went into her room and I heard the door lock behind her. I went to use the bathroom, and after I'd finished, I washed my hands and studied myself in the mirror.

I had left something out when I told her about my time with Max, in part because I knew her reaction would have been even worse. Something had shifted last night after the near miss with the car.

Not just my new appreciation for life, but things between me and Max.

I had been trying to keep our friendship light and easy for my own emotional health, but I was failing in every way imaginable on that front. My defenses had been built out of straw and sticks and it had taken one big gust to knock everything down.

Everything between us had deepened. I'd become even more attached to him.

The problem was I didn't know if Max felt the same.

I might have faced one fear last night, but I wasn't sure if I was ready to try to conquer another.

~

The day flew by in a blur because I had so much to do. Vella was in and out all day shooting me annoyed looks, probably due to my supposed cluelessness when it came to Max. I had my phone glued to my ear as I tried to make so many last-minute arrangements.

I stayed up later than I'd intended and wondered whether I should just remain awake the entire night until Princess Chiara's wedding at four thirty in the morning, or if I should try to get a few hours of sleep before it began.

My mom texted me while I was debating.

IT'S ALMOST TIME! MOM SEND

When my phone had buzzed at me, I'd had a momentary hope that Max would be the one texting me, and I was disappointed that it wasn't from him. He hadn't texted or called all day and I didn't know what to make of it. His radio silence was odd, given that we had been texting and calling on a daily basis. How could he be so sweet and hand-kissy one minute and then ignore me the next?

While I knew that I could have reached out to him first, I needed some kind of sign from him. Something to let me know that I wasn't in this alone.

I awoke with a start on the couch after I heard someone knocking on the front door. I had meant to stay up, but I must have drifted off. I looked at my phone with bleary eyes. It was four fifteen in the morning. I hadn't set an alarm—I would have overslept and missed the wedding.

Had Vella gone out again and forgotten her keys? She'd never done it in the past, but I couldn't figure out who would be knocking so early in the morning.

I padded over to the door, looking through the keyhole.

My heart slammed against my chest when I saw Max standing there, holding bags and a tray.

I looked terrible. I hadn't showered in a couple of days and was wearing my rattiest sweats and a T-shirt of a band my mom had liked when she was younger called Duran Duran. There were so many holes in it that it could have doubled as swiss cheese.

But my curiosity was too great and I had to know what he was doing here at a time when even the sun was still asleep.

I opened the door. "Max?"

"Everly!" He looked fresh and clean, and as he brushed past me to get into the apartment, I noticed that he smelled amazing.

I wondered if I could sneak off and put on some deodorant and brush my teeth without him noticing.

Basta came inside, sniffing every available surface. She nosed me on my leg, and I scratched her ears, still in shock to find them here. She went over to a corner and curled up, quickly falling asleep.

"What are you two doing?"

He gave me a funny look. "We're here to watch the wedding with you."

"We didn't arrange that," I said, watching as he set his bags down on what little counter space he could find in our kitchen. I was pretty sure I would remember if he and I had decided to have our own viewing party.

"That's why they call it a surprise. I thought it would be fun."

What would have been more fun was being able to prepare myself, maybe put on one of my Kat dresses before he came over.

He mistook my silence. "I can go if you want."

"No! I mean, no. I want you to stay. We just can't wake up Vella or else she will do something terrible."

My phone beeped.

ARE YOU WATCHING? MOM SEND

I texted her back.

Yes, I am.

I didn't tell her about Max, though. My mom and meemaw would have died if they'd known I was watching the wedding alongside a real Monterran.

"What is all this?" I asked, watching him unpack.

"I thought I should bring breakfast."

"You know it's just me here, right? I don't have an entire platoon hiding in my bathroom."

He grinned at me. "Leftovers are never a bad thing. I didn't know what you would like, so I brought a little of everything. They're all Monterran dishes. I figured I'd go with a theme."

My mouth parted slightly. What was I supposed to do with this level of thoughtfulness?

"So I have zeppoles, which are basically like doughnuts, cornettos that are croissants but with a Nutella filling, maritozzi, which is a sweet bun with whipped cream, gelato in three flavors—"

"Gelato's not breakfast," I told him.

"It is if you eat it at breakfast," he responded with a grin. "There's also crema frittas, arancini con cioccolato . . ."

So many of the pastries he was pointing at looked like they'd been fried. "Basically you brought me a heart attack."

"But what a way to go."

My heart thudded slow and hard in response.

"I also brought a charcuterie board with cheese and meats. There's prosciutto and sopressata, burrata, fresh mozzarella and Parmigiano-Reggiano, along with olives, figs, grapes, and some water crackers." He sounded so proud of himself.

"Is this what Monterrans eat every day?" I asked in disbelief. There was so much food.

"The typical breakfast would be like cappuccino and biscuits, which I also brought you. We dunk our biscuits in our coffee."

He held something up that was not a biscuit. "That's a cookie," I said. "Whatever you do, don't tell Vella. She has a problem with countries who call cookies 'biscuits.' But cookies for breakfast? I could get on board with that."

"European biscuits are not as sweet as American cookies."

"That's a shame," I told him. "Sugar makes everything better."

His gaze drifted down to my lips. "I do have a special fondness for sweet things."

That thick tension returned, making my limbs feel sluggish. "Thank you," I managed to say. "This was really kind and a very fun surprise."

"You're welcome."

Max leaned his body toward me and I didn't know how to interpret it or respond. I went over to a cabinet and opened it, grabbing a couple of my special plates. "Should we get some food and go watch the wedding?" I asked.

"Absolutely." He took the plate from me, his long fingers brushing against mine, and I nearly dropped it onto the floor. Fortunately he had quick reflexes and caught the plate in time.

I wanted to explain to him that I wasn't normally this clumsy and it was entirely his fault. That kind of confession could only lead to embarrassing places, so I stayed quiet.

We both loaded up our plates, and I was so discombobulated by standing this close to him that I floundered around for a safer topic for conversation. Anything to derail where my mind was headed. "I'm guessing most of this doesn't fall within the healthy spectrum."

"No, Monterrans do things in moderation. We eat our sweets, but not too many."

"Good thing I'm not Monterran," I said. "I may not eat well but at least I'm eating a lot."

He laughed, and it seemed to break that overwhelming tension. Then he finally noticed the plate I'd handed him. "What is this?"

"Commemorative plates from when Nico and Kat, er, King Dominic and Queen Katerina, got married. I have a matching mug that I drink out of every morning. It's basically my version of the good china."

He smiled at me, like he thought I was adorable. "You really are a fan."

I was not going to tell him about my replica of Kat's wedding ring or the many dresses I'd bought to copy her style or how my screen saver was of the royal family's castle.

Or the pen set my mom had bought me when I'd graduated from high school, each one featuring a different member of the Monterran royal family.

"A bit of a fan," I agreed. "Should we turn the wedding on?"

We headed over to the couch and I set my plate on the coffee table in front of me and turned on the TV. I found the channel showing the wedding and put down the remote.

"Should we get Basta something to eat?" I asked.

At the mention of her name, she lifted her head, eyes slightly opening. Then she immediately went back to sleep.

"It's too early for her," Max said. "She'll be begging for treats later, though. Is Vella going to join us?"

"This is too early for her, too. It's usually when she's coming home, not when she's getting up."

He took a bite of one of his pastries and then said, "You mentioned something the other day about how she keeps her bedroom door locked. You've really never seen the inside?"

Finally, someone I could confide in about how weird that was. "Yes! When I first moved in, all I wanted to do was break down her door and find out what she was hiding in there. I even watched some videos online on how to pick locks."

"Which basically makes you an expert on it," he teased.

"Exactly. But now that we're friends, I just respect her need for privacy. I do wonder if she's got some of her ex-boyfriends in there chained to the wall."

"A collection of really creepy dolls?"

"I could see that. Or maybe she's guarding a portal to Narnia. Who knows?"

On-screen, members of the royal family were arriving. The streets had been cleared, but blinding white snow glistened on every rooftop. Crowds lined the streets, holding up signs and cheering for the royals.

"It's so pretty there," I said. "It must be an amazing place to live."

"There is definitely a provincial charm, with medieval buildings and cobblestone streets that make you feel like you've walked into a different time. The sun is different there, this soft golden haze over everything. The people are open and friendly. Monterrans are notorious for their work-life balance."

"I should be better about that."

"Everything has its positives and negatives, and that mentality isn't so great when you need a plumber. Tradespeople don't always come when you call, and it's normal for packages to take weeks to arrive."

"Do you miss it?" I asked.

"The mail system? No. But there are a lot of things I miss about Monterra." He shifted his body to face me, putting his arm along the back of the couch. "Although New York is pretty great, too."

"It's probably due to that fantastic tour guide of yours."

I'd meant for it to be a joke, but my heart untethered itself from my chest and tried to climb up into my throat when he said, "It is due to her, yes."

CHAPTER TWENTY-FOUR

While I sat there not knowing what to say to his comment, I made a mental list of all the reasons why I couldn't fall for Max Colby.

- I had emotional trauma from being repeatedly rejected by men I was attracted to and didn't want that to happen with him because it would be so much worse, given that I liked him more than I had ever liked anyone else.

- He dated around a lot and I'd already lived with one womanizer and was in no hurry to repeat that particularly painful experience.

- He'd let me know repeatedly that he wasn't interested in a commitment, and I didn't want to be one of many.

- He hadn't indicated any interest in me beyond

friendship and had, in fact, eagerly agreed when I'd
told him I wanted us to be friends.

The last one was the one currently weighing most heavily on my
mind. He was flirtatious and fun, but as far as I knew, he was that way
with about half of New York City's population.

It was then that my brain reminded me that I had been quiet for
an unnatural length of time while I composed my list to keep myself
in line.

I cleared my throat and said, "Then maybe you should pay your
tour guide more if she's so good at her job."

He lifted up one of the cornettos and, with a wink, said, "That's
what the pastries are for."

See? No deeper meaning. Just harmless flirtation. Nothing more.

I couldn't let myself get caught up in him, even though I really,
really wanted to. He was so sexy and kind and loved his dog and was
smart and funny, and it was taking all of my self-control to not leap
across this couch and make out with his face.

"The princess is arriving," he said, pointing to the screen.

I'd been so caught up in my lustful impulses that I'd missed the rest
of the royal family arriving for the wedding. Good thing I was recording
this and could pore over everything later.

Princess Chiara arrived in a golden carriage pulled by white horses,
like something out of a fairy tale. The door was opened outside the
cathedral, and a footman assisted her in getting out of the carriage.
She had on a big, princess-worthy wedding dress and a long white cape
lined with faux fur. She was the fashion-loving member of her family,
so it made sense that she'd arrive in so much style. Like all the other
Monterran princesses before her—Kat, Lemon, Genesis, and Violetta—
Chiara had a green sash around her waist.

"The green is for good luck," I told Max. The wedding was probably
the only thing that could distract me from wanting to kiss him. Princess
Chiara looked so happy, and Nico was there to escort her up the stairs.

Her father, the former king of Montcrra, waited at the top for them in his wheelchair. He would be the one to bring her down the aisle.

I knew that her fiancé would wait for her by the altar, not turning around until she was standing next to him. The camera kept panning to his face, waiting for the moment when he would see his new bride. He looked excited and happy and very in love.

"How old is the princess?" Max asked.

"Twenty-two, the same age as me."

"Isn't that a little young to be getting married?"

What was it with this man and not wanting to settle down? Was he trying to send me signals, letting me know that he wasn't interested and my brain should not be heading down the path it already was? "I guess when you find the right person, that sort of thing doesn't really matter."

"If I do get married, I think I'd be like, in my thirties."

"That seems kind of arbitrary," I told him. "If you met your soulmate, you'd be like, 'Oh, sorry, it would be great to celebrate our love and make a lifetime commitment to you in front of all our friends and family but I can't because I haven't reached some imaginary cutoff that I've picked for myself.'"

"I guess you have a point." I nearly missed the mischievous gleam in his eye.

"Of course I do." I paused for a beat and then asked, "Have you been to a Monterran wedding? I'm really curious about what happens at the reception. They usually show the actual ceremony, but I have no idea what the next part is like."

"There's a lot of traditions. Pranks played by the wedding party on the newlyweds, specific dances, favorite dishes. In some places they cut up the groom's tie and the guests buy a piece for luck, and all the money goes to the couple. Usually the bride and groom will break a glass vase, and every piece on the ground represents how many years they'll be happily married. In the northern region some couples plant a pine tree that symbolizes their love. But the final toast is always the same—they'll say per cent'anni. It's a hope that their love will last for a hundred years."

"Per cent'anni," I repeated, liking the way it sounded.

We ate our food and watched the ceremony quietly. Chiara's voice caught several times, like she was so in love with her soon-to-be husband that she couldn't get the words out. I ate up every single second of it.

After the vows had been exchanged, the newlyweds made their way to the front door of the cathedral to greet the waiting crowds. A massive cheer broke out as they emerged outside and waved to everyone. After a couple of minutes, they got into the carriage and drove off to their reception. I turned the TV off, as I knew from past experience that there would be nothing else to report. All the activities beyond that point would be private for the families.

"That was so great," I said as I let out a happy sigh. "I bet my mom's going to call me soon to recap."

It had just been a passing comment, me thinking out loud, but Max took that as some kind of signal that I was throwing him out.

"I should get going," he said as he stood up.

"Oh." I was going to tell him not to leave, but then he went and dropped a nuclear bomb on me.

"I'm assuming today it's going to be another busy day for you."

I nodded. "Yes. Like always. But who needs sleep?"

"Most people do," he said with a smile.

"What about you? What are your plans today?"

"Take a run with Basta, relax for a little bit, and then I have dinner plans with Arabella."

It was like he'd taken a dagger and plunged it directly into my heart.

Dinner plans with Arabella?

Stunning ex-girlfriend Arabella?

I was nauseous. I was going to throw up my zeppoles all over him.

I must have made a face that reflected my feelings because he rushed to add, "She's here in the city and she offered to get together and return some of my things."

Well, she didn't need to take the man on a date to give him back his stuff. And what did she need to return that he'd managed to live without just fine for the last few months?

It was an excuse to see him again. I understood it, I did, but the fiery inferno of jealousy currently consuming me made it so that I felt completely irrational.

I knew I couldn't say anything, though. Friends did not get mad when their friends had dinner with gorgeous supermodels.

If anything, I should probably be high-fiving him and telling him good luck.

Was this why he hadn't called or texted yesterday? Because he was having *let's get back together* conversations with his ex?

Yet another entry for my list of reasons that he and I could not be together—he was still hung up on Arabella.

Resigned to reality, I stood up and nodded. I was going to take a high road here. Maybe not *the* high road, because that would probably consist of telling him to enjoy himself for something that was beyond my current capabilities, but I could take a road near that one.

"That sounds like fun." It did not sound like fun, but that was between me and my brain. "Do you want me to pack up your food?"

"No, you and Vella enjoy." He called for Basta and she got to her feet and came over to him. He clipped her lead into place and I walked them over to the door. He said, "Hey, be sure you don't step in front of any cars today."

I didn't know if I was ready to joke, considering the information he'd just given me.

"Bye," I said, feeling proud of myself for not melting down over Max having dinner with his ex. "And bye to you, Basta." I got down on the floor to rub her head and she gave me cute doggy kisses that made me laugh.

"I'm so glad you like her," he said. "It would be really awkward if you didn't."

"Of course I like her," I said as I straightened up. "She's the most adorable dog ever."

With a grin Max said, "I was talking to Basta."

~

Vella found me surrounded by a graveyard of half-eaten pastries, snoozing on the couch.

"What happened in here?" she asked after she'd woken me up. "Did you rob a bakery?"

"Max came over to watch the royal wedding with me and brought a whole bunch of Monterran breakfast food and I was eating my sorrows."

She sat down on the couch next to me. "Why would you need to eat your body weight in carbs?"

"He's having dinner tonight with his perfect ex-girlfriend and I'm so jealous I can barely see straight. Or my vision impairment might be due to a sugar overload." The one thing I was glad about was that he hadn't told me about his date with his ex until after the wedding was over. His revelation didn't taint the memory I would treasure of eating delicious food and watching something I loved with him.

"Huh."

"'Huh'?" I repeated. "I need let's-light-his-hair-on-fire Vella, not huh Vella."

"I mean, I could do it, but it would probably mar his face and no one in the world wants that."

"Ugh," I groaned. "He and I are just friends, nothing more. I have no right to be jealous. At all."

"You may not have the right, but I am giving you permission to be as jealous as you want."

"I don't think you have the authority to do that," I said with a weak smile.

"Sure I do. I've granted it to myself. By the power vested in me by me, I hereby allow you to be jealous that Max is having dinner with his ex-girlfriend and to be annoyed about it and even petty if you want to be."

"I am feeling very petty. Like, I'd let the air out of her tires if she owned a car and I knew where it was."

Vella made a pshaw sound and opened up the pastry box on the coffee table. "You think way too small." She picked out a treat and started to eat it.

"It's because my brain is too crowded right now. What I am thinking about is how you said stuff is happening between Max and me just because he wants to rescue me."

"I never said that." Her mouth was full when she spoke, but I could make out what she was trying to say.

I ignored her response because she pretty much had, even if she wanted to deny it now. "Does that mean I'm going to have to almost get run over every time I hang out with him?"

She swallowed her bite. "He doesn't like you because he stopped you from getting flattened like Wile E. Coyote. He liked you before that."

"He doesn't try to spend time with me." I crossed my arms, like I was determined to be difficult. At her raised eyebrows, I added, "Other than this morning."

"Maybe that's because you're constantly telling him how busy you are and he's being considerate of your schedule. Wouldn't it be worse if he was always trying to hang out with you and distracting you from your job?"

"I guess," I mumbled. I decided to say the scary part out loud. "But if he does like me, why doesn't he say so? Or try to kiss me?"

"He's probably being respectful or whatever because you told him you only thought of him as a friend. I don't know how people like you do relationships."

"Max Colby doesn't like me." I needed to say it out loud, if only to remind myself.

Vella finished off her food and let out a long sigh. "Let me put it to you this way. Dating is like a foreign country for you. You've never really visited—maybe a couple of day trips, but that's it. I have lived here for most of my adult life. I am fluent in the language and know all the customs. So please allow me to translate this for you. I'll even ignore all the other events and only count what happened today. A man who surprised you with delicious pastries at four thirty in the morning does not want to be just friends. No guy watches a televised wedding of people he does not know and doesn't care about for no reason. He did it to make you happy. *Because he likes you.*"

Surprise gripped my throat, rendering me momentarily speechless. I wanted to protest but found that I couldn't. I forced myself to think about my list of all the reasons things couldn't possibly work with him. I wanted to share it with Vella, but I knew she would just shoot them all down.

I weakly settled on, "I don't have time right now to worry about dating."

"No one is asking you to worry. Dating is in the fun section of the program." She stood up, dramatically smacking her hands together as if she were washing them clean of this whole situation. "Is there more food in the kitchen?"

I nodded. "There's gelato in the freezer, too."

"Oh! Gelato!" She opened the freezer door to survey her choices. She glanced back over her shoulder at me. "I am sorry about the kissing, though. Not only that he's not doing it but, as I said, given how he dances, he probably won't be all that great at it."

I probably should have kept my response to myself but I didn't. "You're wrong. I know that it's going to be so good between us. If I get this excited because he sits close to me or holds my hand, it's going to be Mount Vesuvius good if he ever kisses me."

"Hopefully your love will not bury a bunch of people in lava. Is it okay if I eat the pint of chocolate?"

"Sure." I reached for my pen and notebook on the coffee table. Maybe it was time to make a list of why it would be a good idea to be braver and put myself out there. I had already resolved to do just that—why was I having such a hard time following through?

I tapped the pen against my lips, thinking. I knew why I was having a hard time.

Because I was setting myself up for failure and I didn't like failing.

More importantly, I didn't want to lose what I had with Max.

CHAPTER
TWENTY-FIVE

The rest of the week flew by, my days blurring together. Most of my waking energy was devoted to the two events I had that week—the Origin Telecom event and Hyacinth's birthday. Everything was coming together well for the party, but I knew from firsthand experience how quickly everything could, and often did, fall apart.

Max continued to text and call every day. It was always friendly—sometimes he shared funny memes or pictures of Basta. My responses were usually short. Not only to protect myself, but because I really was that busy. The Origin Telecom conference had many hiccups and stressed me out so completely that I found actual clumps of hair in the shower after it was over.

But it was done and finished and now I could focus on the event I was most excited for—the one that might lead to my promotion.

All of my hard work in New York had led to this single event, and I needed it to be flawless.

The morning of Hyacinth's birthday, Max sent me one single message that was running on a loop in my brain all day long.

Thinking of you.

What was he thinking? How did he mean that to sound?

I wasn't sure.

I got to the hotel early in the morning and directed the vendors on how everything was to be set up. I helped out where I could. It was exhausting but exhilarating work.

Three hours before the event, I got an upsetting phone call. It was from the modeling agency to let me know that half of the models wouldn't be appearing and they didn't have anyone to replace them.

"We can send American models," the agent had said, but that defeated the entire point.

My stomach tied itself up in knots as I realized that I was going to have to find replacements myself. Just as I'd opened my contact list, Max called me. Almost like he'd sensed that I was in trouble.

"Max?" I said, feeling a bit frantic and knowing that just hearing his voice would help me calm down.

"Is everything okay?" His tone was serious and caring.

"I just had three models cancel. Apparently they all went out to dinner together last night and got food poisoning."

"Can you replace them?"

"I can try. But that means I'm going to have to pay a premium to replace them last minute and I've already pushed the limits of this budget. This was like, the one thing Hyacinth was excited about—all her friends getting to take pictures with fake royalty."

"What do you need?"

"A Monterran in a tux."

"I can do that," he said.

Max could do that. Why hadn't it occurred to me before? "You really want to spend your evening at a sixteen-year-old's birthday party?"

"Maybe I'm interested in learning more about event planning."

His reason didn't matter to me. Him showing up was going to save me. "I'll text you the address. You need to be here in three hours."

"I'll see you soon."

I hung up. On the scale of one to disaster, the models canceling was barely even like, a three. Max would fill in and things would be fine. I was going to make sure of it.

That sentiment obviously jinxed me. There was an issue with the quality of some of the flowers that we solved after calling a wholesaler, who delivered fresh blooms within the hour. One of the ice sculptures hadn't been stored properly and was halfway melted. I slightly rearranged the decorations so that it wouldn't even be missed. The napkins were the wrong shade of blue, but I was going to have to roll with it.

I had planned on going home and getting ready. I had picked out a special dress for tonight—it was red and looked just like the one Kat had worn to a special state dinner in England for one of her best friends, Princess Caitlin. It was the most princessy dress ever and I was going to have to work until I was eighty-five to pay back the amount of debt I'd accumulated to buy it, but I loved it.

I didn't have time to go all the way home, get ready, and return before the guests started arriving.

While I was doing final spot checks, I called Vella. When she answered, I said, "Can you bring me my dress? It's on my bed. I don't have time to get it and now Max is coming tonight and I have to look nice."

"I was going to wax various body parts, but I can do that later. Send me the address."

With a sigh of relief, I hung up and texted her.

Things were going to be okay.

Vella arrived very quickly, like she'd grabbed my dress and immediately flown over, which was very unlike her. "Thank you so much! You're an actual lifesaver," I said. I took the dress from her and held it up so that it didn't brush against the ground. I noticed that she had several cases with her. "What's all that?"

"Remember when I went to cosmetology school? I'm going to do your hair and makeup."

She had never done anything like that for me before. "Why?"

"Because tonight I am your fairy goth-mother and you are going to enjoy your ball, Cinderella. Where can we get you ready?"

I could feel actual tears coming on. "I'm going to hug you."

Vella gave me an imperious look. "I will allow it this one time because I deserve it."

I hugged her quickly. "There's a bathroom over here that has a makeup counter," I said. She followed behind me into the bathroom.

"Sit down," she said as she began setting up her equipment. "Find me a picture on your phone of how you want everything to look."

Easy enough. I pulled up a photo of Kat in the red dress and showed it to Vella. She leaned in close to the screen. "I can't do plastic surgery."

"I meant her hair and makeup!" I said with a laugh, and she gave me an evil grin that let me know she'd said it intentionally to give me a hard time.

Vella was fast and efficient. I was actually in awe of how quickly everything got done. I got changed and put on some petticoats so that my dress would be fluffy. She helped me slide the dress on over my hair so that I didn't mess it up. She had created long curls that I wore half-up, half-down. She had put enough hairspray on to make us personally responsible for a hole in the ozone layer. My makeup was dewy and soft-looking.

I hardly even recognized myself. "You do good work."

She agreed with me as she started to pack everything back up. "I do. But didn't anyone ever tell you not to wear a red dress to a bullfight?"

"I don't think that's a saying."

"It is because I just said it. If you only want to be friends with a guy, you shouldn't go out there dressed like that."

I bit my bottom lip before admitting, "Maybe I'm trying to be more than friends with him."

She stopped what she was doing. "Oh, my shriveled black heart just grew three sizes!"

"Which is still smaller than the average heart," I said, and she laughed. Then I added, "Thank you so much for doing this."

"I owed you. I ate the last of the gelato." She closed her cases. "Now go have fun and please do something worthy of reporting back tomorrow."

My phone beeped as I was telling her goodbye. It was Hillary from work letting me know that she'd arrived and asking where I wanted her. I told her to head into the kitchen and make sure that everything was on schedule. I trusted Bartolomeo, but Hillary was excellent at gently reminding and encouraging vendors without seeming pushy. She was one of the people I had recruited from the office to help out tonight because I wanted the extra hands standing by. I would do the same thing in two weeks, when I attended the ambassador's anniversary party—I probably wouldn't be needed, but it never hurt to have backup.

Plus, I wanted to impress Claudia by volunteering for her event.

I checked in with Marie Albrecht, who was helping Hyacinth get ready to make a grand entrance. They had rented a suite in the hotel and were getting their hair and makeup done professionally. Hyacinth was still on her phone, making silly faces and taking pictures. I hoped this evening was everything she wanted it to be.

I headed back into the ballroom, standing in the middle of the room while the band set up. I turned in a slow circle. It was part Wonder Woman, part taking in what I'd accomplished in a very, very short amount of time, feeling unbelievably proud of it.

There was a noise off to the right. I turned to see Max walk in through the door and nearly fell into a heap on the ground.

If a picture of Suit Max had been overwhelming . . . real-life Tuxedo Max was going to be the actual death of me.

My ovaries threatened to wage a revolution, ready to declare independence from my brain if I continued to ignore how hot he was.

He walked over to me, and the closer he got, the more I felt like I was going to pass out.

Then he did something he'd never done before. He greeted me the way a Monterran would, leaning in to kiss one cheek and then the other. His touch was fleeting but it still scalded me, turning my face pink.

"You look . . . Wow," he said.

"No one has ever wowed me before."

"You deserve it. Along with a few other adjectives that I can't say with other people around." My internal temperature rose at his words, and I was concerned that I might break out in a sweat and ruin all of Vella's hard work.

"It's just hair and makeup," I said with a dismissive wave.

He wouldn't let me downplay it. "No, it's you. You're glowing."

Was I? I was excited about how the party would go, putting aside the minor hiccups from earlier. I was happy to be here with him, and my Copy-Kat dress was giving me a much-needed boost.

I didn't respond to his observation, feeling a bit too embarrassed. "Thank you for coming. I didn't want to impose on you and put you in an awkward position."

"No position with you could ever be awkward."

Now my face was fully on fire. Was this a language thing? I wondered if he knew how that sounded.

Or maybe I was reading too much into something that had been innocent, due to my ovarian revolution.

"You've done me such a huge favor with Sunny that this is a very small thing that I could do in return," he added.

Focus on the task at hand, I told myself. "I still appreciate you showing up and helping."

"I'd do anything for you."

My pulse was so wildly out of control that my blood was not flowing properly. Max noticed and took me by my hands. "Are you doing okay? You seem a little jittery."

Now I was out of breath, my limbs trembling.

It was because he was close to me, touching me, saying romantic things to me. Which I, obviously, could not tell him.

"I've been drinking a lot of coffee today." That was true, and safer as far as explanations went.

"How many?"

"I can't remember. Two? Twenty-six? Which means in dog coffees I've only had like, three."

He laughed and it was as glorious a sound as ever. "Where do you need me?"

By my side, I longed to say. I went over to a table and grabbed my clipboard. I didn't need it to answer him, but it made me feel better holding it. Like a shield. "You mingle with the guests. Say hello, speak in Italian, take photos with whoever asks for it."

I wondered if it would bother him to be a walking prop.

"Sounds good," he said with a nod. "What's with the clipboard?"

"My checklists. Making lists helps me feel in control of things even when I'm not. And they're also here in case I have a heart attack and go to the hospital—somebody else from Elevated could fill in for me."

The irony that I might actually be in danger of having a heart attack from Tuxedo Max was not lost on me.

"Has that happened before?" he asked.

"It has. That's why the policy exists."

The alarm on my phone sounded, alerting me that I needed to do one final walkthrough because it was almost time for people to start arriving. "I have to get to work, but I'll check in with you later."

He nodded. "I'll be counting the minutes."

It was silly and romantic and I didn't know how to respond other than to say, "Okay."

So stupid.

I was mentally berating myself as I started toward the kitchen when I heard him call my name. I stopped and he walked over to me, taking my hands again.

He said, "Tonight, after the party? I think you and I should talk."

CHAPTER
TWENTY-SIX

It was a good thing that there was so much to do—it made it so that I couldn't spend my entire evening thinking about what Max had said.

What did he want to talk to me about?

For all I knew he might have wanted me to dog-sit Basta or something. I decided I probably shouldn't read too much into it.

I kept an eye on Max as I took care of the rest of my responsibilities. I had ordered a backdrop specifically designed for photos and social media videos that had a beautiful scenic shot of the Monterran royal family's palace. Max seemed to be spending most of his time there, and it didn't surprise me in the least that Hyacinth's friends wanted to take photo after photo with him.

When dinner was served, I went into the kitchen. Hillary was handling things expertly, but I was desperately hungry and wanted to grab a plate of something before I waded back out into the fray.

I had just served myself a plate when I felt a hand sliding along my back. My entire body tingled in response, knowing it was Max.

"Are you hungry?" I asked.

"Very," he said in a low, growly voice that was doing funny things to the backs of my knees.

"Have a bite of the steak," I told him. "It's delicious." Without thinking, I cut him off a piece and held it out to him. He leaned forward to take the bite, his lips wrapping around the fork, slowly pulling the steak into his mouth, and although I knew he hadn't meant for it to be sexy, it was.

"It is delicious," he agreed. He was so close to me that I could have kissed him if I'd been braver.

"My favorite couple!" a loud voice boomed, and I turned to see Bartolomeo. "How are you this beautiful evening?"

"Wonderful. And the food is divine," I told him.

"This is why you are my favorite customer," he said with a wink.

"I bet you say that to all the girls."

"I do!" He laughed and Max and I laughed with him. "But in your case, it is true. Please excuse me, I have to oversee the next course."

Bartolomeo was an incorrigible flirt. Maybe it was just how men were from that part of the world.

Meaning everything Max said and did were empty gestures.

That thought made me sad.

And he didn't help things when he said, "I get where Bartolomeo is coming from. You're my favorite, too."

My heart seized in my chest, unable to beat. His favorite? Favorite what?

Friend?

Event planner?

Royal-family fangirl?

"People love you," he said. "And I—"

Every cell in my body screamed with anticipation. I told my hormones to calm down. He was not going to say that he loved me. That was ridiculous and I was a complete fool for even thinking it, let alone sort of hoping. "You what?"

"I love that about you. That you light up every room you walk into."

I said, "I do?"

"You do. I've been watching you tonight." He took my fork from me and placed it on the counter.

My appetite was suddenly gone due to the alarm I was feeling. Max had been watching me? Had he seen *me* watching *him*? Was he going to call me out for being a total stalker?

He took my hands in his, and this time I managed just a shiver instead of full-body trembling. "I've seen how everyone responds to you. You make people happy. You make me happy. And I—"

"Everly?" Hillary was standing on her tiptoes to see me over the crowd in the kitchen. "I have a question."

The only thing I wanted was to hear how Max was going to finish that sentence.

But I had a job to do. "I'll be back," I told him regretfully.

He squeezed my hands and released me. I walked over to Hillary, who wanted to know whether Hyacinth had any allergies. She didn't, and that was information I'd already shared with Bartolomeo. I irrationally wondered why Hillary hadn't just asked him instead of interrupting what felt like a very significant moment between Max and me.

I went back over to where I'd been eating, but he wasn't there.

You're not at this party for a boy, I had to tell myself. *You're here to do a job and get a promotion.*

But it was so hard to not get distracted when Max was nearby.

So after I wolfed down the rest of my food, I made sure to keep my distance from him.

Physical distance, because there was no way I could keep my mental and emotional distance from him. I thought about him constantly, and even though he'd told me he'd been watching me, I still found myself searching him out and watching him.

It was like a sickness.

After dinner the baker brought out the absolutely enormous birthday cake for Hyacinth. I was pleased to see that she was off her phone and enjoying the singing, along with the four-tiered cake decorated with wintry snowflakes and a tiny sugar palace. She managed to blow out all of her candles to the delight of her guests and there were waiters ready to cut up and serve the cake. After ensuring that it was passed out to all the guests who wanted a piece, I waited for about ten more minutes to give everyone a chance to eat. Then I went up to the stage to introduce Silver Cup. The band started their set by playing a cover of "Bizarre Love Triangle." It was a perfect song for both the adults and teens and it got a bunch of people out on the floor dancing.

It was all going so spectacularly well that I was worried. I had the feeling that it was all too good to be true.

Which was a feeling I was all too accustomed to lately, given that I had it every time I spoke to or hung out with Max.

I took a very large slice of cake and went into the kitchen to eat it. This particular baker had a gift for making cakes that were both beautiful and incredible tasting. Again, I was pleased with myself and what I'd accomplished.

Max came into the kitchen, as if he'd been following me. His face lit up when he saw me, and his handsomeness again overwhelmed me. Was I ever going to get used to it?

"What are you up to?" he asked.

"I'm eating an irresponsible amount of birthday cake."

"I can see that," he said.

"I'm feeling very guilty about it at the moment. It is probably forty times the recommended daily allowance of sugar."

He shook his head. "You shouldn't feel bad about eating cake. You can just use the science of relativity. Cake is healthier for you than heroin, right?"

Max might have had a point. As I was considering that, he said, "You have frosting right there."

"Where?" I asked, reaching up to feel around for it, growing more concerned with each passing second that I looked ridiculous.

"Here. May I?" he asked, and I nodded.

I held my breath, bracing for impact. He reached up with his thumb and gently rubbed the icing off of my upper lip. His thumb was warm and firm and my lip tingled in response to his touch, my blood heating in my veins.

Then my stomach flipped completely over when he lifted his thumb up to his own mouth and licked off the frosting. Even though he wasn't touching me, it felt like he was. I leaned back against the counter as I didn't know if I was still capable of supporting my own body weight.

The kitchen door opened. My eyes flickered briefly in that direction and I saw Claudia.

I straightened up. I'd had no idea she was coming here tonight. She noticed me and came over, smiling.

"Everly! Tonight has been magnificent. You have done a truly incredible job. I hope you are proud of yourself!"

"Thank you so much," I said, feeling breathless, both from her compliment and from what Max had just innocently done.

"I'm going to personally oversee the cleanup and takedown tonight," she said, and it surprised me. That was the entire point of being senior staff—getting to delegate things like this to the underlings.

I hoped she didn't think I wanted to leave. "I'm happy to stay."

"Oh, this isn't a comment on your performance. I know you would be the last person here if I needed you to be. You did a fantastic job, and I want to end the evening with a senior member of our team as the point of contact. We are trying to win over the Albrechts and their friends, and I think it would be better if I was the one they interact with when tonight ends."

That made sense. It was unusual, but so was this event. We were trying to establish a foothold in this space, so I understood why Claudia, who had a lot more experience with clients, wanted to be the person seeing them off.

"Sure thing," I said, and handed her my clipboard. There wasn't much left to check off.

"You should go and have fun. Celebrate." She shot a meaningful look at Max and I worried that I might have appeared unprofessional. But she smiled, as if enjoying some private joke, and left with the clipboard.

"So you're free?" he asked.

"It would appear so."

"Do you want to go get a drink?"

"I really do." It was exactly what I needed. This had been a long, strange, stressful evening and the idea of unwinding and relaxing sounded perfect.

"I know a wine bar not too far from here."

"Yes to all of it," I said. He came with me while I grabbed my bag and coat, and we left. The night was perfect—cold but clear. Max took my hand and it made things even better. My skin was still flushed with excitement and the chill felt good against it.

"She was right," he said. "You did a great job with the party."

"Thank you." Strangely enough, his praise meant more to me than Claudia's.

"Are you worried that your boss is sticking around to take the credit?"

"Claudia is not my boss and she's not like that. This is a chance for her to network with the other potential clients at the party and schmooze the Albrechts. They will feel special that someone so high up is personally overseeing everything."

"Was tonight a nice change? From what you usually do?"

I let out a little laugh. "Leaps and bounds better. I can freely admit that corporate events are usually total snoozefests."

"You say that like it's a bad thing. I would pay to attend a snoozefest."

I laughed harder this time. "In my experience, snoozefests are not nice, peaceful events. They are stressful. The event I had a couple of days ago was free, no tickets required, and no security. A man showed up and locked himself in the main bathroom. I had to get the manager to help me direct attendees to a bathroom on the second level. I finally managed to coax the man out and he was escorted from the hotel."

"That sounds like the opposite of a snoozefest."

"Definitely much more exciting than anyone had anticipated. I'd told the client that we needed security and tickets, but they didn't want the expense, so they didn't listen to me. It's annoying when you can see so clearly that something's going to go spectacularly bad and nobody believes you. Like I'm Cassandra."

"From Greek mythology?" he asked.

"Yes!" I said, pleased he got my reference. "I used to really love Greek mythology. I even participated in my school's Language Arts Day team and it was my specialty."

"I briefly considered majoring in classical antiquity in college."

"You're lying."

He grinned. "I'm not. I have the textbooks at home to prove it."

I realized that I didn't know where he lived. That seemed like something friends should know about each other. "Where are you staying?"

"We're here," he said, opening the door for me to go into the bar. It was an elegant place and was surprisingly quiet, given how many people were seated. We went over to two empty chairs at the bar and were immediately greeted by a bartender. Max ordered a cabernet sauvignon and I asked for a glass of chardonnay, since it was the drink that Max assumed I would order the first night we met and it seemed fitting to have it now.

Max turned to face me. Our knees were brushing against each other and the contact sent pulses of warmth through me.

"Did you enjoy your evening of being objectified as a glorified photo prop?" I asked him.

"It was strange."

"Definitely weird, but the client liked it. And it's not even the weirdest thing I've done to make a client happy. I once had to drive a live turkey from Connecticut into the city because someone wanted to pardon a turkey at their Thanksgiving event. He rode in the passenger seat. And I didn't have a valid license or car insurance."

"How do you drive without a license or car insurance?"

"Very slowly," I said, and he laughed.

The bartender brought over our wine. We thanked him and I took a sip. Okay, a large gulp. The effect was immediate and I could feel myself relaxing.

"This hits the spot. And just so you know, this is probably wasted on me. Wine is wine to me."

"You mean you can't pick out the region and year the grapes were harvested?" he teased in mock horror.

"No," I said, swirling it around in my glass. "All I'm picking up are subtle notes of 'not from Walmart.'"

He laughed and rested his free hand on the back of my chair.

"So if I wanted to say I loved the wine in Italian, how would I say it?" I asked.

"Italian is not like English. If you say you love pizza and you love your mom, even though those two feelings are different, you use the same word. In Italian we use 'ti voglio bene' when you're talking about tender affection you have for family or friends. You'd use 'ti amo' for someone you're really in love with. Same thing in Spanish with 'te quiero' and 'te amo.'"

"Then I ti amo this wine," I said. I was also probably ti amo–ing him a little bit as well.

He grinned. "I'm really glad I got to see you tonight."

"Why is that?" I asked.

"I enjoyed seeing you in your element. You were born to do this. You told me once that you didn't have a superpower, but you're wrong. This is it. Your ability to lead, to calm other people down, to create beauty from nothing, to make everything work seamlessly. You're incredible."

"Thank you," I breathed. I didn't know what else to say. I gripped the bar to keep myself from reaching for him.

"I'm also glad that I got to see you because I have to leave in the morning."

That was like a bucket of ice being poured over my head. "Where are you going?"

"There's a potential donor who might make a sizable donation, but he's out in Los Angeles and has to be wooed."

There was no one on the planet better equipped to woo than Max Colby. "How long will you be gone?"

"For a few days. I'll be back in time for Sunny's baby shower." He seemed to be studying my face, as if he were searching for something.

"I still can't believe you got her mother-in-law to invite men to the shower."

"She was easy enough to convince."

I believed that he'd had zero issues on that front. I was surprised she hadn't signed over the deed to that palatial apartment of hers to him, too.

He was going to be gone for only a few days, but I hated the thought that he wouldn't be around. I still had an actual mountain of work to do, but I liked knowing that if I wanted to see him, I could.

I realized that I was going to miss him. "You're not going to find another tour guide out there, are you?"

He moved closer to me. "There's only one tour guide for me."

That made my heart feel sparkly and light and I didn't care if I was reading into it. If he flirted with every woman with a pulse. All I cared about was being with him.

"Then let me show you something."

CHAPTER TWENTY-SEVEN

"I've seen the Empire State Building before," Max said as we stood on the sidewalk, looking up toward the top.

"From the main deck observatory?" I asked. "It is my duty as your official New York City tour guide to take you up there. I'll lose my fake license if I don't. Come on."

"Isn't it closed?"

It was well after midnight, so it was a good question. "It's okay. I know a guy."

"Of course you do," he said with an amused grin.

We went into the lobby and were greeted by my friend Hollis. "Hey, Hollis!"

He whooped and then wrapped me into a big bear hug. We were little more than acquaintances if I was being honest, but our common geographical background had bonded us.

"How are you, Everly-darlin'?"

"I'm good." He put me down and shook hands with Max as they introduced themselves.

"How did you two meet?" Max asked, and was it my imagination, or did I detect a tiny note of jealousy?

"At a corporate event where Hollis was working security," I said. "I heard his accent and asked where he was from. He grew up about half an hour away from my hometown and so this made us instant friends. We've kept in touch."

"I'm lucky that I get to call her a friend. Everly is the sweetest girl east of the Mississippi," Hollis said, grinning at me.

"Don't I know it," Max said, his hand tightening around mine.

"Thank you for letting us in after hours," I said to Hollis, telling the part of me that was thrilled by Max's little display of possessiveness to knock it off.

It didn't listen.

"My pleasure, Everly-darlin'." He handed me a key and told me it would open the door to the observation deck.

"Thank you!"

Max and I went over to the elevator and I pushed the button for the eighty-sixth floor.

"Your accent's back," he said.

"Hollis brings it out in me." The security guard's accent was so thick that I couldn't keep my own from emerging.

As the elevator climbed, I remembered earlier, when Max had told me he wanted to talk to me after the party. I wondered if he still did and what he would say. It concerned me because I knew that if we had The Talk, this would all end, and I wasn't ready to lose him.

Max was such a good guy that once he knew that I had developed serious, real feelings for him, that would be it. He wouldn't lead me on. And how could we continue to be just friends when I was head over heels for him? He would back off.

I didn't ask about his dinner with Arabella, the other women in his phone, how he spent his evenings, or where he thought things might go between us. There was so much that I wanted to say, to know, but not at the expense of not having him in my life.

Which was cowardly—I knew that—but no one had ever accused me of too much bravery.

I tried to encourage myself. WWKD? Would she let this opportunity pass her by? Or would she seize the day? Maybe if I couldn't speak the words, there was another way to let him know how I felt.

I unlocked the door and we walked out onto the deck. It was entirely enclosed, but we were very high up.

"This is a great view," he said as he walked over to the edge of the deck, looking out into the night sky. He stood there for a moment before returning to where I had pressed myself against the wall. He laced his fingers through mine.

"A lot of television shows and movies have been filmed here," I said as my heart rate increased, knowing what I was about to do. "On a clear day you can see six states."

"You're taking this tour-guide thing seriously. How are you doing with the height thing?"

"I'm okay because I'm with you."

I saw the moment his expression shifted. The smile fell slowly off his face, replaced by a far more serious and intent one.

"Oh?"

Gulping, I nodded. "But the view and movie stuff is not all this deck is known for."

Okay. This was it. Time to lay all my cards on the table.

"It's apparently good luck to kiss someone here."

The air solidified in my lungs while I waited for his reply.

A smile played at the edge of his lips and he looked extremely interested. "Really?"

"Uh-huh." I wondered if he could feel my clammy anticipation, the fear that coursed through me as I worried that this was all going to turn out badly.

"Do you bring a lot of men up here to kiss?" Now he was teasing me.

"I haven't kissed anyone since I moved to New York," I confessed. It was an embarrassing revelation that I hadn't intended to share with him, but given how ramped up I was, it slipped out.

"That's too long to go without kissing someone." He shifted his body closer to mine. "You should absolutely kiss somebody."

"Any suggestions?" My mouth had gone completely dry and it was hard to talk.

"I'm not busy," he said with a deceptively innocent shrug. "And if we kissed, then we wouldn't tempt fate to give us bad luck."

"Definitely," I agreed.

"I need to ask you something first," he said. He paused for three long heartbeats and then asked, "How do you feel when you're with me?"

I wasn't sure how to answer him. I felt so very many things when I was with him. Was he looking for something specific? I didn't know.

So I finally settled on, "Safe."

"That's good," he said as he smiled softly, somehow managing to move even closer to me. He reached up to trace the outlines of my face with his fingertips and my heart nearly exploded in my chest from anticipation. "But first . . ."

He was still holding my right hand, and he turned me into a spin and then pulled me tight against his chest.

"What are you doing?"

"I wanted to make sure you had courage first from your Wonder Woman spin."

Shaking my head, I said, "I never should have told you about that."

"Probably not." He grinned at me.

That spin had me feeling a bit disoriented, which was bad, given that I knew his kisses were going to make my balance situation worse.

"Everly." He said my name reverently, like a prayer and a wish combined, and it disconnected my legs from my body so that I felt like I was floating. His eyes roamed over my face, and there was the look I'd been waiting for since the first night we'd met. Desire, lust, a promise that he was about to take me in his arms and kiss me senseless.

There was no mistaking it. I wasn't imagining things or hallucinating. It was very real.

A heaviness pressed against me, the type that came from sharing this sort of wanting gaze. My pulse beat slow and thick. Despite the fact that it was freezing outside, my body flushed and I was hot all over, like it was noon and the sun was beating down on me.

He nuzzled his nose against mine, frustratingly ghosting his lips over my mouth. I realized that he was giving me a chance to change my mind, even though I was the one who had orchestrated this entire thing.

I wasn't going to change my mind. I wanted him to kiss me so badly my teeth ached.

He reached up to cup my face, and I noted that his hands seemed to be slightly trembling, as if he wanted this as badly as I did. His thumbs stroked my cheeks while he continued to keep his tantalizing lips just out of reach. He was bewitching my hormones and my soul.

I knew he was taking his time, drawing it out, and I didn't know if that was a good thing or a bad thing. My body voted for bad as it had waited far too long for this moment. He did not need to ratchet up the tension—I was about ready to burst from desperate longing.

"Do you want me to kiss you, Everly?" he asked, the words warm against my lips. I knew why he was asking. This was going to change things. If there was a friendship boundary line, we were about to irrevocably cross it.

"Yes, kiss me." Three one-syllable words. And they were like a match that sparked a flame.

Because his mouth finally descended to mine and the first thing I thought was, *Vella was wrong.*

She had incorrectly surmised that because he was bad at dancing, he'd be bad at kissing, but I was personally discovering that she couldn't have been further off. He had zero coordination or rhythm problems while he kissed me mindless.

His touch was warm and gentle. As far as first kisses went, it was pretty perfect. Like someone had scripted it, directed it, and Max was the award-winning actor who'd been hired solely for his on-screen kissing skills.

It was more than just a kiss. It was like an answer to every question I'd had since I'd met him.

His touch, his kiss, was soft and gentle. Perfect. He held me tight, like I was something precious and special to him. I'd never done drugs, never had the desire to. But if there was a drug that was like kissing him, I might have reconsidered my stance.

"Max," I whispered, in complete awe. "You're really good at this."

I felt his mouth curl up in a smile against my sensitized lips, and then he moved to trace my jawline with the tip of his nose. "Why do you sound so surprised?"

"Vella thought you'd be bad at it. But I knew."

"Knew what?" he breathed, pressing a delicate kiss to my jaw.

I sighed blissfully. "I knew it would be like this."

"So did I," he said before his lips devoured mine, creating shivers that moved in waves up and down my spine.

His kiss was more intense now, and I arched against him, a soft moan escaping from the back of my throat. I parted my lips as an invitation and he eagerly accepted, deepening the kiss. He ignited liquid fire in my stomach and it spread slowly to all of my limbs, burning as it went.

I felt his desire in his kiss. That he wanted me. It was undeniable.

It was also too much.

A still-functioning but frantic part of my brain warned me to protect myself. I didn't want Max and me to be caught up in some fantasy, kissing on the Empire State Building in formal wear. I wanted him to kiss me because I was Everly, and for no other reason.

I pulled my head back slightly. He didn't release his hold on me and took the opportunity to press heated kisses to my cheeks, the corners of my neck, the delicate parts of my earlobe.

"Why didn't you kiss me before this?" I asked, aware of how breathless my voice sounded. "Is all of this because I wore some makeup? The dress?"

That got him to stop kissing me. He still held me close, our chests moving in unison, our hearts thundering against each other. "Is that what you think?"

I shrugged, not able to say the words.

He pressed a soft kiss to my lips and then immediately retreated. "That's not why I kissed you. I kissed you because you finally let me. I would have kissed you every moment since we met if you'd let me." He kissed me again, brief, fleeting, gentle.

"Why?"

He smiled and shook his head like it was a silly question. "Because you are sexy and desirable and it's all I can do to keep my hands off of you."

"Even the morning of the royal wedding?" I asked, remembering how terrible I'd looked then.

He grinned. "Especially the morning of the royal wedding."

I didn't believe him, but it didn't matter. Even if he was saying this because he thought I wanted to hear it, I. Did. Not. Care.

I reached for him, pulling his mouth back to mine, and my stomach jumped when we collided against each other, hungry and wanting. It overwhelmed me, this sensation of my entire body being on fire, like somebody had replaced my bones with molten lava.

I'd predicted Mount Vesuvius and I had not been wrong.

It was so overwhelming, too much and not enough all at the same time. He seemed to sense what I was experiencing and quickly adapted to it. Like he could feel my hesitation and he backed off, gentling his kisses. But then when he intuited my need and enthusiasm for more, he deepened the kiss, engulfing my lips, moving against me in a way that had me panting and desperate for more.

This time he was the one who broke off the kiss, resting his forehead against mine. "I shouldn't be doing this."

My brain was so hazy and fuzzy I couldn't understand him. Why shouldn't he be doing it? I was very enthusiastically into it. Kissing him was the only thing I wanted.

The only thing that mattered.

"Yes, you should," I insisted.

"No, you don't understand—"

But I stole his words by kissing him hard and was rewarded with him groaning against my mouth, the sound reverberating deep in his chest. I showed him how much I'd been dreaming of this moment. I kissed him with all the longing I'd kept buried since we'd met.

He responded, flame calling to flame, burning hotter and higher until I thought I would melt away completely.

His fingers were in my hair, pressing against my scalp, down my neck and arms, creating prickly sensations everywhere he touched. His hand drifted down to my waist and pulled me against him. He turned me so that he could place me against the wall of the building, and I was grateful for the extra support.

Because this man kissing and holding me had caused me to lose touch with the parts of my brain that controlled speech and judgment.

Maybe it was the wine?

No, it wasn't the wine. It was all Max.

"Everly?" It was like an alarm bell suddenly sounded; we weren't alone. It took me a full ten seconds to realize that it hadn't been Max who had spoken my name.

We broke apart, both of us breathing hard, our chests heaving. I was glad to know I wasn't the only one affected this way.

I looked over Max's shoulder and saw Hollis grinning at me. He was the one who had called my name. "I'm about to go off shift. Y'all need to call it a night."

"We'll be there in a second," Max said, his voice sounding rough and tight. When he heard the door close, he turned his head toward me, taking in my face. "Are you good?"

Good? I was ecstatic. Euphoric. I was so far past good it wasn't even funny.

"Yes."

"We should go," he said, then pressed one last kiss on the tip of my nose. It was so adorably sweet and intimate that I shivered again. How long had we been outside? It could have been anywhere from twenty minutes to twenty years. That kiss had somehow simultaneously lasted an eternity and was over far too soon.

He took me by the hand and we met Hollis just past the door. I returned the key and he locked the door and then we all rode the elevator down together. Hollis was speaking, but I couldn't hear him.

My lips were tingling and I reached up to touch them with my fingertips, still in awe over what had just happened between Max and me. I caught him watching me and his expression told me that he wished his lips were doing the exploring instead of my fingers.

I caught my breath and his eyes were lidded, heavy. I could see him breathing faster. His cheek twitched like he was clenching his jaw tightly, barely containing himself.

"Here we are! Y'all have fun," Hollis said when we returned to the first floor, and I heard the teasing in his tone.

"Thank you again," I said, amazed at my ability to walk and speak at the same time.

"Y'all come back anytime!" he said cheerfully as he walked us through the lobby. "Good night!"

I think I returned his farewell, but I wasn't sure. When Max and I got outside, I wondered what would happen now. I didn't want to be separated from him and I knew he felt the same way.

He signaled for a cab and one came over to the curb. He opened the door for me and I got in, scooting over to make room for him. Where would we go now? I was both excited and a bit nervous about what would happen next.

But Max leaned his head in through the open door and told the cab driver my address and then said to me, "I have to get up early for my flight. We'll talk soon."

He closed the door, and the cab pulled away from the curb before I could respond.

What had just happened?

CHAPTER
TWENTY-EIGHT

"Aw, you're home," Vella said with as much disappointment as I was currently feeling.

"Hello to you, too. I do still live here." I dropped my bag on the floor and kicked off my shoes, not even attempting to clean up after myself. I was too depressed.

"I was kind of hoping you'd be having such a good time with Max that you wouldn't come home at all."

A disbelieving sound escaped me, and I reached behind my back for my zipper. I wanted to take this dress off and get rid of it. Maybe I'd burn it. While I was struggling, she gasped.

"You kissed Max!"

I froze. "How can you possibly know that?"

"It was from that time I was training to be a psychic."

"You can't train . . ." I trailed off, not willing to argue. I was too defeated. "Can you please help me with my zipper?"

"Sure," she said, coming up behind me to tug it down. "Too bad Max isn't the one doing it."

"I don't think he would want to," I said with a huge amount of self-pity. With a whoosh, my dress slipped off me, puddling onto the floor. I put on a shirt and yoga pants. Vella was staring holes into my back, obviously wanting me to explain myself.

Now that I wasn't in his arms, it was easy to question everything. It was hard to believe that we'd even kissed, like it had been some kind of waking dream or fevered hallucination. How could he kiss me like that and just put me in a taxi?

Maybe he'd enjoyed himself but hadn't wanted me to get the wrong idea.

And if I was just one of many, as I suspected, it wouldn't have meant anything to him. It would have been no big deal. Just another make-out at another New York City tourist attraction. He probably did it all the time and it hadn't fazed him.

While I felt like my entire world had just completely shifted and been irrevocably altered.

I'd been in the midst of a hormonal Chernobyl, and he'd sent me away without a second thought.

What if he regretted it? Thought it had been a mistake to kiss me?

So many unanswered questions.

"You did kiss him, right?" she asked.

I collapsed onto the couch. My poor spinal column had had too much excitement for one night and could no longer keep me upright. "Yes. We definitely kissed. Like, a lot."

Vella went over to the windows and looked outside.

"What are you doing?" I asked.

"Making sure that there isn't a plague of locusts or a hail firestorm signaling the end of the world. Because I thought that was where we'd have to be before you finally kissed him."

I didn't even smile, and this seemed to alarm her. "Do I need to take my superglue over to Max's place?"

"No."

She sat next to me. "So, are you two like, together now?"

"We just kissed. People can kiss and it doesn't mean anything."

"*Other* people can kiss and have it not mean anything. Not you."

"Okay, you're right," I conceded. "But I don't know what's going on. He kissed me and then he didn't say anything else. He just put me in a cab, mentioned he had an early-morning flight, and sent me home."

"What was he supposed to say? I know it's been a while for you, but guys don't usually give a relationship speech after they kiss you."

I reached for the blanket folded up on the arm of the couch and put it over me. "I'm just confused. Does he like me? Or is he only attracted to me? Does he want something more? Or to casually kiss from time to time while still being just friends?"

"Did you ask him?"

"No, my brain was a little scrambled."

"I'll bet his was, too. And I'll bet that he is interested in more."

I hadn't expected her to defend him or to choose the optimistic route. "Just because we made out doesn't mean he wants to be with me. You know that better than anyone."

"I do." She nodded. "But given that I can't read minds yet, I can't tell you what Max does or doesn't want beyond this. Maybe he's only looking for somebody to hook up with, but he doesn't seem the type. Although he is really good-looking, so we can't rule that possibility out completely."

I was absorbing what she'd said when she added, "But if that was all he was after, he would probably choose someone who is less of a challenge."

"Hey!"

She shrugged. "I'm just saying you're not a casual-hookup kind of person, and he has to know that."

He did know that, in excruciating detail. I'd shared so much of my not-at-all-sordid past with him. I put my hands over my face and let out a groan. "Him and I kissing is basically all your fault."

"How am I to blame? I mean, I accept the actual possibility that I might be, but how?"

I moved my hands and gestured at my head. "You made me look like Queen Katerina and that's the only reason he kissed me."

Vella was looking at me like I was stupid. "Are you serious?"

He had reassured me that it wasn't the reason earlier, but I wasn't feeling particularly rational at the moment. "Yes!"

"Max liked you long before I slapped some mascara and blush on you."

I just grumbled in reply, burrowing myself deeper under the blanket.

"Did you ever see that movie *Dumbo*?" she asked.

It was such a random question, so far from what we'd been talking about, that it kind of snapped me out of my funk. "I have."

"Dumbo didn't need a feather to fly. It was just a prop. You don't have to do your hair and makeup like that queen, or wear clothes like her, to be your best self or to have Max be interested in you. You've always had the ability to fly."

It was one of the nicest things that Vella had ever said to me. "Aww," I said, and she gave me a disgusted look.

"This is the last nice conversation I'm going to have for the rest of the week, so listen up. Don't read too much into tonight. Ask him about it. I mean, maybe there is a possibility that his flight really does leave early in the morning." She immediately stopped herself with a grimace. "Yeah, I heard it. It was an excuse."

"I don't know if I'm ready to have that talk with him."

"If nothing else, you have to take back your edict."

"My what?" I asked.

"You're the one who told him that you wanted to be friends. You need to tell him you changed your mind."

That was entirely possible. She'd pointed it out previously—that maybe he was just being a gentleman and taking me at my word. It scared me to undo it, though. This way was safer, but it was also making me sadder.

"You need to think about what that Kitty person would do."

It took me a second. "Kitty? Do you mean Kat?"

"Same difference," she said. "First you have to figure out what you want. Do you want to be in a relationship with him? I think you do.

228

Decide, and then go talk to him like an actual grownup and have a real conversation about your feelings. If you want to be in a relationship with him, tell him and deal with the fallout."

"I don't know if that's what Kat would do," I said, because she didn't know that it wasn't an apt comparison. "She ran away from Nico when she thought he had rejected her."

And I understood her fear all too well. Because if Max told me *no thanks, not interested*, I was going to crawl into a deep, dark hole and try to disappear completely.

"Why do you like Kat so much? I mean, seriously. Is it that she's a queen? Or is it something else?" Vella asked.

"I admire her. I like that she has her fairy-tale love story."

"There it is," she said, jabbing her finger toward me. "What you like about her is that she's living happily ever after and you want that. Which is not a bad thing to want. It's not for me, but I can understand the appeal. What you want is a successful relationship. Not a castle and ball gowns."

Huh. I'd never examined it that deeply, but I suspected that Vella was right. "Maybe you should reconsider that psychology career."

"Oh no, it would involve way too much of me having to listen to other people talk about their stupid problems and boring lives and I am not interested in that."

"Except for me."

"Except for you and only you. And don't tell anybody."

I made an *X* across my heart. "It just seems a shame because you're so intuitive and smart."

"That's because I've had more higher education than actual professors," she said, and I finally smiled. "You just give me the word and his hair is literal toast."

"Okay. Thank you."

She nodded with satisfaction and got up. "I'm going to bed. If you hear a drill early in the morning, don't worry about it—I'm just making a hole into the neighbors' apartment so that I can drop some stink bombs through the wall."

Now I finally did laugh as she walked away. She always managed to make me feel better.

Until tonight, I would have said the same thing about Max, that he always made me feel better. I had always loved being around him—if he were a song, I would have put him on a loop and happily listened to him all day.

But now I was confused and distraught. Dating really was like a foreign country where I didn't understand the language or the customs. And Vella, who lived there permanently, didn't seem to understand my situation any better.

Which did not bode well.

I would take her advice. I needed to figure out what I wanted and then communicate that to Max.

If it meant that I lost his friendship, that would truly suck.

But what would suck worse was never knowing if we could have had more.

~

I spent the rest of the weekend working and got to the office a little bit early on Monday morning. Vella had yelled through her door that she'd see me there later, and I hoped that by *later* she meant *at a point that might still be considered relatively on time.*

Claudia usually arrived right at nine o'clock, and I wanted to be at my desk, just in case. She wasn't in yet, though.

My desk phone rang a few minutes after I sat down. "This is Everly Aprile."

"It's Mom."

I frowned. She didn't usually call me at work. "Is everything okay? Is Meemaw doing all right?"

"She's fine. You haven't been answering your phone."

That was because I had turned it off. I had been working the last couple of days, but I'd also been thinking about what I wanted to do as far as Max was concerned and I didn't want any outside distractions.

Plus, it had been my cowardly way of avoiding having to speak or interact with him before I was ready.

My decision-making might have all been for nothing—he could have just ghosted me entirely, and then the decision would have been taken out of my hands.

That thought made me feel sick to my stomach. I didn't want him to ditch me.

So I'd avoided giving him a choice by making myself inaccessible. He couldn't ghost me if I was unaware of it.

Not exactly mature, but it had helped me to get a lot of work done.

I turned my cell phone back on and waited a few seconds until it was on. There were a bunch of texts from my mom, a couple of missed phone calls, but nothing at all from Max. Complete and total silence.

My heart fell. I had thought I mattered to him, had hoped that the kisses meant something, but they obviously hadn't. He couldn't have made it any clearer that he wasn't interested in me. That the kisses had been some kind of mistake that would never happen again.

I wanted to start crying.

"Sorry about that," I said to my mother. "What's up?"

"I was calling to see if you got the promotion."

"Mom, it's first thing Monday morning. Nobody else is even here yet. And it'll be a long process." There would be a lot of people who'd have to sign off on it.

"Well, when that Claudia woman arrives, you should go into her office and insist that you talk about it right away."

I tried to not feel completely exasperated with her. That was not how things worked here.

This was the first time my mom and I had chatted since Princess Chiara got married. We'd had an hour-long conversation about the wedding where we'd discussed what everyone had been wearing, how

Princess Violetta seemed to be glowing and had briefly touched her stomach, making us wonder if she might be pregnant, and how Princess Serafina had been on her phone the entire time but tried to hide it from the cameras.

It had been such a fun talk—I wished we could always be like that. I wished that I could talk to her about Max and have her listen, really listen, just so that I could vent. Maybe she'd even have some insight to share and a guess as to why he'd been so weird.

I didn't tell her, though, because I knew how things would go.

"Good morning, doll. Can I see you in my office?"

My mouth dropped open.

Adrian Stone was here and heading toward his desk like he hadn't disappeared for the last two weeks.

"Mom, I have to go. I'll call you later." I hung up the receiver in its cradle, not even bothering to let her respond.

Adrian. It was so weird seeing him. I realized with a start that I hadn't thought about him at all for a long time.

Like I had shoved him completely out of my mind.

He sat down at his desk and turned his computer on. When I entered the room, he said, "Please shut the door."

In all the time I'd worked here, he'd never asked me to do that. I closed the door until it latched into place. I sat down across from him, suddenly a bit nervous. Did he know how Claudia was changing things? Was he going to blame me for it? Be upset that I didn't keep him updated on what was happening at Elevated?

I was glad to see him again, but it was different. I still thought he was handsome, but that fluttery feeling I used to get every time I saw him?

It was gone.

That feeling now belonged to someone else.

But maybe it had been an out-of-sight, out-of-mind situation. What if those feelings came back now that he had returned?

"I wanted to ask you to have dinner with me tonight," he said.

A lance of shock pierced me. "What?"

"Dinner. Tonight. Me." He was being playful and flirtatious. He'd never treated me that way before and I didn't know how to take it.

I wondered if it was even appropriate, given that he was my boss.

As if he could read my mind, he said, "I've already disclosed to HR that I intended to ask you out, if you're worried about that."

I felt like somebody had punched me hard, knocking the wind out of me. I didn't understand what was happening.

Adrian had just strolled back into my life as if he'd never left, and then asked me to have dinner with him?

Maybe I was misunderstanding his intent. "Dinner? Did you want to talk about work?"

"I am asking you on a date," he said. "So that we're clear."

Adrian Stone wanted to take me on a date?

CHAPTER
TWENTY-NINE

Absolutely nothing was clear right now. In fact, him "clarifying" was only making me more confused. "What about Colette?"

A look of pain crossed his face, but it quickly disappeared. "She and I are done."

There was obviously a lot more to that story, but there wasn't time to ask about it now. Adrian was waiting for an answer.

An answer to him asking me on an official date. Something he'd planned to do before he'd ever stepped foot in the office today, given that he'd already told HR.

Unlike Max, who was kissing me while still having dinner with his ex-girlfriend—and who knew what he was getting up to in Los Angeles, how many dates he'd gone on. He hadn't even bothered to reach out to me while he was gone. He wasn't being clear about his intentions with me at all.

And I preferred this.

It was everything I'd hoped for since I'd started working here, but there was no joy here, no excitement.

Just an aching hollowness.

Maybe that would change if I accepted.

"Yes," I said cautiously. "I'd like to have dinner with you."

"Great! How about eight o'clock at my apartment?"

"Sure." I nodded. I waited for a beat, but that hollowness didn't go away. If anything, it got worse.

"Thanks, doll. Can you close the door on your way out?"

I got up, my body feeling unbearably light. Like I was no longer tethered to reality.

I couldn't believe Adrian had finally asked me on a date.

Or that I'd agreed to go.

He buzzed me when I sat down at my desk. I pushed the intercom button. "Yes?"

"I'm going to send over a list of things I need you to get done today."

"Okay."

He hung up his phone and I still had that unreal feeling. An email from Adrian came into my inbox, and I glanced at the very long list. There were a lot of things he had to catch up on. The first item was to order a large bouquet of flowers and have them delivered to the office. He was probably going to give them to Claudia to apologize for taking off for so long. It wouldn't be the first apology bouquet I'd ordered for him.

I went online to my favorite local florist's website and placed the order. The whole time all I could think about was what I had just done and whether or not it had been a mistake. My cell phone rang and my heart leapt with excitement when I saw who it was.

Max was calling me.

I ran into the conference room and closed the door. I wanted privacy.

"Hello?" I said, my heartbeat thundering in my chest. I'd missed him so much.

"Everly? How are you?"

My hands were shaking so bad that I dropped my phone. I swore and grabbed it off the floor and put it on the table. I put it on speakerphone and said, "I'm sorry, I dropped the phone."

"No problem. I was calling to see how things were going. Was your boss happy about the event?"

My boss? Did he mean Adrian? Did he know what had just happened? That was ridiculous. There was no way Max could possibly be aware that Adrian had asked me out on an official date. But it was where my worried mind went. It shouldn't have, though. Max and I were supposed to be just friends.

Right?

But why was he calling me now? Why hadn't he called me at all over the last two days? This just seemed so random.

Or like he somehow knew what I'd just agreed to.

"I haven't seen Claudia yet." I hesitated, not knowing what else to say. Should I tell him? It felt cowardly not to. He'd had no problem telling me about his date with his evil, stupid ex-girlfriend.

But if things really had changed between us . . .

The conference door suddenly swung open and Adrian leaned in. "Everly? What kind of food do you want for our date tonight?"

My mouth dropped open, my pulse hammering so hard in my wrist that I could actually see it, and I glanced down at the phone, fervently wishing that it might have somehow turned itself off.

It didn't.

Max was still there and presumably had heard every word.

Adrian waited for an answer, and I pressed the mute button on my phone and told him, "I don't care. Whatever you want is fine."

He nodded and then closed the door. My heart was in my throat as I unmuted the call. "Max?"

"I'm here." His voice sounded completely different. There was a detachment, almost a coldness, in his voice.

I wanted to ask him if he'd heard Adrian, but then he said, "So you finally got that date with your boss? Congratulations. It's everything you wanted, right?"

My mind was floundering. How did I fix this? Max hadn't reached out to me until this morning. Maybe if I'd turned my phone on and seen a bunch of missed messages from him, I wouldn't have said yes to Adrian.

It wasn't fair to blame him. I had done this. And I didn't know how to undo it.

Tell him. I could actually hear Vella's voice in my mind, encouraging me to say something. But the fear was stronger and paralyzed me into not speaking.

I had to say something, had to explain. I had been so scared that Max would reject me and had wanted so desperately to protect myself that I'd allowed myself to get hurt even worse by not being honest about what I did and did not want.

"Yes, but it's not what you—"

He cut me off.

"I'm about to walk into a meeting, so if there's nothing else?"

"I just . . ." I let my voice trail off. What was I doing? "I'll let you go to your meeting," I said as my shoulders slumped, feeling defeated.

"Talk soon," he said, and hung up.

That didn't feel very relationship-y, either.

A skyscraper had settled in the pit of my stomach, making it difficult for me to breathe properly.

Why couldn't I just say what I wanted? Why was I always like this?

Right as I opened the conference room door, Rodrigo, one of the event designers, entered the room. "Hi, Everly. Did Claudia add you to the committee for the diplomat's anniversary party?"

"No, she didn't. I'm going to be there on Saturday night to help out, though."

He nodded and I added, "I was just making a phone call." I held my cell up like some kind of explanation.

From his expression I could see that I was doing it again. Explaining things that didn't need to be mentioned. I left the conference room and went back to my desk, intent on tackling the list that Adrian had created for me.

That phone call had gone so badly. I still didn't understand how Max could kiss me that way and then ignore me completely.

Maybe this was part of what I needed to figure out. That there might be nothing here and I needed to move on from Max.

Adrian laughed at something. That sound used to make me smile, but it wasn't having any effect on my current mood. It did cause me to pull up the company handbook to see the rules on dating coworkers.

Apparently he'd been right and we could go out, so long as we told Human Resources, which he had already done.

Before I'd even accepted.

What if I'd said no? He was my boss. Wouldn't it have made things really awkward for both of us if I'd turned him down?

I glanced at his office as I realized that he had fully expected me to say yes. It hadn't even occurred to him that I might reject him.

That bothered me.

I knew that he could be entitled and self-centered, but I couldn't help but compare him to Max. There wasn't anything about Max that was entitled or self-centered.

I was trying to work and sort out my feelings all at the same time when Vella buzzed me. "There are flowers for Adrian at the front desk."

"I'll come grab them." I hung up with her and called Adrian. "Your flowers have arrived. Do you want me to take them to Claudia?"

"No. They're for you."

"Me?" I turned my head sharply to look at him. He was leaning back in his chair, grinning at me.

"Yes, you. You didn't think I'd take you out without getting you flowers first, did you?"

He'd had me order flowers for myself? Again, I couldn't help but compare him to Max. Max never would have done that. The hollowness only intensified.

If Max had sent me flowers, it would have meant the world to me. Heck, I would have settled for a single text.

My world felt upside down.

"Thank you," I said, but I didn't mean the words. I didn't want flowers from Adrian.

"You're very welcome."

I hung up the phone and headed toward reception. When I reached Vella's desk, she asked, "Who got Adrian flowers?"

"They're for me," I said, trying to fake an enthusiasm I didn't feel.

She raised a single eyebrow at me. "Adrian, the human participation trophy, went through the effort of getting you flowers?"

"Technically he had me order them but didn't tell me that they were for me," I said. "How nice was that?"

"Zero percent."

"It's the thought that counts." I didn't believe it but I couldn't handle Vella making me feel worse about things.

"Yeah, I'm sure it takes a lot of thought to make a gesture this small, this late. He should have been buying you flowers every day for the last four years to thank you for being such an amazing assistant and for sacrificing so much for him. Why did he finally pony up?"

Just a few weeks ago, I would have been bursting at the seams to share my incredible news. I discovered that I did not want to tell her.

"Adrian asked me out on a date tonight and I accepted." I pushed my shoulders back, waiting for her response.

She just blinked at me a few times and then said, "I'm sorry, did you just say you were going on a date with a man who has the emotional capacity of a doorknob?"

"That's not—"

"What are you planning on doing with him on this *date*?" she demanded, cutting me off.

"We're going to have dinner at his apartment."

It was the first time I'd ever seen Vella look shocked. "You are going to his house, which is filled with sharks and snakes, and he's your employer with a shady past? That's not a date. That's a nineteenth-century Gothic novel. Don't do it."

"You told me to figure out what I wanted and that's what I'm doing," I said defensively. I knew she was upset because she cared about me, but the depth of her reaction surprised me. "I had a crush on Adrian for a long time. Maybe if I spend some time with him, I can figure out my feelings faster."

"That seems like a stupid way to work things out. Like jumping into the ocean to see whether or not you can swim," she said, shaking her head. "Is this because Max went out with his ex? Are you trying to even the score?"

"No." It wasn't, was it? I wasn't a vengeful or petty person. That didn't seem like something I would do, but what if it had been like, a subconscious thing? "Adrian is being up front about what he wants. Max isn't."

"And neither are you!" she practically shrieked. "When have you told Max anything about how you feel?"

She was right. I couldn't say as much, but I knew she was right. It wasn't fair that I expected him to share how he felt when I was too scared to do the same thing.

"Isn't Adrian engaged?" she demanded. "Weren't you supposed to be getting him a ring?"

I had honestly forgotten about that, and other than a couple of random texts from Adrian that had nothing to do with rings at all, he'd never brought it up again. I tried not to drop the ball on things like this, but I'd been so completely caught up in Max that I had totally blocked it out.

"Things are over with Colette," I said.

"So you elected yourself president of Reboundlandia?" A UPS driver arrived with a package, and she stopped her rant long enough to sign for it. But as soon as he was gone, she picked it right back up again. "What I don't get is why you're going on a date with Adrian when you're so pathetically in love with Max."

My heart started banging hard in my chest, preventing my lungs from drawing in breath.

In love with Max?

What?

CHAPTER THIRTY

"I'm not . . ." I tried to protest but couldn't finish my sentence. I wasn't in love with Max.

Right?

"Oh, you are."

"It's only been like, two weeks," I said, finally fixing on an argument she couldn't refute. "That's not long enough to fall in love with someone—that's an antibiotic cycle."

"Did you tell Max?"

Somehow my heart beat even faster and I was having a hard time swallowing. I could actually feel sweat breaking out on my lower back. "That I love him?"

"No, that you're going on this 'date,'" she said, making air quotes with her fingers.

"Not technically. I had him on speakerphone and he heard Adrian saying something about it. Max basically congratulated me."

"Of course he did. He's a good guy. He was sacrificing his own wants for yours. He probably thinks you have real feelings for Adrian and is trying to nobly step aside so that you can have what Max thinks you want."

Her words struck me and I had to sit down on the corner of her desk as I considered them.

Vella's tone softened. "He didn't respond like a fairy-tale prince. He didn't stop you. You wanted him to tell you not to go, that he loves you, too. You were playing a stupid game and now you've won a stupid prize—the man of your dreams stepping aside so you can be with someone who isn't worthy of you."

"You play games all the time." It wasn't much of a defense against what felt like very accurate and true statements, but it was all I had. I felt like I was about to collapse in on myself. What had I done?

"Right. And do you see me in a healthy, happy, long-term relationship? No. Which is good for me, but not for you. You want that fairy tale."

I did want it, but it seemed so far out of reach.

Impossible.

"What did Max say after he told you to go out with Lumpy?"

"He said he had to get to a meeting and he had to go." My voice sounded like I felt—disconnected, worried, unsure.

"At six in the morning?"

"No, it was like, nine."

"Did you forget about those pesky little things called time zones between here and California? If it was nine o'clock here, it was six there."

I had forgotten about the time difference. Had he just woken up? Maybe that was why he'd sounded so strange.

The phone rang and Vella picked up the receiver and immediately hung it back up.

"Aren't you supposed to answer that?"

"In a minute. I just want to know what you're going to do now that you're stuck between a rock and a hard cheese." At my blank expression she said, "Adrian *Stone* and Max *Colby*? Instead of being stuck between a rock and a hard place, I substituted it with *rock* and *a hard cheese*."

"Colby is not a hard cheese."

"I stand by my joke. Just like I'll stand by you no matter what choice you make. The right one or the stupid one."

The phone rang again and she said, "I better get that and blame the disconnect on a technical problem." She picked up the receiver. "Thank you for calling Elevated. This is Vella, how may I assist you?"

Part of me noted that I'd never heard her be so nice or professional before. The rest of my mind was a morass of confusion. She had hit me with so many bombs that I was still reeling from the blows.

That it had been a mistake to say yes to Adrian.

That some part of me had secretly been testing Max.

I headed back to my desk. I hadn't meant to test Max. It was what had happened, though. I had wanted him to tell me not to go out with Adrian.

It really rubbed me the wrong way that I had done it. My dad used to give my mom all kinds of tests to "prove" that she was a good wife to him. She always fell short, never reaching the impossible standard that he'd set, always failing.

And I had done the same thing to Max. It had been unintentional, but my intent didn't change what I'd done.

I sat down in my chair and thought of the biggest piece of ammunition that Vella had launched at me.

That I was in love with Max.

I had wanted to deny it but hadn't been able to.

Because I knew it was true. The butterflies with six-foot wingspans currently flapping in my stomach confirmed that I did love him. I didn't know when it had happened exactly, and I might have lived in denial about it for a long time if my best friend hadn't so forcefully pointed it out.

I'd never been in love before, but that was how I knew this was it. It was completely different than anything I'd previously experienced. There was an emotional connection between Max and me that I didn't quite understand, but I knew it was there.

I definitely lusted after him, but what I felt for him was so much more than that. He was, as Vella had pointed out, my dream man. Kind, affectionate, funny, smart, loyal, selfless, a total gentleman.

That he came in such a shiny package with such a delicious accent was just icing on the cake.

I drew in a shaky breath. Now what did I do? Max had lied to get off the phone with me.

If he had feelings for me, that must have hurt him.

But he'd never said anything to indicate that he wanted to be with me. And as Vella kept pointing out, neither had I. Yes, we'd kissed and it had been mind-bendingly fantastic. But it was possible to be attracted to someone and not actually want to date them.

I thought about what he would look like waking up in the morning, his dark hair ruffled, his face sleepy and soft. The rough stubble on his jaw, his bright blue eyes slowly blinking at me as he would say, "Hey," and pull me down next to him. He would hold me close while he nuzzled my hair, my cheek, and then finally capture my lips in a sweet but fiery kiss. His skin would be warm from sleep and I would melt into him.

Despite how messed up my brain currently was, even I knew that I probably shouldn't be imagining cuddling with one man while planning to go on a date with another.

~

I was again frozen by indecision, not sure what I should do, and so the end result was that I did nothing. I didn't reach out to Max to try to see where he was at, if there was a future for us.

To be fair, Max didn't contact me, either.

Part of me thought I should cancel my date with Adrian, but he was still my boss and I didn't know if there would be consequences for not showing up. This was why people didn't date their bosses. He had power over me that made me feel like I shouldn't refuse.

I didn't think he'd retaliate or make me uncomfortable if I rejected him—Adrian was a nice guy, just spoiled. I recognized that I'd put myself in an awkward position.

No position with you could ever be awkward.

Great. I was hearing Max flirting with me in my head while I knocked on Adrian's door.

Adrian answered and smiled at me. "Hey. Come on in."

I walked into his front room and was flooded with memories of Max. Where he'd sat on the couch. The spot in the kitchen where he'd slipped and fallen. The hallway where I'd smacked into him. The bathroom door where we'd brushed past each other.

How we'd spent the rest of that day together.

Why was I such a bonehead and here with Adrian instead of calling Max?

"Dinner is ready," Adrian said, and I resented him interfering with me thinking about Max.

We walked over to his table and I knew the restaurant he'd ordered it from. I was surprised he hadn't had me order it for him.

I felt chastened over my unkind thought. He had gone to a bit of trouble for me and I should appreciate that at least. We both sat down and I realized that I hadn't said anything yet.

"It looks delicious."

"It does. Dig in."

This was weird. There was a strange vibe here that made it impossible for me to relax. I'd always felt comfortable at Adrian's place, if a bit in awe of it, but now it was like I'd discovered that I was a triangle peg that no longer fit into the square holes here.

"Hey doll, can you pass me the salt?"

I handed it to him and tried to tamp down my annoyance. He was calling me *doll* again. He probably meant it as an endearment, and once upon a time, that was how I'd seen it.

But now it felt demeaning.

Because I realized that I *had* been Adrian's doll. Never speaking up for myself, being there whenever he felt like playing with me, doing whatever I could to please him and make his life easier. I wasn't myself when I was with him. I was just waiting around on a shelf for him to pick me up when he was ready.

I'd had no life outside of the one he'd given me.

I knew everything there was to know about Adrian. How he liked his coffee, what laundry detergent his housekeeper used. What sports teams' games he recorded and his waist size in pants.

I'd had a crush based on nothing.

Because while I knew all those details, I didn't know him as a person.

Not like I did Max.

Adrian wasn't a bad guy. He was just completely different from me. He didn't understand me the way that Max did.

This was a big mistake.

"You're being awfully quiet," he said.

It was true. "I wouldn't let you watch my puppy for a weekend. Or have two drinks with you."

He was completely confused. "I don't understand."

"What happened with Colette?" I asked.

His face fell. "I don't know. Things were going so well, and out of nowhere she decided that I wasn't as serious about our relationship as she was and she broke up with me. I was going to propose to her. I flew across an ocean to meet her family. I dropped everything in my life to go with her to France. How could she think that I wasn't as serious about her?"

"Did you tell her?"

"Why would I have to tell her? She should have been able to see from my actions how much I love her." He paused. "Loved her. Past tense. It's over."

"I don't think it is. Colette needs the words. Actions aren't enough. Tell her that you love her. That you were going to propose. You should go and fix things with her. I can tell that you don't really want me here. You miss her."

He gave me a wry smile. "I knew you had a crush on me. I probably asked you out tonight to stroke my ego a little."

"Used to have a crush," I corrected him. "And I think I had it for so long because you weren't available and commitment has always been scary to me. But I'm in love with someone else. And I think I said yes to you because I was unfairly testing him. I wanted him to tell me not to come, but he didn't. And I didn't use my words, either. I was trying to push him into the response I wanted instead of talking about my feelings."

I stood up. There was no point in staying here and continuing this farce. "I think we should call it a night. Don't lose Colette. If you want, I will order her the biggest and best bouquet of flowers tomorrow. She's the best thing that's ever happened to you."

Adrian smiled at me. "You're a close second. I hope you know that you're an important person in my life."

I was his assistant, nothing more, nothing less. I'd never really mattered to him outside of what I could do for him. I'd made his life as easy as possible. No wonder I was so important to him. But it was kind of him to say as much, no matter how deluded it was.

Then he wrecked what little goodwill I had toward him when he added on, "You've always been so reliable and sturdy. Like a good workhorse."

He saw me as a farm animal. Max treated me like I was sexy and desirable, and Adrian thought I was Mr. Ed.

I didn't tell him that, though. There was no point in insulting him when I was hoping to get promoted. "Thanks, Adrian."

He walked me to the door and we said good night. I briefly wondered if it was the shortest date on record as I walked down the long hallway to the elevators.

I thought of what Vella had said earlier—how I had sacrificed so much for Adrian. Over and over again I'd given him the absolute best of me, giving up so much of my unpaid free time to make him happy, hoping to get some tiny compliment from him.

What had I sacrificed for Max, a man I was actually in love with?

Some of my time in planning the baby shower for his cousin, but I could have done that in my sleep, and I was getting paid for it.

I hadn't given up anything for him.

Maybe it was time that I sacrificed something for Max. My dignity, my fear and insecurities, my sense of self-preservation.

No more putting it off. I was going to be open and honest with the man I loved.

CHAPTER
THIRTY-ONE

There was no word from Max for the rest of the week, and despite me just resolving to do better, I was still too much of a chicken to reach out. I was worried that anything I tried to say in a text would come out wrong and be forever committed to a screen, where I'd have to relive my stupidity over and over again. I wanted to talk to him in person.

I also wanted him to want to talk to me, and his silence made me think that he didn't.

My heart ached and twisted at the thought that things with Max might be over before they'd even started.

The one positive I was currently clinging to was that he had said he was attending Sunny's baby shower. I was going to get to see him there.

I went over early in the morning to the Belmonts' penthouse and quickly realized what our first issue of the day would be.

It was so windy outside that there was no way we could have the event out on their grand terrace. It would knock everything over, send linens flying off the tables, and all of the carnival booths would be flattened.

Rain and snow I could manage and work around. But there was no work-around for wind. Everything would have to be inside.

I had the equipment guys bring everything in. I tracked down Sunny's mother-in-law, Margot, and explained the situation. I told her that I would need to move all the furniture out of the bottom floor so that we could decorate it properly.

"We have guest rooms on the second level, at the top of the stairs, that you can store everything in," she said.

I had been worried she might be upset, but she seemed very understanding and I was grateful for it. After I'd shared the new plans with the movers, installers, lighting techs, and drapery guys, I went into the kitchen to check in with the caterer, Jeanine, to see how things were going.

"Two servers didn't show up this morning," she said. "Not detrimental, but not ideal."

"With this crowd and everything shifting around, we are going to need as much help as possible. Let me make a phone call."

I really had to find more friends than just Vella. She was going to get sick of me asking her for help. She mumbled, "What?" when she answered her phone.

"Do you want to earn some money today as a cater-waiter?"

"It depends. Is this the party that Max is going to be at?"

What difference did that make? "Yes."

"I'm there. Black pants, white dress shirt?"

I glanced into the kitchen. "That is what the other servers are wearing. I'll send you the address. Also, you can't punch anybody in the throat."

"I'm not going to do that." She paused. "Again."

I hung up and texted her the address. I was just going to have to hope that she would behave. Vella arrived when I was helping the balloon supplier gather up some of the balloons that had come free of the arch at the entrance. She slipped her arm through mine and dragged me away with her.

"Have you seen Max yet?"

"Not yet." I was full of bubbly, nervous energy at seeing him again. I couldn't stop tapping my foot every time I thought about him.

Which was constantly and was interfering with my ability to do my job.

"I'm just glad you dumped Lumpy and have publicly admitted you don't have feelings for him. The riddance, it is good."

I couldn't disagree with her there.

"And you're doing a little revenge dressing, I see."

That had me glancing down at my outfit. I'd chosen a black dress. I had picked it so that I would blend in with the staff while still looking professional. The thing that was important about it was that Kat had never worn a dress similar to this one. Like my best friend had said, I didn't need it.

I could face Max and have this conversation with him without relying on my feather to help me fly.

"Revenge dressing?" I repeated. "Is that what you use on the salad of your enemy?"

"At least you're joking again," she said with a note of relief in her voice. It was a fair judgment—I'd been serious and focused all week. I kept running conversations with Max in my head, trying to figure out what I would say to him. What he might say back to me.

No matter how many times I practiced it, though, I knew the first time I laid eyes on him, he was going to knock me off my feet.

"But when I said 'revenge dressing,' I meant you're going to get your revenge on that man ghosting you by looking so amazing he's going to trip over his own dropped jaw."

"This is why we're best friends," I told her.

"That and the cheap rent," she agreed. "You're going to have a conversation with Max today, right?"

"Is that why you came? To get ringside seats to my humiliation?"

Her eyes went wide. "Does that mean you're actually going to talk to him?"

I nodded. "It's time to be honest with him. I can't stay in this weird limbo state forever. It would be better for me to know if he only wants to be friends because then I can start getting over it."

251

"Yes, because your crush on Lumpy was so short-lived." Her observation was full of sarcasm.

"I did get over Adrian," I pointed out.

"Thanks to meeting Max. You do realize that what you felt for Lumpy and what you feel for Max now are not even remotely the same, right?"

It would be like asking someone, "What's hotter, this tiny birthday candle or the surface of the sun?" The two things were not comparable. What I had thought I felt for Adrian was nothing like what I felt for Max. One tiny flicker versus molten, blinding light.

"Yes, I realize that."

"And when Max tells you he likes you, too, you have to spend the rest of our lives telling me how right I was and treating me like the wise sage that I am."

"Deal." If she was right, then I would be too happy to care that I had to pay her homage.

"Where's the kitchen?" she asked. "I should probably go get started."

I pointed it out to her and went back to my clipboard and the million things I still had to accomplish before the party started.

A half hour before the party was to begin, Sunny arrived. She was wearing a bright yellow dress and looked adorable. She rushed over to me. "Everly! This is beyond anything I could have imagined. Thank you so, so much."

It was pretty perfect, if I did say so myself. She didn't need to know about the earlier struggles we'd had—she deserved an amazing day. I didn't want her to stress. As far as Sunny was concerned, everything would go just as we'd planned, no matter what else came up.

"How did you make it look just like a big top?" she asked, turning in a circle to get the full effect.

"Lots of planning," I told her with a smile. I had wanted an upscale circus feel and that was exactly what I had. The main room was breezy and airy, the pastel pink and blue linens draping up toward the center with lines of tiny pastel triangle flags hanging down like tent poles.

Jugglers, balloon artists, a magician, stuffed animals in fancy birdcages that would be perfect to donate after this was over. There were multiple booths set up with carnival games, along with more donatable prizes. A huge box near the door had a sign hung on it with the name of Max's charity and a note that all presents and donations could be left there.

Sunny's eyes welled up with tears, and she started fanning her hands in front of her face as she looked up to the ceiling. "Pregnancy is making me so hormonal, but I love it all. I couldn't have asked for anything better."

"I'm so happy that you like it! Beside the carnival games we've got some fun stations set up," I told her. "Over there we want to have people write a message on a diaper with a permanent marker for you and your husband, but you can't see them until the shower is finished. I've hidden pacifiers all over this room and there's going to be a prize for whoever finds the most. We've got a station for decorating onesies and bibs and a Polaroid station where people take a picture of themselves and write down what day they think the baby will be born. We'll hang their photos up on this line with tiny clothespins," I said. "There should be something to keep everyone entertained and having a great time."

Sunny started to cry more earnestly now. "This is so wonderful. Thank you, thank you, thank you."

A man appeared, carrying a large bag. He was familiar and it took me a second to place him. He was Sunny's husband.

Which he confirmed when he offered me his hand and said, "Hi, I'm Todd Belmont. Thank you so much for pulling this together for us at the last minute." He smiled. " And my wife doesn't usually cry, so take it as a huge compliment."

I smiled back as I shook his hand. "And I'm Everly Aprile. It's good to meet you and thank you."

"Everly?" he said, his eyebrows raising as he turned toward Sunny. "Is that the same one that Max—"

Sunny put both of her hands on my arms and said, "Can I talk to you real fast, Everly?"

She dragged me away from her husband and took me over to the base of the stairs. "Sorry about him," she said. "Men. Always saying things they shouldn't."

That hadn't really been my experience. I couldn't get Max to say anything to me.

"There is something I want to tell you," she went on, "and I hope you don't take this the wrong way."

Now I felt anxious and concerned. "Is there something wrong with the shower?"

"What? No! It's sheer perfection and you are an event-planning goddess. I want to say something about Max."

"You wouldn't be the first person today to do so," I told her.

She frowned slightly but pressed on. "Max has been really hurt in the past. There are people who have taken advantage of him and his good nature. Please treat him well."

"I intend to," I said, feeling a little breathless. Had Max asked her to speak to me?

No, he wouldn't have done that. But they were close, and if Sunny had felt like she needed to say something . . .

She might not be literally speaking for Max, but these could still be his words.

"You make him really happy," she said. "I can't remember the last time I've seen him like this."

While I wanted to discuss this with her until we were both sick of the topic, I heard new voices and realized that some guests had started arriving. I would have to explain the different events to every new person who came in and Sunny needed to say hello to her guests.

"We should get back out there," I told her. "People have started arriving."

It was easy to slip into event planner mode, to make sure that everyone had a glass of champagne and an idea of where they should head next. About half an hour after all one hundred of her guests had arrived, we would start preparing to serve the luncheon. Sunny wouldn't be opening presents as was customary since she planned on donating them all. She had thought it would be a nice touch for the new recipients to leave them in the wrapping paper.

Everything was going perfectly until Max walked in and I suddenly forgot how to speak.

CHAPTER THIRTY-TWO

Max was dressed upscale casual—khaki pants and a light blue button-down that matched his eyes perfectly. While I had known he was going to knock me off my feet, I hadn't adequately prepared myself for how heavy the blow would be.

He handed his coat to the staff member I'd assigned to the job and he turned, his gaze landing on mine.

I stood there and stared at him. What was I supposed to say? Some nagging part of my brain was trying to remind me that I had something important to tell him, but in that moment I could not remember what it was.

He came over to me. "Everly, you look beautiful."

Then he pressed a soft kiss to my left cheek, lingering there, until he pulled back slightly to do the same to my right cheek. My body flushed under his touch and from his proximity.

Max, Max, Max, my hormones called out to him, willing me to throw myself into his arms.

"Thank you," I said after he finished. And whether that was for the compliment he'd paid me or the hello kiss, I wasn't sure.

His lips parted and he took in a short breath, like he intended to do . . . something. Speak?

Kiss me?

But I didn't get to find out because Margot Belmont arrived and claimed him. "Max! I'm so glad you were able to join us. Let me show you around."

Then he left with her. He said nothing to me and just left.

Again.

Which was probably my fault because he knew I'd gone on a date with Adrian. He had been polite and kind, because he was Max, but he might be really upset with me.

I shifted into automatic mode, my brain disconnected from the rest of my body. I continued greeting guests, explaining the different stations and pointing them over in Sunny's direction so that she could say hello as well. I also watched Max the entire time as he interacted with different people, laughing and smiling as he drank his champagne.

Hmph. I wished this weren't an event and that I could knock back a couple of glasses. I felt like I needed something to help me calm down. My poor battered nerves were now completely on edge. It took everything I had to put a fake smile on and pretend like Max wasn't in the same room with me and that I wasn't freaking out.

I counted the hundredth person, a little bit surprised that everyone who had RSVP'd yes had actually showed up. I went into the kitchen to give Jeanine the heads-up that I'd seat the guests in about half an hour.

"Got it," she said. "Oh, and by the way, the mother-in-law was asking about a specific vase that she had in the living room and can't find now. She wants someone to locate it."

That someone would have to be me.

I headed upstairs and into one of the rooms where we'd shoved all the furniture. I hadn't been up here to direct the movers and they had just sort of put things wherever, which made it difficult to get around. I climbed over benches and around tables, looking for the vase. I thought I spotted it behind a couch and had just started to climb over to reach it when I heard, "Everly?"

Of course. Of course Max would come looking for me when I was face down, butt up. I immediately stood and turned toward him.

He closed the door behind him. We stood there in silence for a few beats, a heavy longing filling the space between us. Then he said, "I'm going to kiss you. If you don't want me to, tell me now."

His words thrilled me, the demand and wanting I heard in them. I liked take-charge Max.

With a masculine grace and ease, he started skirting around the furniture like it wasn't even there, never taking his eyes off me.

My heart was thudding so hard that I was sure he could hear it, and my eager anticipation built with each step he took.

When he reached me, he stood so close that I felt a phantom imprint of him on my skin. My heart was stumbling over itself and I could see his pulse beating hard at the base of his throat.

I whispered, "Shouldn't we talk?"

"After."

This time I knew what was coming. And instead of it easing off the anticipation, it made it worse. I wanted his mouth on mine.

Now.

In answer to my unspoken demand, Max slid a hand behind my head and kissed me.

He did it like he'd been trapped underwater for the last five minutes and the only way that he could breathe again was by kissing me. It was desperate and frantic and needy and everything I could have ever asked for.

There was no question that Max wanted me.

It also immediately let me know that our last kiss hadn't been a one-off, or some kind of cosmic aberration. No, Max really did just kiss that well, like he was a professional athlete and this was his event and he'd done nothing but practice for the last ten years straight.

It also meant that Vella was right and I hadn't tricked him into it at the Empire State Building. He hadn't done anything he didn't want to do, given the way he was kissing me right now.

Then everything blurred together as we wrapped ourselves around each other. It would have been impossible to see where one of us began and the other ended. Yet I still needed to get closer to him.

He seemed to have the same need, as his hand found the warm, sensitized skin at the back of my neck, urging me closer.

His scorching mouth was firm, his fiery kisses adding fuel to the fire that was burning between us. I was exhilarated, lightheaded, my nerve endings vibrating with bliss and heat.

I couldn't help but let out a sigh of pleasure that seemed to travel through every part of my body. I had missed him so much.

And I could tell from the fervent, bruising way he kissed me that he'd missed me just as desperately.

He leaned against me and I felt like I was falling . . . until I realized that I actually was falling, that he had accidentally pushed me back onto the couch I'd been climbing on when he entered the room.

"I'm sorry, I didn't mean for that to happen," he said, his low voice sounding chagrined.

I, however, was quite happy with how things were turning out and just smiled at him.

"Are you okay?" he asked, his body pressing mine down against the cushions. I loved the gentle concern in his voice. He started to leverage himself in order to stand up.

"I am very happy right now," I told him, wrapping my arms around his neck to pull him back down to my lips.

Max made a sound in his chest and then deepened the kiss, parting my lips with his. My veins caught fire, burning up with desire and need. I was dizzy from his touch, his kiss, his labored breathing. Everything he was doing told me that he needed me as much as I needed him.

"Whoa!"

Max lifted his head and we both peered over his shoulder to see Vella standing in the doorway. He easily got to his feet but it took some pushing and adjusting to help me stand as well.

Mostly because my limbs refused to cooperate.

Vella was covering her eyes. "You don't know how sorry I am to interrupt you, both because I didn't need to have that image burned into my retinas but I also want you to have your happy reunion. Maybe when I'm clear of this room, though. But I came up here because there's a problem."

"Did you punch somebody?" I asked. I was still so out of breath.

"No," she said indignantly, dropping her hands. "And before you ask, I didn't light anyone's hair on fire, either, even though there are quite a few people at this party that deserve it. I can tell how judgmental all these people are just by looking at them. The issue is that like, thirty more guests just arrived."

It was like getting kicked in the stomach. "Are you serious?"

"A big group showed up after you and Max . . . you know. Apparently they're guests of Margot's and she didn't bother telling you or Sunny that they were coming."

"This is why we have final head counts." I ground the words out, clenching my teeth together in frustration.

"What do you need?" Max asked, squeezing my hand to let me know that he was here for me.

"I have to talk to Jeanine. The food is going to be the major issue right now. I'm also going to need like three more tables set up with chairs to accommodate that many people. We have extra table linens just in case, so we should be good there." I wouldn't have enough centerpieces, but I could just take some of the stuffed animals and use them and hopefully nobody would notice how differently their tables were decorated from the others.

"I'll take care of the tables," he said. "I'll go speak to Margot and see what she wants us to use."

"Tell her I'm going to have to use her personal plates, glasses, and silverware as well." If she wanted to spring a bunch of surprise guests on us, she could provide the things we needed to entertain and feed them. He nodded and I leaned up to kiss him on the cheek to thank him.

I ran downstairs to the kitchen and found Jeanine. She was preparing the first course, an organic mixed greens salad. I quickly filled her in and her eyes got wider with everything I said until they practically popped out of her head.

"But the final head count was a hundred people, not a hundred and thirty," she protested.

"I know. But apparently the mother-in-law invited quite a few more people without telling anyone." Despite begging for final head counts for this very reason, both Jeanine and I had been doing this for long enough that there was already a cushion built in to make sure we had food for a few additional people or to replace a couple of dropped plates.

But she wouldn't have enough to cover thirty percent more guests.

The chef let out a big sigh. "We'll have to rearrange the salads and then I'll cut the meat of the main course in half to make sure we have enough. Maybe put out more bread."

"I don't think these are the kind of people who eat bread."

"Probably not," she agreed. She found her purse and pulled out a credit card, handing it to her sous chef. "You need to go to the nearest store and bring back all the fruits, vegetables, cheese, and crackers you can find. We'll make up some trays and put them on a table near the kitchen in case anyone is still hungry."

The sous chef nodded and took off.

"That's a good idea," I told her. "Give me the receipt so that I can make sure you get reimbursed."

"I'll definitely do that." She tapped her fingers against the countertop. "Dessert shouldn't be a problem. It's a cake, so we'll cut smaller slices."

"If bread's out, sugar probably is, too."

"But they'll drink, right? Tipsy people don't seem to notice as much if they're still hungry." With that she told her servers to go back out and circulate with more champagne.

"I'm really sorry, Jeanine." I could see how visibly stressed she was.

"It's not your fault, Everly. And it sounds like it's not the mother-to-be's fault, either."

"Nope." This was all on Margot Belmont. Who I was sure was a nice person deep, deep down, but I was feeling a bit too stressed to look that hard.

I started raiding kitchen cabinets and found enough plates, cutlery, and glasses for the new guests. There was even a passing similarity to the ones Jeanine had brought with her.

After that was organized, I went out into the dining area and helped Max and two waiters set up the extra tables and chairs. We were as quick and efficient as we could be so that we'd create the least amount of disturbance to the guests, all one hundred and thirty of them.

Somehow everything came together. Jeanine reportioned the salads so that we could serve the first course, and the additional tables looked nice. Not as good as the others that I'd originally set up, but there wasn't much I could do about it.

The sous chef and a waiter finished setting up the grazing table. If it had been left up to me, I probably would have bought prepackaged vegetable and fruit trays, but Jeanine had directed them to create a masterpiece. Everything was artfully arranged and appealing, like it had always been intended to be included.

Max came over to my right and looked over the grazing table and said, "No veggie dip? I don't want to know what celery tastes like."

That made me smile. "What's wrong with celery?"

He grimaced. "It's crunchy water with hair."

"Do you also have strong feelings about the fruit?"

"Fruit is hit or miss. It kind of depends on what season it is and how fresh they are. Sometimes strawberries are amazing, other times they're vile."

I nodded. "That's why you can't go wrong with Oreos. They always taste the same. I also have an appreciation for grapes. Mostly in their liquid form."

"So do I," he said. "Especially when I can taste them on your lips."

A warm tremor passed through me. I couldn't let him distract me by saying or doing sexy things. I welled up all of my courage and let out a deep breath. Now or never.

"Max, we need to talk."

CHAPTER THIRTY-THREE

"About the celery?" he asked with a wicked glint in his eye.

"No. Are you okay to skip lunch?" Jeanine had all of this well under control now. I wasn't going to be needed until after everyone had finished eating, and they'd only begun their first course. We had some time.

"I'm not very hungry," I added.

I was. But not for food. It was hard to stand here and talk to him like everything was normal when all I could think about was his body pressing into mine, pinning me in place, his mouth ravaging mine, and how delicious all of it had felt.

But we'd had the actions upstairs and now it was time for the words.

"I'm fine with skipping lunch. Let's talk."

I led him by the hand to the base of the stairs and sat down. I'd be nearby in case anyone needed me, but not in some closed-door room where I knew he could easily distract me. He stretched out next to me and I tried organizing my thoughts, figuring out the best way to have this conversation with him.

Max beat me to the punch. "How did your date with your boss go?"

"It was not a date," I said, and then had to correct myself. "It was intended to be a date, but I left three minutes after I arrived."

He seemed to consider this information carefully and then announced, "I'm glad. Vella told me he was a bad guy."

"When did you talk to Vella?" I glanced over at her and she immediately swung her gaze away, staring at the ceiling and acting innocent, like she hadn't prepped Max and then sent him over.

She had always told me that she wasn't the type to interfere and yet here we were.

"I talked to Vella earlier, before I went upstairs and found you."

Memories of him finding me were making my knees sweat, so I forced myself to pay attention to the conversation we were trying to have. "Adrian's not a bad guy. He's clueless and helpless, but not bad."

Max had no response to that and just absorbed the information.

I felt compelled to fill in the silence. "And I didn't stay because I don't have feelings for Adrian."

His eyebrows flew up in surprise. "I thought you were in love with him."

"I was never in love with him. I had a crush on him. A crush that very quickly fell apart when I examined it." Especially when I compared it against the way that I was in love with Max. "It was just all smoke and shadows. Nothing substantial."

"I thought you wanted to be with him," he said, like he couldn't understand what was happening.

"I don't." I paused and then added, "Is that why you didn't talk to me after you overheard us?"

He hesitated for a moment and then nodded. "I guess I figured that if you were so willing to go out with him, you weren't interested in dating anyone else."

Did he mean himself? It looked like he was going to join me in beating around this particular bush. "I'm not the only one who went out on a date with someone else."

"Who?"

"Arabella."

"That was not a date," he said. "I told you, she had some things she wanted to return to me. Nothing happened."

"It seemed to me like a convenient excuse to see your extremely gorgeous ex-girlfriend that you dated for forever and I . . ." My voice trailed off at the expression on his face. "What?"

"You're jealous." He said this like it delighted him.

"What? No." This wasn't about my feelings of insecurity when it came to his ex. And he didn't get to be happy about my jealousy when he had felt the same way, even if he hadn't said so yet. "You can't go radio silent because I went out with someone when you did the exact same thing."

"It wasn't the same, though. I don't have feelings for Arabella."

"And I just told you that I don't have feelings for Adrian!"

"Then why did you go?" he asked.

"Honestly?" Here it was. Time to be direct. I willed my heart to stop pounding so hard against my rib cage, but it didn't listen. "I think I wanted you to stop me."

"I would never tell you who you should spend time with."

"Neither would I. I wanted to, though."

"Same." His admission thrilled me. "But I don't want you to go out with him or anyone else. And if I'd known that me seeing Arabella would upset you, I wouldn't have gone."

That was like a confession, right? He didn't want me to date anybody else? And he wouldn't have spent time with his perfect, evil, stupid ex if he'd known I didn't like it? "It wasn't fair for me to test you like that. It's something my dad used to do and I hated it."

"What do you mean?"

"When things started going south in my parents' relationship, he would say things like, 'If you just lose twenty pounds, we'd be happy again.' Or 'if you kept the house immaculate and wore makeup every day for me, things would get better.' She was never good enough and he was constantly moving the goalposts. I don't want to do that, so I'm sorry that I did. I should have told you how I was really feeling."

As if he sensed that I needed the support, he reached out and took me by the hand. "And how are you feeling?"

But there was another explanation that I needed first. "Why are there so many women texting you on your phone?" At his look of surprise, I added, "You date around a lot, right?"

"I already told you that I'm not dating anyone."

"I thought you meant not dating anyone seriously, but like casually."

He glanced down at our joined hands. "Not casually, not seriously. And how do you know who is on my phone?"

I felt my face flame up in response. "I may have inadvertently looked at your phone, which I shouldn't have done and I'm sorry that I did, but in my defense, you should have a password on it."

"I should." He nodded with a mischievous smile, like he knew something I didn't. "The women texting me are people I work with. Most of my colleagues are female."

Oh.

Oh.

I'd held on to the belief for so long that he was a womanizing playboy that I didn't know what to do with this new information other than to explain where I was coming from. "This is more dysfunctional dad stuff for me. My dad used to cheat on my mom a lot and so I distrust men that I think are like him."

Max gave me a small smile. "My dad was the same way, unfortunately. I've never been unfaithful to anyone I've been with, and I never would be."

I believed him.

"But," he added, "that wasn't what I asked you. How are you feeling?"

I could feel a burning sensation at the back of my throat. Like I was trying to hold back tears. Max was so beautiful and so perfect that at some point he was going to realize he was too good for me. I was sure this was more residual stuff from my terrible father, but I couldn't help my insecurity. Even if Max was being so wonderful. "I'm scared that you're going to realize that you should be with your own kind. Like a racing stallion and a donkey would never date."

"Huh. I've never been called a donkey before."

My eyes were still watery, but that made me smile. "Obviously I meant it the other way around. If I tell you what I'm feeling, you'll quickly realize that you're too good for me and—"

He reached up to turn my face toward him, interrupting me. "Everly? You're the one who is too good for me."

"What?" I whispered, in total disbelief. Had he never seen himself in a mirror? Never read his own diary? He was an amazing person in an even prettier package.

"You always look for the best in others," he said. "Why can't you see it in yourself? Because I can. You're smart, funny, kind, generous, thoughtful, and the most scarily organized person I've ever met."

I laughed, but I could see the sincerity in his eyes next to the teasing.

He gently ran his fingers along the side of my face and then reached up to move a lock of my hair that had fallen over my shoulder back into place. "Why don't you believe that you deserve good things?" he asked.

It was like he'd seen straight into my soul and uncovered something I hid from everyone else. Maybe even from myself.

That on-the-edge-of-tears feeling was back, making my throat tight. "Probably because they've been in short supply my entire life."

He nodded. "You expect things to end badly. I understand that because I'm in exactly the same boat. But I have hope that someday it won't end that way."

"I think that's why I try to look at people and the world as being half-full—because deep down I'm convinced that it will always be half-empty."

"And I probably played into that fear when I didn't call or text you this week." His voice was regretful.

Heart racing in my chest, I pushed myself to be braver. "You did. But to be fair to you, I had told you that I wanted us to be just friends."

His expression turned neutral. "And now? Is that still what you want? Because I want you to choose what you want."

I gulped hard. "What if . . . what if one of the things I choose is you? If you're interested."

His smile could have powered the entire New York City skyline. "If I'm interested? What do you think I've been doing this entire time?"

"Being my friend?"

He brought my hand up to his mouth to press a gentle kiss against it. "Everly, I love being your friend. And . . ."

Max left the rest of that sentence unspoken, hanging in the air between us. Why didn't he finish it? Was he scared? Worried? Not quite where I was?

It seemed like he was leaving it to me to spell things out, so I did. "I want to take the next step with you. I mean, if you want that, too."

"The next step?" He grinned. "I already hurled myself down the entire flight of stairs. I'm more than ready for the next step."

I slapped him on the shoulder. "Then why are you torturing me? If you wanted to be more than friends, why didn't you just say something? I only said it because I was worried you would friend-zone me and I didn't want to be humiliated. Especially if you were the womanizing player that I had imagined you to be."

"Maybe I should have said something before. But you said you didn't have much experience and I wanted to take things slow."

"By taking things this slow, you made me think you didn't like me."

He kissed my hand again. "I was trying not to scare or overwhelm you."

So he had been treating me like a skittish horse, too.

Vella was right and we were both stupid.

"And now that we've both admitted that we like each other," he said, "what does it look like moving forward?"

"I don't know."

"Are you scared?"

"More excited than scared," I confessed, and he grinned at me again.

"I can work with that."

"I'm guessing we probably have more to talk about," I said. "Someplace that isn't your cousin's in-laws' home. Maybe you can come over to my place after the shower ends and we can have dinner together and figure things out."

His eyes were intense and hungry. "Yes, there's more that needs to be said. But after we finish talking, I'm going to kiss you until you forget what words are."

My heart fluttered in anticipation. I'd been kissed by him twice now, so I knew it wouldn't take me very long for him to get me to that point. "We should get back to the shower." My voice was breathy and weird but he seemed to like it. "I have to go find out who won the pacifier contest."

"I did."

"How do you know that?"

"Because I have all fifty pacifiers."

I couldn't help but laugh. "What made you decide to dominate the game?"

With a wicked grin he said, "I heard there was a prize involved and I already know what I want."

Then he brought my hand up to his lips again, but instead of a single kiss like he'd already given me, he began to kiss each knuckle. Each press of his warm lips to my skin made me feel like he was marking me his. He turned my hand over and kissed the inside of my wrist, smiling against the way my pulse hammered beneath his mouth.

Each kiss was like a promise of what was to come, and I wished we weren't in a room full of so many other people.

But soon . . . soon I would have him all to myself.

CHAPTER THIRTY-FOUR

Max and I rejoined the shower, which was still going strong. No one seemed to notice or complain about smaller portions at lunch or the mismatched tables and chairs. Everyone seemed to be very happy and Jeanine's idea to keep all of the champagne flutes topped off was an excellent one.

Everywhere I went, every person I spoke to, I could feel Max's gaze on me. There was something slightly predatory and possessive about it that thrilled me, like he couldn't wait to get me alone.

I helped with as much cleanup as I could in the kitchen, away from the guests. We wouldn't be able to start breaking down everything else until most of the people had left.

And apparently the guests were having such a great time that nobody wanted to go. I was going to have to kick them out soon because the vendors were going to show up with their teams, expecting to pack everything back up.

Vella came over to offer me a glass of champagne but I shook my head. I wanted a clear head and to be totally present for Max later on.

"Why are you so giggly-looking?" she asked.

"I can't stop smiling."

"Yeah, you kind of look like the Joker." Then she gasped. "Did you work things out with Max?"

"Yes, but we're going to talk some more."

"Do you mean 'talk,' as in it should have air quotes around it?" she asked hopefully.

"No. Well, maybe."

"Here." She set her tray down and dug into her purse and produced a tube of lipstick. "Hold still."

Before I could react, she was applying it to my mouth.

When she finished I asked, "What did you just do?"

"That shade is Ruby Woo by MAC. This'll get Max where you want him. Red lipstick makes men think about sex."

I shook my head. "Doesn't everything do that?"

"Good point," she responded. "And earlier the other cater-waiters invited me to a party and I wasn't going to go but now I think I should. So you will have privacy." She waggled her eyebrows at me and I couldn't help but laugh.

"Thanks, I think?"

"You're welcome. And Everly, there's something I want you to know."

"I already had the sex talk years ago."

She frowned. "No, that's not it. It's important to me that you are aware of the fact that it is a special burden being right all the time."

I laughed again.

"Plus, I hope you appreciate how much this means you've grown," she said.

"In what way?" I asked, keeping an eye on Max, who was still watching me with that look that made my insides burn and shiver at the same time.

"You started out wanting the prince but you chose the pauper."

"Like you said, the part of Kat's life that appeals to me the most is her being with the man she loves." Max was my fairy-tale prince, too good to be true, and none of the rest of that stuff mattered.

We both noticed Sunny making her way toward us and Vella said her goodbye. "I'm going to help pack up the rest of the stuff in the kitchen and get my money. I am going to need a full report later."

"See you later," I said.

"Everly!" Sunny hugged me for like, the fifth time that day. "You did amazing. I am so sorry about those extra guests. I asked Margot repeatedly for all of her guests' names, told her about the head count, and she still did this."

"I was kind of hoping you wouldn't notice," I said, a bit disappointed.

"Oh! I only know about it because Max filled me in on all the details. Part of me wonders if she did it intentionally just so that things would fall apart, but you didn't let that happen."

"Do you really think she'd do that?"

"I'm not who she wanted Todd to marry and she uses stuff like this to prove to him that he should have married someone more like them. But you showed her up today. In fact, before she came downstairs, she was complaining to Todd's sister that the shower was going to be cheap and tacky, but she shut up as soon as she walked in the room and hasn't said a word about it since."

I was gratified for both me and Sunny. "I just hope that you enjoyed yourself."

"Like I keep telling you, it was absolutely perfect. If you don't mind, I am going to recommend you to all my friends."

"I would love that! Thank you!" Maybe I could bring some new clients in to Elevated. That would definitely make Claudia happy.

"Excellent. And, just to let you know, I transferred over your fee. And I didn't make a mistake—I sent you twice what you asked for. I should be paying you three times but Max said that might be insulting or something, I don't know why, so I'm tipping you a hundred percent and I hope you're okay with it because I will close my bank account down before I let you send that money back to me. You deserve every penny."

"Sunny, I couldn't possibly—"

"Nope! I'm not listening. I one-upped my mother-in-law, who wanted me to fail, and I have this perfect memory of most of the people I love being here to celebrate with me. And I don't mean to be pushy, but I would love for you and me to grab lunch sometime. I have enjoyed getting to know you and I think we should be friends."

I couldn't help but grin at her. "I would like that, too."

"Great! I will text you. Thank you again."

She had doubled my fee? That was a lot of money. What was I going to do with all of it?

Guests finally started saying their goodbyes and I sent out texts letting the vendors know to come inside in about ten minutes to start collecting their stuff. Sunny and Todd were by the door, thanking everyone for coming. The box for Max's charity was overflowing.

Normally I would be with the couple and telling people to take home goody bags, but Sunny had decided to invest that money in congratulations kits for new moms with everything they'd need for the first few days after they got home from the hospital.

The vendors came in through the back entrance and I helped to get everything taken down, making sure that all of the furniture we'd stored upstairs was returned to the correct spot. I was motivated to work quickly and get out of there as fast as possible.

I even found the vase that Margot had been so worried about and returned it to the right place next to an expensive couch in her front room.

After we were finished, you couldn't even tell that an event had taken place.

"Are you ready to go?" Max asked once everything was done.

"Yes!"

We decided to go to a nearby grocery store, presumably the same one that Jeanine's sous chef had shopped at earlier, and picked up some ingredients for dinner. I offered to make him my meemaw's smothered chicken recipe and it felt so domestic to be shopping with him.

Like we were a real couple.

We walked back, hand in hand, to my apartment. It was dreary and cold and the wind was still blowing, but I didn't mind.

I asked Max about his California trip, and he told me all about the donor and the countless meetings, the unending hoops he'd had to jump through.

"Do you see yourself always working for this non-profit?" I asked.

"Definitely. I can't imagine any other job that would bring as much happiness, getting to help people in need. I guess I'm selfish that way."

I smiled at him.

"What about you?" he asked. "Do you envision yourself climbing the ranks at your company?"

"I see a future where I become the boss at Elevated, but if I'm being completely honest, and I've never said this to another person before, it's always been a dream of mine to start my own business. I would focus on baby and bridal showers and call it Aprile's Showers." Getting to be in charge of every step of the process, having no one else I had to check in with or answer to, sounded like heaven to me.

"That sounds perfect! Why don't you do that now?"

"Well, I've heard it's not exactly cheap to start your own business and it's hard to get something like that off the ground. You need clients."

"I'm sure Sunny will tell everyone with a pulse about how amazing you are, so that part's handled. The money thing will be a bit more difficult," he mused. "But you told me the most important parts of event planning are the ability to design beautiful things, being calm in a crisis, and relationships with vendors, and as far as I can tell, you're three for three."

"You're right. I think I'd do a good job. But it'd be a one-woman show and I'm not sure I can be everywhere at once."

"I'd help out."

"You would?" I asked, touched by his offer.

"I would. I'm strong. I can move stuff."

He did have truly excellent arms, which I very much enjoyed.

Max handed me the groceries. "I'll prove it to you."

Then before I could figure out what he was doing, he had swung me up into his arms and carried me as if it were effortless for him. I hadn't known that could happen for someone as tall as me and I was impressed by and thrilled at his strength.

While I would have happily let him carry me for several more blocks, people were staring.

"You've proven your point," I said with a laugh, and he came to a stop. He released my legs but not his arm around my back and we remained close together, unmoving. I pressed my lips against his neck and was rewarded with a sharp intake of breath and his hand flexing against me. I left a faint imprint of red lipstick behind but I didn't say anything. It was like I had marked him as mine.

I wanted to mark up a whole lot more of him.

Given where my thoughts were headed, I was about to get a public indecency ticket if we stayed here any longer. "We should go," I murmured against his skin. He smelled so good that I sighed.

After a few beats he nodded and then released his arm around my waist. He reached for the groceries and then my hand to hold it again. We resumed walking, even though my legs were feeling a bit wobbly.

I tried to think of a topic we could discuss that wouldn't be about how much I wanted him to kiss me, something light and fun. I settled on, "You found all the pacifiers. You never did tell me what you had in mind as your prize."

"What I have in mind and what's actually going to happen are two very different things," he said in a voice that made my blood instantly heat up.

I had the feeling that when we got to my place, despite our best intentions, there wasn't going to be a whole lot of talking happening.

CHAPTER
THIRTY-FIVE

We were both silent as we entered my apartment. He put the groceries on the counter while I took off my coat. He shrugged his off as well and I hung both on a hook near the door. I reminded myself that we were going one step at a time. Even if Max had already tumbled down the stairs, we should take each step carefully.

No rushing.

And then I completely negated my own plan.

I walked over to him and put my hand against his chest, steadying myself. His heartbeat was strong and steady beneath my palm. Then I leaned forward slightly to kiss him. I had never kissed him on the lips before—he had always initiated. It felt brave and bold, but I was still a bit hesitant and unsure of myself.

And he didn't respond the way I might have expected. He kissed me back, but it was gentle and soft and undemanding. Delicious and heady as always, but there was a definite restraint.

Old me might have assumed that he didn't want to kiss me, that I had forced myself on him, but I knew it was something else.

I stepped back and he was watching me carefully. Maybe waiting for my next move?

He had wanted to talk. I should let him do that. But I needed something to do so that I didn't try to maul the poor man, who seemed a bit dubious about what was happening.

Which wasn't like Max.

To be fair to him, though, we were in an entirely different situation than we'd ever been in before. We were alone, we wouldn't be interrupted, and we had admitted that we had feelings for each other and wanted to be in a relationship.

Everything had changed.

I left the kitchen and walked across the living room, over to my alcove. To my surprise he stayed right behind me, like he didn't want to be parted from me.

The sight of Max Colby standing next to my bed was my undoing. I wondered what he would do if I pushed him down on it.

"This is basically my bedroom," I announced, probably unnecessarily.

"Interesting," he said.

"Yep! This is where I sleep." Now I was saying stupid things. Oh no.

"Just sleep?" he said with a tone that let me know he was kidding, but also that he might be open to exploring other activities besides sleep, and my revolutionary ovaries tried declaring war again.

"I'm going to get changed," I told him, desperately needing a diversion. "Go over there."

I pointed in the direction of the living room and he took a few steps back. I grabbed the dressing screen that I occasionally used as a room divider and placed it between us. I could have just gone into the bathroom to get changed, but I realized that I didn't want to be in a different room, separated from him.

I didn't even want this screen between us.

Turning, I grabbed a tank top and soft pants to change into. I slid my dress off but all of my attention was focused on Max. There was only this flimsy thing between us and he could have pushed it aside.

Or I could have.

There was something charged and sexy about changing with him right there but not able to see anything other than a shadowed outline.

I pulled my clothes on, almost regretting doing it. If I walked out in my underwear, there was no way we would take things slowly. Or be able to have a conversation. I was pretty sure about that.

"I'm dressed," I said when I finished. And I meant to move the screen myself, but Max lifted it and tossed it to the side, like he'd been waiting for an excuse to do just that.

He reached for me and I eagerly awaited his mouth on mine.

But he didn't kiss me. Instead he placed his hand on the side of my throat. He moved his hand down, rubbing his thumb across my collarbone, and then he leaned forward to press a hot, delicate kiss to where he'd been touching me.

I grabbed on to his shirt, trying to stay upright. There was a pulling sensation just behind my belly button that grew and blossomed into white-hot heat. I was going to ask him to do it again because of how amazing it had felt, and he did it without me begging. He was excruciatingly tender with me, pressing warm kisses up and down the column of my neck, across my collarbone, on my shoulders. The whisper of his fingertips followed along behind his mouth, touching me everywhere his lips had.

He had turned my entire body into one desperate ache, wanting beating through my blood.

I ran my own fingertips along the planes and contours of his perfect face, then ran my fingers through his dark, silken hair. He was so unbelievably handsome. "I can't believe you want to be with me."

It had been meant to stay inside my brain, but the words somehow came out. And they had the negative effect of making him stop kissing me.

"Why?" He truly sounded dumbfounded.

"Look at you. You are annoyingly gorgeous." As if he didn't know.

He framed my face with his hands. "And you are so beautiful, so sexy, that I have a hard time keeping my hands to myself."

"Really?"

"When I came upstairs today and found you, I wanted to talk. But that all went away the second I saw you."

"Oh." I breathed the word. "You would think someone else would have noticed by now if that was true."

He kissed my forehead softly. "You've surrounded yourself with some very stupid people. I wish that you could see yourself the way that I do."

"How do you see me?" I reached up to wrap my fingers around his wrists.

"Desirable, annoyingly attractive, with a smile that doesn't just light up a room, it illuminates it."

My heart fluttered up into my throat. "My mom spent a lot of money on braces," I whispered, and he grinned at me.

"You are beautiful inside and out. And I would have told you that constantly since we first met but I—"

"Was trying not to scare me," I finished for him. The magnetism of this moment and his otherworldly blue eyes drew me in so completely that I had started to become personally offended by every molecule of air that existed between us.

Max moved his hand so that he could trace the outline of my mouth, the calloused pad gliding along my more-than-ready lips, and my breathing turned shallow. I lifted my face up so that he could finally kiss me, but instead he pressed a kiss to the corner of my mouth. He ghosted his lips along my skin, over my cheekbones, against one eyelid and then the other. My forehead, my temples. I could feel his warm breath in my hair.

It was almost like he was trying to prove something to himself. That he could be restrained, he could touch me carefully and gently without losing his head.

I didn't know if this was for his benefit or for mine, but I felt so frantic for him that I wasn't sure how much more of this particularly exquisite torture I could withstand.

"You said you wanted to talk," I reminded him.

"Right." He dropped his hands and moved a step back. "There's something that I've been wanting to—"

I couldn't have described what possessed me in that moment other than my protesting lady parts were distraught at the loss of his touch and the possibility that I wasn't going to be properly kissed anytime soon.

I threw myself at him, knocking him back against a wall. He swore in three different languages.

"What's wrong?" I asked him. Did I not know my own strength?

"I think I've cut myself." He reached over to his side, just behind his shoulder blade.

"Oh no," I said, suddenly remembering why I shouldn't have pushed him into that wall. "For a few months Vella was going to be a painter and she had all these canvases hanging up and she never took the nails out. Let me see."

He lifted his shirt, and for a good twenty seconds, I couldn't focus on anything but the fact that his torso was the most perfect thing I had ever seen in my entire life. My throat closed and my heart jackhammered in my chest.

Wow.

My fingers actually ached to touch him and I had to ball my hands up so that I didn't attack him.

"Is it bad?" he asked, causing me to remember what I was supposed to be doing.

There was a short scratch, but it wasn't bleeding. He'd only grazed his skin. "You definitely nailed yourself. Sorry about the pun."

"It's okay. It was a good one."

I shook my head. "So I nearly knocked you out and now I've scratched you up."

"I don't mind if you scratch me up," he said in a voice full of promise and longing at the same time.

Without thinking I leaned forward and pressed a kiss to the scratch. Probably not very sanitary but I heard his sharp intake of breath, stronger than when he'd actually injured himself.

I tilted my head to the side to see his face better. The air was thick and heavy with unresolved tension and I could feel my rampaging heartbeat in my toes. A silent agreement passed between us, and the next thing I knew, his shirt was coming off. I honestly didn't know if he had unbuttoned it or if I had done it. But it slid off his shoulders and he asked, "Is this okay?"

"Yes!" So much more than okay. I was going to have myself a field day. I meant to explore him, to kiss every inch of exposed, warm skin, to feel and taste all the ways he was different than me, but my exploration was cut short when his mouth descended quickly on mine and I had to settle for running my fingers along the muscles in his back as I was pressed against him.

We took a couple of stumbling steps, our lips still fused together as we moved. There were no thoughts happening. Just pure, blissful, unadulterated lust.

Not just that, though. There was something more. There was frantic need and desperation but feelings being conveyed, too. He cared about me—I felt it in the way he kissed me, the way he touched me. How he tried to continue to be gentle with me even if every movement was tinged with utter wildness. I reveled in the restraint I felt in every muscle in his body, as if it took everything inside him to hold himself back.

I wondered what an unleashed Max would be like.

My brain would probably overload and explode from it.

The backs of my legs hit my bed and I fell against it with a surprised Max following.

"I'm good," I said before he could ask. It had been my idea, after all. He moved to lie alongside me and I immediately missed his weight pressing me down.

"Everly," he said, and my name was a broken sound in his chest. He rasped my name against my lips a few more times, as if he meant to tell me something but couldn't remember what it was.

I totally understood.

Now that I had Max Colby in my bed, I intended to finally explore him the way I'd wanted to since his shirt had come off. I started off with the area that was closest to me—his throat.

He tilted his head to the side for me, allowing me better access. I kissed and nipped my way down and absolutely loved the hisses and sighs he made. How his muscles would contract when my wandering fingers brushed against them. His every tiny reaction that I was responsible for—it was like finding out you had a superpower you never knew about.

A low, rough sound escaped his throat, something primal, and he pulled my face up to his so that he could kiss me.

Not just kiss me, but kiss me without holding back.

Liquid pleasure pooled immediately in my spine, spreading everywhere and making me feel too hot and my skin too tight. Like I was a star about to go supernova.

I couldn't help but moan into his mouth and he pulled back slightly. He started speaking Italian in between his kisses and I didn't even care what he was saying, only that it was so hot I wanted to spontaneously combust.

His breath was heavy and his hands wandered along the edge of my tank top, and then his fingers were under the hem, pressing into my back as it was his turn to explore. I was completely aflame everywhere he touched me—hot, crackling, burning.

And every kiss and every touch stoked that fire inside me, causing it to grow wilder and needier.

He dragged his lips away from mine and began pressing hungry kisses along my jaw, along the line of my throat. These were nothing like his soft, sweet kisses earlier. They were demanding and consuming and he was murmuring in Italian against my skin. I arched against the sensation, my heart turning volcanic and pumping molten blood through my body.

It was so much but I needed more. I tugged at his shoulders, wanting him to move.

He hesitated for only a moment and then shifted so that he was over me. He braced himself with his elbows, looking down at me with so much desire in his eyes, but with a softer emotion alongside it, one that made me melt inside. He brushed some of my hair away from my face. "Everly."

I swallowed hard. Then I reached up to capture his mouth, urging him to kiss me again. Words turned into heavy breaths and thoughts turned into sensations. There was nothing but Max and his touch and kiss. Everything else ceased to exist.

I tugged at his shoulders again and this time he did what I wanted, his weight pressing down against me, our legs intertwined, my heart beating hard against his. This shifting seemed to be all that was needed to get him to forget all about holding back. He parted my mouth and kissed me deeply, tasting me. His blood-scorching, toe-curling kisses were overwhelming, his fingers perfectly kneading and grazing and pressing me into mindless ecstasy.

When I was nine years old, there had been a freak snowstorm near my house. We'd had to go to the store for supplies. On the way home the roads had looked clear, but they weren't. Black ice everywhere. My mother slid and careened out of control for a few seconds when she hit a particularly bad patch, but it had felt like hours. I remembered the weightlessness in my stomach, the sensation of soaring through space, being out of control but somehow thrilled at the same time. The hollowed-out feeling like you were going way too fast but part of you didn't want that sensation to stop.

It was how I felt now. Careening out of control, weightless, light-headed, stomach floating—and I wanted more.

I reached down for the hem of my tank top, intending to take it off. I had to feel his skin against mine.

His hand went around my wrist, stilling my movement. "Wait, what are you doing?"

"What do you think?" I asked, reaching up to kiss him, but he turned his head slightly so that it landed on his jaw. I furrowed my eyebrows. What was *he* doing?

"I'm trying to be sensitive to your situation," he said. "I know that you don't have a lot of experience—"

"Barely any," I supplied. If we were going to call my non-past out, we should at least do it accurately.

"Barely any experience, and I don't want to put you in an uncomfortable situation or pressure you. Especially because you make me forget myself."

"You make me forget myself, too." I moved against him and he made a sound that was part pain and part pleasure. His hand stayed on my wrist, though, holding it in place.

A section of my brain that wasn't hazy registered the fact that he was trying to be respectful to me and my situation. "You're not taking advantage of me. I'm an adult and I can make my own choices. You don't need to protect me from myself. Speeding cars, maybe. But not from myself."

His chest was still moving back and forth rapidly, like he was having a hard time catching his breath. "I do want to protect you. Even if the person I have to protect you from is me."

"You don't have to do that, either."

"I want to keep you safe and make it so that nothing bad ever happens to you."

Which was very sweet and endearing and my heart turned into a gooey mess. I loved him so much that it felt impossible to keep it contained inside any longer. I tugged my hand out of his grasp and reached up to stroke the side of his face gently. "I know I'm supposed to feel nervous or anxious about escalating things, but when I'm with you, I don't feel that way. I want to be as close to you as I can and everything that entails because I love you."

"You what?"

CHAPTER THIRTY-SIX

If Meemaw were dead, she would have been rolling in her grave right now. It was the one thing she had drilled into my head once I'd become a teenager—I was never supposed to tell a man I was dating that I loved him first. It had always seemed outdated and sexist to me, but given Max's reaction, maybe it had some merit.

My first inclination was to try to retract it. Take it back and pretend I'd never said it.

But that would be lying and I didn't want to do that.

"I have to go," he said.

Now I was the one dumbfounded. "What?"

Max disentangled himself from me, and I was too shocked to react to the sudden loss of his warmth. He stood up and grabbed his shirt and put it back on, doing up only one button, and then got his coat, and the whole time I was thinking he was doing the opposite of what I wanted. I wanted clothes off and him in bed with me, not clothes being put on and him leaving.

My brain was so scrambled from his kisses that I couldn't process what was happening. I tried, though. "Where are you going?"

"I promise I will call you," he said. He lingered in the doorway for a moment to look at me and then he was gone.

I lay in my bed, unable to move, all of my limbs short-circuited and nonfunctioning. What had just happened? Or not happened?

Was he really that freaked out by me telling him that I loved him?

I had thought Max was more mature than that. If he didn't love me back, he could have just said it. Or that he wasn't quite there yet. He didn't have to make a great escape and leave me feeling so depressed and defeated.

It was like I had almost had everything I'd ever wanted and he'd just yanked it away from me.

I couldn't have said how long I lay there for, but eventually Vella came home. When she entered the room, she had one hand over her eyes. "I'm home! And I'm loudly announcing it just in case!"

"Max isn't here," I said.

She dropped her hand. "Why are you lying there like a starfish? Are you having to rest after finally sliding into home base?" At my blank expression she added, "Did you score a home run?"

"Only if a home run is when you hit a foul ball that knocks out a little old lady in the stands and the bat breaks and impales the catcher. Why are we talking about sex like it's baseball?"

"I was doing it for your virgin ears," she said. She grabbed a chair and brought it over to my bed. "What happened?"

"One minute we were making out and then he just stopped. I thought guys didn't do that."

"They usually don't," she said, looking faintly alarmed. "Most guys wouldn't stop even if an asteroid from outer space landed on them. Did you kick him someplace you shouldn't have?"

"No, I . . . I don't think so."

"Maybe he's married?" she offered. "I had a guy abandon me early in an evening once because he had to get home to the wife he didn't tell me he had."

"You seriously find the worst people to date."

"I am in complete agreement with you. But something had to have happened with Max."

"Well, I told him that I loved him, and if a crime reporter had been describing it, they would have said that he immediately fled the scene."

"Wait, you told him you loved him?"

"Yes," I said, worried about her incredulous tone.

"Everly! Why would you do that?"

"You were the one saying that I was in love with him!"

She rolled her eyes. "Which you are, but as my uncle Morty used to say, great Jehoshaphat! I did *not* tell you to tell Max. Have you met a man before? You never fire unless fired upon first."

"I wasn't shooting at him, I was being honest with him about how I felt." I hadn't realized that it would be such a bad thing to tell him. I should have known better. But I had been caught up and not thinking all that clearly. "And we have shared so many intimate things with each other about ourselves—things from our past that no one else knows, our secret hopes and dreams. He doesn't seem to have any problem with those. But we get close physically and he shuts down."

"It usually works the other way around, just so you know. I expected better from him. I never would have figured Max for a walking cliché. You say 'I love you' and he runs out of here like his hair was on fire. Which I might do the next time I see him. Coward."

"The saddest part is that this is probably the best relationship I've ever had with a man. Not that it's been much of a horse race."

She patted me on the arm. "Do you want to watch *The Bionic Woman* with me?"

"Okay." I tested my limbs and all the feeling seemed to have returned to them. Vella put the chair away and I got up slowly and made my way over to the couch.

It probably wasn't fair to Max that I had gone from *yes, let's be more than friends* to *oh, and by the way, I'm also in love with you* in a single day.

As someone who had spent most of her life worrying about what other people thought and putting their feelings first, I hadn't done that at all here. It hadn't occurred to me how Max might take my confession. I probably should have considered it before I said something.

Then again, I couldn't regret telling him. In my quest to be more like Kat, I wanted to be more open about my feelings and the things I wanted, and this was part of it. I did love Max and I wanted him to know that.

Even if it scared him.

My phone started ringing and Vella was the one who located it in my purse, which I had dropped on the floor when I came into the apartment. She glanced at the screen and her eyebrows raised as she said, "It's Max!"

My heart pounded hard and slow and I had to swallow the bitter taste in my mouth. I was afraid of what he was going to say. I waited until the last possible moment and then I answered. "Hello?"

"Everly? I am trying to learn from my mistakes and communicate better. I didn't want to just disappear on you again."

"Why did you run out?" I asked, even though I was pretty sure I knew the answer. "I probably shouldn't have said—"

"No, don't. I don't want you to take it back. I'm not afraid. Not for the reason you probably think, anyway."

"Then why?"

"I need to talk to you, but it has to be in person. And it can't be someplace where we're alone and all I want to do is devour you."

I couldn't help the pleasurable shivers that started running up and down my back. "What if I want to be devoured?"

"That is part of the problem," he ground out, sounding frustrated. "I've discovered that I'm basically powerless to resist you."

"Then don't resist me," I said, only partially teasing. It was an intoxicating feeling to know that someone like Max felt like he couldn't keep away from me. "But if you're worried, maybe we can get together tomorrow in some neutral location where there are other people and talk?"

"I have a bunch of appointments for most of the day, and then a family dinner tomorrow night."

"And I have that work thing tomorrow night anyway, so I wouldn't be able to go even if you were free. What about Sunday?"

"I can do Sunday. Let's have lunch together at Roma Vida."

Aw, that was where we'd kind of had our first date. He was the cutest. "It's a date. And I'm glad you called me. Shutting down and running off is not a way to deal with problems."

"I know. And I'll see you on Sunday," he said. "I'll be thinking about you every second until I get to be with you again."

That reassured me that I hadn't frightened him off completely. "Okay. Bye."

When I hung up my phone, Vella was giving me a surprised face. "Newfound respect for Max Colby. Good for him."

"But what do you think he has to tell me?"

"Like I said, all I've got is 'married.' I don't know what else would be important for him to disclose."

Neither did I. While I was completely relieved that he had called me and still wanted to see me, I felt more confused than ever.

~

My work event the following evening was the anniversary party for Ambassador Preston Wainscott and his wife, Fiona, and it was easily the swankiest event I'd ever attended. There was a lot to oversee and I could tell that Claudia was grateful I had come to help. There were so many moving parts, and the hotel was one of the most expensive ones in New York and the staff were not exactly easy to work with. A bit snobbish, even.

It also wasn't simple coordinating tasks with the other event-planning company. Everybody was being a bit territorial, which I understood. If this were an event I had helped plan from start to finish, I wouldn't want another company coming in at the last minute and putting their fingerprints all over it, either.

Forty different things went wrong and it took all of us to put out each of those fires. Nothing major, just a lot of small annoyances that would have upset our guests of honor if they were aware of them.

For a brief moment I wondered if any members of the Monterran royal family would be at the party. Mr. Wainscott had been their ambassador—it would make sense that he might know some of them and they might come.

A few weeks ago that thought would have filled me with eager anticipation.

But now? I didn't need a Monterran prince. I had Max.

The guests started arriving and I no longer had an assigned task, so I just floated around, letting the other planners know that I was available if they needed assistance. I would have to stay until the very end, as I'd promised Claudia that I would help with takedown. I felt like I owed it to her since she had done it for me at Hyacinth's birthday party.

I was also hoping to finally talk with her about my possible promotion. She had blatantly told me that it would happen if the birthday was a success, and it had been. But she had been so busy this last week with this event that she hadn't had any free time to discuss it with me. I'd checked with her assistant to see her schedule and not a single time slot had been available.

So this would be my chance to make my move.

I was walking around the dance floor, where the DJ was setting up. I had been surprised that this couple didn't want like, an orchestra, but apparently the DJ had been at their request, as they shared a love for 1980s hair bands and wanted those songs played.

The Elevated CEO, Topher Crawley, was here. He nodded at me and came over to say hello. I always felt anxious around him, like I didn't know the correct thing to do or say.

"How are you this evening, Everly?"

"I'm good, sir. How are you?"

He smiled and held up his hand. "I'm not old enough to be a 'sir.'"

What was I supposed to call him, then? If I said "Mr. Crawley," he might tell me it was too formal, or he might be upset if I used his first name. I wasn't sure what the right move here was and I could feel sweat beads starting to form.

Thankfully he moved the conversation along. "It is kind of you to volunteer to help out. This certainly doesn't fall within your job description."

I knew it might not be a good idea to tell the CEO of my company that I was partially doing it for a promotion that I had been promised.

So I settled on, "I like being a team player."

He nodded. "Good. And it was nice to see you."

I let out a sigh of relief when he walked away.

A few minutes later Adrian arrived and I saw that he had Colette with him. I smiled at him, and when he caught my gaze, he smiled back and pointed at Colette. I gave him a thumbs-up. I was glad that they had apparently worked things out.

I was in and out of the kitchen to see where I could help out the most for the next little bit. When I reentered the ballroom, I was shocked to see Sunny talking to Topher Crawley. What was she doing here? Her in-laws had to be friends with the Wainscotts. I could see them being part of the same social circle.

She seemed to notice me at the same time, and her face became more animated. She kept pointing at me and smiling, but Topher Crawley's expression fell the longer she went on.

What was that about?

It was weird seeing her here, like different parts of my life were all converging at this one party.

Too bad Max wasn't here, too.

Then ten seconds later, I saw him. Like I'd somehow personally conjured him up. And he was Tuxedo Max again. I internally swooned at the sight of him. It was a good thing there were five hundred other people at this party. He was drinking a glass of champagne, his free hand in his pocket. He looked bored and annoyed.

I walked over to him, barely able to contain my glee at seeing him. "Max?"

"Everly?"

And the sound of utter shock in his voice made me think that he wasn't quite as happy to see me.

CHAPTER
THIRTY-SEVEN

"What are you doing here?" he asked.

"Working. What are you doing here? Did Vella tell you where I was?" Had he come looking for me? Because he couldn't wait another sixteen hours to see me again? That was sweet.

But his body language and panicked expression told me that he hadn't been searching for me. He was surprised that I was here.

"Your company is not in charge of this party." He made it sound like he had specifically checked.

"No, the ambassador used Melissa Morgan Events as the planner. And Melissa Morgan is a friend of Claudia's and asked us to help out because it had so many moving parts that needed to be taken care of. You met Claudia, remember?"

The panic on his face got worse.

"What is going on with you?" I asked. Hadn't he just told me yesterday that he wanted us to be better about communicating, not shutting down when something happened?

"We need to go somewhere so that we can talk," he said, and the urgency in his voice made me want to dig my heels in and stay put. He was hiding something from me and I didn't like it.

Before I could say as much, Sunny was there hugging me hello, and somehow Max appeared even more freaked out.

"What are you doing here?" she asked, sounding delighted to see me.

"I'm working this event."

"Well, what a coincidence! Max didn't mention that you were hired to work his dad's party."

It was like a giant gong had sounded right next to my head and drowned out all other noise, pinpointing all of my focus to a single white noise roaring inside my head.

His *dad's* party?

What?

"Everly, I can explain," he said.

"What is wrong with your voice?" Sunny said, looking at her cousin. "Why do you sound like that?"

"He always sounds like that," I said. My heart was pounding like a raging animal trapped in a cage, desperate to be set free, roaring and throwing itself against the bars.

He said, "Sunny, can I talk to you for a minute?" but she ignored him, all of her attention focused on me.

"He doesn't have an accent. I don't know why you're doing one," she said, just as confused as I was. He tried again to get her to step aside with him, but I put my hand on her arm. She might have been his cousin, but she was my friend, too.

"Because he's from Monterra," I said.

She replied, "He's American. His dad was the ambassador to Monterra, but Max is not Monterran."

There it was. The secret he'd been hiding from me. I had told him the first night we met that it was important to me that people not lie.

And he had been lying to me from the beginning. Every conversation, every text, every kiss—all of it had been one giant lie.

I was in love with a man who didn't exist.

"Everly, I can explain," he said, reaching for my hand, but I physically jerked myself away from his touch.

"Your father is Preston Wainscott?"

His face was clouded, dark. "Yes."

"And you're not from Monterra?"

"No."

Sunny finally seemed to realize that she had said something Max didn't want her to reveal. She excused herself but neither Max nor I said anything to her as she made a hasty exit.

She wasn't here because her in-laws knew the Wainscotts. She was here because it was her uncle's anniversary party and her cousin had invited her.

I couldn't believe this was happening. He had hidden this from me for weeks.

I felt so humiliated.

"This is not how I wanted you to find out," he said.

I let out a laugh of disbelief. "I'm sure you didn't intend for me to ever find out. Did you enjoy pulling one over on me? You must have thought I was so stupid to fall for your act."

I began to walk away. I couldn't deal with this right now. I was supposed to be working, not watching my whole world crumble and fall apart.

"No, Everly, I was going to tell you. Tomorrow. I've been trying to tell you for so long."

"Oh, yeah, I know just how hard you've tried to tell me. You had so many opportunities and you never did!" I got as far as the edge of the dance floor before I whirled around to face him again. "What is your actual name?"

"Max Wainscott. My mom and dad call me Maximilian."

His mom . . . Colby . . . I knew that name. "Is your mother Serena Colby?"

From his expression I already knew the answer. "Yes."

Serena Colby was the socialite who ran New York City. She was the tastemaker everyone followed, and anything she touched turned to gold. Gossip columnists called her "the queen of New York." She came from extremely old money and was currently married to one of the wealthiest men in the world.

I had once thought Adrian Stone was a prince of the New York City social scene.

But Max was the one who actually deserved that title.

"You're rich, too. This whole time I thought you were poor like me and you let me believe it and make a fool of myself."

He put his hands in his pockets. "You didn't make a fool of yourself."

"Yes, I did."

"I liked how you saw me. I wanted to be that person."

"So for the sake of your ego, you lied to me? Because it made you feel good?" I asked.

"No, I'm not expressing myself well right now."

"Oh, is that because English is your second language?" I asked with a surprising amount of sarcasm. Like I was channeling Vella.

He looked wounded. "I thought you always tried to see the best in people."

"I did. And look where it got me. You lying to me and using me."

"When did I use you?"

"To plan the baby shower for your cousin last minute."

"Everly, I wasn't trying to use you."

It didn't really matter what he had been trying to do. "That's how I feel about it."

I shook my hands once, like they were dripping in gross mud and I wanted to fling it off. Like his lies had covered me in some kind of invisible muck. I was not going to make a scene at this event. I wanted to yell and maybe throw a drink in Max's lying face, but I would keep myself under control. A part of my brain kept reminding me that I was at work right now and it would reflect badly on my company if I behaved inappropriately, even if my personal life had been hit by a wrecking ball.

"Everly—"

"I thought you didn't say things you don't mean," I interrupted him. "Does lying not count?"

Every line on his face reflected his desperation and I could see that he wanted to explain, to make me understand. "Remember how you said that when you get around people from the south, your accent comes back? The same thing happens to me when I get around Monterrans or Italians."

"And? 'Whoops, I had a bit of an accent when we met and you thought I was from Monterra and I let you keep thinking it'? Still a lie."

"I didn't think I'd see you past that first night and that it was a little white lie that didn't matter. But the more time I spent with you, the more I wanted to be with you, and I didn't know how to tell you what I'd done. I didn't know what you would do if I told you the truth and I didn't want to lose you."

Part of my heart twinged. Even if he'd lied before, I wanted desperately to believe him now. I couldn't let myself be swayed, though. "So that excuses it? You lied and lied and I don't know how to get past that."

He took a step closer to me and I knew he wanted to reach for me, but he refrained. "You do. You know me. You know the man that I am."

"No, I don't. That's the entire point, Max." And listening to his unaccented English, I realized that he seemed like a totally different person to me now. "You had to know that I was going to find out eventually. Did you ever think about that?"

"Yes! That was why I wanted us to meet tomorrow. I was going to tell you everything."

Someone came up to my left and it took me a second to register that it was Adrian. I scanned the room quickly, wondering if I had accidentally raised my voice and my boss had come over to scold me.

"Everly, I need to speak with you for a minute," Adrian said, apologetically.

"We're in the middle of something right now," Max said.

"Max! This is my boss."

He looked guilty and immediately backed off. Adrian took me by the arm and led me a few feet away.

"Everly, I'm so sorry that I have to do this, but Topher Crawley told me that I have to fire you and have you escorted from the party."

Adrenaline and shock spiked up my spine until it created a ball in my throat, and for a second I couldn't speak. "What? Why?"

"You have a noncompete clause in the contract you signed when you started at Elevated. Apparently Topher spoke to a woman at this party who said you threw her a baby shower yesterday."

I put a hand over my stomach, unable to believe that this was happening. Surely the universe wouldn't hit me with two such horrific tragedies right in a row. "I didn't know about the clause. I'm not even an official event planner. I did it in my free time."

"Yes, but you met with the woman at Elevated's offices. Which Topher knows because he recognized her from the meeting. He thinks you're trying to poach potential clients for yourself, which also violates your contract."

I knew I should have read that thing before I signed it.

"I'm not trying to steal clients," I said, pleading. There had to be a way out of this. "Claudia specifically told me she wasn't interested in doing showers and that's what this was. A baby shower. I was just trying to do a favor for a friend."

"Did you get paid for it?"

"I—yes. I did."

"I'm really sorry," Adrian said again, and I could see that he was. "You were the best assistant I ever had. I should have promoted you a long time ago. But Topher's made this call and there's nothing I can do."

Correction—there was nothing he was *going* to do. With a sick feeling in my stomach, I realized that Adrian would never stick his neck out for me. Less than a week ago, he had been telling me that I was the second most important person in his life, and tonight he was firing me. I hysterically wondered if he could see the irony in that.

Two men approached, hotel security staff who were probably all too happy to throw me out.

Adrian leaned his head to the side, indicating that these were the people who had been sent as my escorts so that I wouldn't make a scene. "Have a good night, Everly. Keep in touch."

I should have let Vella light his hair on fire when she'd wanted to.

I had worn a side bag tonight that I currently had on, and so the only thing I needed to do was collect my coat from the coat check. I turned my head and caught Max's gaze.

He looked stricken and I could tell that he'd overheard every word. "Everly, I'm so sorry."

I nodded, telling myself not to cry. "So tonight you cost me my heart and my job. If you wanted to find a way to evict me from my apartment, you could go for the hat trick."

When I tried to move past him, he started following me, saying my name again.

"Leave me alone," I said. "I've already been embarrassed enough for one night. I don't want to talk to you about this. I think we've both said everything we need to say, and whatever this was is very obviously over. Enjoy your father's anniversary party."

With my head held up, I walked across the ballroom to the coat check. I didn't lose my security detail until I was out on the sidewalk, asking the valets to hail me a cab. It didn't take long for one to arrive, and as I went to climb into the taxi, I looked back at the hotel lobby.

Max was standing beyond the entrance doors, watching me.

I closed the door hard.

This was over and it had barely even begun.

CHAPTER THIRTY-EIGHT

I cried the entire way home and I think I completely freaked my taxi driver out. He kept asking me if I was okay, but I couldn't talk. I was incapable of forming words. Instead I curled up into a ball in the back seat. I wanted to make myself as small as possible, as if that would some-how prevent me from feeling so much searing, horrific pain.

When I got back to the apartment, I was dismayed to find Vella making out on the couch with Otis.

I just stared at them. I didn't have enough emotional reserves left to even be upset with her for whatever was happening right then.

She took one look at my face and said to him, "Get out."

"But I thought we were going to—"

"Out now," she said.

Otis grumbled and got to his feet, shooting me a dirty look on his way out. He slammed the door shut.

"I thought you were done with him," I said.

"That was like a goodbye make-out session."

"How was he supposed to hear you say goodbye when you had his ear in your mouth?" I asked, grateful for this tiny distraction from the unbearable pain pressing down on my chest.

"Osmosis?"

But I was too defeated to argue with her that she didn't understand how osmosis worked. Instead I dropped my bag and wearily took off my shoes. I went over to curl up on the couch next to her. To my surprise she grabbed the blanket and put it over me.

"Why do you look like a sad raccoon?" she asked. "And who do I need to stab?"

"I got fired tonight." I quickly explained how that had happened.

"Then I quit in solidarity," she said.

"Who are you going to call and tell that you quit?" It was the weekend; there wasn't anyone at the office.

"No one."

"Then how will they know?"

"They'll figure it out pretty quickly when I don't show up Monday morning. But I know that's not why you're this upset. What happened?"

The story of what Max had done tumbled out of me, but I told it robotically, because I was so exhausted that I couldn't cry through it like I wanted to. I didn't have anything left. My tear ducts had tapped out.

The ache in my throat and chest didn't ease, though. Neither did the stabbing pain in my heart.

When I finished, Vella said, "He pretended to be from Monterra? Like that famous actor's wife who pretended she was from Spain but she was just a basic girl from Boston? Is Max from Boston?"

"I don't know where he's from." I wondered if everything he'd told me had been a lie. "This is why you couldn't find anything about Max Colby online. He doesn't exist."

She took her phone out and did a search and made a squeaking sound. "Maximilian Wainscott is like private-jet-and-a-mansion-on-every-continent rich. There are so many photos of him online, so many stories on gossip sites. Wow."

No wonder he'd never told me where he lived. This was probably why I hadn't ever seen his apartment. Why he never gave me any details about his family. Max probably could have picked my mom and Meemaw out of a lineup, I had told him so much about them.

Why hadn't I realized how many things he kept from me? I'd been so distracted by my love for him that I hadn't even noticed.

"What do you want me to tell him when he comes here?" she asked.

"Why would you think he'd come here?"

"Because he's in love with you, too."

I shook my head, hard. "He can't love me. He never would have lied to me if he did. And I told him to leave me alone. That I didn't want to talk to him and that this was over."

She nodded thoughtfully. "I think he'll stay clear for a little while, but he loves you too much to keep completely away from you. But I'm proud of you for standing up for yourself and a boundary that's important to you."

"What do you mean?"

"Everly of a month ago would have found a way to make this all okay. You wouldn't have held Max accountable for what he'd done. And I know making boundaries is hard. Especially for someone like you."

I nodded. She was right. People-pleasing me would have made excuses for Max. And maybe I hadn't handled this in the best way, but it was better than letting people walk all over me.

"Maybe I overreacted, though." I grimaced. There was that people-pleaser part of me that she'd just mentioned, still wanting to make things okay. To take blame for something that wasn't my fault.

"Considering the fact that there wasn't a news report tonight about you locking him up in his apartment and setting it on fire, no, I don't think you overreacted." When I didn't smile at her joke, she added, "Someday you'll look back at all of this and it will just be blood under the bridge."

She was right. About everything. I had to be better about setting boundaries and standing up for myself. I couldn't let myself get into a situation like this ever again.

I curled up on the couch, again trying to shrink away. We both heard my phone buzz in my purse. Vella got up, found it, and shut it off. I wouldn't be able to shut off the outside world for forever, though. At some point I was going to have to figure out what to do about a job because I still wanted to be able to eat and have electricity.

She set my phone down on the counter. "I want to show you something."

"What?"

"My bedroom."

It was so entirely unexpected that for a few beats I didn't react. "Really?"

"It's time. Come on."

Despite my bone-melting sadness, I got to my feet quickly. I didn't want her to change her mind. Would there be a pile of rodent skulls? The dried hearts of her ex-lovers? Barbie posters? I just didn't know.

I wanted to tell someone that it was finally happening—and I was crushed when I realized that the person I most wanted to tell was Max.

"If you have puppies in there and you didn't share, just know that I'm going to be furious," I told her.

She put the key into the lock and swung the door open. "Have a look."

My heart beat so hard as I crossed the threshold. It was a normal-looking room. No frills or expensive furniture—a mattress with a basic frame and a beat-up dresser.

But what drew my eye was four rows of shelves against a wall, stacked with trophies, sashes, and pictures.

And the photos were all of a blonde-haired Vella, wearing high heels, sparkling evening gowns, and tiaras.

"Cosmetology school is not the only reason why I know how to do hair and makeup," she told me.

"You were a beauty queen?" It was so unlike her I couldn't reconcile the idea that the person standing next to me was the same one in the photos.

"Yes. And I keep all this stuff to remind myself on a daily basis of who I used to be so that I'll remember to not be her again."

"You could just keep a scrapbook or a private Pinterest board like a regular person," I said.

"What's the fun in that? Who you used to be doesn't dictate who you're going to be. It's why I can't settle on one job. I'm not sure who I want to be yet, and I'm going to try everything out until I find exactly what I want. It's why none of my relationships work out, either. I don't know who I am, so how can I be with someone else? But you? You already know who you are, Everly. And you're more than just your insecurities and fears. You can deal with anything that comes your way. And I really admire that about you."

Even though I'd thought all my tears had fallen, some reserves showed up. "You're really good at this supporting-your-friend thing. Have you thought about becoming a life coach?"

"Can you even imagine how many people I would permanently mess up if I did that?"

"You'd do a better job than you think."

She shook her head like she didn't believe me.

"So all I had to do to see inside your room was get fired and have my heart broken?" I asked.

"I kept this from you, and you're my best friend. I didn't let you see this side of who I used to be because it would have changed how you thought about me now. And I like the way you see me." She paused for a few seconds and then said, "I would bet Max found himself in the same situation."

"But you didn't lie about what was in your room."

"No, I get that. I'm just saying I understand why someone might do it. Because in a sense I've done it, too."

There was merit to what she was saying. I was focusing solely on the lies Max had told without really wondering why he had done it. Maybe his reasons would matter. Maybe they would even change how I felt right now.

But I was too upset with him, too hurt, to give those thoughts much consideration.

I walked out of her room and to my alcove. I wanted to go to bed and for this day to be over. I didn't want to think about Max anymore.

"Are you mad at me?" she asked, misunderstanding my silence.

"I'm a little upset that we could have been playing princess dress-up with your tiaras this whole time, but no, I'm not mad. It was your secret to keep. I'm glad that you shared it with me, though. But I'm really tired and I want to go to sleep."

"Okay," she said. "I'm here if you need me."

That made my tears well up again, so I just nodded. When I heard her bedroom door close, I collapsed onto my bed.

She was right about Max—he wouldn't stay away forever. I couldn't talk to him right now, though. I didn't have it in me.

In one night I had lost the man I loved and the job I'd adored. I felt like I had nothing left here in New York.

I grabbed my laptop and did the only thing I could think of.

I booked a flight home.

CHAPTER
THIRTY-NINE

"How long are you going to stay in bed?" Meemaw asked as she lowered herself down onto a chair next to me. "I think we need to stage one of those intervention thingies."

"I don't need an intervention, Meemaw. I'm just sad." My dog, Princess, was curled up in bed next to me. She'd been my constant companion since I'd returned home. As if she could sense how unhappy I was.

I tried to think of the last time I'd been sad before Max. It occurred to me that it was the day when my stepmother had posted that happy photo of my dad's new family and when I found out Adrian was going to propose to Colette. But that same night I'd been able to joke, to laugh, to forget about him completely while spending time with Max.

But now? It was like all the color had gone out of the world and I would never smile or laugh again.

"It's been a week, Everly," Meemaw said.

Sometimes it felt like I'd been home for ten years. Or as if I'd never gone off to New York at all.

My mom came into the room and Meemaw turned toward her. "You know, the absence of a strong male father figure causes insecurity in women. I read the Google about it."

"This isn't because Dad sucks," I said. "It's because Max does."

"Have you talked to Max at all?" my mother asked as she sat on the foot of my bed.

My plan had been to ignore him completely. Maybe even block him from my phone. But then I remembered how upset I'd been at him for shutting down and running off, telling him that wasn't a way to deal with problems, and realized that I was doing exactly the same thing.

So I'd texted him after I'd arrived to let him know where I was and that I wasn't ready to talk to him yet. He had immediately responded.

I'm here when you are ready to talk. I want to explain if you'll let me.

He continued to text daily, just to let me know that he was thinking of me and missed me. He didn't pressure me or ask me to respond. It wasn't like he was ignoring what I said, more like he wanted to let me know that he was still there.

It was exactly what I would have wanted him to do, if he'd asked. *Because he knows you,* a voice inside me whispered. I ignored it.

"I texted him," I said. "I'm not ready to speak to him yet."

"But you love him," my mom responded, her voice soft.

"It's only been a month," I said. I had decided that it was far too short a time for me to be in love with someone. It wasn't logical. "You don't love somebody you've known for a month."

My heart didn't agree with me, though.

Meemaw frowned. "I knew your grandfather for two weeks and we got married the night before he was shipped out to Vietnam. We were happily married for thirty-eight years until he passed."

I had a lot of good memories of Meemaw and Papaw and how in love they had been, in sharp contrast to my parents' marriage. My grandparents' relationship was one of the reasons I believed in fairy tales.

Meemaw was slowly getting to her feet while muttering to herself. "We let her go off to the city and she manages to find a rich suitor but still winds up back here."

When she'd left the room, I asked my mom, "Does this mean the intervention failed? Since half of it left?"

"You know, I dated your father for a year and I never felt about him the way you feel about Max. Sometimes I think time is irrelevant when it comes to love. We feel what we feel."

"What I feel is like a total failure." At love, at my job.

"You didn't fail. You got fired because of a rule you were unaware of. That kind of thing happens sometimes. It wasn't because you failed."

This was the encouraging, supportive mother that I felt like I'd waited my whole life for. "Why aren't you always like this?"

My mom seemed startled. "Like what?"

"It's one of the reasons I love talking about royals with you. When we do that, we're just ourselves and we enjoy each other. But any other time, you don't ever ask me questions about my life."

"I do ask you!" she said, sounding a bit indignant. "All the time!"

"No, you ask so that you can tell me what I should be doing differently. I know you love me, but when you do that, it makes me feel really small. I want to be able to talk to you like we are now. Where you listen to me and let me speak and don't try to constantly tell me what to do."

She twisted her mouth to one side and I recognized the gesture as one she made when she was trying not to cry, and now I felt worse.

"I guess because I want your life to turn out differently than mine. Meemaw used to do the same thing to me, only worse."

"Meemaw?" I asked in shock. While my grandmother would make occasional comments, like the earlier one about me going to New York, for the most part she was a really great listener. I'd spent hours growing up pouring my heart out to her.

"She wasn't always the way that you remember her. But now she's old and worried about getting into heaven, so things have changed."

I felt a hint of a smile hovering around my lips. It was the first time I'd wanted to smile in what felt like forever.

"And," my mom continued, "I want you to be happy. I married someone that I shouldn't have. He did give me you, and I'll always be grateful for that, but we never should have been together. I had dreams that I gave up. I wanted to be a lawyer. But after your dad left, I had to find a way to support us. I'm proud of my salon, but it's not what I wanted to do with my life. I've always wanted more for you, my perfect little princess. I wanted you to have a man who would respect you, love you, and be faithful to you."

"Oh, Mom." I reached out for her hand and she grabbed on to me tightly.

"I know I pushed you to join the salon. I thought it would be a good safety net for you while you figured out what you wanted to do. But you already knew, and I should have supported you in that dream. You are so much smarter, so much more talented, than I ever was. I want the biggest and the best for you and I'm sorry if I went about that in a terrible way. I would never want to hurt you. I want you to have the life you want. To have the life I never got to have."

"You can still have all of that," I told her. "You can still meet someone and have a life with them. You can even change careers if you want to. You don't have to live through me."

She held on to my hand with both of hers. "I didn't mean to try and live through you. And I don't know about trying to change what I'm doing. Or dating. I think I'm an old dog and don't have time for new tricks. But I am sorry."

"You had to be my mom and my dad and I love you for doing that. You always made me feel really loved and I think that's the most anyone can ask for."

"I will do better, though. I promise." She stayed quiet for a moment and then, like she couldn't help herself, said, "And I can see how much it's hurting you being apart from Max. And it's up to you whether or not you want to talk to him. And if you do, it'll go one of two ways. Either you'll end things completely and get closure, which will make it easier for you to move on. Or the second option could mean something pretty great might happen."

Her words filled me with hope. "I know I can't hide out here forever. I've been thinking about it a lot lately and I know what my next steps are going to be."

Using the phrase *next steps* made me think about Max, again. And my heart throbbed with grief.

"That's good. And I know you're trying to pattern your life after Kat's. Just remember what her mom told her when she broke up with Nico. She ran home and climbed into her bed and her mom told her to get back out there and make sure that Nico knew what he was missing out on. Maybe that'll work for you, too."

"You're thinking of the British princess, Princess Caitlin. The one married to Alexander. Kat wasn't close to her mom back then, and she stayed away from Nico for months after they broke up. But they worked things out."

That led to a twenty-minute conversation where we discussed royal breakups and how the people involved had dealt with their heartache.

Surprisingly, it made me feel a bit better.

The plans that I had spent the past week forming in my mind were also making me feel better. By day two it had occurred to me that if I was this sad without Max, why was I continuing to be without him? I was going to talk to him. But not over the phone. In person, the way he had wanted to when he was going to tell me that he wasn't from Monterra.

There were other things I had to work out first.

"Well, Meemaw and I are here if you want to talk some more," she said. "I'm going to go start dinner."

She got up and came over and kissed me on the forehead. "I love you, baby girl. And we will always be here for you, anytime you need us."

"Love you, Mom."

She left my room and I lay in my bed, staring up at the ceiling. I was glad I'd told my mom how I really felt and how I wanted things to change. I knew things were going to improve between us.

Because I had talked it out with her.

Just like I needed to talk things out with Max.

Now that I'd finally been able to have that conversation with my mom, it was one thing I could cross off the list I'd been crafting since I'd arrived home.

My phone rang and I looked at the caller ID. It was Vella.

Which was weird because Vella never called me. If we ever talked on the phone, it was because I had called her.

She always just texted. In fact, she had texted me every day since I'd come back to Alabama just to check in on me. Strange coming from her, but it was nice.

It made me worried that something serious was going on. I answered. "Vella, are you okay? Why are you calling me?"

"So, what Max did was bad, but it wasn't he-murdered-somebody or cheated-on-you bad."

"You know those two things are really different, right?"

"Well, sometimes one necessitates the other," she replied. "But yes. I was just trying to say that there are really horrible violations of trust and what Max did was essentially a harmless lie. He wasn't trying to hurt you. He did mislead you, which sucks, and he knows he shouldn't have done that."

"Why are you standing up for him?"

"A couple of reasons. The first is that he's come over every day at seven o'clock at night to see if you're back yet, and the other day I felt bad, so I invited him in. We got to talking and everything just spilled out of him. I don't think he has anyone else to talk to about this situation. Sunny is not speaking to him right now."

That made me feel sad. I hadn't wanted to come between Max and Sunny. I knew how much they meant to each other.

"The second reason," she went on, "is because while my heart has slightly softened toward Max, I still hate everybody and I'm mad at him for hurting you. But you love him and you're my best friend, so I want you to have everything you deserve that will make you happy. Even if what you want is a stupid person."

"I'm so glad we're friends." I was also glad she wasn't here to see my eyes getting all misty. I also thought about how much closer I'd felt to Vella since she'd shared all of herself with me, and given that I was in love with Max, I knew that I owed him that same chance.

"Yeah, yeah. When are you coming back?"

"Tomorrow," I said. I'd already booked my ticket.

"Good. Will your accent be back to normal then? Because you're a lot like this."

"At least I didn't 'y'all come back now, ya hear' you."

"Stop," she said.

"I could say 'bless your heart' and tell you I'm fixin' to come home soon, so stop pitchin' a fit, because I'm happy as all get-out to be headed back up north!"

"I'm going now," she said, and hung up the phone.

Despite what all of my loved ones seemed to think, I hadn't been curled up in my bed stuck in an endless misery loop.

No, I had done what I was best at. I'd planned.

I'd made backup plans for my backup plans, preparing myself for every contingency and problem. I was deciding what I wanted because the event I was planning was my actual life. I would make those calls, and I would live with the consequences of those decisions.

I knew what I would do when I got back to New York, and I had weighed out the pros and cons of each action. I couldn't control other people, but I was in charge of my life. I had needed this trip home to catch my breath. To be able to hear my own thoughts and to pay attention to what I wanted.

While I didn't know how things with Max would go, I would give him a chance to explain himself.

I wanted to smile and laugh again. And I knew the only way that would happen would be for me to hear him out.

CHAPTER FORTY

After I got home and dropped off my suitcase, I went directly to Elevated. There was a new receptionist at the front desk, and she looked overwhelmed. "Can I help you?" she asked.

"I'm here to see Franny." She was the HR manager and had some paperwork for me to sign and a box of my things for me to collect. "I'm Everly Aprile."

The receptionist's eyes widened. "Stay here. I'll be right back."

It was very strange to be left in the lobby. This had been my second home for so many years that it was weird to be an outsider.

When the receptionist returned, she had Claudia with her, which I had not expected.

"Everly! I was hoping that we could chat. Would you mind coming into my office?"

"Sure." I nodded.

When we got into her office, she closed the door and we both sat down. I felt a bit nervous, which was silly because it wasn't like she could fire me.

"I want to hire you," she said.

It was probably the last thing I would have predicted she would say. "What?"

"You will get the title of event planner and you'll be reporting directly to me."

"But what about Mr. Crawley?"

She narrowed her eyes. "What happened to you was wrong and ridiculous. I've already spoken to him and let him know that I would be doing this. You are an excellent employee and team player. It's always been important to me to help other women succeed. You deserve that chance."

A week ago I would have leapt at this opportunity, but now I had different plans. "Thank you so much. I really appreciate the offer, but I've decided to strike out on my own." This had been one of the things I'd been planning over the last week. I knew starting my own company was a big risk, but I was ready to take some really big leaps. And thanks to the money Sunny had given me, I had enough to do it.

"Good for you, Everly. I would be happy to mentor you and help you get everything started."

"Thank you!" Again, I hadn't expected her response. "I will definitely take you up on that. And if you get any clients looking for a baby or bridal shower—"

"I will send them your way," she said before I could finish my sentence. "Not that you're going to need my help."

She reached over and grabbed a pile of paper and pushed it toward me. "The word's already spread, thanks to the work you did for the Belmont baby shower."

"You mean the shower that got me fired?" The irony of that was not lost on me.

"I mean the shower that put your name on the map. Clients have been calling here and asking for you by name. This is a bunch of the messages and emails we've received and I'm giving them to you. This should help you get started."

"But why don't you keep these leads for yourself?" I suspected that it was what Adrian would have done.

"Because that's not the kind of person I am," she said. "Plus, like I told you, we're not doing showers. But we would be happy to partner up with your new company for any clients who may need different types of events."

I took the papers. "Thank you."

She stood up and offered me her hand, and I shook it. I said, "I wish I'd been your assistant instead."

"I wouldn't have let you. I'd have promoted you within three months." We walked over to her door. "Best of luck to you, Everly. You are going to be wildly successful."

Wildly successful. The words pounded themselves into my brain as I walked toward HR.

One of the most amazing event planners in the business thought I was going to be wildly successful.

And she had given me the best start possible.

~

Despite the fact that I had been planning for a week what I would do and say when I saw Max again, all of my plans and backup plans went out the window when I returned to New York.

I considered calling him, but I knew he was going to come by at seven o'clock. I spent time getting ready because this was going to be an important moment in my life, one way or the other, and I wanted to be prepared for it.

Vella told me she was going to go say goodbye again to Otis. I tried to talk her out of it, but she informed me that she had to make her own mistakes so that she could better discover who she was.

Given that I'd made some not-so-great decisions lately, I didn't feel qualified to stop her and just said, "Call me if you need help moving a body."

Then it was just me in the quiet of the apartment, waiting, watching the clock.

Precisely at seven o'clock, Max knocked. I walked over to the door, took a deep breath, and opened it.

"Everly?" His mouth dropped open.

He looked terrible, like he hadn't slept at all the entire week I'd been gone. It was the worst I'd ever seen him look. He was still drop-dead gorgeous, but lines of exhaustion and worry were etched on his face.

"Hi, Max." Well, that was an entirely inadequate response for whatever was happening between us right now as we stood in the doorway.

He shifted his body and I saw his hands raise slightly, like he wanted to touch me, hold me, but he didn't.

"Come in," I told him. "I think we have a lot to talk about."

He came into the apartment and I closed the door behind him. My hands were sweating, my heart racing. I couldn't remember the last time I'd been this nervous.

I walked over to the couch and sat. Max did the same. He took off his coat, laid it on the arm of the couch, and then started wringing his hands.

He said, "I've imagined this moment so many times and now that you're here and willing to talk to me, I don't know how to start."

"You could—"

"First, your job," he cut me off. "Sorry, I didn't mean to interrupt you."

"No, go ahead."

"With your job situation. My dad has a friend who is a friend of Elevated's CEO. I will get your job back."

"I don't need you to do that."

He misunderstood me. "I'm not trying to save the day here or anything, and I'm not trying to rescue you. I want to help you get it back because I am responsible for what happened and I want to make it right."

"No, I didn't say that because I wanted you to stay out of it. I'm saying it because I don't want to go back to Elevated. I think I'm going to try and start my own company. I have some seed money thanks to Sunny and a list of potential clients."

He gave me a shy half smile. "I thought you might say that, so I paid the graphics designer at the non-profit to make these up." He took out his phone and opened an app and handed it to me.

It was a bunch of different logos and business cards with "Aprile's Showers" on them.

My breath caught. This was unbelievably thoughtful and kind.

And exactly the kind of thing Max would do.

I gave the phone back to him, my hand shaking. "Thank you. But you should know that it wasn't really your fault that I lost my job and I shouldn't have blamed you. I'm sorry I did that. I was just really angry with you."

"You had every right to be. And you're not the one who should be apologizing here."

I nodded.

Then he said, "What were you going to tell me earlier? You said 'you could' before I interrupted you."

"Oh. You said you didn't know how to start, and I was going to say that you could start at the beginning."

"Right." He nodded, sliding his phone back into his pocket. "So the night we met at the bar. I saw you crying and how sad you were. When I saw you smile at Basta, it was the most beautiful thing I'd ever seen. And the only thing I wanted in that moment was to keep making you smile."

"Oh." I seemed to be saying that a lot lately. My nervous system was short-circuiting and my heart was thrashing around so hard in my chest I was sure it was going to disconnect itself from some important veins and arteries.

"I dream in Italian. Sometimes I hear someone speak and I translate it into Italian and then back into English. Which I know makes no sense, but I do it. I did live in Monterra for years while my father was the ambassador there. It's where I went to high school. Italian was my primary language for a long time. Monterra feels like a second home to me, but I am American. And like I said, when I get around people speaking it, like everyone in that sports bar, I pick it up without realizing it, including the accented English."

He had already explained this part of it—that the accent had been accidental because of his environment.

"So I didn't set out to deceive you. I was speaking that way without realizing it. And when you pointed it out and you were so happy at the idea that I was Monterran, well, I didn't want to take that away from you. I figured it couldn't hurt anything. I didn't expect to see you again."

"But then you left your phone and coat behind."

A wry smile from him. "And now some part of me wonders if my subconscious did it deliberately because despite me thinking I wouldn't see you again, I really wanted to. I'd had so much fun talking to you and I wanted it to continue. I wanted to see you again."

My heart was bonging loudly in my chest, strong enough to reverberate through the rest of my body.

"And again and again. And even when you said you were only interested in being friends, I kept coming back because I knew I wanted more. I knew that you were scared, but I wasn't sure why. But one thing I was certain of—I thought that if I told you the truth, that I wasn't from Monterra, you would stop spending time with me. I didn't want to lose you. You told me the first night we met how much you hated people lying to you—that you couldn't tolerate it. I couldn't see a way to tell you and not lose you. It was selfish of me."

"You know, there's something Vella recently shared with me," I said.

"The beauty pageant thing?" he asked.

My eyebrows lifted. "How do you know about that?"

"She showed me. I think when I was sharing with her about you and our situation, she felt obligated to return the favor. And she said she assumed you would tell me eventually, anyway."

I shook my head. I would have kept her secret. "She didn't want me to know about it because she thought it would change how I saw her. And it wouldn't have. I would still like her regardless. It wouldn't have changed anything. I would have liked you and wanted to be with you even if you weren't from Monterra."

"It's more than that," he said. "You were the first woman I'd ever dated who'd never heard of me."

"Because Max Colby doesn't exist," I reminded him. His country of origin wasn't the only thing he'd lied about.

"I know. I'm sorry about that, too. My whole life people wanted to be friends with me because of who my parents are. Paparazzi used to follow all of us around constantly. Especially during my parents' divorce. Arabella loved it and couldn't get enough of it. My 'friends' loved the money, the lifestyle, the attention. What I could give them instead of who I was. Since moving to New York, I've been using Max Colby. And you liked me. Not Maximilian Wainscott. You don't know what that means to me."

I wanted to comfort him, so I followed my instinct and reached out and took his hand. He gripped me tightly, the look of hope and surprise on his face making my heart ache.

He swallowed hard before continuing to speak. "You said once that you didn't respect people with trust funds and I wanted your respect. Not just your respect. Your admiration. Your heart. I kept that part of me hidden from you because I was afraid."

I looked at our joined hands, the way he held on to mine like they were a lifeline. "And again, it doesn't matter to me that you come from money. I thought that we had similar backgrounds, but I don't care that we don't. It never mattered to me if you were rich or poor."

He stayed quiet for a few seconds, as if considering what I'd said. "After we kissed that first time, I felt like such a jerk. I was lying to you but kissing you like that? It wasn't fair to you and I didn't know how to tell you. I knew I had to, but like you said, I was running away instead of dealing with my issues. Then before Sunny's shower, when I heard your boss talking about taking you on a date, I thought I had lost you. I was so unbelievably relieved that you chose me that I couldn't think clearly. All I knew was that I wanted you so badly that I couldn't even remember where I was, let alone that I should be telling you the truth."

He glanced over his shoulder at my bed. "I'm so drawn to you—you're like this magnet that I can't stay away from. I tried to put you out of my head after I found out about that date and I couldn't do it. You were always there, no matter what I did. You were all I could think about. Then when things heated up here at your apartment, I again had to deal with the fact that I was lying to you, but I knew I wouldn't be able to confess when all I want to do is touch you and kiss you whenever you're close."

I understood that sentiment all too well.

"When you told me that you loved me"—his hands squeezed mine again—"I was in shock because I'd known for a while that I had fallen in love with you and it was incredible and overwhelming to realize that you felt the same way."

That revelation was a complete shock, like an arrow piercing my heart, sharp and fast and unexpected. I couldn't breathe. Max loved me?

"And how could I lie to someone I love? A relationship is supposed to be based on trust, and I was lying. Over something so stupid and inconsequential. And I—"

"You love me?" I stopped him mid-rant, wanting to make sure that I'd heard him correctly. That I wasn't imagining things.

"Of course I love you." He said it like I should have known that already. "Who wouldn't love you? You're the most incredible woman I've ever met."

"You've never said that to me before."

"I haven't? That was another thing that I should have been telling you repeatedly once I realized it. It just all happened so fast and I fell so hard and so quickly."

This was one of the variables I hadn't been able to plan for. I knew Max liked me, was attracted to me, cared about me, but I didn't know whether or not his feelings were as deep as mine. I'd hoped they were, but I hadn't known.

"I'm really glad you love me," I confessed.

"Why?" he asked, a hint of a laugh in his voice.

I had missed his laughter so much. "Because I was scared that you didn't."

He hesitated for a moment and then reached over to me, holding my face with his hands. "Everly, I will love you every minute of every day for the rest of my life. I will love you until my final, dying breath, and then whatever happens after that, I will still love you. If I was given an entire eternity to love you, it wouldn't be long enough."

Tears fell down my cheeks and he rubbed them gently away with his thumbs.

"In addition to always loving you," he said softly, "I want to spend the rest of my life making you smile."

"You're not doing a great job right now," I said through my tears, and this time he did laugh.

He leaned forward and pressed a soft, tentative kiss to my cheek. "Everly Aprile, I have been head over heels for you from the very beginning. Including literally when you nearly knocked me out in your boss's apartment."

"That was an accident," I protested.

Max smiled at me again, but then his face quickly sobered. "I don't know the exact moment that I fell in love with you, and I also don't remember what my life was like before you came into it. I can't bear the thought of having to spend another moment without you. I am so sorry for lying to you. Can you forgive me?"

"I love you. And Max, I've already forgiven you. But you have to promise to never lie to me again."

"Never," he promised.

"If I ask you whether or not you like my shoes—"

"I will tell you that I don't care about shoes and have no opinion one way or the other and that you're beautiful no matter what you're wearing."

"What did I just say about lying?"

He kissed my cheek again. "It's not a lie, la mia lei. It is the truth."

I remembered that phrase from our first night. It meant "my her." That I was his, out of all the women out there.

A surge of joy and love filled me up, making me feel unbearably light and happy. "It's okay with me if you still want to do the accent."

"Really?" He sounded intrigued.

"Yes, feel free to whisper sweet Italian words anytime you'd like."

Then he said something, but it was in a bunch of different languages and one word seemed to meld into another and I didn't know what he'd just said.

"What does that mean?" I asked.

"I just promised you in every language I speak to never lie to you again. And Everly, ti amo. Te quiero. Wǒ ài nǐ. Je t'aime. Eu te amo. I love you in every language, too."

What else could I do but kiss him? I leaned forward and softly pressed my lips against his. I heard his breath catch, how he held himself so still, as if he were trying not to scare me off.

It was a sweet little peck, but his entire body relaxed when I pulled back. When he finally seemed to understand that we were going to be okay. That I really did forgive him.

He said, "You know, you made me rethink everything in my life. What I thought about relationships, about marriage, about loving someone. You said I should find someone I enjoy being with all the time, someone I wanted to build a life with, someone who shared my goals and aspirations. My best friend. You were right. And that person is you."

"Max," I said, so touched.

We kissed again, gently, slightly longer, but still tentative on his part.

He rested his forehead against mine. "You thanked me once for saving you."

"When that car nearly flattened me like Gumby?"

He smiled. "Yes. But you're the one who saved me, and I didn't even know that I needed to be saved. I am sorry that I'm not royalty, though."

"I was waiting for a fairy tale, but you're so much better than some story because you're real. I would take every hardship and obstacle and misunderstanding if it means I get to be with you in the end."

"And I would face down every evil queen and wicked stepmother, slay every dragon, to be with you," he promised, kissing my hands.

"But I also want to be with you through all the mundane, routine, and ordinary moments, too."

"So do I, la mia lei."

"And speaking of hardships and shared aspirations, if I start my own business, I am going to have a crazy schedule," I warned him. "I'll never know when I'll be able to see you. I'll have to constantly work evenings and weekends to get it up and running."

"I will support you a hundred percent in everything you do, and I will take whatever time you can give me. I'll even rearrange my schedule so that I can be available whenever you are."

"You would do that for me?" The tears were going to start falling again.

"I would do anything for you, Everly."

"There is one more thing," I said, scooting closer to him. "As you know, I don't have a ton of experience when it comes to the more physical side of relationships. Maybe you could help me out with that."

He gave me a wolfish grin. "You know how much I love helping others."

"I'm counting on it," I told him.

Then he kissed me for real and made the rest of the world completely fade away. Max was mine and I was his and nothing else mattered.

I had just climbed into his lap when he pulled his head back. "Did you make a list for today?"

At my expression, he laughed.

"Yes, I made a list," I admitted.

"Am I on it?"

"You are the list," I said. "I listed out the pros and cons of us being together and tried to write down all the ways this conversation might go. The only thing I didn't know was how it would end."

There was so much love in his bright blue eyes as he looked at me, gently caressing my face. "You know how our fairy tale ends. Happy Everly after."

EPILOGUE

Two years later...

"They really do tours here?" I asked as we stepped out of our rental car in front of the Monterran royal palace.

Max proposed to me three months after I came back to New York City. He'd had the ring with him the day we worked things out and got back together, but he wanted to wait for a perfect moment.

That perfect moment never came because we were both so busy. We were at a bridal shower in Central Park, where he had volunteered to help out with the heavy lifting. While everyone was eating, he took me into a wooded area and said, "You need to plan your own bridal shower."

"What? Why?"

Then he got down on one knee and I knew why.

We were married six months later because neither one of us saw the point in a long engagement. It was relatively easy to organize everything quickly because I was the best client I had ever worked with. I went along with every decision I made.

Vella had agreed to be my bridesmaid but only if I let her wear black. Which I was fine with.

Max's mother? Not so much.

Sunny, however, thought it was a lot of fun to wear black as a bridesmaid and made many funeral jokes throughout the reception.

Her little girl was officially our flower girl, even though she couldn't walk yet.

My mom and Meemaw adored Max and spent more time talking to him on the phone than they did to me. Max's father and stepmother were friendly, while his mother was more polite but reserved. They were going to be tough nuts to crack, but I figured, given enough time, I could do it.

We'd had to wait more than a year to go on our honeymoon. I had apologized so many times to him, but he said he didn't care and only wanted me to be happy. My business took off so quickly and there was such a high demand for my services that I was booked solid for months and months. I currently had six full-time employees and was thinking about taking on more.

Aprile's Showers had succeeded beyond my wildest expectations.

When Max had told me that we could honeymoon anywhere in the world, there only one place I wanted to go.

Monterra.

And now we were here at the royal palace. It had snowed several days in a row, which was fine by us—we had an excellent hotel suite and lots to keep us busy—but the roads had cleared and Max said that he'd gotten us tickets to do a public tour of the palace.

The palace was just the way I'd imagined it, only better, because it was real. Snow glistened off turrets and slanted roofs. It looked like something out of a book, with its high walls made out of gray, sparkling stone. I reached out to touch one of the stones, just to reassure myself that I wasn't imagining it.

"This way," Max said.

"Have I told you lately that you're the best husband in the whole world?" I asked him, snuggling against his arm. This was so exciting. I knew we would only be in the parts of the palace that were public, but I'd never gone inside an actual castle before.

"You have, and that's high praise coming from the best wife in the world," Max replied, kissing the top of my head.

Being married to him was the most incredible thing that had ever happened to me. I felt like I should kneel in prayer every night to thank whatever heavenly being had sent him my way. He was still too good to be true, in every way imaginable.

We walked across a courtyard, past some guards, and over a drawbridge. We passed through twenty-foot-high doors and then down a long hallway that contained actual suits of armor. The ceilings had to be like, thirty feet high, and there were flags and tapestries draped along the walls.

A group had gathered and Max and I joined them. A woman was speaking in Italian and English, welcoming us to the tour and to the palace. "Please stay with the group and follow me!"

While I'd seen every image that the royal family had let be published of the castle, it was even better in person. It was just like I'd pictured. Stately and important while still having a magical charm and family feel to it.

We walked through several receiving rooms and a ballroom where King Dominic and Queen Katerina had had their wedding reception. I took way too many pictures of that room.

We had just entered a parlor when Max tugged on my hand. "Come with me."

"Where are we going?" I asked, giggling as I followed him. I imagined he'd found some secret alcove and was going to kiss me senseless and then we'd rejoin the tour.

But he didn't lead me to an alcove. Instead he was walking through rooms and down hallways.

"Max!" I protested. "Is Monterran prison bad? Are we going to be locked up for trespassing? Oh! Or beheaded? What do they do to people who wander through palaces in this country?"

"La mia lei, you don't need to worry. Have I ever gotten you arrested?"

"It only takes one time," I said.

"I have something I want to show you." He was trying to reassure me, but it wasn't working.

"Just so you know, I am not standing on any glass ledges."

"You'll like it."

We walked into a room decorated in dark reds and gold, and I saw a short, bald man in a very expensive suit waiting for us. Oh no. My stomach dropped down to my feet. Was he the head of security? Was this it?

Max and the man spoke in Italian, too fast for me to understand. I'd been trying to use an app to learn the language, but so far all I knew how to say was "Where is the bathroom?" and "Can I have more pizza?"

The man turned to face me. "Buongiorno. My name is Giacomo Rossi and I'm going to give you a private tour of the palace."

"Private tour?" I nudged Max. "You really are the best husband ever."

He grinned at me. "I told you I'd do anything for you." Then he kissed me breathless. It was over far too quickly because despite his stature, Giacomo was fast and we had to run to catch up with him.

More hallways, up two flights of stairs, and then we were standing in front of another set of massive doors.

"Right in here," Giacomo said, opening the door for us.

Max let me walk in first.

"Is this . . ." The words died in my mouth.

Sitting on a couch, looking at me, were King Dominic and Queen Katerina.

Nico and Kat.

Oh . . . my . . .

Max walked over and shook their hands, and introductions were made. I stayed where I was, not able to process what was happening.

Nico and Kat?

What?

Kat came over to me with a big smile. "You must be Everly."

"I'm Kat. I mean, you're Kat and I'm Everly."

"I'm glad we figured that out," she said with a wink that put me at ease. She was tall, in her early thirties, with long dark hair that fell in perfect waves past her shoulders.

Okay, I was absolutely going to gush. "You must get this all the time, but I am such a big fan of yours. Right after I met my husband for the first time, I realized I was messing up my life and so I made this list of how to be more like you. I called it What Would Kat Do?"

Why was I saying these things?

And why was Max letting me? He knew better.

Kat was still smiling, so I figured that was good. "I am such a mess you should never pattern your life after me."

Her handsome husband, who just like Max had black hair and light blue eyes, joined us and put his arms around her shoulders. "Nonsense. You are utter perfection, cuore mio. The world would be a better place if everyone tried to be like you."

"He's biased," she stage-whispered to me, and I laughed. I'd never really seen them be affectionate in pictures or when they were being filmed, and it was both a bit weird and profoundly sweet to see how much they loved each other.

"I'm sorry, but can I get a picture with you?" I asked.

"Of course!" Kat said.

Giacomo materialized, reaching for my camera.

"Max, come here," I said, beaming at him. He had been standing back, letting me have my moment, taking it all in. It didn't seem like he cared much about meeting heads of state—he was far more interested in how excited I was.

"How did you do this?" I asked him as he slid his arm around my waist.

"My dad made some phone calls. I knew you would love this."

"I do. And I love you."

Kat stood on my right and I realized that I didn't know if it was okay to touch her. "Should I . . ."

She put her arm around me first while also holding on to Nico. "This one can be stiff and formal, but despite his and Giacomo's best efforts, I'm still a regular person."

Giacomo held up my phone and said, "Di cheese!"

We all said cheese and he took several photos before returning my phone to me. "Thank you," I said.

I scrolled through the photos and sent one to my mom. Despite the time difference, she responded immediately.

WHAT? TELL THEM I'M THEIR BIGGEST FAN! MOM SEND

She attached a photo that she'd taken last year of her wearing all of her Monterra gear, including her sweatshirt with Kat and Nico's picture on it, surrounded by her pillows and commemorative plates.

I showed Kat the text. "My mom wants me to let you know that she's actually your biggest fan."

Kat laughed and then showed the photo to Nico, who grinned.

"Please tell your mother that she is welcome to visit us anytime," he said.

"Absolutely," Kat agreed, nodding.

My mother was going to have an actual heart attack.

Giacomo made an angry sound and we all looked over at him. He was glaring at his phone.

"Are you watching the game?" Nico asked, and the shorter man nodded. Nico went over to see Giacomo's screen.

"What's the score?" Max joined the other two men, peering over Giacomo's shoulder.

"I will never understand the appeal of soccer," Kat said.

"Me neither. But I still can't believe I'm meeting you. This probably sounds cheesy, but like I said, I have looked up to you for such a long time. I wanted a marriage just like yours. And while he's not royalty . . ." I glanced over at my husband, who seemed to sense that I was watching him. He shot me a secret smile and went back to his game. "He's the

330

most amazing man I've ever known, and I didn't know that I could be happy like this."

I had put my hand over my stomach and Kat understood what this meant. "Are you pregnant?"

I shushed her. I was shushing a queen. "I am. But I haven't told Max yet. He's going to be so excited, though. He really wants to be a dad, but we only just started trying. I haven't been able to decide on the best way to tell him."

"Can I tell you a secret?" When I nodded, Kat said, "I'm pregnant, too. Three months along."

"Congratulations!" I said to her.

"And to you! I tried to be creative this time when I told Nico. I wrote it on these little flags that I put on top of cupcakes, but he just yanked the toothpicks out without even looking at the notes and just mindlessly ate everything I put in front of him! I finally had to tell him to read them. He was so happy."

My first inclination was to find the nearest bakery and do the same thing for Max. He did love sweet things.

But no, I was going to find my own way to tell him, and it would be perfect for us.

I didn't need to copy anyone else.

Kat reached over to me and grabbed my hands. "Would you like to stay and have dinner with the whole family?"

"The whole family?" I almost choked on my own saliva. "As in, everybody?"

"Serafina's not home from university yet, but I think everyone else is here. It's almost Christmas and they all come back for the holidays. Christmas is a big deal in Monterra."

"We would love that," I told her, feeling like I might pass out.

"Let me go to tell Giacomo to set a couple additional plates," she said with a smile.

Max came over and I threw myself into his arms. "They invited us for dinner! This is so exciting."

He kissed me and then said, "I'm so glad that you're happy."

This was it. The moment when I could make him as happy as I was. Our proposal had been impromptu, so why not this? And was there a better place than to tell him in the private family rooms of the Monterran royal palace? "Maybe I should tell Kat to set three places at the table for us."

"Three? Why would she set three . . ." His voice trailed off and I saw on his face the moment he connected the dots. "Are you telling me that you're pregnant?"

I nodded and he picked me up and hugged me tightly.

"You already made me the happiest man alive when you married me, but somehow you just made it even better," he said. "I feel like I'm going to burst."

"After dinner we should call our families and let them know."

"Let's tell them when we get back," he said as he nuzzled my cheek. "For now, this will be just for us."

Well, and the queen of Monterra, but I didn't think this was the right time to tell him that.

A woman came into the room carrying a tray of champagne flutes. Kat took two and handed me one. "Apple cider," she said quietly. Nico had handed the extra one to Max so that we all had one in our hands.

Nico held his drink aloft. "To Max and Everly, thank you for joining us today and congratulations on your wedding and your honeymoon. Kat and I wish you all the happiness in the world. For a hundred years! Per cent'anni!"

It was the toast we had done at our own reception. "Per cent'anni!" everyone responded, clinking our glasses together.

After we took a drink, I slid my hand into Max's and led him away from the others.

"I can't thank you enough for this," I said. "But I'm certainly going to try later on."

His eyes gleamed with anticipation. "I don't know, this may be your last chance to try and land one of the king's cousins and wind up with an actual prince."

"I don't need a prince because I've got something even better."

"How did I ever get so lucky?" he asked, smiling at me.

"You better get used to it. Because I'm yours. For a hundred years," I promised him.

"And I'm yours. For a hundred years," he agreed, and then he kissed me.

AUTHOR'S NOTE

Thank you for reading my story! I hope you enjoyed reading Max and Everly's love story. If you'd like to find out when I've written something new, make sure you sign up for my newsletter at www.sariahwilson. com, where I most definitely will not spam you. (I'm happy when I send out a newsletter once a month!)

And if you feel so inclined, I'd love for you to leave a review on Amazon, on Goodreads, with your hairdresser's cousin's roommate's blog, via a skywriter, in graffiti on the side of a bookstore, on the back of your electric bill, or any other place you want. I would be so grateful. Thanks!

If you'd like to read more about the royal family of Monterra, you can start with *Royal Date*, which is the story of Nico and Kat falling in love: https://www.amazon.com/Royal-Date-Royals-Monterra-Book-ebook/ dp/B00QXUN5Y4/

ACKNOWLEDGMENTS

For everyone who is reading this—thank you. It's kind of miraculous that I've been able to make writing my career, and it's due to readers like you. Thank you for making all of this possible. I appreciate you so much!

My thanks to my editor Alison Dasho—you have done so much for me and have been such a support and guiding light. I love your insight and input and writing things that I know will make you smile. A huge thank-you to the entire team at Montlake for doing everything you can to make my books successful. Charlotte Herscher—I can't imagine that there's a better dev editor than you out there. You always make my stories so much stronger!

Thank you to the copyeditors and proofreaders who find all my mistakes and continuity errors and gently guide me in the right direction, especially when you think I've made a chronological error (and big thanks especially to Kellie for getting my voice and style!). A special shout-out to Caroline Teagle Johnson for the gorgeous cover!

For my agent, Sarah Younger—you know how much you mean to me and how much I rely on you. I'm so glad that you're on my side and we're making this journey together. I can't wait to see where else it will lead!

Thank you to Jessica and Kristin of Leo PR. I'm grateful for your efforts and guidance!

A big thank-you to Michelle Leo of Michelle Leo Events in Utah. I so appreciate you taking time out of your busy schedule to chat with me about event planning. For the readers—Sunny's carnival baby shower is based on a wedding reception that Michelle did, and you can check out the amazing photos on her website. My gratitude to Michelle for allowing me to include her party in my book!

For my kids—I love you, I love you, I love you.

And for Kevin, I'm so glad that I get to live happy Everly after with you.

ABOUT THE AUTHOR

Photo © 2020 Jordan Batt

Sariah Wilson is the *USA Today* bestselling author of *The Hollywood Jinx*, *The Chemistry of Love*, *Cinder-Nanny*, *The Paid Bridesmaid*, the Royals of Monterra series, and the #Lovestruck novels. She happens to be madly, passionately in love with her soulmate and is a fervent believer in happily ever afters—which is why she writes romance. She currently lives with her family and various pets in Utah and harbors a lifelong devotion to ice cream. For more information, visit her website at www.sariahwilson.com.